SPHERE OF MAGIC

"Let the sentence be carried out!" the Angostin called. The men took hold of Megan and, unresisting, she was led to the pyre and forced to clamber high upon the piled wood before her hands were unbound and lashed to the stake.

It was then that I saw the floating sphere gliding effortlessly over the heads of the spectators. Sometimes it hovered over individuals before moving on. Perfectly round and swirling, like smoke encased in glass, the Search-spell moved on.

Suddenly the Search-spell found its prey, and a shaft of white light flashed into the evening air, hanging for several heartbeats above the head of Jarek Mace. In sudden fear the mob melted away from him and the white light became golden, bathing him. Already handsome, he appeared at once godlike, his fringed buckskin shirt of molten gold, his skin of burnished bronze. And he smiled as he executed an elaborate and perfect bow.

"It's the Morningstar!" the Angostin bellowed. "Take him!"

MORNINGSTAR

David Gemmell

A Del Rey Book

BALLANTINE BOOKS • NEW YORK

A Del Rey Book
Published by Ballantine Books

Copyright © 1992 by David A. Gemmell

All rights reserved under International and Pan-American Copyright Conventions. Published in the United States of America by Ballantine Books, a division of Random House, Inc., New York. Originally published in Great Britain by Random Century Group in 1992.

Library of Congress Catalog Card Number: 93-90187

ISBN 0-345-37909-8

Manufactured in the United States of America

First Ballantine Books Edition: October 1993

DEDICATION

Morningstar is dedicated with great affection to a man
who can't stand heroic fantasy and who will never read
this novel. But despite his aversion to this kind of
fiction he has actively supported my work—and the work
of other British writers—for many years.
Roger Peyton and his staff at Andromeda Bookshop
in Birmingham helped me get my first American sale
and ensured Gemmell books were on display long before
they were available even in my own hometown.
Fortunes are made when the big stores back an author.
But Andromeda is where the dreams begin.
My thanks to Rog, his partner Rod Milner,
and all the guys in Brum.

ACKNOWLEDGMENTS

My thanks also to my editor Oliver Johnson, copy editor Jean Maund, proofreader and researcher Stella Graham, and test readers Val Gemmell, Tom Taylor, and Edith Graham.

Special thanks to Vikki Lee France for continuing support and encouragement.

Prologue

YOU KNOW ME, then? I thought so. It is rare for travelers to journey to the high lands at the start of winter. What are you—a scholar, a historian, both? I know you are no magicker, and you appear to be weaponless. Ah, a storyteller! Well, there is honor in that.

I have been a storyteller for sixty-eight years. Aye, and a magicker of some talent. Not great talent, mind you. But I could work the Dragon's Egg. Not many could do that right. Have you seen it? Well, perhaps it is not as popular as once it was. But I could make the dragon break clear of the egg without the shell turning to dust. First the head would come clear, then one tiny, beautiful wing. At last he would ease himself from the shell and then devour it with tongues of fire. It required great concentration, but I could never get the scales right; they would shimmer and fade.

I cannot do it now, of course. The power is almost gone from me.

So, what stories can I give you?

The Morningstar? Everything is known of him—his courage, his battles, his rescues. There are no new stories.

The truth, you say? Now, that is novel. Perhaps unique. Why would you be interested in the truth? Of what use is that to a storyteller? Your listeners will not want the truth. They never do, and they never did. They want heroes, boy. Men of wonder, handsome and tall, men of honor. The Highlanders of legend. They would sweep the truth from the table and stamp it beneath their feet like a beetle. Truth has an ugly face, you see.

There are few still living who remember the Morningstar.

Some are blind, some senile. Whisper his name in their ears and you will see them smile, watch the strength flow back into their limbs. That is real magick.

No, you don't want the truth. And neither do I.

Do you like my house? It was built a half century ago. I wanted to be able to see the sun rise over the eastern lakes, to watch the new pines grow on the flanks of the mountains. Mostly I wanted a home surrounded by trees—oak, beech, and elm. It is a simple house. At least by your standards, for you are a nobleman. How do I know? Your boots alone would cost two years' wages for a workingman. But this house is comfortable. I have three servants, and a local farmer supplies all my food. He charges me nothing, for his grandfather marched with the Morningstar and his father once sat on the great man's knee.

Each year at the harvest feast I sing for my supper. I stand at the head of the farmer's table, and I speak of the old days. Do I tell the truth? After a fashion. What I tell them is a history they all know. It is comfortable; it fills them with pride. There is no harm in that.

But the truth? Like a poisoned dagger, boy.

Yet still you want to hear it . . .

No, I will not speak of those days. You may stay here the night and join me for breakfast in the morning. Then you will go.

Do not be disappointed. I am favoring you with a kindness, though you cannot understand it. You see, the world knows the Morningstar. He lives in the hearts and souls of his people.

You know the song-prayer:

> *He is the light reborn*
> *that shadows fear; when*
> *night descends on us,*
> *he will be near.*

Do I believe that? Of course. I wrote it.

Midnight. A time for memories. My visitor is abed, his disappointment shrouded by sleep and the dreams of the young. There is a log fire behind me, filling the room with warmth and a golden glow. Shadows flicker by the rafters like old ghosts.

It is an effort, but I push open the window, dislodging the

snow from the sill. The cold, skeletal fingers of winter reach in, whispering against my shirt. I shiver and stare out over the bleak glens to the ice-covered lakes and the mountains beyond.

Steep snow-covered peaks are silhouetted against the moon-bright sky, and I can just make out the trees in their winter coats of fallen cloud. And there is a mist—a Highland mist—stretching into the distance, covering the ice-filled gulleys and the silent glens.

On, the Highlands. The people have forgotten now that I ever was Angostin. After sixty-eight years they treat me as if I were born into the old nobility. And I, for my part, have learned all their customs: the dance of the swords, the blessing of the oak, the slashed palm of brotherhood. At the celebrations I always wear the war cloak of the Raubert clan given to me by Raul himself ten years ago.

I wonder sometimes what my family would think of me, were any left alive to see me now. There are no sword dances among the Angostins. So serious are my southern kin, excelling only in battle and in the building of monstrous fortresses of gray stone. A dour people are the Angostins, with an uneasy dislike of song and laughter.

Somewhere a wolf howls. I cannot see him from here.

The truth. How could I begin to tell it? Yet there is a need in me to speak of it, to release it into the air. There is a deep armchair by the fire, covered in soft leather, filled with horse-hair. It is a comfortable chair, and I have spent many a long hour in its depths, my head resting on its curved cushions. It is empty now. But I will use the remnants of my power to fashion a listener. I will create a ghost of the future. He shall hear the true tale of the Morningstar.

I do not wave my hands or speak the words of power. That is for firelit evenings in taverns, entertaining the gullible. They like to see a magicker perform. But this is no performance, so I will merely concentrate.

There he sits, sculpted in light, crafted from magick, silent and waiting. I have given him an intelligent face with keen gray eyes, like the nobleman in the guest room upstairs. And he is young, for it is the young who shape all tomorrows and only the old and the weary who twist our todays—stunting them, holding them back, making them safe. There he sits, waiting, ghostly and transparent. Once I could have dressed him in purple, and any who saw him would marvel at his appearance. Now he shifts and fades. But that, I suppose, is how a ghost should look.

Where shall I begin, spirit? What would you like to hear?

Naturally he does not answer, but I know what he would be thinking were he able to think.

Begin at the beginning, storyteller. Where else but Ziraccu?

◇ 1 ◇

I T IS ALL ruins now, but back then, under a younger sun, the city walls were strong and high. There were three sets of walls on different levels, for Ziraccu was an ancient settlement, the first of its buildings raised during the Age of Stone, when neolithic tribesmen built their temples and forts on the highest hills of this Highland valley. Hundreds of years later—perhaps thousands, for I am no expert on matters historical—a new tribe invaded the north, bearing sharp weapons of bronze. They also built in the valley, throwing up walls around the four hills of Ziraccu. Then came the Age of Iron and the migration of the tribes that now populate the mountains of the north. The painted warriors of bronze were either killed or absorbed by these fierce new invaders. And they, too, built their homes in the high valley. And Ziraccu grew. On the highest levels dwelled the rich in marble palaces surrounded by fine gardens and parks. On the next level down dwelled the merchants and the skilled crafts-men, their houses more homely yet comfortable, built of stone and timber. While at the foot of the hills, within the circle of the lower walls, were the slums and tenements of the poor. Narrow streets, stinking with sewage and waste, high houses, old and dilapidated, alleys and tunnels, steps and stairways, dark with danger and bright with the gleam of the robber's blade. Here there were taverns and inns where men sat silently listening for the watchmen.

Ziraccu, the merchant city. Everything had a price in Ziraccu. Especially in the years of the Angostin War, when the disruption to trade brought economic ruin to many.

I was young then, and I could weave my stories well. It was

5

a good living, traveling from city to city, entertaining at taverns—and occasionally palaces—singing and magicking. The Dragon's Egg was always a favorite, and I am sorry it has fallen into disregard in these latter days.

It was an evening in autumn in Ziraccu, and I was hired to play the hand harp at a wedding celebration in the south quarter. The daughter of a silk merchant was marrying the son of a spice trader. It was more an alliance than a marriage, and the bride was far from attractive. I will not dwell on her shortcomings, for I was, and am, a gentleman. Suffice to say that her ugliness was not so great as to be memorable. On the other hand, I felt great pity for the groom, a fine upstanding youngster with clear blue eyes and a good chin. I could not help but notice that he rarely looked at his bride, his eyes lingering on a young maiden seated at the foot of the table.

It was not the look of a lascivious man, and I knew instantly that these two were lovers. I felt for them but said nothing. I was being paid six silver pennies for my performance, and that, at the time, was more important than true love thwarted.

The evening was dull, and the guests, filled with good wine, became maudlin. I collected my fee, which I hid carefully in a special pocket in my right boot before setting off for my lodgings in the northern quarter.

Not a native of Ziraccu, I soon became lost, for there were no signs to be seen, no aid to the wanderer. I entered an ill-smelling maze of alleys, my heart pounding. My harp was slung over my right shoulder, and any who saw me would recognize the clothes of a bard—bright yellow shirt and red leggings. It would be most unusual to be accosted, for bards were rarely rich and were the only gatherers of news and gossip. We were welcome everywhere—especially those of us who knew a little magick. But—and this is the thought that occupied me—there were always those who knew nothing of tradition, some mindless robber who would plunge his knife into my belly before he realized his mistake.

Therefore, I walked with care through the dark alleyways, drawing myself up to my full height, pulling back my shoulders so as to appear tough, strong, and confident. I was not armed, not even with a short knife. Who would need a knife at a wedding?

Several rats scurried across my path, and I saw a corpse lying by the entrance to a short tunnel. In the bright moonlight it was easy to see that the corpse had been there for some days. His boots were gone, as was his belt.

I turned away my gaze and strode on. I never did like to look upon corpses. No man needs such a violent, visual reminder of his mortality. And there is no dignity in death. The bladder loosens, the bowels empty, and the corpse always assumes an expression of profound idiocy.

I walked on, listening for anything that might indicate a stealthy assassin creeping toward me. A foolish thing to do, for immediately the thought comes to you, the ear translates every sound into a footfall or the whisper of cloth against a wall.

I was breathing heavily when at last I came out onto a main thoroughfare I recognized.

Then the scream sounded.

I am not by nature heroic, but upbringing counts for much in a man's life, and my parents had always made it clear that a strong man must defend the weak. The cry came from a woman. It was born not of pain but of fear, and that is a terrible sound. I swung around and ran in the direction of the cry; it was a move of stunning stupidity.

Turning a sharp corner into a narrow alley, I saw four men surrounding a young woman. They had already ripped her dress from her, and one of the attackers had loosened his leggings, exposing his fish-white legs and buttocks.

"Stop that!" I shouted. Not the most powerful opening line, I'll admit, especially when delivered in a high-pitched shriek. But my arrival stunned them momentarily, and the naked man struggled to pull up his leggings, while the other three swung to face me. They were a grotesque bunch, ugly and filthy, dressed in greasy rags. Fight them? I would have given all I had not to touch them.

One of them drew a dagger and advanced toward me, grunting out some kind of inquiry. The language he used was as foul as his look. The strangest thoughts come to a man in danger, or so I have found. Here was a man with no regard for his appearance. His face and clothes were filthy, his teeth blackened and rotting, yet his dagger was sharp and bright and clean. What is it that makes a man take more care of a piece of iron than this own body?

"I am a bard," I said.

He nodded sagely and then bade me go away, using language I would not dream of repeating.

"Step away from the lady, if you please," I told them. "Otherwise I shall call the watch."

There was some laughter at this, and two of the other three advanced upon me. One sported a hook such as is used to hang meat, while the second held two lengths of wood with a wire stretched between them. The last of them remained with the girl, holding her by the throat and hair.

I had no choice but to run, and I would have done so. But fear had frozen my limbs, and I stood like a sacrificial goat waiting for the knife and the hook and the wicked throat wire.

Suddenly a man leapt from the balcony above to land in their midst, sending two of them sprawling. The one on his feet, he of the meat hook, swung his weapon at the newcomer, who swayed aside and lashed out with a sword belt he was holding in his left hand. The buckle caught the man high on the left cheek, spinning him from his feet. It was then that I saw that the newcomer was wearing only one boot and was carrying his sword belt in his hand. Hurling aside his scabbard, he drew his blade, lancing it through the neck of his nearest foe. But the first of the villains I had seen rose up behind the newcomer.

"Look out!" I cried. Our unknown helper spun on his heel, his sword plunging into the chest of his opponent. I was behind the man, and I saw the blade emerge from his back; he gave a strangled scream, and his knees buckled. The warrior desperately tried to tear his sword loose from the man's chest, but it was stuck fast. The rogue with the throat wire leapt upon the newcomer's back, but before he could twist the wire around his intended victim's throat, the newcomer ducked and twisted, hurling his attacker into a wall. As the villain rose groggily, the newcomer took two running steps, then launched himself through the air feet first, his one boot cracking against the base of the man's neck and propelling his face into the wall. There was a sickening thud, followed instantly by the crunching of bones. The sound was nauseating, and my stomach turned.

The last of the villains loosened his hold on the girl, throwing her to the ground and sprinting away into the shadows. As the girl fell, she struck her head on the cobbles. I ran to her, lifting her gently. She moaned.

"You bastard! I'll see you dead! You'll not escape me!"

shouted a voice from an upper window. I glanced up to see a bearded man upon the balcony. He was hurling abuse at the newcomer.

It did not seem to perturb the fellow. Swiftly he wrested his sword clear of the corpse, then gathered his second boot, which was lying some distance away against a wall.

"Help me with her," I ordered him.

"Why?" he asked, pulling on his boot.

"We must get her to safety."

"There he is! Take him!" screamed the man on the balcony. The sound of running footsteps came from the alley.

"Time to go," said the newcomer with a bright smile. At once he was on his feet and running.

Armed men rushed into sight and set off after him. The officer of the watch approached me. "What is happening here?" he asked.

I explained briefly about the attack on the girl and of our sudden rescue. He knelt by the still-unconscious woman, his fingers reaching out to feel the pulse at her throat. "She'll come around," he said. "Her name is Petra. She is the daughter of the tavern keeper Bellin."

"Which tavern?"

"The Six Owls; it is quite close by. Come, I'll help you carry her there."

"Who is the man you are chasing?"

"Jarek Mace."

He said the name as if it were one I should know, but when I professed ignorance, he smiled. "He is a reaver, a thief, an adulterer, a robber—whatever takes his fancy. There is no crime he would not commit if the price were worth the risks."

"But he came to our aid."

"I doubt that. We had him cornered, and he ran. I would guess he jumped from the window to escape us and landed in the midst of a fight. Lucky for you, eh?"

"Extraordinarily lucky. Perhaps it was fate."

"If fate is kind to you, bard, you will not meet him again."

That was the first time I saw the Morningstar.

The officer of the watch was a kindly man. I do not recall his name, but I remember how he covered the unconscious girl with his gray cloak before lifting her into his arms. I thought this a gallant act. He was a strong man and had no need of my assistance as we walked through the alleys, coming at last to a wider street where three inns were situated. The Six Owls was centrally placed, the building—three floors high—stretching across an arched tunnel that led to the stables. Heavy curtains covered the many ground-floor windows, but the sound of raucous singing could be heard from within.

We took Petra, who was by then recovering, to a door at the rear and entered a wide kitchen. Two middle-aged women ran forward as they saw the girl, but the officer comforted them, his voice soothing.

A serving girl ran to fetch the owner of the tavern, a colossal man named Bellin. Bald as a rock and round as he was tall, he had huge arms and his face was moon-shaped and pale.

"What's this? What's this?" he boomed, his small brown eyes glinting with what I took to be ferocity.

"This gentleman rescued the young lady," said the officer. "She was being attacked by a gang of ruffians. I fear they were intent on rape. But no harm has been done."

"They didn't . . . ?" began Bellin.

"No," the officer answered.

"The gods be praised," said the innkeeper, stepping forward and taking his daughter into a suffocating embrace. Her senses had returned, and she looked toward me. Easing herself clear of her father's arms, she curtseyed prettily. She did not seem in the least troubled, and I guessed then that she had recovered far more swiftly than any of the men had guessed. Her eyes were upon me, and I thought I saw an invitation there, but I was young then and found it hard to believe that any attractive girl would give me a second glance.

"I thank you, sir, for your kindness and your bravery," she said. What could I say? I recall mumbling some nonsense and wishing I were gone. The innkeeper moved his great bulk toward me, then thumped me on the shoulder. It was the most painful moment of the night, but I grinned foolishly and basked in their praise. "Where did this happen?" asked Bellin. Petra took hold of the officer's arm.

"Baker's Alley," she said swiftly. I saw the officer's reaction and knew at once that this was not the place of the incident. But he said nothing, and neither did I.

It seemed the young lady had been visiting her grandmother,

having taken a basket of pies and fruit for the old woman. It was a fine story, but both the officer and I knew she had detoured to meet some young suitor. The officer waited while Petra removed herself to her room to dress, but when she returned his cloak, he bowed and left to resume his duties. After he had gone, I asked Bellin if he could supply directions back to the inn where I had purchased lodgings. When I named the place, he guffawed.

"You cannot stay in such a cockroach-infested hovel," he insisted, and offered me, free of charge, his best guest room, slipping two gold coins into my hand as he ushered me through the main drinking hall. I am ashamed to say that I did not even make a polite attempt to refuse either.

But then, times were hard in Ziraccu.

The room was low-ceilinged and boasted two windows, one narrow and leaded, the other large and leading to a small balcony. The bed was softer than I liked, but the mattress was thick and clean. There was a table, four leather-covered chairs, and a stool set before the stone fireplace. A fire had been recently lit, and the room was still cold. I sat down upon the stool and sipped a goblet of fine wine.

These lodgings were far better than those for which I had paid. Banking the fire, which by now had fulfilled its purpose and warmed the room, I took off my coat and undershirt, laying them carefully upon the back of a chair. The boots, complete with the wedding silver and the two gold coins, I left under the bed.

All in all it had been a fine day. It was not often that a bard was treated like a hero, and though I find compliments embarrassing, I am forced to admit that I enjoyed the praise. There was a little guilt also, for it was not I but Jarek Mace who had saved the girl. But I consoled myself with the thought that it was I, Owen Odell, who had first rushed to her rescue.

A copper warming pan had been left in the bed. I removed it, slid under the heavy blankets, and closed my eyes, seeing again the tall man leaping to our aid. I have seen many troupes of dancers in my life, yet rarely have I watched so graceful a human being. He had moved with great economy, always in balance, his confident skills wondrously displayed.

I pictured him again in my mind. Somewhat above six feet tall, wearing a common soldier's jerkin of dark leather and be-

neath it a white blouse with puffed sleeves, slashed with . . .
silk? Probably. But his dark leggings were of cheap wool, frayed
at the knee, and his boots were those of a cavalryman. You know
the old style, worn high over the knee to protect the rider but
folded down when afoot. Expensive boots.

A curious mixture, to be sure! But could I make a song of it?
The hero bard and the wolfshead swordsman.

I doubted it, for there was no suitable ending. The swordsman
had not fallen in love with the girl, and the tale was too swift in
the telling.

Snuggling down, I slept without dreams until somewhere close
to dawn.

I was awakened by a hand that closed over my mouth. "Do
not cry out, goat face, or I shall slit your throat!"

The hand moved away from my mouth, but I felt the point of
a dagger against my neck. The room was dark, and I could see
nothing save a black silhouette above me.

"What do you want?" I managed to ask.

"The gold. Where is it?"

"Gold? What are you talking about?"

"Don't bandy words with me! I rescued the wench; the reward should be mine."

"Jarek Mace?"

"You know me?" asked the man, surprised. Stepping back
from the bed, he opened a tinderbox and struck his flint. Flames
sprang up within the iron box. Lighting a taper from them, he
moved to the three lanterns hanging upon the whitewashed walls.
Soon the room was bathed in light, and I sat up, watching him.
He was wide-shouldered yet narrow of hip, long-legged, and—
as I have said—exceedingly graceful in his movements. His hair
was light brown, worn long to the shoulder but cropped above
the eyes. There was nothing special about the shape of his head
or his eyes or mouth, yet the combination of his features created
a remarkably handsome face. Turning back to the bed, he
grinned, and such was the power of the smile that I returned it.
Pulling up a chair, he sat beside me. "I have seen you before,"
he announced. "You do magicker's tricks and tell stories."

Thus was my life described, and irritation began to grow
within me. I had been called goat face, and my skills, which I
had given some fifteen of my twenty-five years to learn, had
been dismissed in one short sentence.

However, I felt it wise to bear in mind that my unwelcome guest was a known killer of men and was currently sitting alongside me holding a sharp dagger. "My name is Owen Odell."

"I don't care about that, bard. But how do you know of me?"

"The officer of the watch told me your name soon after you rescued me."

"Ah! Then you accept my point? As the rescuer, the gold is mine."

"It was given to me," I pointed out. His expression hardened, and he lifted the dagger, tapping my naked arm with the tip.

"Let us not quibble, Master Odell. I do not wish to kill you, but it would not worry me overly much. I have killed men for less than two gold coins."

"You couldn't possibly kill me," I said.

"Really?" he answered, the dagger point rising to rest on my neck. "Pray explain?"

"You saved my life."

"What has that got to do with it?"

"There are many religions that point out that a rescued man is the responsibility of the rescuer. Our lives are now linked."

"I am not a religious man—nor especially patient. And if you do not surrender the gold to me at once, I shall sever whatever links there are with this dagger."

The words were spoken with great sincerity. I glanced around the room. My clothes had been thrown from the chair, and the drawers of the small dresser lay open. My boots had been pulled from beneath the bed and were lying by the fire. "You have searched the room, and you can see that I am naked. There is no money here; I spent it."

"You lie! He gave you two gold coins."

"Indeed he did."

"It is not possible for you to have spent such an amount in such a time."

"I paid for this room for a month." The lie came easily to me, yet I felt no guilt, for this, I understood, was a kind of game, a battle of wits. I was sure that in such a contest I could outwit the fellow.

"Right, you die," he said, rising. Before I could speak, he pushed me to my back, his dagger pressing against the base of my throat. "Last chance," he told me cheerfully.

"It's in my boot," I said.

"I am losing patience. I've already looked in your boots." The dagger point nicked the skin, and I felt the blood flow.

"There is a special pocket," I told him.

He moved away from me and knelt by the boots, examining them. "Clever," he muttered, finding the pocket and tipping out the contents.

"The silver is mine!" I said, rolling from the bed.

"Wrong. You tried to cheat me. You deserve to lose it all."

"That is hardly fair!" I argued.

"It is not my business to be fair. I am a thief."

There was a certain logic to the argument that was hard to dispute, but my temper was rising. As I said, I am not by nature heroic, but neither am I cursed with cowardice. The gold I would not fight for, but the silver was mine and well earned. I saw his eyes narrow, and I knew he had read my intentions. I would not say he was alarmed, but I am not a small man, and in those days, filled with the strength of youth, I would have been no easy victim.

"Do not be foolish, now," he warned me. "You could die here!"

I was about to leap upon him when I heard the sounds of footsteps upon the stairs. Then soft tapping came at the door. "Are you awake?" called Petra.

"Yes," I answered. I heard Jarek curse softly and watched with relief as he slipped the dagger back into its sheath.

The door opened, and she stepped inside. Her blond hair was brushed back now and braided, and she wore a flared skirt and a pretty blouse of blue wool and linen. "Oh!" she whispered. "I didn't realize you had some . . ." Then she recognized him. "It is you! Oh, Jarek!" she cried, running forward to embrace him.

"That's the kind of welcome I like," he said, mystified.

"You rescued me . . . and I thought you didn't care. You were so fearless. My father has put aside five gold pieces for you as a reward—if that is all right. I would not wish you to feel insulted."

"Insulted? Not at all. It would hardly be civil to refuse. Is he awake?"

"No. I am always the first to rise. I milk the cows. I just wanted to . . . thank the bard."

"Of course you did," he said smoothly. "And your father awakes at . . . ?"

"It will be several hours yet. But sit down with your friend and I shall bring you an early breakfast. Cold meat and cheese with some fruit? And of course a jug of the best ale."

"Very kind," he told her, bowing once more. She curtseyed and backed out of the room.

"My silver and gold, if you please."

"What?"

"There are six silver pieces," I explained, "and two gold coins. If you wish to keep them, you can. But I shall tell the girl's father of the attempted robbery and of the fact that your rescue was merely an accident as you tried to escape the watch. On the other hand, return to me my coins and you will be the richer by a breakfast and five gold pieces."

He chuckled then and tossed my money on the bed. "I like you," he said. "I may kill you one day, but I like you."

I have known many men of violence in my long life—cruel men, brave men, evil men, noble men. Never have I met any who matched the complex amorality of the Morningstar. That first meeting remains etched in my mind. I can still see the dawn light seeping into the night sky and my guest kneeling before the embers of the fire, expertly blowing the dying coals to life and adding fuel. I can taste the dark bread that Petra brought, fresh and warm from the tavern bakery.

Why that meeting should remain so clear while other, greater events are lost in the misty recesses of memory is a mystery to me. We sat and talked like old friends, discussing the weather and the state of the war. He had been a soldier in the army of the king but had despaired of the generals and their stupidity. After one defeat too many he had deserted. I am not now—nor ever was—a lover of wars. I see no need for them. And this one was more foolish than most.

These northern lands had been conquered by the Angostins more than two hundred years before, and all the nobility were now of their race. It was a complicated issue, but let me explain swiftly. This large island of ours had once been split in two, the lush south ruled by the Ikenas, and the barren, mountainous north by Highland tribes, mostly of Pictish and Belgaic origin. Then the Angostins crossed the narrow sea and conquered the

Ikenas. This third force was led by Villem, the battle king, an Angostin prince of great strategic skill. He crushed his enemies without pity and crowned himself king of Ikena. His descendants attacked the north and conquered this also. But as the years passed, the Highland nobles—all now Angostins and thus lovers of battle—decided to set their own king upon a throne in the north. This led to civil war.

Why was it more foolish than most? Well, think of it: an army of conquered Ikenas led by Angostins from the south against a force of conquered Highlanders led by Angostins from the north. The slaughter was great among Ikenas and Highlanders, while the Angostins in their mighty armor were rarely slain. When captured, they were held for ransom and later released after enjoying banquets in their honor served by their captors, many of whom were distant cousins of their prisoners. Nonsense . . .

And grisly nonsense at that.

Jarek Mace, at first a foot soldier in the army of the south, had deserted to join the army of the north as a cavalryman. The pay was better, he said, but the generals worse. It was while talking about the war that I began to notice changes in his speech patterns. When he was angry, his voice would lose its cultured tone and he would fall into the slang I had heard south of the border. It was thus when he spoke of the generals and the butchery that was the Angostin War. But at other times he would sound like a minor Angostin noble. He was a great mimic.

"Why is the watch seeking you?" I asked him.

He chuckled. "You remember the bearded fellow at the balcony window? I paid court to his wife. A pretty young thing she is, full-breasted and never happier than when on her back, legs spread."

"I do not appreciate coarse language," I told him sternly, "especially when speaking of a lady."

"I shall bear that in mind, bard. Now, where was I? Oh, yes. I met her in the marketplace. She was looking at some Frankish jewelry. I spoke to her, and we struck up an instant friendship. One of the pleasures of life is striking up instant friendships with women. Anyway, I walked her to her home and noted, as a man will, that several large trees grew close to the south of the house, their branches touching the walls at many points. The house itself was stone-built. Not exactly a palace, but there were many ornate carvings in the stone. That evening I climbed into the house and found my way to her room. Her husband was absent. I woke her and declared—as one must—my undying love for her and enjoyed a fine night.''

''You are in love with her?''

''Did I say I was?''

''That is what you told her.''

He smiled and leaned back in his chair. ''I see you are not a man of the world, bard. Have you never slept with a woman?''

''That is a singularly intrusive and impertinent question,'' I told him.

''Then you have not. I see. Is it boys, then?''

''It is not! How dare you?''

''Oh, I am not criticizing, man. I was merely trying to ascertain your knowledge of affairs of the loins. There are rules, you see, governing all things. If you wish to bed a lady, you must first declare your love. If you wish to bed a peasant, you must first declare your wealth. You understand? Well, this one was a lady. So I told her I loved her.''

''And she believed you?''

''Of course. She wanted me in her bed. I knew that from the first moment in the marketplace.''

''What happened?''

He sighed. ''Women play by different rules. She decided she wanted to run away with me, to live in some distant place where we could walk naked among the flowers or suchlike. In short, she became boring. So I left her.''

''And then?''

''It always happens. Her love turned to anger, and she told her husband about me. It is partly my fault—I should not have taken all her jewelry. But I had gambling debts, and anyway, I think I earned some reward for the pleasure I gave her.''

''You stole her jewels? What kind of a man are you?''

''I thought we had decided that question. I am a thief.''

''It sounds to me as if you broke her heart.''

''I never touched her heart,'' he said with a chuckle. He stood and walked to the window, gazing out over the city. ''This will not last long,'' he whispered, his voice losing its lightness of tone.

''What do you mean?''

''Ziraccu is finished. The war will come here. Siege engines will sunder the walls; armed troops will rampage through the streets."

"But this is not a battlefield," I said.

"The Ikenas have a new king. Edmund, the hammer of the Highlands, he calls himself. He says he will not rest until the northern kingdom is overcome. I believe he means it. And that will mean new rules of engagement."

"How so?"

"A lot more death, bard," he said cheerfully. "You can forget about set battles and ransomed knights. This Edmund believes in victory, and he'll not stop until all his enemies are worm food. Mark my words. He'll attack the cities and raze them. He'll end the Angostin Wars once and for all. But I'll not stay to see it. I have no wish to be trapped here like a rat in a pipe."

"Where will you go?"

"Somewhere where the women are warm and the gold is plentiful."

"I wonder if there is such a place," I said, forcing a smile. "But tell me, how did you know I received two gold coins as a reward?"

"Bellin's wife whispered it to me just after . . . but you don't want to hear about that."

"His wife?"

"Yes. Nice woman. Very open. But I'd love to have her and the daughter in the same bed. Now, wouldn't that be a pretty sight?"

"No, it would not. And you are a disgraceful man."

"I try," he said, laughing aloud.

◇ 2 ◇

JAREK MACE RECEIVED his reward from the innkeeper and, with a fine smile and a wave, walked away from the tavern. I felt a sense of loss at the time and could not understand it. But life moved on. I stayed several days at the Six Owls and even entertained the regulars on my last night.

They were common men and women, and I did not bore them with the Dragon's Egg, which is for the cultured. I gave them what they required—the Dancing Virgin. It is a simple piece of magick involving a silver tray that floats in the air while a girl no taller than a man's forearm dances upon it, her body swathed in shimmering veils of silk.

It was not a great success, for there are many talented magickers who have debased the piece, introducing male partners and allowing them to simulate copulation. I could, of course, have duplicated such a scene, indeed, achieved a far more powerful display of the erotic. But I had always felt it wrong to pander to the lust of the mob. There were several coarse shouts during my performance, which unsettled my concentration, but I continued and finished the display with a burst of white fire, a glowing ball that circled the room before exploding with a mighty bang.

Even after this the audience was apathetic in its applause, and I leapt from the table and walked to the long bar feeling somewhat depressed.

Few understand the emotional strain of magicking, the sense of fatigue and weariness of the soul that follows a performance. I drank heavily that night, and it was very late when Bellin informed me that he would need my room for guests arriving the following day.

It seemed I had outstayed my welcome.

For the next few months I performed at several weddings and two funerals. I like funerals; I enjoy the solemnity and the tears. I do not mean to sound morbid, but there is something sweet and uplifting about grief. The tears of loved ones are more powerful than any epitaph on a man's life. I have seen the funerals of great men, with many carriages following the hearse. Great speeches are made, but there are no tears. What kind of a life must it have been that no one cries for you? There is an eastern religion that claims that tears are the coins God accepts to allow a soul into heaven.

I greatly like that idea.

Man being what he is, of course, the eastern men pay people to cry for them at their funerals.

However, I digress. The months flowed by, and I struggled to earn enough money to pay for my meager requirements. The war was affecting everyone now. Food was in short supply, and the prices rose. The Ikenas king, Edmund, had been true to his word. His army swept through the land like a forest fire, destroying towns and cities, crushing the armies of the north in several pitched battles, coming ever closer to Ziraccu.

There were tales of horror, of mutilation and torture. A nunnery, it was said, had been burned to the ground, the abbess crucified upon the main gates. Several noblemen captured at the Battle of Callen had been placed in iron cages on the castle walls and left to die of cold and starvation.

The Count of Ziraccu, one Leonard of Capula, declared the city neutral and sent emissaries to Edmund. The emissaries were hanged, drawn, and quartered. Left with no choice but to fight, Leonard began hiring mercenaries to defend the walls, but no one believed they could resist the might of the southern Angostin army.

It was not a good time to be a bard. Few wanted to hear songs of ancient times or listen to the music of the harp. What they desired was to realize their capital and head for the ports, setting sail to a continent where the baying of the hounds of war would not carry.

Houses were being sold in Ziraccu for a twentieth of their worth, and rich refugees left in their hundreds every day.

I had intended to wait in Ziraccu until the spring, but on the seventh day of midwinter—having not eaten for several days—I realized the time had come to make my way north.

I had no winter clothing and stole a blanket from my lodgings that I used as a cloak. I wrapped my hand harp in cloth, gathered my few possessions, and climbed from the window of my room, sliding down the roof and jumping into the yard.

The snow was deep everywhere, and I was faint from hunger by the time I reached the northern gate. Three sentries, sitting around an iron brazier glowing with coals, were eating warmed slices from a large meat pie. The smell of beef and pastry made my head spin, and I asked them for a slice. Naturally they refused but, recognizing me for a bard and a magicker, told me they would give me food if I performed well. I asked them what kind of performance they required.

They wanted the dancing girl and her partner, several partners, in fact.

I learned then that principles rarely survive an empty belly, and for a large slice of meat pie I gave them what they required. No subtlety, no silken veils. A small orgy performed above a brazier of coals. Warmer and with a full belly, I walked out into the night, leaving the lights of Ziraccu behind me.

When I reached the foothills, I turned for one last look at the city. Lanterns were glowing in the windows of the houses on the heights, and Ziraccu appeared as a jeweled crown. The moon hung above the highest hill of the city, and spectral light bathed the marble walls on the count's palace. It was hard to believe in that moment that this was a country at war. The mountains loomed in the distance, proud and ageless, in what seemed a great circle around Ziraccu. It was a scene of great beauty.

Two months later the city was conquered by Edmund and his general, Azrek.

The slaughter was terrible.

But on that night all was quiet, and I walked for upward of an hour toward the distant forest. The temperature had plummeted to well below freezing, but a magicker has no fears of the cold. I cast a small spell that warmed the air trapped within my clothing and strolled on.

The night was clear, the stars bright. There was no breeze, and a wonderful silence lay upon the land. There is such beauty

in night snow, it fills the soul with music. I had a need upon me
to lose the images I had created for the guards, and only music
could free me. I waited until I had reached the outskirts of the
forest; then I found a hollow, cleared away a section of snow,
and magicked a fire. There are some who can hold the fire spell
for hours, never needing fuel. I could not achieve this, but I
could maintain the flames for long enough to burn into gathered
wood. I found several broken branches and added them to my
flames. Soon I had a fine small blaze. I did not need the heat,
but there is a comfort in fire, especially in lonely places. I did
not fear trolls or demons, for they rarely came close to the hab-
itats of man, and I was but two hours from Ziraccu and still on
the trade route. But there were wolves and wild boar in the
forest, and my fire, I hoped, would keep them from me.

Unwrapping my harp, I tuned the strings and then played
several melodies, tunes of the dance, light and rippling. But
soon the unheard rhythms of the forest made themselves known
to me, and I began to play the music the forest wished to hear.

I was inspired then, my fingers dancing upon the strings, my
heart pounding to the beat, my eyes streaming tears. Suddenly
a voice cut through my thoughts, and my heart lurched inside
my chest.

"Very pretty," said Jarek Mace. "It will bring every robber
within miles to your fire!"

His appearance had changed since last I had seen him. He
had grown a thin mustache and a small beard shaped like an
arrowhead; it gave him a rakish, sardonic look. His hair had
been expertly cut, and he wore a headband of braided leather.
His clothes were also different, a sheepskin cloak with a deep
hood, a woolen shirt edged with leather, and a deerhide jerkin.
His boots were the same, thigh-length, but he had gained a pair
of leather trews that glistened as if oiled. A scabbarded longsword was belted at his waist, and he carried a longbow and a
quiver of arrows. He was every inch the woodsman.

"Well, at least one robber has been brought to my fire," I
muttered, angry at the intrusion.

He grinned and sat down opposite me, laying his bow against
the trunk of an oak tree. "Now who would rob you, bard? You
are all bones, and your clothes are rags. I'll wager there is nothing left in the pocket of your boot."

"That's a wager won," I told him. "I did not expect to find you here."

He shrugged. "I stayed for a while in Ziraccu, then headed north after the suicide."

"Suicide? What suicide?"

"The woman whose jewels I stole. The stupid baggage tied a rope to her neck and threw herself from the staircase. After that they were really after my blood. I can't see why; I didn't ask her to do it."

I sat and looked at him in disbelief. A woman who had loved him so desperately that she had killed herself when he left her. And yet he showed no remorse or even sorrow. Indeed, I don't think the event touched him at all.

"Did you feel nothing for her?" I asked him.

"Of course I did; she had a wonderful body. But there are thousands of wonderful bodies, bard. She was a fool, and I have no time for fools."

"And who do you have time for?"

He leaned forward, holding his hands out to the fire. "A good question," he said at last. But he did not answer it. He seemed well fed and fit, though he carried no pack or blankets. I asked him where he was staying, but he merely grinned and tapped his nose.

"Where are you heading?" he asked me.

"I am heading north."

"Stay in the forest," he advised. "The Ikenas fleet attacked Torphpole Port and landed an army there. I think the forest will be safer for a while. There are plenty of towns and villages here, and the tree line extends for two hundred miles. I can't see the Ikenas invading it; it will be safer than the lowlands."

"I need to earn my bread," I told him. "I do not wish to become a beggar, and I have little skill at husbandry or farming. And anyway, a bard is safe even if there is a war."

"Dream on!" snapped Mace. "When men start hacking away with swords, no one is safe, not man, woman, or child. It is the nature of war; it is bestial and unpredictable. Face it, you are cut off here. Make the best of it. Use your magick. I've known men to walk twenty miles to see a good ribald performance."

"I do not give *ribald* performances," I told him curtly, the memory of the meat pie display surging from the recesses of my mind.

"Shame," he said. "Perhaps you would consider the shell game. A magicker ought to be magnificent at it. You could make the pea appear wherever the least money was bet."

"Cheat, you mean?"

"Yes, cheat," he answered.

"I . . . I . . . that would be reprehensible. And anyway, the magick would soon fade if I put it to such use. Have you no understanding of the art? Years of study and self-denial are needed before the first spark of magick can be found in a soul. Years! It cannot be summoned for personal gain."

"Forgive me, bard, but when you perform in taverns, is that not for personal gain?"

"Yes, of course. But that is honest work. To cheat a man requires . . . deceit. Magick cannot exist in such circumstances."

He looked thoughtful for a moment, then added several small sticks to the fire. "What of the dark magickers?" he asked. "They summon demons and kill by witchery. Why does their magick not leave them?"

"Shh," I said, alarmed. "It is not wise to speak of such as they." Hastily I made the sign of the protective horn and whispered a spell of undoing. "They make pacts with . . . unclean powers. They sell their souls, and their power comes from the blood of innocents. It is not magick but sorcery."

"What is the difference?"

"I could not possibly explain it to you. My talents are from within and will harm no one. Indeed, they could not cause pain. They are illusions. I could make a knife and thrust it into your heart. You would feel nothing, and no harm would come to you. But if . . . one of them were to do the same, your heart would be filled with worms and you would die horribly."

"So," he said, "you will not play the shell game. Well, what else can you do?"

"I play the harp."

"Yes, I heard that. Very . . . soulful. Sadly, bard, I think you are going to starve to death. Gods, it is cold!" Adding more fuel to the fire, he once more held out his hands to the flames.

"I am sorry," I said. "I have forgotten my manners." Lifting my right hand, I pointed at him and spoke the words of minor enchantment that warmed the air within his clothes.

"Now, *that* is a talent!" he exclaimed. "I hate the cold. How long will the spell last?"

"Until I fall asleep."

"Then stay awake for a few hours," he ordered me. "If I wake up cold, I'll cut your throat. And I mean that! But if I sleep warm, I'll treat you to a fine breakfast. Is it a bargain?"

"A fine bargain," I told him, but he was immune to sarcasm.

"Good," he said, and without another word stretched himself out on the ground beside the fire and closed his eyes.

I leaned back against the broad trunk of an oak tree and watched the sleeping man, my thoughts varied but all centered on Jarek Mace. My life as a bard and a storyteller had been filled with tales of men who looked like Jarek, tall and spectacularly handsome, confident and deadly in battle. It had almost become second nature in me to believe that a man who looked like him must be a hero. Part of me still wanted—needed—to believe it. Yet he had spoken with such lack of care about the poor dead woman back in Ziraccu. I did not know her, yet I could feel her grief as she tied the noose around her neck. I tried to tell myself that he did care, that he felt some sense of shame but was hiding it from me. But I did not believe it then, and I do not believe it now.

He had been drawn to my fire by the sound of the harp, but he had come to rob a lone traveler. And had I been carrying a coin, I don't doubt he would have taken it and left me, throat slit, on the snow of the forest floor.

Now he lay still, his sleep dreamless, and I, frightened of his threat, remained awake, my spell keeping him warm.

I thought back to our conversation and realized that I had seen yet another Jarek Mace. His speech patterns were subtly altered. In Ziraccu he had sounded for the most part like an Angostin, except in those moments when anger had flared and his voice had lost its cultured edge. Now, in these woods his speech carried the slight burr of the Highlander. I wondered if he even realized it. Or did he, like the chameleon, merely adjust his persona to suit his surroundings?

A badger moved warily across the hollow, snuffling at the snow. She was followed by three cubs, the last of which approached the sleeping man. I created a small globe of white light that danced before the cub's eyes, then popped. The cubs scampered away, and the mother cast me a look that I took to be admonishment. Then she, too, disappeared into the bleak undergrowth.

I was hungry again and growing cold. Two spells of warming were hard to maintain. Banking up the fire, I moved closer to the flames.

My father's castle on the south coast would be warm, with heavy velvet curtains against the narrow windows, huge log fires burning in the many hearths. There would be wine and spirits, hot meats and pastries.

Ah, but I forget, ghost! You do not yet know me save as the threadbare bard. I was the youngest of three sons born to the second wife of the Angostin count, Aubertain of WestLea. Yes, an Angostin. Neither proud nor ashamed of it, to be sure. My eldest brother, Ranuld, went to live across the sea, to fight in foreign wars. The second, Braife, stayed at home to manage the estates, while I was to have entered the church. But I was not ready to wear the monk's habit, to spend my life on my knees worshiping a God whose existence I doubted. I ran away from the monastery and apprenticed myself to a magicker named Cataplas. He had a twisted back that gave him constant pain, but he performed the Dragon's Egg like no one before or since.

That, then, was me, Owen Odell, an Angostin bard who in that dread winter was unable to make a living and who was sitting against a tree, growing colder by the moment, while his powers were being expended on a heartless killer who slept by his fire.

I was not a happy man as I sat there, hugging my knees, my thin, stolen blanket wrapped tight around my bony frame.

An owl hooted in the branches above me, and Jarek stirred but did not wake. It was very peaceful there, I recall, beneath the bright stars.

Toward dawn Jarek awoke, yawned, and stretched. "Best sleep I've had in weeks," he announced. Rolling to his feet, he gathered his bow and quiver and set off without a word of thanks for my efforts. My power had faded several hours before, and I had barely managed to keep Mace warm, while I was almost blue with cold. With shivering hands I threw the last small sticks on the fire and held my numbed fingers above the tiny flames.

The morning sky was dark with snow clouds, but the temperature was rising. Standing, I stamped my feet several times, trying to force the blood through to the frontiers of my toes.

Walking deeper into the forest, I began to gather more fuel. The weight of the recent snow had snapped many branches, and the smaller of those I collected in my arms and carried to my campsite, returning for larger sections, which I dragged through the snow. The work was arduous, and I soon tired. But at least I was warmer now, save for my hands. The tips of my fingers had swelled against my nails and throbbed painfully.

But all my discomfort was forgotten when the three men emerged from the forest to approach my fire.

There are times when the eyes see far more than the mind will acknowledge, when the heart will beat faster and panic begins at the root of the stomach. This was such a time. I looked up and saw the three, and my mouth was dry. Yet there was nothing instantly threatening about them. They looked like foresters dressed in homespun wool, with leather jerkins and boots of soft hide laced at the front with leather thongs. Each of them carried a bow, but they were also armed with daggers and short swords. I pushed myself to my feet, sure in my heart that I faced great peril.

"Welcome to my fire," I said, proud that my voice remained steady. No one spoke, but they spread out around me, their eyes cold, faces grim. They seemed to me then like wolves, lean and merciless. The first of them, a tall man, looped his bow over his shoulder and knelt beside the fire, extending his hands to the flames. "You are a bard?" he said, not looking at me.

"I am, sir."

"I don't like bards. None of us like bards."

It is difficult to know how to react to an opening like that. I remained silent. "We come a long way in search of your fire, bard. We seen it last night, twinkling like a candle, built where no sensible man would. We walked through the night, bard, expecting a little coin for our trouble."

"I have no coin," I told him.

"I can see that. It makes me angry, for you've wasted my time."

"How can you blame me?" I asked him. "I did not invite you."

He glanced up at one of the others. "Now he insults us," he

said softly. "Now he says we're not good enough to share his fire."

"That's not what I said at all."

"Now he calls me a liar!" snapped the man, rising and moving toward me, his hand on his dagger. "I think you should apologize, bard."

It was then that I knew for certain they planned to kill me.

"Well?" he asked, pushing in close with his hand on his dagger. His breath was foul upon my face, his expression feral. There was nothing to say, and so I said nothing. I heard his knife whisper from its sheath, and I tensed myself for the lunge.

Suddenly his head jerked, and I heard a soft thud and the crack of split bone. I blinked in amazement, for an arrow had sprouted from his temple. He stood for a moment, then I heard his knife drop to the snow; his hand slowly moved up to touch the long shaft jutting from the side of his head. His mouth opened, but no words came, then he sagged against me and slid to the ground with blood seeping from his shattered skull.

The other two men stood transfixed.

And Jarek Mace appeared from behind a screen of bushes, walking forward to the fire with his bow looped over his shoulder. Ignoring the corpse, he approached the two men. "Good morning," he said, his voice smooth, his smile in place. "It is cold, to be sure."

In that moment everything changed. The two robbers, who had looked so threatening and tough, appeared suddenly to have lost their power. I looked hard at them but could see only unwashed peasants, confused and uncertain. What strength they had had was gone from them, their power leached away. They were wolves no longer.

"I think," said Jarek Mace, "it is time for you to move on. You agree?"

They nodded but said nothing. "Good," Mace told them. "Very good. Leave your bows behind and take the body with you."

Dumbly they dropped their bows to the ground, then walked slowly to where I stood. They did not look at me but hauled the corpse upright and half carried, half dragged it away.

Within moments the little clearing was bare, and apart from the dropped bows and the blood by my feet there was no sign of the intruders.

"Thank you," I managed to say.

"You are most welcome," said Mace, "but it was nothing."

"You saved my life. He would have killed me."

"Yes. Now for the breakfast I promised you."

"Breakfast? Shouldn't we be gone from here? They might come back with others."

"They won't come back, bard," he assured me.

"How can you be certain?"

"They don't want to die." Standing, he strolled back to the bushes, returning with a small deer slung across his broad shoulders. Thankfully he had already gutted and prepared it, but even then I could not tear my eyes from the deer's delicate features. I have no aversion to eating venison, but I prefer it skinned and boned. It does my digestion no good at all to see the meat in its original form, and it is hard to appreciate food when its owner's head lies close to your fire.

Even so, the meat was good, and Jarek cut the remaining portions and wrapped them in the hide for later use.

"Well, what are your plans?" he asked me as we finished our breakfast.

I shrugged. "I was told there was a village some six miles to the north. I intend to walk there and try to earn my supper."

"And then?"

"I have thought no further on the subject. I would have starved in Ziraccu had I stayed much longer. Perhaps I will try for the ports and seek passage south."

He nodded. "That's good thinking. No one in his right mind would want to stay in this war-torn land. Is your power returned yet? I'm getting cold."

"No," I lied, basking in magick warmth. "Not for another hour, maybe two."

"Then let us be moving," he grunted, pushing himself to his feet and swinging the hide sack to his shoulder. Taking up my harp bag, I walked alongside him.

"Where are we going?"

"To the village you spoke of. I have friends there."

I said nothing more and trudged silently behind him down the narrow trails through the trees. After a while we heard voices and laughter and emerged into a clearing beside the forest road.

It was a scene of murder and pillage. A score or more of rough-garbed woodsmen were moving among the bodies of the slain, ripping away rings and boots, cloaks and jerkins. Two wagons stood by, piled high with furniture and chests. I glanced at the dead—several men, three women, and beyond the road a monk in a bloodstained habit with an ax still jutting from his back.

"Good morning, Wulf," called Jarek, striding across the murder site and hailing a hunchback with a forked beard.

The man looked up and grinned. "It is so far, Mace," he said. Lifting a small hand ax, he brought the blade down on the hand of the dead man below him. I grunted in shock as the fingers were sliced in half. The hunchback lifted them, pulling the rings loose before discarding the shattered bones. "Who is your squeamish friend?"

"He is a bard and a magicker," Jarek told him. Then he pointed at the corpse. "You've missed an earring."

The hunchback grunted and tore the gold loose; the dead man's head flopped in the snow. "I wouldn't have missed it for long," Wulf muttered. "What's in the hide?"

"Venison."

"Looking to share it with friends?"

"Are you looking to buy it?"

The hunchback let out a cackling laugh. "Why should I not take it? There's twenty of us, and only a fool would fight. You are no fool."

"No, I am not," Jarek agreed, smiling. "But I would kill you, Wulf, then offer to share it with the others. You think they'd fight to avenge you?"

"Nah," said the hunchback. "What do you say to this here brooch?" His bloody hand flicked the gold through the air. Jarek caught it with his left hand, then hefted it for weight.

"Nice. It's a bargain." Dropping the sack, Jarek walked on, stepping over the body of the priest. I hurried after him, keeping my mouth shut and my disgust to myself until we were some distance from the scene.

"At least he didn't rape the women," said Jarek. "He's very moral that way."

"Are you using that as an excuse for him?"

"He doesn't need me to excuse him," he answered. "Wulf is a woodsman—and a good one. But the war has taken its toll, even in the forest. The Count of Ziraccu needed money to hire his mercenaries. So even a count has a limited income: he could not afford to maintain his work force here. Wulf has no job now. Food supplies are scarce, and prices have risen fourfold. He has a family to feed yet no coin to buy food. What else could he do but take to the road?''

"He has become a murderer!"

"That's what I said, didn't I?"

"You condone the murder of innocent women?"

"I didn't kill them," he said. "Don't vent your anger on *me*."

"But you were happy to trade with their killers."

He stopped and turned to face me, the smile, as ever, in place. "You are angry, bard, but not with me. You were filled with horror back there, and loathing and disgust. But you said nothing. That is what is burning inside you . . . not the trade."

I let out a long sigh and looked away.

"Come on," he said cheerfully. "It is a short walk to the village."

The village was a collection of some twenty-five dwellings, some of simple wood construction beneath sloping roofs of thatch, others more solidly built of clay, mixed with powdered stone, beneath wooden roofs weighted with large stones. They were all single-story but equipped with narrow lofts where the children slept. The settlement was situated on the western shore of a long lake, and a dozen fishing boats were drawn up on the mud flats by the water's edge.

Jarek and I walked into the village, passing a group of children playing by the open doors of the central hall. There was much giggling as the youngsters, dressed in simple tunics and trews of wool—most of them grime-ingrained—chased each other around the building. An old man sitting in a narrow doorway nodded at Jarek and lifted a weary hand in greeting. Jarek waved and moved on.

A young girl, scarcely in her teens, watched us as we passed. Her blond hair was cropped close to her head, and her eyes were wide and frightened. She shrank back against the side of the building, her gaze locked to us. I smiled at her, and she turned and sped away between the houses.

"Ilka," said Jarek. "The village whore."

"She is but a child."

"Fifteen or thereabouts," he said, "but she was raped two

years ago in the forest and left to die. She is an orphan with no hope of marriage. What else could she become?''

"Why no hope of marriage? She is comely.''

"The rapists cut out her tongue,'' he answered.

"And for that she is condemned?''

He stopped and turned to face me. "Why do you say condemned? She has employment, she earns her bread, she is not despised.''

I was lost for words. I could see from his expression that he was genuinely curious and lacked any understanding of the girl's grief. Her future had been stolen from her, the gift of speech cruelly ripped from her mouth. Yet she was the one who faced a lifetime of punishment. I tried to explain this, but Jarek merely chuckled, shook his head, and walked on. I wondered then if I had missed some subtlety or overlooked an obvious point. But her face stayed in my mind, haunted and frightened.

We came at last to a narrow house built near the water's edge. Beyond the dwelling was a tall net hut and a fenced area that had been dug over and shaped for a vegetable patch. Nothing was growing now, but inside the house there were sacks of carrots and dried onions and various containers filled with edible tubers that were unknown to me. It was a long one-room dwelling with a central hearth of fired clay and stone. Screens had been set around the hearth, and there were four rough-hewn seats close to the fire. Against the far wall was a wide bed. Jarek loosened the string of his bow and laid it against the wall, his quiver and sword alongside it. Shrugging off his sheepskin cloak, he sat beside the fire, staring into the flames.

"Who lives here?'' I asked, pulling up a seat alongside him.

"Megan,'' he answered, which told me little.

"Is she your lover?''

He chuckled and shook his head; he had a fine smile, warm and friendly. "You'll meet her soon enough,'' he said. "Show me some magick. I have been here for only a few moments, and already I'm bored.''

"What would you like to see?''

"I don't care. Entertain me. Pretend I'm a full audience in a tavern.''

"Very well . . .'' I sat back, thinking through my repertoire. Then I smiled. Before his eyes on the dirt floor a small building appeared, then another, and another. Between them was an alleyway. A young girl, no taller than the length of my hand, came running into sight, pursued by ruffians. A brightly garbed young man carrying a harp entered the scene. "Stop that!" he cried, his voice thin and reedy and far away. The ruffians advanced on him, but suddenly a tall hero leapt from an upper balcony. He moved like a dancer, yet his sword was deadly, and soon the ruffians were either dead or fleeing. I let the scene fade from sight. It took great concentration, but to have enchantment merely vanish always seemed to me to be the mark of a clumsy magicker.

He was silent for a moment, staring at the dirt floor. "That's good, bard," he said softly. "That's very good. Is that how it looked to you?"

"It did at the time."

"How have you lived so long?" he asked me.

"What do you mean?"

"The romance in your heart. This world of ours is a garden of evil. You should have been a monk, locked away in some gray monastery with high walls and strong gates."

"Life can be like the stories," I said. "There are still heroes, men of great soul."

"You have met them?"

"No, but that does not mean they do not exist. Manannan, the last knight of the Gabala, and Rabain the Vampyre slayer, both walked these woods, saw the stars above the same mountains. It is a dream of mine to see such a man, perhaps to serve him. A soldier or a poet, I do not mind. But someone with the courage to change this world, a man with a soul as bright as the last star of the morning."

"Dream on, bard. Morningstar, indeed! You know much of weapons?"

"Very little. My older brothers were trained to be knights. Not I."

"A morningstar is a terrible weapon. It has a short handle of iron, and attached to it is a chain; on the end of the chain is a ball of spiked metal. It is a kind of mace. When a man is struck by it, he dies, his skull smashed to fragments."

"That is not the morning star I spoke of."

"I know, but you spoke of a dream. I am giving you the reality."

"Only your reality."

"What is it you are looking for? Glory? What?"

I shrugged. "What do all men seek? I want to be happy. I would like a wife and sons one day. But I want them to grow in a land where there is hope for the future, where men do not take to the road. If that is a hopeless dream—and maybe it is—then I will sire no sons. I will wander, and play my harp, and weave my magick until the end."

I expected him to laugh or to say something scornful. But somehow what he did was worse. He stood and walked to a nearby water butt, lifting a copper gourd and drinking deeply. "You think the weather will break soon?" he asked me.

I did not answer him. I felt a sudden need for music and took my harp outside, walking to the water's edge and sitting beside a long, narrow boat. The wind was rippling the water, and small sections of ice came floating by on the gray surface. Snow began to fall, and I played for the snow, my fingers plucking daintily at the shorter strings, the higher notes, the music drifting out over the lake. Darker, deeper tones crept in as the storm clouds gathered.

Several villagers came by as I played, but I ignored them. The first person I noticed was the whore, Ilka. She crept in close and sat hugging her knees, her huge blue eyes fixed to my face. The music changed as I saw her, becoming wistful and sad. She shook her head and rose, beginning a curious dance in the mud. I saw her then as a nymph, a magical eldritch creature trapped in a world that understood nothing. And the music changed again, lifting and swelling, still sorrowful but filled with a promise of new tomorrows.

At last my fingers became tired, and the music died. Ilka stopped, too, and looked at me with those wide, haunted eyes. Her expression was hard to read. I smiled and said something— I don't remember what it was—but fear came back to her then, and she scampered away into the gathering dusk.

Toward evening I saw Wulf and his killers striding toward the village.

For a moment only I was filled with stark terror, but then I saw the children running up to meet them. The hunchback lifted one small boy high into the air, perching him on his twisted shoulder, and the sound of laughter filled the village.

Jarek was right, in part at least.

This forest was a garden of evil.

◇ 3 ◇

I SEE THAT you are quizzical, my ghostly friend. How, you wonder, does the laughter of children in such circumstances denote evil? Well, think on this . . . is it not comforting to believe that all acts of murder and malice are committed by brutes with no souls? Worshipers of unclean powers?

But how dispiriting to see a group of men coming home from a day of toil, ready to play for an hour with their children, to hold their wives close, to sit at their hearth fires, when their work has been the foul slaughter of innocent travelers. You take my point? Evil is at its most vile when it is practiced by ordinary men.

We can excuse a demon who stalks the night seeking blood. It is his nature; he was created for just such a purpose. But not a man who by day commits acts of murder and by night returns home to be a good, loving husband and father. For that is evil of a monstrous kind and casts doubts upon us all.

But I am running ahead of myself. Where was I? Ah, yes, the village by the lake. I had watched the whore dance, and I had seen the return of the village men. And now, as the winter sunlight faded, I was standing outside the hut staring out over the cold lake.

An old woman came walking across the mud flats. She was tall and thin, her bony body covered with a long woolen gown, her shoulders wrapped in a plaid shawl. Upon her head was a leather cap with long ear pieces tied with thongs beneath her chin. She was carrying a sack, and she walked with the long strides of a man. I took her to be more than seventy years old.

"Do you not bow in the presence of a lady, Owen Odell?" she asked, stopping before me.

I was shocked and did not move for a moment; then good manners reasserted themselves. "My apologies," I said, extending my left leg and bowing low, sweeping my left arm out in a graceful half circle. "Have we met before?"

"Perhaps," she answered, smiling. Her face was lined, but good high cheekbones prevented the skin from sagging. Her lips were thin, and her eyes, deep-set beneath shaggy brows, were bright blue. Forty years before she must have been a handsome woman, I thought.

"Indeed I was," she said brightly. "Thank you for looking beyond the crone and seeing the true Megan."

"You are a magicker, then?"

"Of sorts," she agreed, walking past me to her hut.

Jarek was asleep on the bed. Megan carried her sack to the rear of the room, tipping the contents onto a wide table. All kinds of leaves and roots had been gathered, and these she began to separate into small mounds. I moved behind her, looking down at the first mound. I recognized the flowers instantly as eyebright, downy leaves with white petals tinged with violet and with a yellow spot at the center of the bloom.

"You are a herbalist also, madam?" I inquired.

"Aye," she answered. "And doctor, meat curer, midwife. You know this plant?"

"My nurse used to make an infusion of its leaves for winter colds," I told her.

"It is also good for preventing infection in wounds," she said, "and for relieving swollen eyes."

I cast my eyes over the other plants. There was wild thyme, figwort, dove's foot, woundwort, sanicle, and several others I could not recognize.

"Your magick is strong, Megan," I said.

"There is no magick in gathering plants," she muttered.

"Oh, but there is when it is winter and none of them grow. You have a spell garden somewhere, and your enchantment works there even while you sleep."

"You have a long tongue, Owen Odell," she said, a short curved blade hissing from the leather scabbard at her waist, "and I have a sharp knife. Be advised."

I looked into her eyes. "An empty threat, madam," I told her, keeping my voice low.

"How would you know?" she asked. "You cannot read my thoughts."

"No, but I like you, and that is purely on instinct. My magick may not be strong, but my instincts usually are." She nodded, and her eyes lost their coldness. Smiling, she slipped the skinning knife back into its sheath.

"Aye, sometimes instincts are more reliable than magick. Not often, mind! Now make yourself useful and build up the fire. Then there are logs to be cut. You will find an ax in the lean-to behind the house. After that you can help me prepare the hanging birds."

I learned something that evening: Physical labor can be immensely satisfying to the soul. There was a stack of logs, sawn into rounds of roughly two feet in length. They were of various thicknesses, and the wood was beech, the bark silvery and coarse but the inner bright and the color of fresh cream. The ax was old and heavy, with a curved handle polished by years of use. I placed a log upon a wide slab of wood and slashed at it, missing by several inches. The ax blade thudded into the slab beneath, jarring my arms and shoulders. More carefully I lifted it again, bringing it down into the center of the log, which split pleasingly.

As I have said, I was not a small man, though I had little muscle. I was tall and bony, but my shoulders were naturally broad, my arms long, and my balance good. It was a matter of a few minutes before I was swinging the ax like a veteran woodsman, and my woodpile grew.

I worked for almost an hour in the moonlight, stopping only when my fingers became too sore to hold the handle. There was a deep ache in my lower back, but it was more than matched by the pride I felt in my labor.

For the first time in my life I had labored for my supper, working with my hands, and the flames of tonight's fire, the warmth I would know, would be the result of my own efforts. I laid the ax against the lean-to and began to stack the chunks I had cut.

Megan walked out into the night and nodded as she saw all that I had done. "Never leave an ax like that," she said. "The blade will rust."

"Shall I bring it inside?"

She laughed then. "No, young fool, leave it embedded in a log. It will keep the blade sharp."

She waited as I stacked the firewood, then bade me follow her to a small hut at the rear of the building. Even with the winter wind blowing, the stench was great as she opened the door. There were some twenty geese, seven turkeys, and more than a dozen hares hanging there. I cast a swift spell, and the aroma of lavender filled my nostrils.

"Have you ever prepared a goose?" she asked.

"For what?" I answered, forcing a smile.

"I thought not. Nobleman, are you? Servants to run your errands, build your fires, heat your bed? Well, you will learn much here, master bard."

Stepping forward, she lifted a dead goose from a hook and pushed it into my arms. The head and neck flopped down against my right thigh. "First pluck the bird," she said. "Then I will show you how to prepare it."

"It is not a skill I wish to learn," I pointed out.

"It is if you want to eat," she replied. After working with the ax, I was extremely hungry and did not argue. My hunger, I should point out, did not last long. Plucking the bird was not arduous, but what followed made me wonder if I would ever eat goose again.

She carried the carcass to a long, narrow bench. I followed her and watched as she sliced open the skin of the creature's neck. Then she cut away the bones and head and pulled clear the crop bag, which she flung to the floor. "Useless," she said. "Even dogs wouldn't touch it. Now give me your hand," she ordered me, and took hold of my wrist. "Insert two fingers here on either side of the neck and rotate them inside the beast." It was slimy and cold, and I could feel the bird's tiny tendons and veins being torn as my fingers slid over the brittle bones. She pulled my hand clear, then inserted her own fingers into the hole. "Good," she muttered, "you have released the lungs, the gizzard, and the heart."

"I'm so pleased."

Turning the goose, she took up a small knife and then pushed a finger into its body. Extending the skin, she cut a circular hole at the rear and discarded the sliced flesh. "Push your hand in and pull out the insides," she ordered me. I swallowed hard and did as she instructed. My stomach turned as the oily, dark, and bloody mess pulled clear. I stepped back from the table.

"Don't you vomit in here!" she snapped. Stepping forward, she continued to clean out the goose, removing what appeared to be oceans of fat. "Good tallow," she said. "Candles, grease for leather, ointment for the rheumatic. Liver, heart, and lung make for good broth. A fine bird."

I couldn't speak and turned away to where the hares were hanging head down. Each of them had a small clay pot suspended from its ears. Walking toward one, I glanced into a pot; it was full of blood, but worse than this, there were maggots floating there. I watched another emerge from the hare's nostril and drop into the congealing blood. Sickened, I leapt back.

"This one's rotten!" I said.

Megan walked over to where the creature was hanging. "Not at all. It is just high. The meat will be soft and full of flavor. Wulf will be coming for it tonight. We'll prepare that next."

I could not watch and, without the usual courtesies, ran from the hut.

The sound of Megan's laughter echoed after me.

It is hard for a young man to discover that he is useless. We have such pride when young. I was a good bard and a fine musician. As a magicker? Well, there might have been twenty or thirty men in the southern kingdom who were better than I, but not more.

Yet here in this village I was little more use than a mewling half-wit. It galled me beyond words. I wanted to leave, to march away to some larger settlement. But the forest was vast, and my knowledge of it scant.

That evening I sat disconsolately before the fire tuning my harp and thinking back to the days of childhood in the south. Jarek awoke sometime before midnight and, without a word to Megan, took up his cloak and walked from the house.

"Where are you from?" I asked the old woman.

"Not from here," she answered. Her speech was clipped, the pronunciation good. But the voice was disguised, I felt.

"Are you noble-born?" I inquired.

"What would you like me to be?" she responded.

"Whatever you wish to be, madam."

"Then take me as I am. An old woman in a small village by a lake."

"Is that all you see when you look in the mirror?"

"I see many things, Owen Odell," she told me, an edge of sadness in her voice. "I see what is and what was."

The fire was crackling in the hearth, the smoke spiraling up through the small hole in the high thatched roof, the wind hissing through cracks in the wooden walls.

"Who are you?" I asked her.

She smiled wearily. "You want me to be some mythic queen or ancient sorceress? Do you seek always to make the world fit into a song?"

I shrugged. "The songs are comforting, Megan."

"You are a good man, Owen, in a world where good men are few. Take my advice and learn to use a blade or a bow."

"You wish me to become a killer?"

"Better than to be killed."

"Are you a widow?"

"What is this fascination you have with my life? I grow herbs and prepare meat for the table. I weave cloth and cast an occasional spell. I am not unusual or in any way unique."

"I do not find you so."

She stood and stretched her back. "Go to bed, bard. That is the place for dreams." Wrapping her shawl about her, she walked out into the night.

I don't know why, but I was convinced she was leaving to meet Jarek Mace. Taking her advice, I stripped off my clothes and stretched out on the bed, pulling the goose-down quilt over my body.

Sleep came swiftly, and I dreamed of a lost swan, circling and calling in the sky above an ice-covered lake. I knew he was searching for something, but I did not know what it was. And then I saw, beneath the ice on the water, a second swan, cold and dead. But the first bird kept calling out as he flew on weary wings.

Calling . . . calling.

There are, it seems to me, two kinds of pride. One urges a man to disguise his shortcomings for fear of looking foolish. The second spurs him on to eliminate those shortcomings. Happily, I have always been blessed with the latter.

I set to work during the winter months to learn those skills which would make me a valuable asset to my neighbors. Despite my loathing of carcasses and blood, I taught myself to gut, skin, and prepare meat for the table. I learned to tan hides, to make tallow candles, to identify medicinal herbs and prepare infusions and decoctions.

And I labored with ax and saw to supply Megan with firewood aplenty.

The villagers also taught me something valuable: how to live together in harmony, each man and woman a link in a chain, each dependent upon the other for food, clothing, shoes, bows, medicines. There was only one piece of communal property— a large cast-iron oven. It had been bought in Ziraccu and carted into the forest, where it was leased to Garik the baker. The rest of the huts made do with field ovens, bricks of clay erected over tiny trenches. Garik would make bread and cakes for the villagers in return for meats, hides, and home-brewed ale. Megan earned her living by supplying herbs and curing meats. Wulf, the hunchback, brought in venison and boar meat. Each person had developed a skill that enhanced the lives of the other villagers.

Even Owen Odell found his niche. Each week, on the holy day, I played my harp in the village hall, creating new vigorous melodies so that the villagers could dance. I was not popular, you understand, for I was an Angostin among Highlanders, but I was, I believe, respected.

In my spare moments, which were few, I sat and watched the village life, observing my neighbors, learning about them, their fears and their hopes. Highlanders are a disparate people, a mixture of races, and the ancestry of many could be seen in their faces and builds. Garik the baker was a short, powerfully built man with flat features, a jutting brow, and a wide gash of a mouth. It took no great imagination to see him dressed in skins, his cheeks painted blue in the spiral patterns of his Pictish ancestors. There were several like Garik, whose bloodlines ran from the earliest human settlers; they were dour men, hard and tough, men to match the mountains. Others, like Orlaith the cattle herder, were taller, their hair tinged with the red of the Belgae, their eyes dark, their souls fiery and passionate. A few showed Angostin lines—long noses and strong chins—but they admitted to no Angostin heritage. This was hardly surprising, since the Angostins were the most recent invaders, a mere few hundred years before. And Highland memories are long indeed.

My reputation among them was raised several notches when I used a search spell to locate a missing child. She was Wulf's youngest and had wandered off into the forest during a cold afternoon. Wulf and a dozen of his fellows set off to look for her, but the temperature was dropping fast, and most of the men knew the child could not survive for long.

A search spell is not difficult to cast when one lives in a forest and people are few, though only the very best magickers could cast a successful search spell within a city. This one was slightly more difficult for me because I blended the spell with one of warming. Even so, an apprentice could have cast it.

Essentially one pictures the object of the search and creates a glowing sphere of white light. The image of the object—in this case a yellow-haired child—is set at the center of the light sphere. Then the light is sent out into the woods, seeking to match the image at its heart to an outside source. It is not an unusually complex spell, and if by chance there were several yellow-haired children in the forest, it would probably alight on the wrong one. But on this day there was only one lost little girl, and the sphere found her wandering beside a frozen stream, her fingers and lips blue with cold.

It touched her, and the second spell became active, covering her with a warm, invisible blanket while the search sphere rose up above the trees, blazing with light and drawing the rescuers to the toddler.

The child was unharmed, and such was Wulf's delight that he made me a present of an ornate dagger with a leaf-shaped blade and a ruby encased in gold at the hilt. He also grabbed my shoulders, dragged me down, and kissed me on both cheeks, an altogether unpleasant experience.

But in the days that followed, when I was out among the villagers, I would be greeted with smiles and people would inquire politely after my health.

It was two months before news of the war filtered through to the village. A travelling tinker, well known to Wulf and therefore allowed to pass through, came to us one bright cold morning. He told of the fall of Ziraccu, the slaughter of its inhabitants. Count Leopold had been found hiding in the granary; his eyes were put out, and he was placed in a cage and hanged from the ruined walls. Then the army had moved on to the north. Thankfully, they had avoided this part of the forest.

During the evenings I would sit with Megan, listening to tales of the Highlands. They were fine, companionable times. Jarek Mace was often absent, traveling to other settlements yet always returning with news, or coin, or venison.

"What were you like when younger?" I asked Megan one evening when Jarek was abroad on one of his journeys.

"I was like this," she answered. Golden light bathed her from head to toe, and her short-cropped iron-gray hair was replaced by golden curls hanging free to milk-white shoulders. Her face was beautiful beyond description, her eyes blue as the summer sky, her lips full. Her figure was slim, but the breasts were large in comparison; her neck was long and sleek, the skin smooth as porcelain.

I was lost for words—but not at her beauty. This was one of the seven great spells, and only masters of the craft could weave one so casually.

"Where did you learn such a piece?" I asked.

The beautiful woman shrugged and smiled. "Long ago, from a man named Cataplas."

"He was my teacher," I told her.

"I know."

"But I had not the skill to learn the seven."

"There is yet time," she said, letting fall the spell.

"You are noble-born," I pointed out. "The gown you conjured was purest satin, and there were pearls at the neck and cuff."

"You think I would create sacking to wear?" she countered.

"Why must you be so mysterious, lady?"

"Why must *you* be so inquisitive?"

"The first words you spoke to me were, 'Do you not bow in the presence of a lady?' Not a woman—a lady. That intrigued me at the time; it still does. You were not born in the village."

"You are wrong, master bard. My family was traveling at the time of my birth, and I was born in a village such as this. Far to the north. But I came here twenty years ago, and I have been content."

"But what is there here for you?"

"Peace," she answered.

"Why does Jarek Mace stay with you? Is he a relative?"

"No. Just a man."

"I wish you would tell me more, Megan. I feel . . . there is so much more to know."

"There is always more to know," she chided. "Even as you lie on your deathbed there will be more to know. Are you another Cataplas in an endless search for knowledge? It is not the mark of a wise man, Owen."

I shrugged. "How can the search for knowledge be foolish?" I countered.

"When it is conducted for its own sake. A man who seeks to learn how to irrigate a field in order to grow more crops has not only increased his knowledge but found the means to make life better for his fellows. Learning must be put to use."

"Perhaps Cataplas will do exactly that when he believes he knows enough."

She did not answer me at first but stirred the coals in the fire, adding fresh wood to the flickering flames. "There was once a prince in this land, to the north of here, who was on a quest for knowledge. He was a good man, a kind man, but his quest became an obsession. His brothers, also good men, tried to sway him; he was a fine magicker, and he became a great sorcerer. But even this was not enough. He traveled across the sea, passing from land to land, ever seeking; he journeyed into desolate mountains and subterranean caverns, sought out lost cities, and communed with spirits and demons. After twelve years he returned, late one night, to the city of his birth. His brothers ruled that city wisely and well. In the summer the water was clean, filtered through sand and shale. In the winter the storehouses were full, and no one starved. But then he returned. Within the week travelers began to notice that the gates of the city were always shut, and woodsmen carried tales of screams and sounds of terror within the gray walls.

"The days passed into weeks. No one left the silent city. People began to gather from the villages and towns, staring at the towering walls, wondering what secrets were hidden there. Several men scaled those walls, but none returned.

"And then one night the gates opened. And the people saw—"

At that moment the white face of a Vampyre appeared in front of my eyes, his teeth white, the canines long and sharp and hollow. I screamed and fell back, toppling from my chair. Megan's laughter filled the cabin as I scrambled up, embarrassed and yet still fearful, my heart hammering.

"That was unkind," I admonished her.

"But wondrously entertaining." Her smile faded, and she spread her hands. "I am sorry, Owen. I could not resist it."

"You had me convinced the tale was true. You are a fine storyteller."

"Oh, it was true," she said. "Have you not heard of Golgoleth and the Vampyre kings? Two thousand years ago these lands knew great terror and tragedy. For the prince, Golgoleth, had returned as a creature of darkness, a Vampyre. He tainted the souls of his brothers, joining them to him and bringing them the dark joys of the undead. And then the evil spread throughout the city and ultimately throughout the land."

"I have heard of Golgoleth," I told her. "It is a tale to frighten naughty children: Be good or Golgoleth will come for you. But I doubt the truth of the story as it is now told. I see him as an evil man and a practitioner of the black arts but not as an undying immortal feasting on blood."

"He did not feast on blood, poet, but on innocence. But perhaps you are right. Perhaps it was fable."

Talons scraped upon the wood of the roof, and I leapt from my seat. Then an owl hooted, and I heard the flapping of wings in the night.

"Just fable," said Megan, smiling, her eyes mocking. "Will you sleep now, or perhaps you need a stroll into the forest. It is very pleasant in the moonlight."

I grinned then and shook my head. "I think I will just go to sleep and save my walk for the dawn."

Spring came early, the thaw swelling the mountain streams, bright beautiful flowers growing on the hillsides. It was on the third day of spring that Garik's sheep were slaughtered, and great excitement followed. Huge tracks were found near the two butchered animals, and Wulf, the senior woodsman, pronounced them to be troll spoor.

There were three of the creatures, probably a mated pair with a cub. They were far from the troll passes, the high cold peaks of the northwest, and it was rare, Wulf informed me, to find the beasts so far south.

The men of the village armed themselves with bow, spear,

and ax and set off in pursuit. I went with them, for I had never
seen a troll and was anxious to increase my knowledge. There
are many tales of the beasts in legend, almost all of them involving the kidnapping and eating of children or maidens. But
in all my long life I have never come across a recorded incident
where trolls feasted on human flesh.

We followed the trail for two days as it wound higher into the
mountains. One of the beasts walked with a limp—probably
the male, pronounced Wulf, for his track was the largest. Often
the cub's spoor would disappear for long periods, but this, I was
told, only showed that the female was carrying him.

On the second night we came upon the remains of their camp
fire, the ashes surrounded by splintered sheep's bones.

"No point looking for them in the dark," said Wulf, settling
down beside the dead fire and building a fresh blaze upon the
remains. There were ten men besides myself and Wulf in the
hunting party, and they stretched out around the fire and began
to talk of better days. Garik the baker was there, and Lanis the
tanner. The others I forget.

"Have you ever seen a troll?" I asked Wulf as we sat together.
The hunchback nodded.

"The last time was ten years ago, up in the high country. Big
fellow, he was, gray as a rock, with tusks curling up from his
jaw, just like a boar. I didn't have my bow strung at that moment, and so we just stood and looked at each other. Then he
said, 'Go.' So I went."

"They truly have the power of speech? I thought that was
myth."

"Ah, they can talk, right enough. Just a bit. When I was a
tiny lad, my father took me to Ziraccu Fair on Midsummer Day.
They had a young troll there, caged. He could speak a fair bit."

"What happened to him?"

"They had a tourney for the knights, and before it there was
a troll baiting. Hunting hounds were set on the beast. He fought
right well for a while—too good, really. Killed four o' the
hounds. So the knights came in and hamstrung him. It was more
even then, and the hounds tore him apart. It was good sport.
My father told me I should feel privileged to have seen it. There's
not so much troll baiting nowadays—less of 'em, you see. They
do it with bears now, I'm told, but it's not the same."

I moved away from the fire, and as the others slept, I idly cast a search spell, picturing a fanged snout on a flat gray face. The sphere floated away, then stopped no more than twenty feet from the fire. I sat bolt upright, hand on dagger, and considered waking Wulf.

But first I sent out a questing spell, small as a firefly, and watched it as it flew to where the troll was hiding. The spark did not change color, nor did it speed away from the hiding place. I brought the tiny flame back to me and opened my mouth. It flew in and settled on my tongue. There was fear there, and resignation, but no feeling of impending violence. I sighed, for it came to me then that the creature in the bushes was the crippled male, and he was there to die in order to save his family.

I stood silently and crossed the small clearing, halting just before the dark undergrowth. The troll got to his feet. He was upward of eight feet tall, and there was only one tusk growing from his lower jaw, curving out, wickedly sharp, to a point level with his eye. The second horn had been sheared off, the stump brown and pitted. His skin was covered with hundreds of nodules and growths that on a human would have been termed warts. A roughly made sheepskin loincloth was tied around his waist. I beckoned him to follow me and walked away from the campsite. I don't know what possessed me to do it, but truly, there was no fear. I did not expect to be harmed, nor was I.

The beast followed me to the crown of a hill, where I sat upon a boulder and faced him. He squatted down in front of me, and in the moonlight I saw that his eyes were distinctly human, huge and round, and gray as an autumn storm cloud.

"Do not remain here," I said. "It is not safe."

"Nowhere safe," he replied. He was, as Wulf had described, stone-gray and hairless, and upon the calf of his huge right leg there was a vicious scar, serrated and long, the muscles around it withered and weak. But his arms and shoulders bulged with muscle.

"What happened to your leg?"

"Fought bear. Killed it," he grunted. "Why you talk?"

I spread my hands. "I have never seen a troll."

"Troll?" He shook his head. "A bad name. But we call you *Uisha-rae*, the pigs-that-walk-on-two-legs. Why you follow us?"

"You killed two sheep belonging to Garik the baker."

"For this we must die?"

"No," I said. "Go with your . . . family into the north. No

one will find your tracks. Go tonight. I will hold them sleeping until you are far away.''

"Why?"

"I don't know. Go now.''

The beast reared up on its hind legs, turned, and limped away from me. I returned to the campsite and cast a sleep spell that kept the hunters snoring until around noon. Once they began to wake, I pretended sleep and lay quietly as they argued among themselves. They could not believe they had slept so long. Back in the village each of the men would have risen before dawn and been working for a good hour before the sun climbed into sight.

With the trail cold, Wulf at last called off the hunt, and we set off toward the village.

By midafternoon we were joined by Jarek Mace, who came loping along the trail carrying his longbow. He joked with the others for a while, then dropped back to walk alongside me at the rear of the group.

"You keep curious company," he said softly.

"What do you mean?"

He smiled and tapped his nose.

"You saw them?" I asked him.

"Yes.''

"You did not kill them, did you?"

"You are a strange man, bard," he answered. "The male could have killed you, Owen, and if any of the others had found the tracks as I did and known that you spoke to the creature, then they would have killed you. Why did you take the risk?"

"I don't know," I told him honestly. "It just seemed . . . somehow sad. Here was a small family being hunted by armed men, and the male—the father—was ready to give up his life to protect his wife and child. I felt it would be wrong to kill them.''

"They were only trolls," he whispered.

"I know. Why are they so hated?"

"They talk," he answered.

"That makes no sense.''

He shrugged and walked on in silence. I thought long and hard about the trolls, and I realized he was right. Man is the only animal capable of hate, and in the main he reserves his hatred for his fellow man. No one hates a bear or a lion; they might fear them for their power and ferocity, but they will not hate them. But the troll . . . Grotesque and powerful, yet with the capacity for speech, he is the perfect target for all man's resentments.

It was a dispiriting thought as we trudged on along muddy trails.

We camped by a swollen stream in a small hollow surrounded by beech trees. The night was cool, but there was little breeze and the camp fire gave a pleasant glow to the hollow. I sat with Wulf and Jarek Mace while the others slept.

"The Angostins have gone," said Jarek, "but they left behind an army of occupation under three generals. Ziraccu is being rebuilt, and they are allowing Ikenas to move north and settle there."

"Who cares?" responded Wulf. "As long as they stay away from the forest, I don't give a good God damn."

"I don't think they will stay clear," Jarek told him. "Edmund has given the entire forest to the new count, Azrek. He was responsible for the sacking of Callen Castle and the murder of the nuns and priests at the monastery there. He is a greedy man by all accounts; he will want his taxes paid."

"We paid this year's taxes to Leopold," said Wulf.

Jarek chuckled. "That will not concern Azrek."

"If there's nothing to take, what can he do?" responded the hunchback.

Jarek said nothing. Wrapping himself in his sheepskin cloak, he lay down beside the dying fire and closed his eyes.

It was midmorning on the following day when we topped the last rise before the lake. Black smoke was billowing from the village, and we could see several buildings ablaze.

Wulf and the other villagers ran down the slope, but Jarek Mace stood quietly on the brow of the hill, scanning the distant tree line. Swiftly he strung his longbow and notched an arrow to the string. Then he walked slowly down the hill, angling to the south. I followed him, dagger in hand.

We found Ilka, the mute whore, hiding among the thick bushes at the foot of the hill. Her face was bruised, and an arrow was lodged in the muscles behind one shoulder blade. The wound was not deep, and it seemed the shaft had struck her at an oblique angle. Jarek broke the arrow but did not pull it clear. "It needs to be cut free," he said. "If we drag it out, she could bleed to death."

The girl could hardly stand, and so I lifted her into my arms and carried her into the ruined village. Bodies were every-where—women, old men, and children, scattered in death. Wulf was kneeling by his murdered family, cradling his yellow-haired daughter in his arms and weeping.

Jarek Mace walked to Megan's house. It was undamaged, and the old woman was sitting by her fire; she was unharmed. I carried Ilka inside, laying her on the wide bed, turning her to her side so that the broken arrow jutted upward. Jarek Mace had run to the far wall, pulling open a hidden compartment. It was empty, and he cursed loudly.

"What happened, Megan?" I asked.

"Soldiers from Ziraccu. There was no warning; they merely rode in and began the killing. There was no resistance."

"Why did they spare you?"

"They did not see me," she said wearily, pushing herself to her feet and approaching the injured girl.

Jarek Mace stormed out of the hut. Once more I followed him. It was the first time I had seen him genuinely angry. I knew it had nothing to do with the slaughter of the villagers; he was furious because the soldiers had found his cache of stolen gold and jewels.

Running to the weeping hunchback, Jarek dragged him to his feet. "They had horses," he shouted. "That means they must keep to the road. We can cut them off by taking the hunting track."

"Leave me alone!" screamed Wulf.

"You will let them die unavenged?" hissed Jarek Mace. The hunchback froze, his dark eyes gleaming. Then he took a deep, shuddering breath.

"You are right, Mace. Let's kill them all!"

I had no wish to remain in this village of the dead, and when the fourteen hunters loped off, I followed them. It was a grueling run, down through glens, up over hills, through dense under-growth, finally crossing a wide, shallow river and wading to the far bank and the road to Ziraccu.

Wulf ran down to the road, kneeling to examine the tracks. "They've not yet passed," he told Mace. "See, this was their outward journey."

"How many?"

The hunchback moved back and forth along the road, study-ing the hoofprints. "Maybe thirty, perhaps less. But no more."

Jarek called the men together, ordering six to take cover on the right of the road, seven on the left. "Do not let fly until I do," he commanded them.

"What about me?" I asked. "What should I do?"

"Stay with me," he answered, then sat down at the side of the road with his longbow beside him.

"How can we fight thirty?" I asked him as the fear started to gnaw at my belly.

"You just keep killing until there's none left," he answered grimly.

He was in no mood for conversation, so I sat in silence for a while, watching the north, listening for the sound of hoofbeats.

"Why did they kill everyone?" I asked at last.

"Azrek is encouraging immigrants from the south to settle here; they will pay good money for tracts of forest land. Wulf and the others were tenants of Count Leopold. They have no rights."

"They could have been ordered off. There was no need to kill."

"There is rarely any *need* to kill," he said, "but men still do it."

"As you are intending to now?"

"They stole my gold," he hissed, as if that were answer enough.

We sat for perhaps an hour, and then I heard them, the slow clopping of hooves upon the dirt road. My heart began hammering, and my mouth went dry.

Jarek stood and notched an arrow to his bow before stepping out into the middle of the road. I could not seem to move my legs and sat for a moment staring at him. He seemed so relaxed as he waited, his bow held by his side, a slight smile showing on his handsome face. Drawing my knife, I climbed unsteadily to my feet.

"Stay where you are," he ordered, "and when the battle starts, run back into the undergrowth. No horse will follow you there."

Then they came in sight, more than twenty horsemen, the front three in full armor with plumed helmets upon their heads. Behind the trio were men-at-arms in breastplates and helms of leather, and bringing up the rear was a wagon loaded with booty.

"Good day, gentlemen," called Jarek Mace.

◇ 4 ◇

THE KNIGHT RIDING at the center of the trio, a huge man wearing a shining breastplate of silver and a helmet sporting a horsehair plume, lifted his arm and halted the convoy. The visor of his helmet was raised, and I could see a corn-yellow mustache and eyes the color of a winter sky, gray and cold. Reining in the giant black stallion, he leaned forward on the pommel of his saddle and gazed upon the tall, lean form of Jarek Mace.

"What do you want, fellow?" he asked, his voice as deep as distant thunder.

"When you travel upon my road, Sir Knight, then you must pay my toll," Jarek answered.

"A toll, is it?" responded the knight as laughter sounded from the riders behind him. "Tell me, fellow, how it is that you came to . . . own this road. For I was under the impression the forest was ruled by Count Azrek."

"He is—for the present—the Count of Ziraccu," Jarek told him. "I am the lord of this forest."

"And what might your name be, my lord?" asked the knight.

"Why, I am the Morningstar."

The knight leaned back, removed his right gauntlet, and opened a purse tied to the sword belt at his waist. "And what will the toll cost us?"

"All that you have," said Jarek.

"Enough of this nonsense," snapped the knight. "I would have given you a silver penny for your impudence. Now step aside or feel the weight of my whip!"

"Certainly, Sir Knight." Jarek moved to his right and then

swung back, the longbow coming up, the string stretching, the notched shaft leaping from the bow. The knight swayed back as the arrow slashed by him to punch through the helmet of the young knight to his left. Without a sound the surprised victim slid from the saddle, pitching headfirst to the ground.

Shafts flashed from both sides of the road, plunging into men and horses. The pain-maddened beasts reared, throwing their riders to the road. More arrows tore into the men-at-arms.

The two knights had both drawn their swords, but instead of entering the fray, they spurred on their mounts toward Jarek Mace. The young bowman sprinted toward me, ducking just as a longsword hissed toward his head.

Instead of giving chase, the knights galloped on toward Ziraccu. Jarek cursed and ran back into the road, notching a second arrow to his string. His arm came up, and I watched him take aim and loose the shaft, which sang through the air and thudded into the back of the second knight. The man straightened in the saddle, then swayed, but clung to the pommel as the horses moved out of range. Jarek turned.

The villagers had dropped their bows and charged the demoralized men-at-arms. Several of the enemy threw down their weapons and began pleading for mercy. There was none to be had, and they were all butchered.

It was not a pleasant sight.

At last Wulf the hunchback, covered in blood, approached where Jarek was sitting at the roadside.

"My children are avenged," he said softly. "Thank you, Mace." Jarek merely nodded, but the hunchback remained where he was. "What do we do now?" he asked.

"Do? Take the booty and get away from this place as soon as possible. Those knights did not ride back for an early supper."

"Yes," Wulf agreed. "Yes, you're right."

Two of the villagers moved up to the driving seat of the wagon and turned the horses back toward the north, while Wulf and the others began stripping the dead of valuables and weapons.

Jarek loped to the wagon, pulling himself over the tailboard. I ran to join him. He was sitting beside some thirty small sacks of coin; scattered around him were golden ornaments, statues, bracelets, bangles, and brooches.

"I'm a rich man, bard," he said, chuckling. "I think I'll buy a castle by the sea."

"Why did you talk to the knights?" I asked him. "Why not just attack?"

"They were moving. A walking horse, when frightened, breaks into a run. A standing horse will usually rear. It is that simple. I wanted the convoy halted."

"You are an amazing man," I told him. "What made you give the name Morningstar?"

He laughed and clapped me on the shoulder. "I thought it would amuse you, Owen. And anyway, the odds were that someone would escape. I didn't want anyone rushing to Azrek with the name Jarek Mace, now, did I?"

"You think he won't find out eventually?"

"By then I will be long gone. What a fine day, to be sure!" With his dagger he ripped open a coin sack. Silver pennies tumbled out. He grabbed a handful and tossed them in the air, where they spun in the sunlight before tinkling down to the wagon boards. "I love money," said Jarek.

Jarek Mace was in high good humor as the iron-rimmed wagon wheels rolled slowly along the forest road. Wulf and the others—having stripped all valuables from the twenty-two dead Ikenas—set off back over the hills to the village. They would arrive hours before us, but I was tired and had no wish to walk too soon among the bodies of the slain. The aftermath of revenge leaves no sweetness in the mouth, and a wagon full of gold was no recompense for a village of the dead.

The sun was low in the sky as we rounded the last bend, and I saw the glittering lake and a large crowd awaiting us. Jarek was sleeping, and I did not at first wake him.

The valuables in the wagon had come, I knew, from more than one settlement, and I guessed—rightly—that in the waiting throng were representatives of those other villages and towns. I could see Megan standing beside a tall woman dressed in the severe black habit and white head scarf of the Order of Naesar nuns.

As the wagon hove into sight, the crowd pushed forward, yelling and cheering.

Jarek awoke at once. "What the devil?" he said, sitting up.

A great cheer went up as he stood.

"Morningstar! Morningstar!" I saw Wulf and the other warriors at the front of the crowd with their arms raised, the last of the sunlight glinting on their stolen weapons.

Nimbly Mace leapt from the wagon to stand with hands on hips, accepting their tribute. The crowd parted, and the abbess strode forward; she was around sixty years of age, stern of face, her eyes deep-set and glacial blue. Moving past Jarek, she opened the tailboard of the wagon and reached inside. Lifting clear a small golden statue of the blessed Saint Katryn and holding it aloft, she turned to the crowd.

"She is returned to us," cried the abbess, and a section of the crowd cheered.

An elderly man approached. His face was lined, his right eye dead and useless. With difficulty he bowed, then took Jarek's hand.

"You have saved our lives," he said, his voice breaking with emotion. "We have had a bleak winter, and the money they robbed from us was to have been used to buy food. Without it our community was finished. I have no way to thank you, but we will not forget you, Morningstar."

Jarek was speechless, but I saw his eyes darken as men and women crowded around the wagon, lifting out goods and coin.

Megan came through the crowd, taking Jarek's arm and leading him away from the throng. "Keep calm!" I heard her whisper. "It is only money."

"*My* money!" he hissed.

I almost felt sorry for him then. Not quite . . . but almost.

Back in Megan's home we sat beside the fire. The young whore, Ilka, was sleeping, her back bandaged; the wound, Megan assured us, was free of infection. Jarek stared gloomily into the flames.

"It was a fine act," I told him, making sure to keep the smile from my face. He glanced up at me, then grinned.

"Easy made, swiftly lost," he said.

"What will you do now?" asked Megan.

Jarek shrugged. "I'll head deeper into the forest. No point staying here; the village is finished."

"They didn't kill everyone," said Megan. "Many people escaped into the undergrowth where the horses would not follow. We can rebuild."

"That is not what I meant. The killers will be back."

Megan nodded. "What would you advise?"

"It is not for me to give advice," answered Jarek. "Who am I but a wandering mercenary with no ties here?"

"Silly boy," she told him. "You are the Morningstar!"

"Oh, stop this nonsense," Jarek snapped. "It was a jest, nothing more."

"I know," replied Megan, "but you should have heard the men talk about it. You called yourself the lord of the forest. You demanded that the Angostins pay a toll to pass. You stood alone at the center of the road. Can you not see it, Jarek? You took on the mantle of leadership, albeit for your own purposes."

"Well, I ended up with nothing as a result of it," he said.

"Nothing?" whispered Megan. "All those people thanking you, looking up to you. That is worth more than gold!"

"Nothing is worth more than gold," he said, his smile in place. "But yes, I'll grant you it was more pleasant than having a boil lanced." He swung to me. "Did you enjoy the day, bard?"

"I don't enjoy watching men kill one another, but it was rewarding to see the joy on the faces of those who believed they had lost everything only to find a hero had rescued them."

"Does it not strike you as . . . unfair . . . that this hero is the only one to lose money on the venture?"

"You didn't lose," I told him. "As soon as I saw that crowd, I guessed what would happen, so I stuffed my pockets with coin and I kept this." Reaching inside my tunic shirt, I pulled clear a small pouch. Opening it, I tipped the contents into Jarek's outstretched hands; there were rings and necklets, brooches and bracelets, all of heavy gold, several studded with gems, emeralds and rubies.

His smile widened, and he winked at me. "By heavens, Owen, I like you more and more. I hope you have deep pockets."

"Deep enough, I would say, for around fifty silver pieces."

"There is hope for you, my friend, in this wicked world of ours."

"Maybe," muttered Megan, rising and stretching her back. Without a word to us she walked to the wide bed and laid herself down beside the sleeping Ilka.

Jarek returned the gold to the pouch, then slipped it inside his jerkin.

"Why not travel with me, Owen?" he asked. "We'll see the high country, the lonely passes, the stands of pine."

"I think I will," I told him.

Toward midnight, with the women sleeping, the hunchback Wulf came to the door. "I need to talk with you, Mace," he said.

Jarek ushered him to the hearth, where the hunchback sat awkwardly, his twisted back unsuited to the chair. "I've nothing here anymore," he said. Jarek nodded but remained silent. "Most women turned away from me, but not my Tess. A good woman, and I treated her right. Good young'uns, too. Pretty— not like their sire. But they are gone now. Gone." His voice trailed away, and he cleared his throat and spit into the dying fire. "Anyways, what I'm saying is that I've no holds here."

"Why tell me?" asked Jarek, not unkindly.

"You're a wandering man, Mace. There's nothing here for any of us now, so I guess you'll be traveling on. I'd like to accompany you."

"You don't even like me, Wulf."

"True enough, but I liked what I saw on the road. I liked it when you stopped them—right well I liked it. You ain't one of us, Mace—more like you are one of them. But by God's holy eyes, you were a Highlander at that moment."

Jarek Mace chuckled, then reached out and laid his hand on Wulf's twisted back. "You are the best woodsman I've ever known," he said. "Having you with us will mean good food and less time lost. You're welcome. But know this: I don't intend taking on the Angostins again. There's no profit in it."

"Time will tell about that, Mace," said Wulf.

We stayed for two more days, helping the surviving villagers pack their belongings for the trek into the depths of the forest. Hut walls were dismantled and loaded on roughly built carts, and even Garik's iron stove was hauled clear of the bakery and manhandled onto the wagon.

The dead were buried in a mass grave at the edge of the trees, and the Naeser abbess, Ka-Piana, spoke movingly about the journey of the souls to the far river. Many tears were shed.

At last, on the morning of the third day, Lanis the tanner came running into the village. His face red from exertion, he sprinted across the clearing and stumbled to a halt before Jarek Mace.

"They are coming!" he said between great gulps of air. "Maybe a hundred horsemen."

Word spread swiftly, and the villagers grabbed the last of their belongings and filed away toward the north and the deep forest. Within minutes only Jarek, Wulf, and myself were left in the clearing by the lake. I glanced around. Already the settlement had a lonely feel, abandoned and desolate.

"Time to go," said Mace. Swinging on his heel, he loped away to the northwest and the hills, carrying his longbow in his left hand, his right rested on his longsword, pushing down on the hilt and keeping the scabbard high so that it would not clatter against his leg. Wulf followed him in an ungainly run; he, too, carried a longbow, and a short, single-bladed hand ax was thrust into this wide leather belt.

As usual I brought up the rear. I had no sword or bow, bearing only my harp, a money pouch, and the leaf-shaped dagger Wulf had given me. I no longer wore the clothing of a bard; the red and yellow would stand out amid the greens and browns of the forest. Now I was clad in leaf-green trews and an oiled jerkin of deep brown, worn over a rust-colored woolen shirt. In truth, I was a different man from the Owen Odell who had come to the village in the depths of winter. The constant work with the ax had built muscle in my arms and shoulders, and my stamina had increased so that I could run for an hour without being winded.

Which was just as well, for as we reached the hillside, we heard the thunder of hooves on the cleared ground behind us. I glanced back to see men-at-arms riding toward us. The trees were not far ahead now, but even so I experienced a moment of panic.

Jarek and Wulf did not even bother to look back, but I increased my pace, passing them both to reach the tree line some thirty paces ahead. There I stopped and waited for the others.

Mace came to a halt and strung his longbow. Wulf did the same.

Three of the leading riders were galloping their lathered mounts up the hillside. Jarek hefted his bow, pulled an arrow from his leather quiver, and swiftly notched it to the string. The bow came up. Apparently without aiming, he loosed the arrow, which plunged home into the chest of the leading rider. He pitched from the saddle, closely followed by a second man, shot through the throat by a shaft from Wulf. The third rider dragged on the reins, turning his horse so fast that the beast fell and rolled over him.

Jarek and Wulf spun on their heels and moved back into the undergrowth, angling away from the route taken by the villagers and leading the enemy farther into the forest.

Within the hour, all sounds of pursuit had faded and we were far into the hills, following game trails and narrow tracks totally unsuited to travel on horseback.

The Highlands are beautiful in spring, ablaze with color and life. From the high mountainsides the forest below becomes an ocean of green flowing through countless valleys, vast and breathtaking, held in check only by the white-topped mountains standing like snow giants of legend.

For days we wandered, traversing steep slopes or scrambling down into the deep glens, camping in hollows or caves. Wulf caught several hares, and on the third day Jarek killed a bighorn sheep; we dined that night on fat mutton and fried liver.

I had no idea where we were heading, nor did I care. The air was fresh, my limbs were young and full of strength, and my eyes could scarcely drink in the wonder of my surroundings.

I know it may seem callous considering the tragedy so recently behind us, but it seemed to me then that nothing could surpass my joy. I was alive and surrounded by beauty on a massive scale.

But then we met Piercollo . . .

Of us all he came closest to being the reality within the myth. There are more stories about him than any of us, including the Morningstar. And while the greater part of them are inventions or distortions, if life had placed him in those fictitious situations of peril, he would have reacted just as the storytellers claim.

Added to which, there was never any malice in Piercollo. I do not believe he ever truly learned to hate. And what a voice! When he sang, such was the warmth and emotion that he could stave off winter. I'd swear that if he burst into song in an icy glade, the snow would melt and spring flowers would push up through the frozen earth just to hear him.

Of them all, I miss him the most.

We were walking down into a shaded glen. The sun was high, just past noon on a warm spring day. Jarek Mace was leading us, and we were moving northwest toward the distant market town of Lualis. As usual I brought up the rear, walking behind Wulf, whose mood on this day was sullen, the loss of his family heavy upon him.

Then we heard the sound of a man singing, his voice rich, the language unknown to me. But the song soared out above and through the trees with a power I could scarcely believe. My skin tingled with the excitement of it, and I knew that this unknown singer was performing for the forest, just as I had months before with my harp. He was singing from the heart, carrying the music from the well of his soul and releasing it into the air like a flock of golden birds.

Mace dropped back to where Wulf and I stood spellbound.

"What the hell is that?" asked Jarek Mace. Wulf's hand slashed the air, commanding silence, and we stood for several minutes and listened. At last the song faded. Mace looked at us both, then chuckled and shook his head. Stringing his bow, he strode off in the direction from which the song had come. As we followed him, there came the aroma of roasting meat. We had breakfasted on wild turkey and were far from hungry, yet the smell made the mouth water and the stomach growl. Suddenly it was as if I had not eaten in days, such was my newfound appetite.

We came to a clearing beside a swiftly flowing stream. There, beside a trench fire pit upon which a whole sheep was being turned on a spit, sat a huge black-bearded man. He was wearing a purple shirt and hose of wool, and about his shoulders was a black-and-white checkered shawl. He glanced up as we emerged from the trees but did not stand or greet us.

"Good day to you," said Jarek Mace. "I see we are in time for lunch."

"You are in time to watch me eat *my* lunch," agreed the man amiably. The voice was deep and heavily accented. He smiled as he spoke, but the smile did not reach the somber brown eyes.

"That is hardly civil," Jarek told him. "Here we are, three hungry travelers, and you with a complete sheep almost ready for the carving." He moved to the fire trench, where several pots bubbled beside the sheep. "Ah, liver broth, vegetables, wild onions, and herbs. Quite a feast for one man."

"Yes, I am looking forward to it. But I prefer to eat in privacy. So why not be on your way."

Mace grinned and stepped back from the fire trench. "Has it

occurred to you, my large friend, that we could just confiscate this meal? You are one against three.''

The large man sighed and rose ponderously to his feet. Sitting down, he had seemed large enough, but now, standing, he was an alarming size. He was somewhere around seven inches above six feet tall; his breadth of shoulder was immense, and he towered over Mace.

"How would you do that?'' he asked, the words spoken softly. "With your bow? You think an arrow could stop me reaching you and breaking your arms and legs?''

"Good point,'' Mace agreed, laying aside the bow and drawing his longsword.

"No good, either,'' said the man. "One cut, one thrust, is all you get. And I have been cut before.''

"Turn the spit,'' said Mace. "The meat is charring.''

The giant glanced back, saw that it was true, and moved to the roasting sheep, turning the iron handle with one hand.

"Now,'' said Mace, "it would appear that we are in somewhat of a quandary. We are hungry; you are loath to share your food. We do not want to kill you or to be killed. Therefore, let us wrestle for it.''

The man stared at him without expression for several heartbeats, then shook his head in disbelief. "You would wrestle *me*?''

"Best of three falls,'' offered Mace. "What do you say? If you win, we'll be on our way. If I win, we share the meat.''

"Agreed,'' said the man. Turning to me, he pointed to the spit. "You think you can keep her turning?''

"I'll do my best,'' I told him. He moved away from the spit to stand before Mace, looming over him and dwarfing him.

"First let us talk about the rules,'' said Mace, stepping in close. Suddenly he hooked his foot behind the giant's leg and hammered his elbow into the man's face. As he stumbled back, Mace leapt feet first at him, his boots thundering against the huge chest. His opponent toppled like a tree, hitting the ground with a bone-jarring thud. "Rule number one—there *are* no rules!''

The giant was unperturbed. Raising himself to his elbows, he gave a low, rumbling laugh. "Had you asked for a one-fall advantage, I would have given it to you,'' he said, climbing to his feet. Mace ran forward and once again leapt at him feet first.

This time the man swayed and caught the flying figure, holding him in his arms with no more effort than if he had been holding a child. With a sway of the hips and a grunt of effort, he hurled Mace high into the air.

I winced at the thought of the landing that would follow, but Jarek Mace was a man of surprises. His body twisted in the air in a full somersault, and he landed perfectly on his feet.

"Very good," said his opponent, clapping his hands. "Now let us be serious."

They circled one another for several moments; then Mace darted in, dropped to his knee, and hurled his full weight against the giant's legs. The man did not move. Reaching down, he grabbed Mace by the jerkin, hauling him to his feet—and beyond.

"A nice try, but you are competing at the wrong weight." With infinite lack of speed the giant lifted his arms and slammed Mace to the ground. Then the stranger stood and walked back toward the fire trench. Mace rolled to his knees, drew his dagger, and was about to rush in and stab his opponent in the back when the man, without looking back, spoke again.

"I like you, little fellow," he said. "Let us call it a draw and eat."

I never knew whether Piercollo heard the whisper of iron hissing from the sheath; he never spoke of it. But I saw the light of anger fade from Mace's eyes.

"It is safe now, I think," called the stranger, and a group of women and children came out from their hiding places in the trees. There were three elderly women, four younger wives, and eight children ranging in age from around four to twelve. Mace stood openmouthed as they appeared, and I looked toward Wulf; there was no reaction from the hunchback, and I guessed he had known of their presence all along.

"Let us eat!" said our host. There were no plates, but the children had pulled sections of bark from the surrounding trees and scrubbed them clean, and the succulent mutton was placed upon them.

It was a feast as fine as any I have tasted, the meat rich and full of flavor, the broth divine, the wild onion soup without peer. At last replete, I sat back against a tree and took out my harp.

The giant approached me as I tuned the strings. "You are a lover of music, eh? Good! After a fine meal there should always be music. My name is Piercollo. You play and I shall sing. Yes?"

"I would be honored," I told him. Wulf joined us and from his small pack took a flute. He smiled self-consciously. "I have heard you play, Owen, and I am not as skilled. But if you will bear with my lack of talent, I would like to take part."

"What shall we play?" I asked them, and we discussed the merits of various songs until at last we decided upon "The Forest Queen." It is not performed much in these more enlightened days, but it was a good song with a simple chorus. You know it?

> She walked within the forest fair,
> the stars of night upon her hair,
> and dreamed of sorrows none could share,
> Elaine, the forest queen.

It was a song of the Before Times, when the land of the Ikenas was said to have been peopled by an elder race who knew great magic. The last queen was Elaine, who, betrayed in love, walked through the forest, becoming at last a restless spirit whose song could be heard in the rushing of the streams and the wind whispering through the branches of the trees.

I set a slow and haunting melody. After several quavering, uncertain notes, Wulf joined in. Then Piercollo sang. The children gathered around us and, after a while, began singing the chorus.

It was more beautiful than you could possibly know: the sun shining on the hollow, the whispering of the stream, the harp, the flute, and the majestic voice of Piercollo ringing out in the mountains. I remember that day more brightly than any that followed, for it was full of enchantment that not even Cataplas could have duplicated.

We sang and played for more than an hour until dusk. Several of the children were asleep by the fire trench, and I saw Jarek Mace stroll away from the hollow to walk to the brow of a nearby hill.

I joined him there and sat beside him. "Thank God all that wailing is over," he muttered. "It was driving me insane."

I felt a great sadness come over me then. For all his charm and courage, Mace had no concept of the beauty of music; nor,

indeed, had he taken any joy in the comradeship and the close-
ness the music had generated. He was a man apart.

"What are you looking for, Jarek?" I asked him.

He shrugged. "There is a castle I want to own. It stands on
the cliff tops overlooking the western sea, far down in the south."

"Why that castle?"

"Why not?" he answered, looking away.

Changing the subject, I mentioned the wrestling bout and the
incredible balance and dexterity he had shown when thrown into
the air.

"I used to be a tumbler," he told me, his smile returning.
"And a juggler and a walker upon the high rope."

"You have had an interesting life."

"Have I?" he said with genuine surprise. "Yes, I suppose I
have. Tell me, Owen, are you happy?" The question surprised
me, and I looked into his eyes, seeking any sign of mockery,
but there was none. He was genuinely—at that moment—interested.

"Yes," I told him. "Very. You?"

He shrugged and turned away. "I will be when I have my
castle. You know, I used to think that music was some sort of
trick, that people only pretended to enjoy it. For me it is a
meaningless series of discordant sounds. I hate it, for its beauty
is denied to me."

"It is a great loss," I agreed, "but did you not find the com-
panionship agreeable? The children sitting around the fire, the
wood smoke, the security?"

"Ah, the romantic in you again, eh, Owen? It was just a roast
sheep, my friend, on a warm afternoon. Nothing more."

"I think you are wrong. I think I will remember this day all
my life."

"You should eat roast sheep more often," he said, thumping
my back. Then he stood, took his bow, and wandered off into
the forest.

I helped Piercollo clean the pots and scrape the animal fat from
the disassembled spit. He gathered the iron rods, bound them
together, and carried them to an enormous pack he had left
under a tree.

"You are a cook?" I asked him.

"Not just a cook. *The* cook. I was known as the finest food maker in Tuscania. I should have stayed there. But no, when the Angostins visited my duke, they clamored for my services. Great golden coins they laid under my nose. Come to Ikena, they said. Serve us and become rich. Foolish Piercollo! He listened, and he liked the touch of their gold.'' He shook his great head. ''I should have stayed in my own land.''

''It is not so bad in Ikena,'' I told him. ''I grew up there, on the southern coast.''

''No, it is not so bad,'' he agreed. ''But the weather? Rain and fog, drizzle and mist. And the people! Pigs would have a better understanding of food. They bring me across the continent, across the ocean, and for what? Burned meat and soft vegetables. There is no skill in such meals. Even that I could have borne, but not Azrek. Oh, no. Not him.''

''Tell me of him,'' I urged Piercollo.

''Believe me, Owen, you would not wish to hear.''

''Tell me.''

''He is a torturer. Every night the screams could be heard from the dungeons. Men and women . . . and even little ones. Very bad, Owen. I think he likes to hear people scream. Well, I do not like it. One day I look for my implements, they are gone. I ask where they are. I am told the count has them. You know what he does? He is roasting a man on my spit! That is enough for Piercollo. I left.''

''Sweet heaven! But surely anyone roasted like that would die swiftly.''

''Yes, but not this time. The count has a sorcerer, a vile man. He kept the prisoner alive for hours, alive to suffer as no man should suffer. I am glad to be free of such a lord. All I wish for now is to return to Tuscania.''

''Where did you come upon the children?''

He smiled, his teeth startlingly white in the gathering dusk. ''They hear Piercollo sing as they are wandering in the forest. The women tell me their village was attacked some days ago. Now they head for the town of Lualis. I, too, will go there; it is a river town, and rivers lead to the sea. From the coast I shall find a ship to take me home.''

''You have family in Tuscania?''

''I have a sister. A good woman—big, well made. Eight sons she has borne and not a single daughter. I will stay with her for a while. What of you? Where are you heading?''

I spread my hands. "Everywhere and nowhere. I live in the forest."

"It is not so bad a place. Many deer and wild pig, rabbits and mountain sheep. Good onions and herbs. I like it here also. But it will not be peaceful for long—not now that the rebels have made it a stronghold."

"Rebels?" I inquired. "I have heard of no rebels."

"I was in Ziraccu when the news came in. There is a rebellion here, led by a hero called Morningstar. He and a hundred men attacked a convoy led by the count's two brothers. One of them was killed. Azrek has offered a thousand crowns' reward for Morningstar's capture. And an army is being raised to rush the rebellion."

I said nothing as my mind reeled with the news, but Piercollo continued to speak. "I would like to meet this Morningstar," he said. "I would like to shake his hand and wish him well."

"Perhaps you will," I whispered.

◊ 5 ◊

THERE ARE FEW still living who remember the old river city of Lualis, with its round castle, its wharves and lanes, its timber yards and stock paddocks, and its profusion of building styles—Angostin brick, Highland wattle and clay, timbered roofs, tiled roofs, thatched roofs.

In those days, before the Deeway had become full of silt, seagoing ships could moor at Lualis, putting ashore cargoes of silks and satins, ivory, spices, dried fruit from the Orient, iron from the Viking mines of the northern continent. The city was filled with sailors, merchants, farmers, horse breeders, mercenary knights, and street women who would sell their favors for a copper farthing.

There were several inns on every street and taverns where drunken men would gamble and drink, argue and fight. Very few of those taverns did not boast fresh bloodstains nightly on their sawdust-covered floors.

Lualis was a glamorous place, so the stories would have us believe. And they are correct. But it was not the bright glamour that shines with golden light from all great sagas. It was the kind that attaches itself to acts of violence and men of violence. The city was dirty, vile-smelling, lawless, and fraught with the risk of sudden death.

Jarek Mace loved it . . .

We arrived on the first day of the spring fair, when the city was swollen with revelers. Three ships were moored at the wharves as our small party trooped in from the forest. The women and children bade their farewells to us and made their way to the more sedate northern quarter, where some had relatives. Mace, Wulf, Piercollo, and I strolled to the nearest tavern, where we found a table near an open window and ordered meat broth, fresh bread, and a huge jug of ale.

All around us people were talking about the fair, the contests to come, the prize money to be won. I saw Piercollo's dark eyes brighten with interest at the mention of a wrestling tourney and the ten gold pieces waiting for the winner. He ate with us, then said his good-byes and wandered out of the tavern in search of his fortune. Mace watched him go, then ordered more ale.

"What will we do here?" I asked him.

"There is always an archery contest," he said. "Wulf and I will win some money. Then we'll rent a couple of women and relax for a few days." He smiled. "We'll get one for you, too, Owen."

"I do not need such a companion," I told him rather too primly.

"As you wish," he answered.

I was ill at ease in the tavern, surrounded by men with loud voices, and I left them to their drinking and strolled through the city streets to the meadow where the fair was under way. There was a dance pole set at the center, hung with ribbons, and a dancing bear was performing for a small crowd at the western end of the fairground. Tiny ponies were tethered nearby, awaiting their child riders, and there were stalls of sweetmeats, sugar apples, lard cakes, honey loaves, and the like. The day was bright, the sky cloudless. People were enjoying themselves.

Several magickers were exhibiting their skills, but the crowds were thin as yet, and the performers either lacked any genuine skill or were saving their efforts for later in the day.

Carpenters were busy building a long raised platform where the knights and their ladies would sit once the entertainments commenced. A canvas canopy, painted red and hung with white streamers, was being raised above the platform. No sudden shower would be allowed to dampen the enthusiasm of Angostin nobles.

There were soldiers everywhere, strolling through the meadow, moving in groups of three or four. I counted at least fifty on the fairground alone, and I had seen more in the city itself. Their presence made me uncomfortable, though in truth, I should have had little to fear.

Toward dusk I made my way back to the tavern. Mace had

booked a room for us on the upper floor, and I mounted the stairs, thinking only of sleep. The moonlit room was small, with three pallet beds set against the inner walls. A rough-hewn table and two chairs completed the furniture, and there was a single tiny window with open shutters. The room smelled musky and damp, but I did not care. The two larger beds had been claimed by Mace and Wulf, their longbows laid upon the single blankets. I moved to the third and stretched out, not even bothering to remove my boots.

Sleep came swiftly, but I awoke when Mace and the hunchback returned after midnight, drunk and laughing. Mace tripped and fell upon me as he tried to remove his boots. Wulf made a gallant effort to fall upon his own bed but missed and sank to the floor, where he curled up happily and slept.

"Not . . . a . . . bad night," said Jarek Mace with a lopsided grin. "I like this place."

"There is blood on your hand," I told him, sitting up.

"It's not mine," he answered cheerfully. With great dignity he pushed himself to his feet, swayed, then staggered to his bed.

"Wake me early," he called. "The first cull of the archers is before noon."

"You'll be in no fit state to take part," I warned him.

"I could beat most of them in the state I'm in now," he replied. For a little while there was silence; then he spoke again. "Have you heard? The Morningstar is really a Highland noble of the old blood. He is Rabain reborn, come to free the north."

A cloud passed before the moon, and we were plunged into darkness. I lay back, thinking about what he had said.

"The legend is growing," I said at last.

He did not reply, but I knew he had heard me.

True to his word, Jarek Mace awoke bright of eye and in high good humor. I, who had consumed no alcohol, had a splitting headache and could have stayed in bed until well past noon, while Wulf awoke with a curse and remained silent and sullen for most of the morning.

We walked to the meadow, where I watched Jarek register for the tournament. An elderly clerk lifted a quill pen, dabbed it into a clay pot of ink, and glanced up at the bowman.

"Name?" he asked.

"Garik of Pottersham," answered Mace easily.

"Next?"

"Wulf of Pottersham."

The clerk scribbled the names on the scroll, and we moved on. The wrestling had begun, and we waited by the rope boundary for Piercollo to make his entrance. He won his first bout easily, and Jarek and I decided to wager two silver pennies on the Tuscanian's next contest.

Wulf declined to bet. "All he has is strength," muttered the hunchback. He was proved wrong twice more, and Jarek and I earned ten silver pennies each. But the last fight had been tough for Piercollo, his opponent almost managing to use the Tuscanian's great weight against him. Jarek did not agree and wagered the ten pennies on the final contest. It was over swiftly. Piercollo was matched against a man of almost equal size, and the two giants circled each other warily. This opponent was an older man, wily and skillful. Piercollo rushed in like an angry bear, and the man sidestepped, grabbed the Tuscanian's outstretched arm, and spun him from his feet. Piercollo rose swiftly. Too swiftly, as Wulf pointed out, for he was still groggy from the fall. The older wrestler threw himself at the Tuscanian, hammering his forearm into Piercollo's face while at the same time hooking his foot around our friend's ankle. Piercollo fell like a toppled tree. Mace cursed roundly when the Tuscanian failed to rise before the count of ten.

Then the first names were called for the archery cull. There were more than a hundred bowmen, and the first targets were set at around thirty paces. Mace and Wulf scored gold and were told to return in half an hour for the second round.

By now the workmen had almost completed the knights' platform, and bench seats were being lifted onto it. I strolled across, past the piled wood of a huge bonfire, to where a dozen servants carrying cushions were arguing with one another as to which of their knights were to have the best seats. It was a common enough scene. Those knights sitting closest to the manor lord were seen by the populace to be favorites. No one wished to be placed at the end of the bench. But it would be unseemly for knights to be seen squabbling over such matters, and therefore cushion-carrying servants were sent with orders to obtain for their masters places near the manor lord. I sat down with other interested—and knowing—fairgoers to watch. The arguments became more fierce until finally a young man in yellow livery struck an older man wearing a blue tunic. The older man staggered, then struck back. Within seconds, the cushions had been hurled aside and the servants were whacking out at one another, kicking and punching.

The crowd cheered them on, and at last, with the fighting over, the cushions were placed. The boy in the yellow livery looked more than downcast as he tossed his cushion to the end of the bench. When his master saw his place, he would probably be in for a worse beating than the one he had already taken.

At that moment three soldiers approached, striding to the platform and climbing the wooden steps. The leader—a lean, fierce-looking individual with a jagged scar from his right brow to his chin—was carrying a satin cushion of rich scarlet. Casually he pushed aside the cushions already there, creating a gap at the center of the first bench. No one said a word, and not one of the servants moved as the man dropped the scarlet cushion into the gap.

"Who are they?" I asked a man standing beside me.

"Count Azrek's men. He must be coming to the fair."

The news made my heart hammer. I don't know why, for Azrek would not know me and I had no reason then to fear him. Still I backed away as if the count's arrival were imminent, my eyes scanning the crowd. None of the nobles would attend until well into the afternoon and the knights' tourney. And yet I could not control my fear. I sought out Jarek Mace and told him what I had heard, but he seemed unconcerned.

"What difference can it make?" he asked.

"I don't know," I answered. But the unease remained.

On impulse I returned to the tavern and gathered my harp, stopping only to pay the tavern keeper for our lodgings. "Will you want the room tonight?" he asked.

"Probably."

"You're not thinking of leaving today?"

"We may. Not sure. My friends . . . are traveling men. Don't like towns, you know."

"You'll miss the burning."

"Tragic, I know, but still . . ."

I stepped out into the open and drew a deep breath, fighting for calm.

Back at the fair Wulf and Mace had progressed through to the last sixteen of the bowmen and were thus guaranteed at least a penny for their efforts. When I found them, they were discussing the merits of the other archers.

Piercollo joined us. "Not enough for a ship," he said, opening his huge hand and showing us the four silver coins he had won.

"You did well," I told him. Mace said nothing to the big man, and I knew he blamed him for the loss on his bet.

The archery tourney continued, and Wulf reached the last four but was eliminated by a tall forester wearing a black eye patch. This infuriated the hunchback.

"Everyone knows a good bowman needs two eyes to judge distance. How does he do it?" he complained. But he was four pennies richer, and his mood had improved.

The final was set just before the knight's tourney. Mace and Eye Patch were matched against each other.

Legend has it that Jarek Mace won by splitting his opponent's shaft from fifty paces. He didn't; he lost. They loosed some twenty shafts, then the string of Jarek's bow snapped, his arrow falling some ten paces forward. That should have disqualified him, but Eye Patch opened the pouch at his side and removed a spare string, which he handed to Mace. Swiftly Jarek restrung his bow, but his next arrow was two fingers' width outside the gold, and Eye Patch won the tourney with a splendid shot that struck dead center.

Jarek Mace swung away without a word of congratulation and collected his two gold coins; then, with a face like thunder, he strode to where we waited at the edge of the crowd.

"Shorter string," he snapped. "Different tension. He should have allowed me a practice shot. Bastard!"

"He needn't have allowed you anything," I pointed out. But Mace was not to be mollified. He was never a good loser.

We purchased meat pies and sat in the shade some thirty paces from the knight's platform. Crowds were now filling the meadow, and we saw the nobles arriving and taking their places on the dais.

"That is Azrek," muttered Piercollo.

I looked up and saw a tall young man with straight black hair and a long, curved nose. He wore a simple tunic and leggings of black satin, edged with silver thread, and a black shirt that glistened like the finest silk. My blood felt cold, and I looked away.

"Handsome fellow," said Mace. "Lacks color, though. The shirt should have been cream, with puff sleeves, shot with gray silk. Now, *that* would have been stylish."

The jousting that followed lasted for several hours, but none of us was interested, and we strolled through the crowds, playing occasional games of chance at the gambling stalls.

But just before dusk the stallholder refused another wager.

"There's time for one more game, surely," said Mace, who had lost several pennies.

"No, it'll be the burning soon," answered the man, "and I want to get a good position."

"Who is for burning?" asked Wulf.

"They caught a witch; they say she's a friend of the Morningstar."

"Her name?" whispered Jarek Mace. .

"Name? Hold on, I did hear it . . . Margan, Macan . . . something like, anyway. You know the name?"

I was about to speak, but Mace's elbow struck me painfully in the side.

"No," he said, and turned away.

I moved swiftly after him, grabbing his arm. "That's Megan! They're going to burn Megan!"

"I know," he answered.

"What are we going to do?"

"Well, we have two choices," he said grimly. "First, we can fight our way through the fifty soldiers and the crowd, cut her free, kill all the knights, and make our escape on stolen stallions. Or else we can forget it, buy some food, and have a quiet evening remembering past friends. What would you choose?"

I swung to Wulf. "What about you?"

"What about me?"

"Is she not a friend of yours?"

"Aye, she is. But Jarek is right. There's nothing we can do—save die with her. You think she'd want that?"

Their reaction to Megan's plight stunned me. What kind of men were these? I wondered. The answer was not long in coming. Jarek Mace was a wolfshead who cared for nothing and no one save himself, and the hunchback was a man whom I had first seen cutting the fingers from one of his victims in order to steal the dead man's rings. What more could I have expected?

And yet I was still surprised and deeply saddened by their easy acceptance of the cruel fate awaiting the iron-haired witch woman. I stood, my legs trembling, and walked back into the throng, wishing I had never ventured into this dark forest.

On the far side of the meadow, before the knights' platform, a large crowd had assembled to watch the burning. There was blood upon the grass, and a man in the crowd informed me that moments before a lance had pierced the helm of a young jouster, putting out both his eyes. I arrived in time to see the corpse being carried away by stretcher bearers. A sudden trumpet blast rent the air, and two soldiers marched into sight. Behind them, being led by a rope around her neck, came Megan, her hands bound behind her.

She moved like a queen, stately and slow. There was no sign of panic in her, nor did she look at the crowd. Upon her tall, thin body she wore only the single white robe of the condemned. The crowd was hushed, awed, I think, by her dignity. My eyes strayed to the waiting stake atop a mass of dry wood some six feet high. My mouth was dry, my heart heavy.

The soldiers and their prisoner halted before the Lord of Lualis and the black-garbed figure of Count Azrek. The Lord of Lualis, a round-faced, balding Angostin, rose ponderously to his feet. "Do you have anything to say to your judges, witch?" he said, his voice booming like a drum.

If Megan answered, I did not hear her. She stood straight of back, her head held high. The Lualis Lord cleared his throat and addressed the crowd. "This woman has been found guilty of witchcraft and treason," he shouted. "She practiced black arts and, in communion with the murderous outlaw known as Morningstar, has overseen the butchery of the honest men and women of her own village and others who traveled the forest roads. The sentence is just. Is there any man here who would cast doubt upon the verdict?"

"I would!" I called. The Lualis Lord looked surprised, but in truth he was less surprised than I. The crowd parted before me as if I had the plague, and I walked forward, stepping over the rope that held back the spectators.

I cannot explain now why I ventured out, save to say that I could not bear for Megan to be killed without at least showing that I cared. It was folly and could achieve nothing. For a successful defense against conviction I would have needed witnesses or at the least a champion.

As I moved nearer, I avoided Azrek's dark eyes, but I could feel his venomous gaze upon me. Soldiers around the platform tensed and took up their weapons, but they did not look at me. Instead they spread out and scanned the crowd.

"And who might you be, peasant?" the lord asked.

"No peasant, my lord. I am Owen Odell, an Angostin from the southern coast. My father is Lord Aubertain, thrice decorated by the father of our glorious king, Edmund."

It was—even at that moment of tension and fear—more than irritating to use the name of my father as a talisman. I did not like the man, nor ever did, I think, and as a child I was determined one day to ride away where men would never have heard of his name. Yet here I was, making the sound of it a shield.

"You have proof of identity?" asked the lord.

"I need none, sir, for I am not on trial here," I answered. This show of arrogance was convincing of itself, and he fell silent for a moment.

"How do you know of this woman?"

"I spent the winter in her village—before it was sacked and destroyed not by the Morningstar but by the soldiers of Count Azrek. I saw the results of *their* butchery. And at no time did I witness the practicing of dark magick by Megan or any other in the village. Nor did I hear talk of treason."

"You are suggesting that soldiers in the service of the king would attack and kill innocent people? Are you mad, sir?"

"I saw what I saw, my lord," I told him.

"Is there any other witness to corroborate your accusations?" I watched his eyes scan the crowd. Azrek, too, was sitting forward, his body tense, his eyes gleaming.

"No," I said. "I am alone."

For a moment there was silence, and I sensed disappointment in the Lualis Lord. He turned to me, his small round eyes bleak and angry. "Without corroboration I have no choice but to let the verdict stand. Are you sure there is no one else you would wish to call upon?"

And then I knew. They were waiting for the Morningstar to make his appearance. Had the situation not been so tragic, I believe I would have laughed aloud. Instead I shook my head.

Count Azrek leaned forward, tapping the fat man's arm. There followed a brief whispered conversation. Finally the lord nodded and sat down, allowing the count to rise in his place.

"You have spoken with great calumny against me," he said, his voice emotionless, his unblinking eyes staring into mine. "I demand the right of challenge."

Strangely I felt no fear. "As you wish," I told him, "but even though I die here, nothing will cloak for long the evil that seeps out from you."

He showed no expression and transferred his gaze to the soldiers holding Megan.

"Let the sentence be carried out!" he called. The men took hold of Megan, and, unresisting, she was led to the pyre and forced to clamber high upon the piled wood before her hands were unbound and lashed to the stake.

It was then that I saw the floating sphere gliding effortlessly over the heads of the spectators. Many people paused to look up at it, pointing to it as it passed. Several times it hovered over individuals before moving on. Perfectly round and swirling, like smoke encased in glass, it glided to a halt above a tall man in a buckskin shirt. At first I thought it was Jarek Mace, but the man turned toward me as he looked up at the sphere, and I saw that he was beardless and wide-jawed. The search spell moved on.

Even within my grief and anger I was impressed by the skill of the unknown magicker who had cast the spell. A searching is always difficult, but in a crowd such as this only the very best would dream of sending out a sphere.

A great cry went up from the crowd as the two soldiers pushed burning torches into the dry wood at the base of the bonfire. Flames licked at the sticks and timbers, smoke drifting lazily up to swirl around the white-garbed woman. Her face was serene, showing no fear, and as her eyes met mine, she smiled. Then the thick smoke enveloped her.

At that moment the search spell found its prey, and a shaft of white light flashed into the evening air, hanging for several heartbeats above the head of Jarek Mace. In sudden fear the mob melted away from him, and the white light became golden, bathing him. Already handsome, he appeared at once godlike, his fringed buckskin shirt of molten gold, his skin of burnished bronze. And he smiled as he executed an elaborate and perfect bow.

"It's the Morningstar!" bellowed the Lualis Lord. "Take him!"

Soldiers ran forward as the light faded. An arrow from Wulf took the first low in the groin, and the man pitched to the ground and began to scream. With no time to string his bow, Jarek Mace swung the weapon like a staff, knocking a man from his feet. Then his sword flashed into the air, and the clanging of blades rang across the meadow. Another arrow sliced the air, this time from Eye Patch, and a soldier fell, pierced through the temple.

Mace backed away before the attack of five men, and I saw the immense figure of Piercollo lift a barrel of beer above his head and run forward to hurl it at the soldiers. It hammered into the first, catapulting him into his fellows, then shattered, spilling foaming ale on the fallen soldiers.

A crossbowman in the black livery of Azrek sent a bolt toward Mace. It missed and thudded into the shoulder of a woman in the crowd. Panic followed, and the mob ran in all directions, hampering the efforts of the gathering soldiers. Mace ducked his head and disappeared into the throng.

An arrow sailed over my head, and I swung to see it miss Azrek by a hand's breadth, punching through the throat of a man sitting behind him. Now the knights, too, and their ladies, scrambled for cover.

"Don't stand there gawping, child, untie me!"

The voice appeared inside my head. Swinging to the fire, I ran to the rear, where the flames had not yet reached. Scrambling up to the stake, coughing and spluttering, I reached Megan. Around her there was no smoke; it swirled just out of reach, as if she were standing inside an invisible globe.

"Your powers are great," I said.

"What a fine time for compliments!" she snapped. "Perhaps we should sit down here and discuss the finer points of magick."

I cut through her bonds and took her by the hand. Swiftly she cast a spell. Instantly, her white robe changed to the color of rust and a leather cap appeared, covering her white hair. Smoke billowed around us like a mist as we descended to the meadow, dispersing only when we were some distance from the pyre. People were running and screaming around us, and we were not challenged as we slowly made our way across the meadow, past the outskirts of the river city, and on into the sanctuary of the trees.

At last safe, we made camp in a shallow cave, lighting no fire and needing none.

"It was a foolish act," she told me, "but I am grateful for it."

"I could not stand by and watch you murdered."

"I know, Owen. You have a fine soul."

Always uncomfortable with compliments, I changed the subject. "I hope Mace escaped from them."

She chuckled. "Yes, he did. Did you like the way I changed the sorcerer's search spell?"

"The golden light? It was a master's touch, and I should have known it was you. He looked like a hero from legend."

"The people will long remember it."

"Perhaps, but the memory will fade once Mace is gone, when they see he is no Morningstar."

"If they ever see it. He chose the name, Owen, and now, I think, the name has chosen him."

"That is a riddle I cannot fathom."

"Give it time, my boy. Tell me, how will the events of today be seen?"

I smiled then. "A dramatic rescue by the lord of the forest. Not all the count's men could prevent it."

She nodded, her face solemn. "Mace was lucky today. They didn't need a search spell. He was in full view all day at the contest."

"Why, then, did they not take him? Were you using your powers?"

"No. There was no need. Azrek has a serpent's subtlety, and he assumed Mace would be more . . . circumspect. He believed there would be a rescue attempt but probably expected Mace to come disguised and arrive only when the crowds were thick. Hence the search spell. But Mace, with his casual arrogance, chose the best place to be, hiding in plain sight where no one would look."

"As you say, Megan, he is a lucky man."

"Luck has to be paid for, Owen," she whispered, "and sometimes the price is very high." Without another word she lay down and closed her eyes.

I shivered, for in that moment, my ghostly friend, I think my soul caught a glimpse of the future.

Then I, too, slept.

* * *

I awoke in the night to find a cool breeze whispering across the mouth of the cave, bringing with it the stealthy sounds of men moving through the undergrowth. Reaching out, I touched Megan lightly on the shoulder. Her eyes opened, and in the moonlight she saw me touch my fingers to my lips, warning her to keep silent.

Dropping to my stomach, I wormed my way to the cave mouth, peering out at the silhouetted trees. At first I saw nothing, but then the dark figure of a soldier, his breastplate gleaming in the eldritch light, edged forward. He was joined by another . . . and another. The first knelt, his pale hand extending down to the ground, tracing a line. Then he took a shining object from the pouch at his side and laid it on the ground. Immediately a faint blue-white light sprang up from the track. I swallowed hard, realizing that Megan and I had walked from that direction and feeling instinctively that the hunter was examining a footprint, mine or Megan's, and was carrying a search stone.

The cave itself was partly screened by thick bushes, but in the bright moonlight there was no hope of the entrance escaping the keen eyes of the hunters.

It is a fearful thing to be hunted, but it is doubly unmanning during the hours of night. I don't know why this should be so, save to note that our most primal fears are of the dark. Moonlight, though beautiful, is cold and unearthly. Nothing grows by moonlight, but all is revealed.

I glanced up, praying for clouds and total darkness, an all-covering blanket of black that would shield us from the soldiers. But almost immediately my fears welled anew, and I imagined the hunters, aided by the search stone, creeping forward purposefully within that darkness, unseen and deadly, their cold blades seeking my heart. No, I prayed again. No darkness. Please!

I was trembling now, but Megan's hand came down upon my arm, gripping my wrist, then patting the skin. I glanced toward her and licked my dry lips with a dryer tongue.

"Fear not," she whispered. "They will not see us." Extending her hand, she pointed at the leading soldier. He cried out and dropped the stone, which fell to the earth and blazed with a fierce light, causing the soldiers to shield their eyes. Leaning her back against the cave wall, Megan gestured with her right hand. The entrance shimmered, and as I looked toward the soldiers, it seemed I was viewing them through a screen of water.

Slowly they approached the rock wall. There were some twenty of them gathered now, lean and wolflike, swords in their hands. They halted some few feet before us, scanned the ground, then moved on.

After a while there was silence beyond the cave.

"What did you do?" I ventured at last.

"Think through your fear, Owen," she advised. "Do not let it master you. The illusion is no more than you could have achieved. Any man who can create the Dragon's Egg should find little difficulty in displaying a wall of rock where there is none."

I felt foolish then, for she was right. The rock face was dark; it would take little skill to cast an image across the cave mouth, and the soldiers had been half blinded by the destruction of the stone.

"But I could not have destroyed their stone," I pointed out defensively.

"No," she agreed, "that you could not do. Azrek has a powerful magus at his side, and I think you will need my . . . skills before this game is played out."

"What you did was sorcery," I said softly. "No trick with light and gentle heat. You burned a stone to dust and ash."

"I am allied to no dark powers, Owen. Sorcery and magick are not as far removed from one another as you would like to believe. Magick is, as you rightly say, merely tricks with light, illusions. But sorcery is a different kind of . . . trick. All I did with the stone was to create enormous heat. It is not difficult; it is merely a more powerful variation of the warming spell."

"How is it done?" I asked her.

"I cannot teach you sorcery in a single night, Owen, nor would I wish to try. But here is your first lesson: When you rub your hands together, you create heat. Well, a stone is not as solid as it looks. It is made of more component parts than there are stars in the sky. I make them rub against one another. The heat generated is immense."

"You are mocking me, lady. A stone is a stone. If it was, as you say, made up of many parts, then air would be trapped within it and it would float on water."

She shook her head. "All that you see in this world is not all that there is, Owen Odell. And your logic is flawed. I can make a stone float or give a feather such weight that you could not carry it. But these lessons can be for another day. For now I want you to tell me why *you* did not create the rock wall illusion."

"I did not think," I admitted. "I was frightened—close to panic."

"Yes, you were. Fear is good, for it makes us cautious and aids survival. Not so with terror. It is like slow poison, paralyzing the limbs and blurring the mind. You have courage, Owen, else you would not have stood up for me at the burning. But you are undisciplined. Never, when in danger, ask yourself, What will they do to me? Instead think, What can I do to prevent them? Or did you think that magick and all the connected powers were merely discovered in order to entertain revelers in inns, taverns, and palaces?"

I was ashamed of my cowardice and said nothing, my thoughts hurtling back to childhood, when my father had constantly berated me for lack of skill in the manly arts. I did not climb trees for fear of the heights or learn to swim for fear of drowning. High horses frightened me, and the clashing of sword blades made me cry. My brothers took to the game of war like young lions, and upon them he showered praise. But Owen was a weakling, worthless, a creature to be avoided. The great Aubertain—how I hated him for his cruel courage, his arrogance, and his pride.

I gloried in his one weakness—fire. A long time before, when he himself was a child, he had been burned upon his left arm: The scars were still visible, white, ugly, and wrinkled, stretching from wrist to elbow. Even into middle age he would jump if a fire log cracked and spit sparks.

And then, one summer's evening, a storehouse near the castle caught fire. Every villager and soldier ran to the blaze, human chains forming to ferry buckets of water from the deep wells to the men at the head of the lines. The fire was beyond control, and bright sparks flew into the night sky, carried by the breeze to rest upon the thatched roofs of nearby cottages.

My father, brothers, and I organized work parties, carrying water into homes as yet untouched and drenching the thatch. There was a two-story house close by. Sparks entered through an open window, igniting the straw matting that covered the ground floor. Flames billowed up.

I remember a woman screaming, "My baby! My baby!" She was pointing to an upper window. My father was standing beside me at the time, and I saw upon his face a look of sheer terror. But then, with a snarl, he tore loose his cloak, wrapped it around his face and shoulders, and ran into the burning building.

Moments later I saw him at the upper window with the babe in his arms. Climbing to the sill, he leapt to the yard below, his hair and beard on fire. He landed awkwardly, and we heard his leg snap, but he twisted his body as he fell to protect the infant he held. Men ran forward then, smothering the flames that writhed about him. The mother retrieved her babe, and my father was carried back to the castle.

I am ashamed to say that my hatred for him swelled, roaring up like the blaze around me.

"Why so melancholy?" asked Megan, and I shivered as my mind fled back to the present.

"I was thinking of my father." I told her then of the unhappiness of my childhood and the story of the great fire that all but destroyed the estate.

"Do you still think you hate him, Owen?"

"No, but his treatment of me still causes me pain. The memories are jagged and sharp."

"You are much like him."

"You misread me, Megan. He is a warrior, a killer, a knight. I am none of these things, nor would I wish to be."

"What do you wish to be?"

I looked out at the night sky, considering her question. "I would like to be content, Megan. Happy. I have known in the woods moments of genuine joy, like when Piercollo sang or when Mace brought the treasure back to the people. But not the happiness I dream of."

"And what would bring it to you?"

"I do not know. Love, perhaps. A family and a quiet home. Fame. To be known as the greatest bard in the Angostin kingdoms."

"These will not bring you what you seek," she told me, her voice soft.

"No? How can you be sure?"

"There is a man you must first find. He will give you the answers."

"He would need to be a great teacher, this man. Who is he?"

"You will know him when you meet him," she answered. "Is your father still alive?"

I shrugged. "I have no knowledge of his affairs. I have not contacted my family for more than six years. But yes, I would think he is still alive. He was strong as an ox and would now be only forty-two years of age."

"When this is over, Owen, seek him out."

"For what purpose?"

"To tell him you love him."

I wanted to laugh in her face, to ram home the stupidity of her words. But I could not. And anger flared in me then, a hot silent fury that was washed away by the sudden tears stinging my eyes.

◊ 6 ◊

I WEPT, AND Megan moved alongside me, her arms around me. "Let it go, Owen. Release it." My head dropped to her shoulder, my eyes squeezed shut, and painful sobs racked my frame. At last I felt the cool breeze upon my back and sensed the coming of the dawn. Pulling back from her, I forced a smile.

"I am ashamed of myself, wailing like a child."

"Where there is pain, there is often a tear or two."

"Yes, but the pain is gone now, back to whence it came, locked away. Where do we go today?"

"We find Mace," she told me. "But first let us view the enemy."

Moving back from me, she watched the sun rise behind a bank of clouds that turned to gold before my eyes, the sky around it turquoise and blue. I felt my soul swell at the beauty of it. Slowly the sun rose through the golden cloud, and its rays pierced the flesh of vapor, spearing down to strike the rock face and the cave, illuminating the rear wall.

Megan gestured with her right hand. The wall shimmered, flattened, glowed . . . and disappeared, becoming a window that looked down upon a long hall. There were flags and pennants hung from poles on both sides of the hall and a long table that ran down its center. At the head of the table sat Azrek, eyes downcast and expression brooding. His fist crashed down upon the wood, and a golden goblet was sent spinning to the floor.

"I want him dead. I want his death to be hard."

"We are seeking him now, my lord," came a voice, but the speaker was not in view.

"Send out the Six."

84

"I shall see that they are fed and then released, lord."

"No!" stormed Azrek, rising to his feet, his pale face gleaming in the torchlight, his black hair hanging lank about his lean features. "I don't want them fed. Let them feast on his heart."

"Yes, sir . . . but . . ."

"But what, fool?"

"They are hungry. They will need to eat before they track down the Morningstar."

"Then let them hunt their meat in the forest. There is plenty there. Succulent meat. Highland delicacies." Azrek laughed, the sound echoing through the hall and whispering out into the cave. The unseen servant departed, and we heard the door close, then creak open moments later.

"What is it?" demanded Azrek.

"You will wish me to mark the Six with the soul of the Morningstar," came a soft voice that seemed all too familiar. Yet I could not place it.

"Yes. Imprint the smell of it upon their senses."

"There is no smell, sir, merely an aura that is his alone."

"Spare me your pedantry. I pay you well, magicker, and what do you offer me in return? You promised me the Morningstar. Well, where is he?"

"Surely you do not blame me, sir. My light shone over him. It was then left to your soldiers to apprehend him. They failed, not I."

"You all failed," snarled Azrek, "and I will not tolerate it. The soldiers who fell back before his blade are now hanging by their heels, their skin flayed from their bodies. Be warned, magicker, I do not like to lose. And this task should be simplicity itself. One man in a forest. One creature of flesh and bone and sinew. Is that too much for you?"

"Not at all, sir. But using the Six will prove costly. They will not return; they will stay in the forest, hunting and killing, until they themselves are slain."

"What is that to me?"

"It cost many lives, more than forty if memory serves, to create them."

"They were only lives," answered Azrek. "The world is full of *lives*."

"As you say, sir. The Lord of Lualis has sent out criers to announce a larger reward of two thousand sovereigns for infor-

mation leading to the apprehension of the Morningstar and
twenty gold pieces for his companies—the hunchback, the giant,
and the bard, Odell.''

"Ah yes, Odell . . . I would like to hear him sing. There are
notes I shall teach him that he would not believe he could reach.''

"I am sure of that, my lord," said the other smoothly, "but
there are two other matters to which I must draw your attention.
First, the woman Megan. I had the ashes raked, but there were
no bones evident. She did not die in the flames.''

"How could that be? We saw her tied to the stake.''

"Indeed we did. I believe Odell, hidden by the smoke,
climbed the pyre and freed her as the soldiers pursued the Morningstar.''

"So where is she now, magicker?''

"Why, sir, she is watching us," he answered, his voice remaining even. The window in the wall appeared to tremble, and
the castle hall beyond spun and rose. Down, down swept the
image. Azrek seemed to swell and grow.

"Get back!" shouted Megan, but my limbs seemed frozen
and I was unable to tear my eyes from the scene. Azrek looked
at me—saw me as if from across a room. A second figure moved
into view.

"How are you, Owen?" said Cataplas amiably.

He seemed unchanged from the master I had known, a long
purple velvet robe hanging from his lean frame, his gray wispy
trident beard clinging like mist to his chin. His hand came up
with fingers spread. A small ball of flames flickered on his palm,
swelling and growing.

Megan grabbed my arm, pulling me back. "Run, Owen!"
she screamed.

Idly Cataplas tossed the flaming globe toward us.

We were at the cave entrance when it sailed through the window. Megan hurled herself at me, spinning me from my feet,
just as a great explosion sounded and a tongue of flame seared
out from the mouth of the cave, scorching the grass for twenty
feet.

I rolled to my back. Megan was lying some way from me,
her white robe smoldering.

"No!" I shouted, scrambling to my feet and running to her.
In taking the time to push me clear she had suffered terrible
burns to her left side. Her arm was blackened and split and

bloody, and most of her hair had been scorched away. Her eyes opened, and she groaned.

I was no healer, but like all magickers I knew the simple spells of warming and cooling, both of which are used by those whose skills are directed toward healing the sick. Swiftly I covered her burns with cool air, and she sighed and sank back to the grass.

"I am sorry, Megan," I told her. "I am so sorry."

"I can heal myself," she whispered, "given time, that is. But it is taking all my power, and I can be of no use to you for a while. Mace is on his way here—I reached him last night. When he arrives, I will be sleeping deeply. Take me to the town of Ocrey. It is north of here, perhaps a day's travel. Do not seek to wake me but carry me to the house of Osian. It is built beside a stream to the west of Ocrey. There is an old man living there; he will . . . care for me. You understand?"

"Yes. I will do as you say."

"And warn Mace of the Six. He must be prepared."

"Who are they?" But she was sinking fast, and I had to lower my ear to her mouth to hear the softest of whispers.

"The Satan Hounds," she murmured.

The name sent a shiver through me, but before I could question her further, Megan closed her eyes, passing from consciousness. I had no idea what she had meant, but there was no way she could have spoken literally. The Satan Hounds, more often called the Shadows of Satan, were mythical creatures said to have walked the earth beside their master after his fall from heaven, when the world had been but a glowing ball of molten rock lashed by seething seas of lava.

I guessed that the pain must have made her delirious. The Six were probably no more than warhounds. Even so, they would be dangerous, for Cataplas had imprinted upon their minds the image of Mace. The talk of souls and auras was, I was sure, a lie to fool only the uninitiated.

Mace arrived within the hour, Piercollo and Eye Patch with him. The hunchback had been left at their camp some two hours' march to the west. Piercollo lifted the sleeping Megan and cradled her to his chest, her head upon his massive shoulder. She did not wake, and none of us spoke as we walked out into the morning.

Mace took the lead, moving smoothly across the forest floor.

He was wearing a black sleeveless jerkin of well-oiled leather and a green woolen shirt with puffed sleeves and cuffs of black leather that doubled as wrist guards. As usual he wore his high riding boots and trews of green. He had no cap today, and the sun glinted on blond highlights in his auburn hair. Wide-shouldered and slim of hip, he looked every inch the hero that he ought to have been—the warrior of legend, the forest lord.

I looked away and thought of Cataplas. I had been surprised when I saw him in the service of Azrek, and yet, upon consideration, I should not have been. He was an amiable man, yet remote. Polite and courteous, but without feeling, lacking understanding of human emotions. His skills had always been awesome, and his search for knowledge carried out with endless dedication. I can remember many pleasant evenings in his company, enjoying his wit and his intelligence, his skills as a storyteller, and his incomparable talent. But I cannot remember a single act of simple kindness.

We entered the outskirts of the town of Ocrey, located the home of Osian—a slender old man, toothless and nearly blind—and laid Megan carefully upon a narrow pallet bed. Osian said nothing when we arrived but waited, silent and unmoving, for our departure. We slipped away into the gathering darkness, crossing several hills and streams before Mace chose a campsite in a sheltered hollow.

Piercollo built a small fire, and we settled around it.

I was saddened by what had happened to Megan but also irritated by the lack of reaction in Mace. This was his friend and I had rescued her, yet not a word of praise was forthcoming. His head pillowed on his arm, he slept by the fire. Piercollo nodded off, his back to a wide oak tree, and I sat miserably in the company of Eye Patch, who had said not one word on this long day.

"Where are you from?" I asked him suddenly as he leaned forward to add a dry stick to the fire.

His single eye glanced up, and he stared at me for a long moment. "What is it to you?" he responded.

It was not said in a challenging way, and I shrugged. "I am just making conversation. I am not tired."

"What happened to the old woman? Mace said she was unhurt by the burning."

"She was, but a sorcerer cast a spell of fire."

He accepted that without comment, then hawked and spit. "You can't deal with magickers," he said at last. "Not one of them has a soul. Their hearts are shriveled and black."

"A generalization, I think."

"A what?"

"You are putting all magickers together, saying they are all the same. That is not so."

"An expert, are you?" he hissed.

"I would not say so. But there are men who learn the art of healing, spending their lives in the service of others. They are magickers."

He thought for a moment. "They are doctors," he announced as if that ended the discussion. "Sorcerers are different."

"Indeed they are," I agreed. He seemed pleased.

"My name is Gamail, though most call me Patch."

"You shoot well. How can you judge distance with but one eye?"

He chuckled and removed the patch, tossing it to me. "Put it on," he ordered. Holding it up to my eye, I saw that it was virtually transparent. Then I looked at his face, to see two good eyes staring back at me.

"Why do you wear it?"

"Three years ago I was fighting in the Oversea War, and the eye was infected. After that it would take no strong light but would weep and blur. I met a doctor who made that for me; it dulls the light."

An eerie howl echoed through the night, followed almost instantly by a high-pitched scream.

Mace awoke. "What in hell's name was that?" he inquired. I shook my head.

"I never heard nothing like it in my life," whispered Patch.

"How close was it?" asked Jarek Mace.

"Difficult to say up here," Patch told him. "Maybe a mile, maybe two."

"Have you heard of the Shadows of Satan?" I asked softly.

"Tell me a story on another night," grunted Mace, settling down once more.

"I do not believe it is a story. Megan used her powers to overhear a sorcerer talking to Count Azrek. The count ordered the release of the Six, and they were to hunt you down. I asked Megan about the Six; she said they were the Shadows.''

Jarek Mace rolled to his feet. "Why didn't you tell me before this?" he stormed.

"I thought she was delirious. What are these beasts?''

"How should I know? But would you want creatures called Shadows of Satan hunting you in the night?"

"No."

The howls came again, closer this time. "Wolves?" I whispered.

"No wolf I've ever heard made a sound like that," muttered Patch, rising.

Swiftly we woke Piercollo and set off into the darkness.

The moon was high and three-quarters full, moon shadows lacing the track at our feet as we moved on into the night. Mace and Patch notched arrows to their bows and carried them ready for use. We traveled at speed, stopping often to listen for sounds of pursuit.

At first we heard nothing, then came the eerie howling from left and right. Jarek Mace swore and pushed on down a long slope to a stream that rushed over white rocks and pebbles. Mace splashed into it, running swiftly toward the west, the water spraying up around his boots like molten silver. I followed him, Piercollo behind me and Patch bringing up the rear.

We ran in the stream for several hundred yards until it curved north, then Mace scrambled up the opposite bank, taking hold of a jutting and exposed tree root and hauling himself clear. Reaching out his hand, he pulled me up after him. Piercollo jumped for the root, his huge fingers snaking around it, but the wood snapped with a loud crack that echoed in the night. The big man slid backward, cannoning into Patch, and both men tumbled into the stream.

A dark shadow moved on the opposite bank. I blinked and stared at the spot. At first I saw nothing, then a massive, horned snout pushed clear of the undergrowth.

How can I describe it without chilling your blood? It was both the most loathsome and the most terrifying sight my eyes had yet beheld. The face—if face it could be called—was pale and hairless, the nose distended and flattened. Long, curved tusks extended up from the lower lip. But it had fangs also, like a wolf. In weight and girth it was the size of a great bull, but there were no hooves, the legs being thick and heavily muscled above great paws similar to those of a lion. In all it was a grotesque deformity, a meld of many creatures.

Yet it was the eyes that sent ice into my soul. For without doubt they were human, and they gleamed with malevolent intelligence.

"Behind you!" I yelled at the struggling men. Piercollo was hauling himself from the stream, but Patch swung, his bow still in his hand, the arrow lost in the swirling water. He saw the beast and reached instantly for his quiver.

With a terrible cry the creature charged, uprooting bushes and snapping a young sapling in its way. An arrow from the bow of Jarek Mace flashed across the water, burying itself in the left eye of the monster, causing it to rear up on its colossal hind legs. Seizing his opportunity, Patch sent a shaft thudding into its exposed black belly, and the creature came down on all fours. It was covered in matted black fur and had a massive hump on its neck. The hump writhed, and two long arms unfolded from it, the fingers long and pale, curved claws clicking together. Charging once more, it bore down on Patch.

Piercollo, unarmed, hurled himself at the beast, meeting its charge. He was swept aside like a leaf in a storm, but his attack caused the creature to swing its huge head, seeking out this new enemy. Patch cooly shot an arrow into its throat, and it screamed again, its ghastly jaws opening wide.

Jarek Mace sent a shaft into the open mouth . . . it vanished from sight, feathers and all.

Piercollo rose from the water, raising a jagged boulder above his head and crashing it down upon the beast's skull. I heard the bone splinter, and the creature's front legs folded. Without a further sound, it died.

The Tuscanian dragged himself over the crest of the bank, Patch nimbly following him.

Mace notched another arrow to his bow, his keen eyes staring back down the trail. Without a word he swung back to the west and set off through the forest.

We followed him in silence.

And the howling began again.

The night has a capacity for terror that the day can never match. Often in my life I have woken in the dark to hear some sound, some creaking of a shutter, or the soft whispering of the wind through dry leaves. In the dark it is easy to picture a stealthy assassin, an undead Vampyre, stalking through the house.

But in the forest the power of the dark swells. Silhouetted trees are eldritch giants with waving arms and sharp talons; the rustling of the undergrowth becomes the stealthy slithering of giant serpents. The hoot of an owl, the fluttering wings of a bat cause icy fingers to pluck upon the strings of the soul's fears, unearthly and threatening.

I shall never forget that midnight run through the dark of the forest with the beasts from the pit upon our trail, the fickle moon hiding often behind thick clouds and forcing us to halt, standing stock-still, blind and terrified. Then she would shine again, and our trembling legs would carry us on, following the narrow deer trails ever west.

Piercollo suffered the most, for his enormous bulk, despite its prodigious strength, was not made for running and he began to fall behind. I shouted to Mace to wait for him, but he ignored me until the next eerie wail sounded from some way ahead of us. Only then did he halt. Another cry shattered the silence of the night, this time from our left.

Piercollo staggered up to us. "I . . . can . . . go no . . . farther," he said, the breath wheezing from his lungs.

Mace swung, his eyes raking the trees. "Over there," he said, pointing to a circle of oaks. Forcing our way through the undergrowth, we reached the trees. Mace climbed the first, ordering Patch to scale the tree opposite; since Piercollo and I were unarmed, he ignored us and we climbed a gnarled oak at the edge of the circle, seating ourselves on a broad bough some fifteen feet from the ground. Piercollo leaned back against the trunk of the tree and wiped the sweat from his face.

"This is not to my liking, friend Owen."

"Nor mine," I admitted. "But the creatures cannot climb."

Piercollo sighed. "He is not what I expected."

"Who?"

"The Morningstar."

"He is what he is," I told him. He nodded and closed his eyes.

The moon disappeared once more, and darkness descended. A cool breeze fluttered across me, causing an instant shiver, for sweat had drenched my clothing. I cast a warming spell and relaxed a little.

Then came the sound of bushes being uprooted and cloven hooves beating upon the soft ground. Leaning back, I took hold of a branch, gripping it with both hands and hugging myself to the tree.

The moon eased herself clear of the clouds, and I glanced down to see the monsters come to a halt, their great heads angled up, staring at Jarek Mace as he sat in full view of them. His bow bent back, and a shaft slashed through the air to bury itself in the throat of the lead beast. It reared high, then charged the tree; the oak was old and firm, yet the vibration almost dislodged Mace. Patch loosed an arrow that sliced into the hump of a second beast. While the first circled the oak Mace had climbed, the remaining four rushed toward where Patch was hidden. There was a tremendous crash as two of the creatures butted the oak and Patch lost hold of his bow, which fell to the ground; he grabbed at a branch to stop himself from falling. Now the beasts moved slowly against the base of the tree and began to push. At first the oak withstood the pressure, but soon I saw one root appear above ground, then another.

Suddenly the tree yawed. Patch's legs swung clear, and he was now hanging by his hands some twenty feet above the ground. An arrow from Mace slashed into the side of one of the beasts, but it showed no sign that it felt any pain.

With a wrenching groan the oak gave way, tumbling Patch to the ground. He hit hard, rolled, and came to his feet running toward the nearest tree.

The beasts set after him . . .

Taking a deep breath, I concentrated hard. The spell of light was not easy, though neither was it the most difficult. But what I wanted now was not just illumination. Forming the spell, I held it for several heartbeats, letting it swell until I could control it no longer. My hand flashed out.

The spell sped from me like a flash of lightning, bursting in the space between Patch and the pursuing monsters, blinding them and causing them to swerve away from their victim. For one brief second I was exultant. But I had forgotten the first beast, the one that had been circling Jarek Mace. Unseen by me, it had cut across the small clearing, and just as Patch leapt for an overhanging branch, it caught him, the taloned arms dragging him back, the awful jaws closing on his waist. With one dreadful cry the bowman died, his corpse ripped into two.

The other creatures gathered around and began to feed. I could not watch, and I tried to close my ears to the sound of ripping flesh and snapping bone.

"Fire! We need fire!" shouted Jarek Mace. "Can you do it, Owen?"

At the sound of his voice the five beasts moved away from their grisly feast and rushed at the oak in which he had taken refuge. Hurling their huge bodies against the trunk, they sought to dislodge him as they had the unfortunate Patch. But this tree was older and more firm, and it did not budge.

Two of the beasts then began to pound their hooves at the base of the tree, digging away at the roots, exposing them, then ripping at the soft wood with their fangs.

"Fire, Owen!" bellowed Mace.

I took a deep breath and tried to concentrate. Creating a fire was a variation on the spell of warming, but the power was condensed, focused on a very small point, usually a fragment of dry bark or shredded leaf.

I stared intently at the twisted hump on the back of the nearest monster, concentrating on the mass of black, matted fur—holding back the spell, allowing it to build, feeling the pressure grow within my mind. When I could hold it no longer, I threw out my arm, pointing at the beast. Blue flame crackled out, lancing down to strike the hump. Smoke billowed from the fur, and the monster reared up, screaming, the sound almost human.

I had expected a few small fingers of fire, but what followed astounded me.

Flames roared out, blazing with white light—more powerful than any beacon fire, brighter than daylight. The creature rolled to its back, but nothing could extinguish the blaze. In its panic and pain it ran into the other beasts, and the flames spread to engulf three of them; then dried leaves on the ground ignited beneath the hooves of the fourth monster, whose legs caught fire, sheets of flame searing around its body.

An unholy glow filled the clearing, and the heat was so intense that Piercollo and I eased our way around the tree, putting the trunk between us and the scorching flames. Even so, the heat was almost unbearable, the light so bright that both of us squeezed shut our eyes.

The blaze lit the sky for several minutes, the flames reaching thirty feet or more into the air. Then they died, swiftly dwindling. I climbed around to the front of the tree. There were no leaves now—the branches smoldering, the tips glowing red with hot ash.

Writhing on the forest floor were a score of blackened shapes. One looked like the burned carcass of a dog, another a horse, yet another a man. One by one they ceased all movement.

Suddenly the last creature emerged from the undergrowth. How it had escaped I do not know, but it advanced into the smoldering clearing and stood, its grotesque arms unfolding from its hump. Jarek Mace sent his last two shafts into the flanks of the beast, but it ignored them and advanced on the tree, continuing to dig at the roots.

"Piercollo has had enough of this," said the giant. Taking hold of a long partly burned branch, he wrenched hard, the dry wood snapping with a loud crack. The branch was some six feet in length and as thick as four spears bound together. He proceeded to strip away the twigs and shoots growing from it. "Give me your dagger," he ordered me, and I did so. Resting the broken length of wood in the crook of the bough on which we stood, Piercollo began to cut away at the tip of the branch, shaping it to a rough point. I could see that he was trying to craft a weapon, but what kind? It was too large for a spear and too unwieldy to be used as a lance.

At last satisfied, he returned my dagger, then hefted the branch and edged out along the bough some twelve feet above the ground.

"Ho, there!" he called out. "Creature of ugliness! Come to Piercollo!"

The beast lifted its grotesque head, its huge eyes focusing on the Tuscanian. Piercollo stood very still with the huge spear held vertically, the point aimed at the ground below. At first the creature just stood, staring up at him, then it moved across the clearing.

"That is it, monster! Come to me!"

With a roar it charged at the tree.

Gripping the weapon with both hands, Piercollo dropped from the bough, his enormous weight driving the huge spear deep into the creature's back, through its enormous belly, and into the ground beneath. The monster's legs buckled, and it sank to the earth with blood pouring from its mouth.

Slowly I climbed down and walked among the many corpses.

Megan had said that magick and sorcery were more closely linked than I knew. But as I gazed upon the dreadful fire-blackened bodies, I hoped—prayed, almost—that she was wrong.

Five years before, when I had been living with Cataplas at his home by the Sea of Gaels, I had watched him experiment with dead mice, dissecting them, examining the innards. Then he had laid the bodies side by side.

"Look at them, Owen, and tell me what you see."

"What is there to see, save two dead rodents?"

"Use your talent, concentrate. Think of colors, auras."

I stared at the mice, and true enough, they glowed with a faint light radiating out from their tiny bodies. "What is that?" I asked, amazed.

"The essence of life," he told me. "You will see that light for three days more, then it will be gone. But watch this!"

With a sharp knife he cut the bodies neatly in two, then took the hind legs and rear body of the first and laid it against the severed front torso of the second. Cataplas took a deep breath, and I felt the gathering of his power. The light around the two halves swelled, and I watched the skin of the bodies writhe together, the edges meeting, joining. The rear legs twitched; the head moved. The hybrid struggled to rise, took several weak steps, then fell again. Cataplas clicked his fingers, and the light faded, the twinned beast ceasing to move.

"You are a sorcerer!" I whispered.

"I am a seeker after knowledge," he replied.

Here, in this clearing, I could see the result of his quest, and it sickened me.

Jarek Mace moved alongside me. "Where do they come from?" he asked. "There are at least three men here, and several hounds."

"The beasts are . . . were . . . merged . . . creations of sorcery. Hounds, horses, men, boars, bonded together into . . ." I turned away, desperate to put the hellish scene behind me.

"Sorcery or not, we killed them," said Mace, slapping my shoulder. "The fire you sent was unbelievable. I did not realize you had such power."

"Neither did I. Can we leave this place?"

"Presently," said Mace with a smile.

I watched in disbelief as he searched the remnants of what had once been the body of Patch. He returned with the bowman's money pouch.

"Should have been mine," he said, "and would have been had my string not snapped. Let us go."

The attack left me in a state of numbed shock, the passing of terror leaving in its place an emptiness, a void that could not even grieve for the ghastly death of the archer, Patch. I stumbled on behind Jarek Mace and Piercollo, scarcely noticing the journey or the rising of the sun and the warmth of a new day.

Cataplas had moved from amorality to evil and was apparently unmarked by the process. Throughout my years with him I had never sensed his capacity for darkness, and none of his actions had hinted at the horror of which he was capable. Often we would journey on foot across the land, stopping at wayside taverns to entertain revelers or in castles to perform for the nobles and their ladies. Always Cataplas was punctiliously polite, soft-voiced, and charming. I never once saw him lose his temper.

Yet here he was practicing the darkest sorceries, merging men and beasts, blood-hungry creatures who lived only to kill. I wondered then—hoped might be a better description—if he himself had been put under a spell. But I knew it was not so.

Long-forgotten memories came back to me. A performance had been canceled because of the death of a child; the parents were grieving and had no wish to be entertained. Cataplas had been irritated by what he saw as their lack of good manners. "Did they not realize," he said to me, "that I have walked thirty miles to show them my magick?"

"But their son is dead," I answered.

"I did not kill him. What has it to do with me?"

All that interested Cataplas was the pursuit of knowledge. Magick he had mastered as no man before or since. But magick was, he said, merely a game played with light, illusory and—artistic consideration aside—worthless.

We parted company one winter's evening just after a performance at the royal court in Ebracom. He had filled the great hall with golden birds whose songs were a joy to the ear and the heart and concluded with the creation of a golden-scaled lion who leapt upon the table before the king, scattering pots and dishes. Women screamed and men leapt back, tipping over chairs and falling to the floor, alarming the warhounds that sat beneath the table feeding on scraps. Only the king remained seated, a grim smile upon his cruel mouth.

The lion rose up on its hind legs and became a huge silver eagle that soared into the air and flew around the rafters, devouring the golden songbirds.

At the end of the performance there was tumultuous applause. Cataplas bowed, and we left the hall.

Outside, in the shadows of the corridor, he said his goodbyes. "I have taught you all that you can learn," he said. "Now it is time for you to walk your own path." He bowed stiffly, turned, and walked away, his long velvet robe brushing the cold stone of the walls.

As I lay in bed that night, I pictured again the golden lion. I can remember a cold chill sweeping over me, and I sat up, rigid with fear. The lion had scattered the dishes!

It was not a trick played with light, not a creation of magick. In the seconds before Cataplas transformed it into an eagle it had been real, solid, the golden claws and fangs capable of rending and tearing.

Not magick at all, but sorcery.

Now Patch was dead, as the burned corpses in the clearing were dead. I looked ahead to where Jarek Mace and Piercollo were walking in the sunlight . . . and I shivered.

In a world of violence, war, and sudden death these men could hold their own. But against Cataplas and all the demonic powers he could summon, what hope was left for them?

And for me.

Fear returned then with great force.

Toward midmorning we crested a tall hill and gazed out over the slender lakes that shone like silver in the valleys of the central forest. The land stretched away in great folds in a hundred variations of green and brown speckled with the hazy purples of bracken and golden-yellow splashes of gorse. The trees were thinner here, and we could see at least two settlements by the largest of the lakes—wooden houses, single-storied, built along the shoreline. Boats and coracles were out on the lake, fishermen casting their nets for the red-fleshed fish that journeyed in from the sea in late spring.

All in all it was a quietly beautiful sight.

"Not a single tavern," grunted Mace. "And I doubt there's a whore to be had."

He was wrong. One of the first people I recognized, apart from the twisted figure of Wulf, was the blond mute, Ilka. She stood with arms folded across her chest, her great blue eyes watching us as we strolled into the settlement.

"You're a sight for sore eyes, Mace," shouted Wulf. "Where's Megan?"

Mace explained, then told the story of the monstrous creatures that had hunted us. Wulf's face was set and grim as he listened.

"We've heard of them," he grunted. "They struck a family of tinkers the night afore last—ripped them to pieces. At first we thought it was trolls, but they've no cloven hoofs. There are hunting parties out, five in all. I was with one of them. We just got back."

"Well," said Mace with a grin, "they won't be needed. Owen cast a mighty spell that burned them up like great torches. And our singing friend here took out the last with a spear the size of a small tree."

Piercollo chuckled. "Life is not without excitement in your company, Morningstar."

"Don't call me that!" snapped Mace, uneasy. "It began as a jest, but it is no longer amusing." Then he spotted Ilka and smiled, his good humor restored. Waving her to him, he took her arm and led her off into the trees. She glanced back once, and her eyes held mine. I cannot say what the look meant, but I sighed and my spirits plummeted.

Mace was gone for most of the afternoon, and Wulf took us to his campsite outside the settlement. He had crafted from woven branches a lean-to shelter with a sloping roof and two movable windbreaks. A fire was burning with a circle of stones, and six rabbits were hanging from a tree branch nearby.

"Welcome to my hearth," he said, settling himself beside the fire. Piercollo and I lay down on the dry ground. Immediately fatigue overtook me, and I fell asleep to the sound of Wulf's flute and the deep tenor beauty of Piercollo singing a gentle ballad.

It was dark when I awoke. Mace was back and sitting with

the others, throwing dice and betting on the result. Ilka sat apart from them, hugging her knees and rocking gently from side to side. I stretched and sat up, smiling at her. She did not respond, but her eyes remained locked to mine.

Lifting my head, I signaled to her to join me, but she shook her head and looked away.

"Ah, the mighty magician is awake," said Jarek Mace, "and he has missed his supper."

"I'm not hungry," I told him.

The stars were out, the moon a glorious crescent, the light so strong that it cast shadows from the trees to the silvered ground.

More than a dozen men came moving from the undergrowth, grim men, dressed as foresters in leather jerkins and trews with daggers at their belts and longbows in their hands. I froze. Mace moved easily to his feet and waited. The newcomers walked slowly, purposefully, their eyes watching Mace. Piercollo eased himself to his feet, but Wulf sat very still, his hand on his dagger.

A tall bowman, his hair silver in the moonlight, strode forward to stand before Mace. "So you'd be the Morningstar?" said the newcomer, looking Mace up and down. "Why is it that I am not impressed?"

"I have no idea," responded Mace, "but your wife was impressed the last time I bedded her. But then, the competition was not fierce."

Even by the light of the moon and stars I saw the man redden. "Be careful, Mace! I am not known for my patience."

"You are not known for anything, Corlan," snapped Mace. "Now say what you have come to say and then begone!"

"You think I won't kill you? You think your life is charmed?"

"I know that if you try, I'll cut your throat," Mace told him.

Corlan's gaze swept to the dagger at Mace's belt; it was still scabbarded.

"You think you are fast enough to beat an arrow?"

"I know I am. Now speak your piece."

"I want some of the profit from this . . . Morningstar game of yours. Let us face facts, Mace. Whatever plan you have cannot be carried off without men. And you have only Wulf. He's good, and so are you. But you need more. I have them. All we want is a share. Isn't that right, men?"

"Aye," the foresters chorused.

"And if I don't agree?"

"Then you die here. And perhaps so do I. Now, do we have an agreement?"

Mace swung to me. "Well, Owen, do we have an agreement?"

For a moment I was thunderstruck, but then I saw the look in Mace's eyes—sharp, direct—and I knew he was warning me to be careful. Beyond that I could not guess at his reasons for drawing me into the discussion.

"Who in the devil's name is he?" asked Corlan.

"It is his game," answered Mace easily. "The Morningstar was his idea."

"What is the game?" asked the forester, turning to me.

In that moment I set my foot on a perilous path. I am not sure now how far ahead I could see; I like to think that a small part of my mind, a deep dark corner close to the soul, inspired me. But I fear it was merely self-preservation that made me speak as I did.

"It is the greatest game of all," I said, "and the profits will make beggars of kings."

My voice was firm and resonant, deep and compelling, and the ease of the lie surprised me. I excused it then—as I do now— by saying that as a bard I was also a performer, and I was performing before an audience that, if it did not like my words, might kill me.

Corlan looked at me with fresh eyes. He saw a tall, dark-haired young man of Angostin countenance, straight of nose, strong of chin, keen of eye, and my confidence grew. "You are correct, Corlan, we will need men, but far more than you have here. These will come in time, but you will be the first—after you have pledged the soul oath."

"I want to hear about gold, not oaths," he said.

"You will hear all you need to in good time," I told him. "Gather around me." I moved away and sat, not looking at any of them. Corlan was the first to sit before me, the others forming a semicircle on either side of him. Mace, Wulf, and Piercollo placed themselves behind me. By now I had thought out my plan of action, one that would take the outlaws as far from us as was humanly possible. Better than that, it would also involve them in tackling Azrek and his men and perhaps diverting his attention from us. I was mightily pleased with myself as I began to speak. "The Highlands have been burned by war, the nobles scattered or slain. The land is in turmoil, and foreign lords have control of the cities. Taxes are ungathered, cattle unbranded, homes left empty, fields lie fallow. Here in this forest are many settlements, and the Angostins will seek to loot and plunder, thus paying their mercenary armies. But how many roads are there to Ziraccu? Only a handful that can be used by wagons laden with gold and coin. The first moves of the Morningstar will be to close those roads, to exact a toll from the Angostins."

"What kind of a toll?" asked a lean, hatchet-faced man to the left of Corlan.

"All that they have."

"We could do that without you," said Corlan. "Where does the Morningstar fit in this?"

"Be patient, Corlan, and listen. You will take their gold. Half you will hide; the other half will be returned to the people. You will be known as the men of the Morningstar, and you will let it be known in the settlements that you are fighting for the freedom of the land. You will be heroes. When you need food, you will pay for it. You will steal nothing from the settlements; there will be no looting or rape. You will walk the forest with heads held high, and you will bask in the acclaim of the people."

"I still don't understand," snapped Corlan.

"What is there to understand?" I answered him. "You will have gold and honor. And when the time is right you will know the full plan. And you will be rich, as all of you will be rich, with more gold than a man could spend in twenty lifetimes."

"So you say. But you have told us nothing," put in another man.

"You know all you need to know. How can you lose? If I am wrong or my plan is flawed, you will still have the profit from your raids."

"Why the men of the Morningstar?" asked Corlan.

"You have heard the legends growing. You know what the people think of Jarek Mace. He is seen as the banner of rebellion; he is the heart of resistance to the Angostin evil. In his name you will be welcome everywhere. They will hide you and feed you; they will die to protect you; they will beg to join you."

"Do you trust him, Mace?" Corlan swung to stare into Mace's eyes.

"He has been proved right so far."

"I don't know. You are a canny man, Mace. I don't like you, but you fight like a demon and you've the mind of a wolf. You believe we'll be rich as kings?"

"Why else would I be here?"

Corlan nodded. "I would guess that's true. What of you, Wulf?"

The hunchback shrugged. "I follow the Morningstar," he said with a twisted grin.

"Then we'll do it," said Corlan, making to rise.

"Wait," I said softly. "First the soul oath."

"I need no oaths," hissed Corlan.

"But I do," I whispered. Raising my right hand with palm upward, I stared down at the skin, holding myself still, forcing my concentration to deepen. Blue and yellow flames leapt from the palm, bright and hurtful to the eyes.

Corlan fell back, dropping his bow. "You are a sorcerer!" he shouted.

"Indeed I am," I said, my voice deep as rolling thunder. It was a fine performance, and I risked a glance at the other men, seeing the fear in their faces. "This is the flame that cannot die. This is the light that feeds on souls. Each man will reach into this flame, taking it into himself. It will sear the flesh of oath breakers, spreading like a cancer through the body. Any man here who betrays another of the company will die horribly, his soul burning in the pit of a thousand flames. His spirit will fly screaming to the realm of the Vampyre kings. There will be no escape. Once you have touched this flame, the soul oath will have been made. There will be no turning back from it."

"I'll not touch it!" roared Corlan.

"Then you will not be rich," I said, smiling.

"Have you done this, Mace?" he asked.

"Of course," answered the warrior. "Would you like to see me do it again?"

"Yes! Yes!"

Mace leaned forward, and his eyes held mine. With my head turned away from Corlan I winked. Mace grinned and thrust his hand into the flame. A small tongue of fire leapt to his palm. It did not burn him, but then, it could not, for it was but an illusion. The flame danced upon his arm, moving to his chest and vanishing into his clothing above the heart. "I am no oath breaker," said Mace softly.

"Nor am I!" insisted Corlan, kneeling before me and extending his hand. I could not resist adding a fraction of the warming spell to the fire, just strong enough to cause a little discomfort. Corlan tensed as the fire touched him, but he did not move as the flame glided along his arm. Silently, almost reverentially, each of the men accepted the flame until at last a young dark-haired warrior pushed out his arm. I saw that he was sweating heavily. The fire touched him, and he screamed, hurling himself back from me and slapping his hand against the grass. The fire slid over him. I increased the size of the flame and the power of the warming spell.

"Take it away!" he begged.

"Speak the truth and save yourself," I said, though I knew not why.

"They made me do it! They have my wife!"

The flames disappeared, and the man rolled to his knees, facing Corlan. "I didn't want to betray you, Corlan. But they told me they'd kill Norin. And it's not you they want but the Morningstar!"

"I understand," whispered Corlan. "I wondered why you spent so long in Ziraccu. How do you communicate with them?"

"I mark the trees. And they gave me this!" He opened his shirt, and I saw a black stone suspended from a length of twine. At the center of the stone was a small white crystal.

"The man who gave you this," I said. "Was he tall and slender, dressed in flowing purple robes?"

"Yes, yes, that was him."

"Give it to me!"

The man pulled it clear, tossing it across the clearing. Catching it by the string, I dashed it against a rock. The crystal shattered, the stone splitting in half.

"What was it?" asked Jarek Mace.

"A simple find stone. The sorcerer places a spell upon the crystal, and no matter where it is carried, he can always locate it."

"I am sorry," said the man, "but they have my . . ." Corlan moved behind him, and his words were cut off by a sharp knife slicing across his throat. Blood gushed from the wound, and the dying man's eyes opened wide. Then he pitched forward to his face and lay twitching upon the grass. Corlan wiped his knife on the dead man's tunic and rose.

"We will do as you say, sorcerer. We will close the roads. We will be the men of the Morningstar. But if you play us false, it will take more than a spell to save you."

I ignored the threat. Fear had risen too fast in me to risk any speech.

"When do we meet, and where?" Corlan asked.

"When the time is right," said Jarek Mace. "And we will find you."

Corlan nodded and strode back into the forest, his men following. Wulf and Piercollo dragged the corpse back into the undergrowth and returned to the dying fire.

"That was impressive, Owen," said Mace, squatting down beside me. I said nothing, for I could not pull my gaze from the blood upon the ground. "I don't know how you knew he was a traitor," he continued, patting my shoulder, "but you did well."

I did not know what to say. Yes, I had suspected the man. Something in the eyes, perhaps, the sheen of sweat upon his brow, the trembling of his hand as he accepted the illusion of fire. But the truth was hard. His guilt had betrayed him, and the mere fact that he had felt guilt showed that he was at heart a good man. And I had seen him slain, probably dooming his family.

Did I do well?

I still recall his face and, worse, the look of relief that touched him as the knife released his soul.

For several weeks we journeyed through the high country, stopping at lonely hamlets or small villages, passing through more open areas where dry-stone walls dotted the hills like necklaces and crops grew on plowed fields.

Ilka traveled with us, though none, I think, invited her. She helped Piercollo with the cooking and stayed close to me as we walked. For a while her company disconcerted me, for whenever I looked at her, I found her eyes upon me, the gaze frank and open. But without language the meaning was lost, and I found myself hating anew the brutal men who had robbed her of both her childhood and her voice.

Sometimes in the night she would suffer tormented dreams and make sounds that were more animal than human, her mutilated tongue trying to form words. I went to her once in the night and stroked her hair to calm her. But she awoke and waved me back, her eyes full of fear.

I think she was content in our company. Piercollo liked her, and when he sang, she would sit close to him, hugging her knees and rocking gently to the music.

Slowly we worked our way northwest. We did not have any set destination that I can recall; we merely wandered, enjoying the sunshine, moving from town to village, village to town. Occasionally I entertained villagers, offering them the Dragon's Egg, the Tower of Rabain, and various other well-known enchant tales. Often I would ask for requests from the audience. The farther north we traveled, the more the villagers asked for tales of the Elder Days, the great wars of the Vampyre kings, the heroism of Rabain, the enchantment of Horga.

These tales were not as popular in the south, where the Angostins wished to hear of their own heroes, but the Highlanders loved them. It took me time to learn to fashion the magick images of Rabain and Horga. I practiced nightly by our camp fire, with Wulf and Mace staring intently at the ghostly forms I created.

"Take away the beard," suggested Wulf.

"The beard's fine," insisted Mace, "but he is too stocky. The man was a swordsman, long in the arm, well balanced. Make him taller."

Horga, they agreed, was spectacular. I did not tell Mace that I based her on the image Megan had showed me of herself when young, glorious of face and slender of figure.

On the first performance, in a small river town in the shadow of the Rostin Peaks, I received a fine ovation, but the audience wanted to see the great battle that had destroyed the Vampyre kings. It irked me that I could not oblige them. Rarely have I been able to sustain more than a few distinct and moving images. Instead I chose to show Rabain's fight in the forest with the undead assassins. I stumbled upon the best technique almost by accident; I believe it is still used by magickers today.

At first I had Rabain fighting a single opponent, a vile white-faced creature with long fangs and a black cloak. Mace found the scene risible.

"He doesn't look undead, he looks half-dead," he said, chuckling. "And so thin. Your audience will have sympathy only for the assassin."

I was deeply irritated by this observation. But he was quite correct.

"Have more attackers, six or seven," he advised.

I tried—I thought unsuccessfully. But the reaction from Wulf and Mace was extraordinary. They were transfixed by the scene. What had happened was that I could not retain detail in all six assassins, and therefore they became blurred and indistinct, their cloaks swirling like black smoke, unearthly and unreal. This in turn made them demonic and terrifying.

Mace schooled me in the sword-fighting techniques my Rabain figure could use against his attackers, spinning on his heel, reversing his sword, diving and rolling to hamstring an opponent. All in all it was a fine fight scene, and I used it to conclude all my performances.

I earned more coin during our few weeks in the north than in all my time in Ziraccu. And I almost forgot Azrek and Cataplas . . .

But of course they had not forgotten us.

One morning, just after dawn, as we lay sleeping in our beds in a small hut on the edge of the village of Kasel, a young boy ran inside, shaking Mace by the shoulder.

"Soldiers!" he screamed. Mace rolled to his knees and fell, then staggered upright. He had downed enough ale the previous night to drown an ox. Shaking his head, he kicked out at the still-sleeping Wulf; the hunchback swore but soon roused himself. Piercollo, Ilka, and I were already awake, and we gathered our belongings and followed Mace out into the trees.

The thunder of hooves came from behind us, but we darted into the undergrowth and slid down a long bank out of sight. The twenty or so soldiers left their mounts in the village and set off after us on foot. Wulf was contemptuous of them at first, leading us deeper into the trees along rocky slopes that would leave little sign for our pursuers. But as the day wore on, they remained doggedly on our trail. We splashed along streams, climbed over boulders, zigzagged our way through dense undergrowth. But nothing could shake the soldiers.

"Are they using sorcery?" asked Wulf as dusk fell.

"I do not know," I answered him, "but I do not think so. If there was an enchanter with them, they would have caught us by now. I think they must be accompanied by a skilled tracker."

"He is certainly good," grunted Wulf grudgingly. "Let's be moving!"

On we traveled, coming at last to a steep slope curving down into a dark valley. Wulf traversed it, then made as if to lead us back the way we had come. Mace ran alongside him.

"Where are you going? That's where they are!"

"I know that!" snapped Wulf. "I'm going back to kill their scout."

"Let's just get down into the valley," said Mace. "There will be plenty of hiding places there."

"No! I'm not running any farther."

"What the devil's the matter with you?" roared Mace. "We can't take on twenty men."

"I'm not going down there."

"Why? It's just a valley."

"I'm not going there, and that's all there is to it," answered Wulf.

"Listen to me," said Mace, his voice soothing. "If we stay here, we're going to die. Now, that's fine for an ugly little man like you who has nothing to live for. But for someone like me—tall, handsome, and charming—it's a galling thought. Now, you wouldn't want to be responsible for the tears of a thousand women, would you?"

Wulf's answer was short, to the point, and utterly disgusting. But he laughed, and the tension eased.

Slowly we made our way down into the valley. It was cold, the night breeze chilling as it whispered through the trees.

"What is this place?" I asked Wulf.

"You perform it often enough, Owen," he replied. "This is where Rabain fought the assassins. We just entered the realm of the Vampyre kings."

The valley floor was lit by moonlight that turned the streams to ribbons of silver, the grass on the hillside to shards of shining iron. I shivered when Wulf spoke, the cold wind blowing around my back and legs. He laughed at my fear, but I could see his own in the gleam of his eyes and the wary way he glanced around at the shadowed trees.

The Vampyre kings! Dread creatures, the fabric of nightmare, but dead now for a thousand years, I told myself, seeking comfort in the thought.

How could I be frightened?

Yet I was. Rabain had killed the Three on the fabled Night of the Seventh Star, after the Battle of Coulin. He and his men had stormed the gray castle, dousing the great gates with oil and setting them ablaze, fighting their way through the courtyards and alleyways into the palace keep. Jerain the archer had slain the first of the kings, a shaft of silver piercing his eye. Boras the Cyclops had killed the second, catching him upon the battlements and hurling him to oblivion on the rocks below. But it was Rabain who had slain the last and greatest of the Vampyre kings. Golgoleth had taken refuge in his throne room, surrounded by demons sharp-fanged and armed with serrated swords. Rabain and the enchantress Horga had come upon them as they were in the midst of creating a dark enchantment that might have turned the battle. Horga's spells sundered the demons while Rabain and Golgoleth did battle.

It was a fine story, incorporating trolls and elven princes, vicious sorcerers and cunning demons. And very popular in the northlands, where they take their fables seriously.

Yet here was Owen Odell, Angostin by birth and temperament, trembling with terror in a dark valley, victim to barbarous superstition.

"Why is it so cold?" I asked Wulf as we walked deeper into the darkness.

"Sorcery," he whispered.

"Horse dung!" declared Jarek Mace. "The valley is deep. Cold air falls; hot air rises. Cast a warming spell, Owen. You'll feel better."

"Piercollo does not like this place," stated the Tuscanian. "It has the smell of decay."

"Mildew," said Mace. "You can see it on the bushes."

We crossed the valley floor, and Wulf glanced back to the crest of the valley. He pointed at the soldiers lined up there, small as children's toys in the distance. They made no attempt to follow us.

"More sense than we have," Wulf muttered.

Their lack of movement troubled me, and I spoke to Mace about it, but he merely shrugged. "Superstition. It is just a valley, Owen, leading to the troll reaches. About sixty miles from here is the source of the Deeway River, and beyond that the cities of Casley and Keras. No demons, just thick forest and a few trolls. The trolls will not bother us. They fear men—and rightly so.''

Looking back, I saw that the soldiers had gone. I spoke to Wulf as we walked on. ''Why did we come here?''

''Mace's idea,'' he answered. ''Don't blame me!''

''No, I meant why did we move in this direction at all?''

''No choice. The soldiers were behind us all the way.''

''But we could have cut to the east or the west.''

''I tried that, but they were circling behind. I couldn't be sure where they were.''

''Then perhaps we were steered this way.''

Wulf halted, then turned to me. ''You could be right, bard.''

''No, he is not!'' hissed Mace, looming out of the dark. ''You are like two children trying to frighten one another. *We* chose which way to run; they merely followed us. And now they are too cowardly to follow further. And if I hear one more word about Vampyre kings, ghosts, spirits, or trolls, I shall crack a skull or two!''

We trudged on in silence, Ilka staying close to the huge form of Piercollo, Mace leading. Wulf, his bow strung, walked just behind me.

The clouds gathered, and it began to rain—thin, icy needles, driven by the wind, instantly soaking through our clothes. Lightning forked across the northern sky, and soon the ground below our feet became sodden and we walked ankle-deep in mud.

After about an hour we finally crossed the valley floor and began the long climb through wooded hills until we reached the far crest and gazed down on a second valley and a small lake, black as jet. Beside it was a ruined keep, its wall crumbling, its gates sagging and rotten. The style was ancient, the towers square-built, not round as with Angostin architecture.

''You know who built that keep?'' asked Wulf.

''Don't say it!'' warned Jarek Mace. ''All I know is that we are going to be warm and dry for the night. And I don't care if it was built by the devil himself. I'm soaked through, cold, and in an evil temper. So keep your mouth shut and let's get in there and start a fire.''

''It'll be haunted,'' whispered Wulf to me as we followed Mace down into the valley. ''Mark my words.''

But at that moment Wulf slipped in the mud and slid down the hillside past Jarek Mace. For a moment we watched in stunned silence, then Mace's laughter roared out above the rain. "Give my regards to the Vampyre kings!" he yelled as the hunchback hurtled toward the keep.

The sight was so ludicrous that all fear fled from me, and I bent double, laughing fit to burst. Even Ilka was smiling as we followed the hunchback down, finding him sitting at the foot of the hill staring at his broken bow.

"We'll buy a new one at the next town," said Jarek Mace, but Wulf was inconsolable.

"Best I've ever had," he muttered. "Had it blessed by the abbess. It's never let me down before. Witchcraft, that's what it is!"

"You fell on it!" said Mace. "That's not witchcraft; that's just clumsiness."

Wulf shook his head. "It was blessed," he repeated. "Nothing blessed can survive in this place. That's why no one lives here, no crops grow. Even the trees are covered with mildew, and most are rotten."

"I'm not listening to any more of this," snapped Mace, walking through the stone gates.

We followed him across a paved courtyard. The stones were uneven, grass pushing up between them. The rain hissed down, the castle walls gleaming in the faint light that pierced the clouds. Lightning flashed across the sky, sending dancing shadows behind the broken columns to our left.

Jarek Mace climbed the steps leading to the hall of the keep and kicked the rotted doors, the wood splintering and falling to the thick dust beyond, which rose like smoke around his boots. A rat scurried for shelter, and then we were inside.

"Make light, Owen," ordered Mace.

I sent a small shining sphere floating into the hall.

The floor was wooden, and I stepped gingerly upon it, but it seemed solid enough.

For me it was—but not for Piercollo.

Advancing into the middle of the hall, he let fall his pack, which hit the floor with a resounding thud. This was followed by a sudden creaking, then a series of explosive cracks—and the Tuscanian disappeared from sight.

◇ 7 ◇

WITH GREAT CARE Mace, Wulf, and I eased our way across the floor to the jagged hole. I brought the sphere of light closer, and we lay on our bellies gazing down into a pit some twelve feet deep. Piercollo lay stunned, his pack beside him. The light did not penetrate far, and I could see little more save that one of the joists had given way, leaving the timbers with no support where Piercollo had fallen.

"There must be another way down," said Mace.

"I'll find it," Wulf told him, moving back from the hole.

"He might be dead," I whispered.

"More likely a broken leg," Mace told me. "We'll soon know. Stay here and call me if he wakes."

"Where are you going?"

"I'm going to build a fire. I'm cold and I'm hungry. Wulf will find the way in below, then we'll get him out."

Piercollo lay unmoving, and I watched Mace cross the hall to a huge hearth, where he gathered tinder and splinters of rotten wood. The Tuscanian groaned and stirred.

"Don't move for a moment," I called down. "You may have broken bones."

Slowly he rolled to his back. I moved the sphere down into the hole, and Piercollo sat up, then ran his hand down his right leg. "There is a small scratch," he said. "It is not much. Nothing, I think, is broken. Bring the light closer."

I did as he asked, and slowly he stood. "There is no door," he called.

"There must be."

"Piercollo is not blind, Owen. There is *no* door."

112

Moving back from the hole, I made my way to where Mace was slowly adding fuel to the small fire. "He is all right," I told him, "but there is no way out of the cellar."

"That makes no sense," muttered Mace. Leaving Ilka to tend the fire, he returned to where Piercollo waited. The sphere was less bright now, and my concentration was fading. "Is there anything down there you can use to climb out?" called Mace.

"Many boxes, but they are rotten. There is a broken table and some weapons. No. Nothing I can use."

Wulf returned and stretched out alongside Mace. "There's no stairs down. Nothing."

"How are we going to get him out?" I asked.

Both men ignored me. Mace sat up and looked around the hall. There was no furniture save a broken chair covered in cobwebs and a few threadbare cushions thick with dust and mildew. Standing, he made his way to the far wall and lifted an ancient torch from its iron bracket. Dusting off the charred, loose strands from the tip, he held it over the fire and it caught instantly, flaring up with long tongues of flame.

"Move aside," he ordered us, and walked to the edge of the hole. "Stand back," he told Piercollo. Then he jumped into the cellar, landing easily with knees bent to take the impact of the ten-foot drop. A few sparks fell from the torch, but those he stamped out. With this new light we could see the full area of the cellar; it was no more than twenty feet long and about half as wide. Weapons and armor had been piled around the walls: helms, bows, swords, daggers, axes. All of them were jet-black and unadorned.

Holding aloft his torch, Mace studied the ceiling, examining the remaining joists. "They seem sound," he announced. "I don't think they'll give way." Moving to the Tuscanian's pack, he hefted it, then passed it to Piercollo. "Throw it through the hole," he said. The Tuscanian swayed to his left, then sent it sailing up over the rim.

Placing the spluttering torch in an upturned black helm, Mace moved beneath the hole, cupping his hands. "Come, my large friend," he said, "it is time for you to leave this place."

"You cannot take Piercollo's weight," the Tuscanian warned him.

"Well, if I can't, then you'll just have to sit down here until you grow thinner. Would you like us to come back in a couple of months?''

Piercollo placed his huge hands on Mace's shoulders, then lifted a foot into the cupped palms. ''Are you ready?'' he asked.

''Do it, you big ox!''

Piercollo tensed his leg, pushing his weight down onto Mace's locked fingers. Mace groaned but held firm, and Piercollo rose, his right arm stretching toward the rim of the hole, his fingers curling over the edge. I gripped his wrist to give him support while Wulf took hold of the Tuscanian's jerkin and began to pull. At first there was no discernible sign of movement, but with Mace pushing from below and the two of us pulling from above, Piercollo managed to get one arm over the rim. After that we dragged him clear in moments.

Mace sank to the floor of the cellar, breathing heavily. ''One more minute and he would have broken my back,'' he said at last. Then he rose and, torch in hand, moved among the weapons.

''A new bow for you, Wulf,'' he called, hurling the weapon through the opening. This was followed by several scabbarded swords, daggers, and two quivers of black-shafted arrows. Lastly a small box sailed over the rim, landing heavily and cracking open.

''Keep back!'' yelled Mace. ''I'm coming up.'' Dousing the torch and stamping out all the cinders, he leapt to grab the rim, then hauled himself smoothly clear of the hole. He was covered in dust and cobwebs, but his grin was bright as he dusted himself down. ''Let's see what treasure is in the box,'' he said. The wood was rotten, but what appeared to be bands of bronze held it together. Mace ripped away the lid and pulled clear a large velvet pouch. The leather thongs were rotten, the velvet dry and ruined, but something creamy white fell clear, rolling from his hands to bounce on the wooden floor.

''May the saints protect us!'' whispered Wulf, backing away.

On the floor at our feet was a skull, the lower jaw missing but the upper intact. Teeth were still embedded in the bone, most of them apparently normal. But the two canines on either side of the incisors were twice as long as the others and wickedly sharp.

Mace picked up the skull, turning it in his hands. ''These teeth are hollow,'' he said, tapping the canines.

"Leave it be, Mace," hissed Wulf. "You can see what it is, damn you!"

"It's a skull," said Mace. He swung to me. "Vampyre?"

I nodded dumbly. "I would say so."

"Well, well! Do you think it's worth anything?"

"Not to me," I told him.

"Throw it back into the cellar," urged Wulf. "It is a thing of evil."

"Perhaps," said Mace, dropping the skull back into the shattered box. Picking up the bow he had found for Wulf, he crossed to where the hunchback stood. "Take a look at this. It's metal, but it weighs next to nothing, and I cannot see how it was strung."

Wulf, with one last nervous glance at the box containing the skull, took the weapon, and I moved forward to examine it with him. Much shorter than a longbow but longer than the hunting bows used by Angostin scouts, it was sharply curved, the string disappearing into the bow tips.

"No range," said Wulf. Pulling an arrow from his quiver, he notched it and drew back the string, aiming the shaft at the frame of the door. The arrow leapt from the bow, struck the beam, and shattered.

"Try one of these," offered Mace, pulling a black-shafted arrow from one of the quivers he had thrown from the cellar. The arrow was of metal; even the flights, which looked like raven feathers, were in fact metallic and stiff.

Wulf drew back on the string once more, and the shaft sang through the air, punching home into the wood of the frame and burying itself deep.

Not one of us, not even the mighty Piercollo, could pull it loose.

"Have you ever seen weapons like these, Owen?" Mace asked me.

"No. According to legend, the swords and arrows of Rabain's men were of the purest silver in order to slay the undead. They were said to shine with starlight when Vampyres were near. I doubt it was true. More likely Horga cast an enchantment, an illusion to lift the spirits of the warriors."

For some time Wulf and Mace examined the weapons. The swords and daggers were lighter than any I had seen and incredibly sharp. Mace put aside his own longsword, replacing it with a black blade and scabbard. The hilt was wound with black wire, and there was even a dark gem in the pommel that reflected no gleam of light from the fire. Wulf took two short swords, and I acquired a long hunting knife, double-edged. Piercollo refused a weapon, but Ilka also chose a short sword, curved like a small saber, which she belted to her slim waist.

We ate sparingly, for our supplies were low, and then sat talking for a while. Mace asked me to tell a story about the Elder Days, one he had not heard. I could think of nothing new, and so I told him of the death of Rabain, murdered by his son two years after the great battle and the ending of the reign of the Vampyre kings. The son died soon after, slain, some fables have it, by Horga the enchantress. And the land descended into bloody civil war.

"That's a fine tale to end a day with," grumbled Mace. Piercollo and Wulf were already asleep, while Ilka sat staring into the dying fire, lost in thoughts she could not share.

"I am sorry, Jarek. My mood is dark. What would you like to hear?"

"Tell me of the great parade when Rabain was made king."

"I've told you that a score of times."

"I know, but I like parades. I like the idea of riding into a city and having the crowds throw flowers before me, making a carpet of blooms. And young women waving from balcony windows, blowing kisses and promises."

I looked at him for a moment in the dying light. "Who are you, Jarek Mace?" I asked him.

"What a strange question, Owen. What would you have me say? I was born in a village that was too insignificant to have a name. My mother was a whore—at least that's what the villagers believed, for she bore a son out of wedlock. I used to dream that my father was the lord of the manor and that one day he would acknowledge me, take me into his own home, and name me as his heir. But he wasn't, and he didn't. My mother died when I was twelve. I found work in a traveling circus, walking the high wire, juggling, and tumbling. Then I became a soldier. Then I came here. That is me . . . that is Jarek Mace."

"Of course it isn't," I told him. "That is merely a précis of a life. It says nothing of the man. What do you believe in? What do you love? What do you aspire to be?"

"I want my castle by the sea," he said with a rueful smile.

"What about a wife, children?"

He shrugged. "I had a woman once, lived with her for months. I cannot see that there will ever be anyone to keep me content for longer than that."

"What happened to her?"

"I have no idea, Owen. She got fat and pregnant, so I left."

"You never went back?" I asked, amazed.

"Why should I?"

"You have a son somewhere—or a daughter. You don't wish to see your child?"

"I think I have many children; I hope to have many more. But I don't wish to see them grow, to smell their soiled wrappings, to listen to them mewling and crying."

"And friendship?" I inquired. "Does that mean anything to you?"

"What is friendship, Owen? Two men each requiring something from the other. Well, I require nothing from anyone; therefore, I need no friends."

"You have never known love, have you, Jarek? You have no conception of what it entails. Just as when you talked of Piercollo's songs; for you they were meaningless sounds. I feel great pity for you. You are not really alive. You are a man apart, self-obsessed and, I would guess, very lonely."

"You would guess wrong," he said. "I know what love is. It is a swelling in the loins that is soon satisfied. It is a stolen kiss under moonlight. Nothing more. But you bards build it up with sweet words and many promises, songs of broken hearts and true love. It is all dung. I never met a wife who wouldn't succumb to my advances while her husband was away. So much for marital love!" He leaned forward and shook his head. "You don't pity me, Owen. You envy me. I am everything you would desire to be."

For a moment I was silent, but I held his gaze. "I think you need to believe that. I think it is important to you."

"What is important is that I get some sleep," he said. Sitting up, he wrapped a blanket around his broad shoulders and threw several chunks of wood on the fire. Just as he was lying down, I saw his eyes narrow. "Look at that," he said softly, and I turned.

The arrow Wulf had fired into the door beam was glowing with a gentle white light. Throwing back his blanket, Mace reached for his sword. As he pulled the blade clear of the scabbard, it was no longer black but shining as if made from starlight.

"What is happening, Owen?" he whispered.

My mouth was dry, my heart beating wildly as I drew my own hunting knife. It, too, shone brilliantly. "I don't know."

Smoothly he rose and, sword in hand, moved toward the ruined doors. Holding my dagger before me, I followed him. As we neared the doorway, we heard sounds from the courtyard beyond, scraping and rustling, the shuffling of boots upon the stones.

A figure loomed up before us. Dirt and mud clung to his helm, and the hand that held the rusted sword wore what appeared to be a tattered gauntlet. But it was no gauntlet. The skin of the hand hung in flapping tatters, the tendons twisted. Worms and maggots glided between the bones.

I gagged and fell back before the apparition, but Mace leapt forward, his sword fashioning an arc of light as it cut through the cadaver's shoulder, cleaving down to exit under the left arm. The undead warrior made no sound as the body fell. Mace stepped across the corpse and raised his sword high.

Bright light shone in the courtyard, and I saw a host of the undead gathering before the keep.

In the instant when the light of the sword fell upon them I saw Cataplas standing beneath the ruined gates, his arms raised. The corpses shuffled forward with rusted weapons in their hands.

"Get back!" I yelled to Mace.

He took a step back, his face ashen, then I saw his jaw tighten. Spinning on his heel, he ran into the hall, shouting to Wulf and the others.

The hunchback rolled to his feet. "What is happening?" he asked, reaching for his bow.

There was no need to answer, for the first of the undead warriors reached the door, his face a twisted black mask of horror. More of the cadavers crowded in behind the first, and Wulf sent a gleaming silver shaft into the chest of a tall, skeletal figure. The arrow passed through the rotted body, which collapsed into the doorway. Piercollo lifted a burning brand from the fire and threw it into the surging mass of corpses, but they were mud-covered and dank, and the torch sizzled and died.

"To the stairs!" shouted Jarek Mace, taking up his bow and

quiver. Behind us, to the left, was a set of stone steps, the wooden banisters torn down, probably used for firewood by some ancient travelers. Piercollo and Ilka were the first to climb the stairs, followed by Wulf and myself. Jarek Mace was the last, and he moved slowly, backing up the stone steps, an arrow notched to his bow.

At the top of the stairs was an empty door frame, bronze hinges bent and warped, evidence of the door having been ripped away. There was a section of battlement beyond some five feet wide and twenty long. Piercollo moved out along it.

A blackened arm reached over the crenellated battlement, then a helm appeared, partly rusted, the bronze ear guards glowing with a green patina. The face beneath it was almost completely corrupted, the nose and eyes long disappeared. It hauled itself onto the battlements, and Piercollo ran at it, swinging his enormous pack and hammering it against the creature. The dead warrior was hurled back over the wall to fall without a sound.

More arms and hands and heads appeared. Piercollo reached the far end of the battlements to find a locked door. Stepping back, he lifted his leg and kicked out; the lock bar shattered, the door caving in. The giant stepped into the doorway and climbed the winding stairs beyond, the rest of us following. I did not dare to look back. At the top of the stairs was a second door, also barred.

"Don't break it!" ordered Jarek Mace. Swiftly he eased himself to the front, pushing his dagger between the dry timbers of the door and plunging the blade into the wooden lock bar. Then he lifted it clear; the door creaked open, and we found ourselves on the roof of a square turret, bathed in the light of a cold moon. A skeletal warrior, cold and still, lay with his back against the wall, a ring on his signet finger glowing in the moonlight.

"There's already one of them here!" said Wulf, backing away from the corpse.

"No," I told him. "The ring he is wearing—it carries enchantment. I do not think he is a danger to us."

"You're sure?" the hunchback pressed.

"Not entirely," I admitted.

Mace shut the door, forcing the lock bar back into place, then ran to the battlements and leaned out. I moved alongside him. Below us the cadavers had started to climb the walls, their dead faces looking up, their skeletal fingers finding the cracks in the mortar and hauling themselves ever closer.

A hammering began on the barred door behind us. "There's no way out!" screamed Wulf.

"Be silent!" Mace roared.

In the bright moonlight I saw the graveyard beyond the castle, the ground heaving and moving as corpse after corpse pushed up from the soft earth.

"How can we hold them?" I asked Mace, fighting to keep my voice calm.

"You're the magicker! You tell me!" he replied.

There was nothing I could say. I had no experience with sorcery and had never desired to acquire such experience. Illusions with light and heat were all that I knew.

"How long till the dawn?" I asked.

Mace stared up at the sky. "Four hours. Maybe five."

The first of the undead reached the top of the battlements. Drawing my dagger, I thrust it at the blackened face. As the blade touched the decaying skin, the creature's hold on the stone loosened and it fell. A second appeared, and Mace beheaded it with a savage cut. Still, more and more reached the tower. Unarmed, Piercollo took hold of one undead warrior, throwing him back over the parapet. Wulf, short sword in hand, moved back and forth across the tower, plunging his blade into undead bodies.

Piercollo swept up a rusted sword and cleared the rib cage of a tall skeleton, but the creature moved on as if nothing had happened. Ilka ran in, the shining silver saber sweeping across the skeleton's back. Instantly it crumbled to the battlements.

I do not know how long we struggled and fought, for time seemed to drag by ever more slowly as we tired. Mace was indefatigable, his shining sword a blur of light as he darted across the tower. But eventually the attack slowed and then faltered. I risked a glance over the battlements but could see no more dark shapes clinging to the walls.

The graveyard was also still, the churned earth unmoving now.

Some corpses still lay on the tower, and these we threw over the walls. The skeleton that had been there when we arrived, we let be. In ages past he had barred the door against an attack and had died there, lost and alone, his flesh devoured by carrion birds, his bones white and clean. It seemed right somehow to let him lie.

On the ramparts below the corpse warriors still gathered, huddled in a silent mass, faces staring up at us.

Cataplas moved out into the open by the graveyard, a tall, slender figure. Looking up, he saw me. "You are in bad company, Owen!" he called, his voice pleasant as always.

"You vile creature!" I stormed. "How dare you say that? I at least stand alongside men of courage, not torturers like Azrek. You disgust me!"

"There is no need for rudeness," he admonished me. "You are an Angostin. How is it that the son of Aubertain could seek the friendship of a murdering peasant, a known robber and rapist?"

I was astonished. Here was a sorcerer leading an army of the undead, daring to speak to me of manners. I stared down at him. He was too far away for me to be able to see the wispy beard and the sad gray eyes, but the robe was the same, faded velvet trimmed with gold. "The company I keep is my own affair, Cataplas," I called out. "Now, say what you have to say, for I do not wish this conversation to last a moment longer than necessary."

"As you wish," he replied, no trace of anger in his tone. "You seek to thwart me in my quest for knowledge, though for what purpose I cannot ascertain. I have two now in my possession; the third I will find. Nothing you or your band of petty cutthroats can do will stop me. And what will you do with the last should you find it before me? You cannot use its power. The three need to be together. You are a magicker, Owen, with little gift for sorcery. What is your purpose in opposing me?"

I could not fathom the riddle of his words, but I answered as if I understood his every phrase. "I oppose you because you are evil, Cataplas. Perhaps you always were."

"Evil? A concept invented by kings to keep the peasants in order. There is only knowledge, Owen. Knowledge is power. Power is right. But I will not debate with you. I see now that you are no threat. Have you yet found a god to follow?"

"Not yet," I told him.

"Then find one swiftly—and send up your prayers, for you will meet him soon."

He raised his arm, and I watched the fireball grow upon his palm, then soar into the sky toward us.

Jarek Mace leapt to the battlements, bow bent and arrow aimed at the sorcerer.

"No!" I shouted. "Strike the fireball!"

At the last moment he twisted his arm, sending the silver shaft singing through the air. It smote the glowing fireball in the center, sundering it, and the arrow exploded in a brilliant burst of white light that nearly blinded us. Jarek Mace stumbled upon the battlements, and I threw myself forward, grabbing at his jerkin and hauling him back to safety.

He notched a second arrow to his bow and sought out Cataplas.

But the sorcerer had gone.

Piercollo moved forward, his face gray with weariness. "Will they come again?" he asked.

I shrugged, but Mace clapped the giant on the shoulder. "If they do, we will turn them back."

Unconvinced, Piercollo merely nodded and walked back to the ramparts, sitting down with his back to the wall. Wulf settled down opposite him, lying on his side with his head on Piercollo's pack. Ilka squatted between them, staring down at the saber in her hands.

"The enchanted blades saved us," I told Mace.

"Yes, they are sharp and true."

"It was not the sharpness. We did not even have to plunge them home. As they touched the corpses, all sorcery was drawn from them."

"A lucky find," he agreed absently, "but what did the old man mean about the three and the one?"

"I don't know."

"You must," he insisted.

"Truly, I don't."

"Then think on it!" he snapped. Turning from me, he began to pace the battlements, keeping a watchful eye on the cadavers below. I sat down with my back to the cold stone wall and thought of all Cataplas had said.

I have two now in my possession; the third I will find. Nothing you or your band of petty cutthroats can do will stop me. And

what will you do with the last should you find it before me?
You cannot use its power. The three need to be together.

Two in his possession. Two of what? *You cannot use its power.*
What power?

No matter how much I forced my brain to concentrate, I could
make no sense of the words. *The three need to be together.*

Stretching out on the wooden floor, I pillowed my head upon
my arm and slept. Mace woke me with a boot in the ribs, and I
grunted and rolled, scrabbling for my dagger. "Are they back?"
I whispered hoarsely.

"No, but I'm getting bored with my own company. Have you
thought about the problem?"

"I have, but to no avail."

He sank down beside me, his handsome face taut, the eyes
red-rimmed and tired. "The old man wants something, and he
thinks we know more than we do. Why? What have we done to
make him think so, save by coming here?"

"You think these ruins are the key?" I asked him.

"They must be. I do not believe he came here just to kill us;
he wanted to make a bargain. You said he was a man interested
in knowledge. Power. He wasn't here looking for gold or treasure, but something else entirely. I would guess it is in that
cellar. Something we didn't find—a magical trinket, perhaps. A
holy relic."

"I don't believe so. There are few such pieces, save in myth.
The cup of Arenos, the spear of Gtath. And as for holy relics
. . . Cataplas has moved beyond such things. They would burn
him now, were he to touch them."

"Then think, Owen! What is there about this place? What is
its history?"

"How many times must I tell you that I don't know!" I said,
my voice rising. Piercollo stirred but did not wake, but Wulf
grunted and sat up.

"How long now to the dawn?" asked the hunchback.

"Another hour," Mace told him. Wulf rubbed circulation
back into his cold limbs, then joined us.

"I told you no good would come of entering this place," he
grumbled.

"We're alive, aren't we?" responded Jarek Mace.

"For now," muttered Wulf. "We'll all end up like him," he added, pointing to the skeleton.

"No, we won't," said Mace forcefully. "That graveyard does not contain an inexhaustible supply of corpses, and we have enchanted blades to cut our way through what remains of them. And we will, come daylight. Put aside your fears, Wulf. Think of this: There may be many of them, but what opposition do they offer? Their muscles are rotten; they move as if through water. Not one of them has so far laid a blade upon us, and if they did, they are so rusted as to be useless. They do not pose a real danger, save for the terror they inspire in us with their appearance. But they are not real. They are filled with sorcery, but they are not the men they were. You might just as well fear a few sticks joined together with rotted string."

There was truth in what he said, and I was surprised that it had not occurred to me before. Without the blades of power the dead would have overwhelmed us, but with them we were relatively safe. It was irritating that Mace had understood this simple fact whereas I, a schooled Angostin, had been swept away on a tide of superstition and terror.

Wulf, though, was not entirely convinced. "This is an evil realm," he said. "The Vampyre kings laid great spells upon it. They live in the ground, in the trees and valleys."

"Their spells died with them," said Mace. "Is that not so, Owen?"

"Yes. All sorcery fades with the passing of the sorcerer. A spell is a creation of the mind, held in being by the concentration of the magicker. When the mind ceases to operate, the spell is gone."

"Who is to say when the mind ceases to operate?" asked Wulf. "Perhaps the Vampyre kings did not cease to be when their bodies were slain. Have you ever thought of that, bard?"

"You are a happy companion," hissed Jarek Mace. "What do you think these undead kings have been doing for the last thousand years? Playing dice? Counting trees? If they are still alive, I think we would have heard of them." He swung to me. "I wonder where your sorcerer friend is hiding. I want to see no more globes of fire."

"I do not think that you will. Such a spell takes a toll even on a sorcerer of his dark skill. Raising the corpses weakened him, and the fireball was not as fast or as deadly as it might have been. I would guess he has gone somewhere to rest, perhaps even returned to Ziraccu.''

"That would take weeks," said Wulf.

"Not by the paths he will travel," I told him.

"I know all the paths there are," the hunchback insisted.

I shook my head. "Once, when I was apprenticed to him, we were commissioned to entertain at a castle on the west coast. It was two hundred miles away, but we made the journey in less than an hour. First he blindfolded me, then led me by the hand. All I remember was the terrible cold and the sibilant hissing of what I took to be beasts around me. But nothing touched me save Cataplas. Suddenly I felt the sun on my back, and Cataplas removed the blindfold. We were on a cliff top overlooking the sea, and to our right was the castle.''

Wulf shivered and rose, rubbing at his neck, which I later learned gave him great pain and was probably the cause of much of his ill humor. The twisted hump upon his back put pressure on the thick, corded neck muscles, and little could be done to alleviate it. Still rubbing at the muscles, he wandered away.

"I think I'll leave this forest and head south," said Jarek Mace. "The north is becoming altogether too perilous.''

"I do not think that would prove a wise decision," I told him.

"It is my experience that the best defense against danger is distance," he said with a smile.

"There is no distance that will keep Cataplas from you. Azrek wants you dead, Jarek. Through Cataplas he can send demons to hunt you down wherever you are—even across the sea. If you leave, you will be alone and easy prey.''

"This is your fault," he said, his eyes showing anger. "You and that foolish Morningstar dream. Am I doomed, then, to walk this forest, killing enemies already dead, fighting monsters and demons?''

"Perhaps, but my father, for all his faults a great general, would have offered you some simple advice. He would have said, 'Jarek, when your enemy's strength is overwhelming, when you are surrounded by foes, there is only one choice for the brave. Attack.' ''

His smile was genuine. "You are a wonderful fool, Owen. What would you have me do? Raise an army from among the peasants and the Highlanders and sweep the Angostins from power?''

"Why not?" I asked him.

"You see me as a king, perhaps? King Jarek?"

"It hardly matters how I see you. It is how *they* see you."

The smile faded. "I am a man, Owen. You heard what the sorcerer said, and I would admit to being a murderer. As to rape . . . that was untrue. I have never needed to force myself on a woman. But I have stolen, and I have deceived, and I have lied, and I have cheated. I say this without shame. This land of ours is made for strong men, and strong men will always take what they want from the weaker. I know what I am, and I am not your Morningstar."

The sky lightened, pink and gold seeping above the eastern mountains. I rose to my feet and stretched. The sun slowly filled the sky with light, and the dawn was majestic. I leaned over the parapet and gazed down at the ramparts.

The host of the dead were gone. All that remained were a few rusted helms, broken swords, scraps of leather, and white shards of bone.

The sun was bright upon my face, its warmth pure, its light healing to the soul.

The rays fell upon the skeleton by the door, and I saw again the gold ring upon a finger of bone. No longer glowing, it was of thick, red gold set with a white stone. Reaching down, I drew the ring clear, lifting it close to my eyes. On the inner rim the goldsmith had engraved a line of verse in the ancient tongue of the Belgae. The rhyme is lost in translation, but it read

Guard am I, sword pure, heart strong.

The circle of the ring was tiny, but when I touched it to the tip of my signet finger, it slid into place, fitting snugly. I gazed down at the skeleton. "I think you stood at your post when all others would have fled. I think you were a brave man and true. May you know rest!"

Ilka was awake, and I felt her eyes upon me. I smiled at her, embarrassed now for speaking to the dead who had no ears to hear. For the first time she returned my smile, and I found her to be beautiful.

The shock was both exquisite and curiously debilitating. My mouth was suddenly dry, and I found myself staring at her, wondering how I had never before noticed her loveliness. The smile faded as I stared, and she turned away and walked to the battlements, looking out over the wooded valley and the shining lake.

"Let's be moving," said Mace. "I don't want to be here when real warriors arrive."

Piercollo shouldered his pack, and we returned to the hall of the keep. Mace jumped down into the cellar and rummaged among the weapons, gathering two more quivers of black arrows and a second dagger.

I looked around, aware that something was missing.

Then I remembered.

It was the skull.

And it had gone . . .

◇ **8** ◇

IT WAS HIGH summer when we finally reached the town of Pasel, a river settlement in the high country some three days north of Rualis. The economy of the town was based on timber. The loggers would cut the tall pines and strip them of branches, then haul them to the river, where they would be floated down to Rualis on the wide Deeway. Pasel was a rough town, not as violent as Rualis, but there were many fights and much blood shed during the summer, when itinerant workers would journey north seeking employment and the town swelled with whores and merchants, tinkers and thieves. The mountains here were rich with game, and hunters would gather to trap beaver and bear, lions, and wolves. And when hungry for pleasure the hunters and trappers would converge on Pasel to rut and fight and gamble away their hard-won coins.

Beyond the town, upon a gentle sloping hill, there was a round keep manned by twenty militia soldiers. These men, led by a taciturn captain named Brackban, maintained what order they could in such a rough place.

Mace knew the town well and led us to an ill-smelling tavern on the east of the settlement. It was some two hours after dusk, and the huge ale room was crammed with customers: loggers in their sleeveless leather jerkins, trappers in furs, whores with earrings of brass and necklets of copper and lips stained with berry juice.

There were no tables free, and I saw Mace's mood begin to darken. He moved to the rear of the room, where three men were sprawled across a bench, drunk and insensible. Mace seized the shoulder of the first, dragging him clear of the seat

and dumping him upon the floor. The man stirred but did not
wake. When the second man was hauled from his place, he
awoke and tried to rise but slumped back, grumbling incoher-
ently. The third came to with a start and tried to strike Mace—
it was a mistake. Mace leaned back, and the blow missed wildly;
his fist cannoned into the man's jaw, snapping back his head,
which cracked against the wooden wall behind. He sagged side-
ways; Mace hit him twice more, then threw him to the floor.

Sliding into the now-vacant seat, Mace leaned upon his fore-
arms and bellowed for a serving girl. As we seated ourselves, a
plump woman wearing a dress of homespun wool and a leather
apron pushed her way through to us. She was tired, her eyes
dull, but she forced a smile, took our order, and vanished back
into the throng.

Ilka was nervous and sat close to Piercollo, her eyes glancing
from left to right at the milling men. His huge arm moved around
her shoulder, and he patted her as one would a frightened child.
She smiled up at him. I almost hated him then and wished that
I, too, could be seen as a guardian of the frightened, a warrior
of note.

It was impossible to hold a conversation in such a place, and
when the ale and food were carried to us, we ate and drank in
silence, each with his own thoughts.

A young man, slim, his face scarred, put his hand on Ilka's
shoulder and leaned down to whisper in her ear. She shook her
head, but his hand slid down over her breast. Piercollo moved
swiftly, pulling the man clear. The Tuscanian said nothing, but
his arm tensed and jerked, and the unfortunate suitor flew back
into the throng as if launched from a catapult. Mace chuckled
and shook his head.

The noise behind us faded away, and I turned to see the scarred
young man moving forward again, but alongside him was a huge
trapper dressed in a wolfskin coat. The man was bald and beardless, but he sported a long red-gold mustache braided at the
ends.

He reached Piercollo and tapped the giant's shoulder. "You
have insulted my brother," he said.

Piercollo sighed and stood. "Your brother has the manners
of a donkey," he told him.

The newcomer smiled. "True, but he is still my brother. And
while Karak is here, no one lays a hand on him." Even as he

spoke the man launched a punch. Piercollo swayed back, his own hand sweeping up, the fingers closing around Karak's fist and catching it easily. I saw the Tuscanian's knuckles whiten as he squeezed the captured hand.

"Piercollo does not like to fight," he said softly. "Piercollo likes to sit and drink in peace." The man's face twisted in pain, his right hand reaching for the dagger at his belt, but Piercollo squeezed harder, and I heard a knuckle crack. Karak winced and groaned, and his hand fell away from the dagger. "It would be good for us to be friends," said Piercollo, "and perhaps drink together. Yes?"

"Yes," agreed the man, the word almost exploding from between clenched teeth.

"Good," said Piercollo with a wide smile. Releasing Karak, he patted his shoulder almost affectionately and turned back to his seat. In that moment the man drew his dagger. Piercollo, his back turned, rammed his elbow into Karak's face, catching him on the bridge of the nose. Everyone in the room heard the bone break. Karak staggered back with blood pouring from his nostrils. Then, with a wild cry, he leapt at Piercollo. The Tuscanian stepped in to meet him, his fist thundering against the man's chin. There was a sickening crack, and the attacker fell, his knife clattering across the floorboards.

"You've killed him!" shouted the scarred young man, dropping to his knees beside the body. For a moment we all thought this might be true, but the injured Karak groaned and tried to move; his jaw was shattered, his nose broken. Several men moved forward to aid him, turning him to his back, where he lay gasping for some time before his friends gathered around him, carrying him from the room.

"If you could have made that fight last a little longer, I might have won a few bets," said Jarek Mace.

"I do not like to fight," repeated Piercollo, downing the last of his ale.

"For someone who doesn't like it, you are rather good at it."

Piercollo shrugged, and it seemed to me that a great sadness had fallen upon him.

"You had no choice," I told him. "He intended to kill you."

"I know, Owen, but it gives me no pleasure to cause pain. You understand? I like to hear laughter and song. He was so foolish; we could have sat together and had a drink, told stories, and become friends. But no. Now he will spend months with broken bones. And for what? Because he has a brother with bad manners. It makes no sense."

"You are a good man," I said. "You were not to blame."

"I am not good man. Good men do not break the bones of others. I am weak, friend Owen."

The doors opened, and a group of men entered. I tensed, for one of them was the scarred young man and he was carrying a sword. "Oh, no!" I whispered. Mace saw them and turned his attention to his ale; in that moment I knew he would leave the Tuscanian to his fate. I tapped Piercollo on the shoulder and pointed to the new arrivals. There were five men, all armed with swords or daggers. Piercollo pushed himself to his feet, and I rose with him, my hand upon my dagger. Ilka also stood, but Mace and Wulf remained where they were, studiously ignoring the proceedings.

Piercollo said nothing as the men advanced, but I pushed my way to the front. "He is unarmed," I said, keeping my voice even.

"He is going to die," said the scarred youngster.

"You think so? Let us see," I said, raising my hand palm upward. First I created a flash of white light, spearing up from the palm to the ceiling—I always find this focuses the attention of the audience. The five men jumped back in shock. "And now the future!" I said this in a loud voice, keeping their gazes locked to me. Instantly the image of Horga formed upon my palm, the enchantress standing just over two feet tall, a white dress billowing in an unseen breeze. "I call upon you, Horga," I said, "to tell us the future if you will. Are there any here who will die tonight?" She floated from my hand, circling the room, pausing now and again above grim-faced men who looked away, licking their lips, trying to still the terror in their hearts. Finally she returned to my hand and shook her head.

"But there is to be a fight," I said. "Surely if such a battle takes place, someone will die."

She nodded and spun on my hand, her finger pointing to the scarred youngster. Golden light blazed from her finger to engulf the young man, and above his head appeared a skull, the universal sign of impending doom.

"Thank you, Horga," I said, bowing to the image. She lifted her arms and disappeared. I turned my attention to the warriors.

"There has already been a fight," I told them, smiling. "An even contest that ended with broken bones. There is no need now for further violence. But if you wish it, we will oblige you."

"I am not afraid to die," said the youngster, but his eyes betrayed the lie.

"Of course you are not," I assured him. "You are a brave man. You are all brave men. But death is eternal, and I like to think that when my time comes and the maggots feast upon my eyes, I will have died for something worthwhile. And I want my sons, tall sons, to stand beside my bed and bid me farewell with love in their hearts."

"He should apologize to me!" said the young man, pointing to Piercollo.

The giant spread his arms. "If that is what you wish, then I do so gladly," he said. "I am sorry that you were offended and doubly sorry that your brother is hurt. And I am deeply glad that I do not have to kill you. Will you drink with us? Piercollo will pay."

The man nodded and sheathed his sword, the others following his example. They did not stay long, but they drank with us and the enmity ended there.

Just before midnight a young nun entered the tavern and moved between tables, collecting coins. Stopping before us, she held out a leather pouch. "To feed the poor and the sick," she said.

Each of us gave a silver penny, and she smiled her thanks and moved away.

Mace's eyes never left her. "What order was she?" he asked me.

"I think she is a Gastoigne. They have braided belts with three tassels."

"Celibates?" he asked. I nodded.

"What a waste," he said. "I wonder if she lives nearby."

I know what you would be thinking, my dear ghost, were you capable of thought: Where is the princess? Where is the great love of the Morningstar for whom he risked his life on a score of occasions, climbing tall towers under silver moonlight, journeying into deep spirit-haunted caverns, fighting men and beasts conjured by sorcerers?

I could tell you with a degree of truth that she didn't exist. Or at least not as the myths would have you believe. I will say no more now. For Mace's great love is both a part of my tale and yet not. But I will leave that riddle to be explained in its proper place.

The woman who gave life to the stories was quite different. To begin with, her hair was not spun gold, nor was her skin alabaster white. She was not tall, standing at just over five and a half feet, and her beauty did not make men gasp. She was what some men call a handsome woman, her features regular, her mouth full and sensual. As to her eyes, they were hazel, the brows heavy—indicators, in my experience, of a passionate nature.

Her name was Astiana, and she was the Gastoigne sister seeking alms in the tavern. And while it is true that Mace noticed her, it was only in the way he noticed most women. He gave no other thought to her that night and indeed spent it in the company of a buxom serving girl with a gap-toothed smile and welcoming eyes.

There were no rooms in the tavern, and Wulf, Piercollo, Ilka, and I left the place just after midnight and slept in a field close by.

Mace found us just after dawn, and we sat and talked for a while. Piercollo wanted to buy supplies, and since it was market day, we decided to stay in Pasel. By midmorning we were bored and anxious to be on our way. The town offered little in the way of entertainment, and the market was dull. Piercollo obtained two sides of ham, a sack of oats, some sugar and salt, and various dried herbs and seasonings. He was content, and we were all ready to move on when Astiana came to the marketplace.

She climbed the wooden steps to the auctioneer's platform and began to preach to the crowd, who gathered around to listen. She spoke of love and caring, of the need to help those less fortunate. Her speaking voice was good though not powerful, and her delivery was less than perfect. But she made up for this with passion and belief, her every word hammering home into the hearts of the listeners.

Even so I was surprised that the crowd remained, for she began to criticize Angostin rule—the unfair taxes and the criminal behavior of the conquerors. Then she spoke of the hope of the people and cried out the name of the Morningstar. A great cheer went up.

This was dangerous talk, and I looked around, seeking out the militia.

They were there, lounging against the walls of nearby buildings, but they made no attempt to stop her. At last a tall officer with braided blond hair beneath a helm of iron stepped forward. "That is enough, Sister!" he called.

Astiana turned to him. "You should be ashamed, Brackban," she chided. "You serve the cause of the evil upon this land."

"You have had your quarter hour, Astiana, and now the auctioneer is waiting and there are cattle to sell. Step down, if you please."

The slender nun raised her hand and blessed the crowd, then walked swiftly from the platform, and I saw Brackban wander away into the nearest tavern.

The cattle auction had no interest for me, and I returned to my companions, who were sitting at a bench table near the town center, enjoying a late breakfast of bread and cheese. "She spoke well of me," said Mace. "Fine sentiments."

"She was not speaking of you, Jarek," I told him coldly.

"You are in a foul temper this morning."

"Not at all. It is just that I see things more clearly now."

"Have I done something to offend you, Owen?"

Piercollo had wandered to the edge of the crowd, watching the auction. Ilka was beside him; both were out of earshot. "Offend me? Last night our friend could have been slain, and you did nothing. You left him to his fate. I find that despicable."

"You did well enough without me," he pointed out, "and why should I risk my life for the man? I did not ask him to break the fellow's jaw; it had nothing to do with me."

"Had it been you under attack, would you have expected us to stand with you?"

"No," he answered simply. "Nor would I have asked you."

We were ready to leave when a troop of soldiers rode in, scattering the crowd at the auction. Hauling on their reins, the fifty men sat their mounts while their officer dismounted and climbed to the platform, pushing aside the auctioneer.

"By the order of Azrek, lord of the north," he shouted, "the town of Pasel is now under direct military rule. The militia is hereby disbanded. My name is Lykos, and town leaders will assemble this evening one hour after dusk at the keep, where I shall inform them of the new laws and taxes decreed by the Lord Azrek. There will be a curfew at dusk, and anyone found abroad after this will be arrested. There will be no public meetings and no gatherings until further notice.''

I saw Brackban walk from the tavern and stand with arms folded before the newcomer. "Pasel is not in your lord's domain," he said. "You have no authority here.''

"Azrek is the lord of the north, a post given him by Edmund, the high king. Do you dispute the king's right by conquest?''

"Pasel is a free town, also by decree of the king," argued Brackban. "Our taxes are paid in full and held for you at the keep. But we report to the Lord of Rualis. I repeat, Azrek has no authority here.''

"Who are you, soldier?" asked Lykos.

"I am Brackban, captain of militia.''

"The same Brackban who allows sedition to be preached in the town center by outlawed sects?" Lykos sneered.

"Since when have the Gastoigne nuns been outlawed?" answered Brackban.

"Since their abbess was nailed to the gates of the abbey," shouted Lykos. "Arrest him!" Several soldiers leapt from their mounts and ran at the captain.

Brackban jumped back, his sword hissing from its scabbard. The first man to rush in died instantly, his neck half-severed, but before the sword could rise again, Brackban was overcome and borne to the ground.

The crowd stood by, silent and uncertain. "There is a reward of twenty silver pieces to the man or woman who identifies or captures the traitress known as Astiana. She will be brought to the keep this evening or this entire settlement will be judged as traitors, their property forfeit.''

"I am Astiana," came a high clear voice, and I saw the young nun step forward from the back of the crowd. Two soldiers moved alongside her, pinning her arms.

The crowd surged forward, and the soldiers swung their mounts, many of which were frightened by the sudden movement. One horse went down. I don't believe the crowd intended violence at that moment, but in the confusion the soldiers drew their swords and lashed out at the town dwellers nearest to them.

What followed was panic, rearing horses, and people running in every direction, trying to escape the swords of the soldiers.

It was a miracle that no one was killed, though many were later treated for wounds, deep cuts caused by the slashing sabers.

I saw Piercollo shepherding Ilka from the scene. Then a horseman moved in, his blade slicing down. Piercollo swayed back from the cut, then grabbed the man by his cloak and hauled him from the saddle. Instantly soldiers bore down on him. Ilka tried to draw her sword, but Piercollo pushed her from him, sending her sprawling to the ground.

I made to rise and run to his assistance, but Jarek Mace grabbed my shoulder. "Wait!" he ordered.

"Take him alive!" yelled Lykos, and more soldiers leapt from their mounts to rush in toward the Tuscanian. Two he felled with sweeping punches, but he was tripped from behind and fell heavily, striking his head upon a wooden post. Then he was still.

Rolling him to his belly, they bound his hands.

Mace pulled me back from the table where we sat into the shadows of the eating house. Wulf was nowhere in sight.

Lykos strolled down to the now nearly deserted square and stood before the bound giant. Piercollo was conscious now, and three soldiers hauled him to his feet. "I saw you in Rualis," he said. "You were with the man known as the Morningstar. Where is he?"

Piercollo said nothing, and Lykos struck him savagely across the face.

"You will tell me all you know," he said. "Take him away."

Mace dragged me back inside the deserted eating house as the soldiers prepared to depart. Wulf emerged from a shadowed alcove.

"What now, Mace?" he asked.

The warrior released his hold on me and rubbed his chin, his eyes thoughtful. "No matter what that officer said, the town leaders will have a meeting. Find out where it is to be held and when and try to gauge the feeling of the militia. Is this Brackban popular? And the nun; how do the townspeople feel about her?"

"What are you planning?" I inquired.

He smiled at me. "Why, I shall attempt to rescue our friend, of course. Is that not what you would expect from the Morning-star?''

"Yes, it is, but not what I would expect from you.''

"Life is full of surprises, Owen.''

Ilka came in, her eyes wide and fearful but her expression determined. She stood before Mace, and he glanced down at her. "We will do what we can to free him,'' he told her. She nodded and tapped the hilt of her saber.

"Even to fighting for him,'' agreed Mace. She smiled then and took hold of his hand, kissing his fingers.

The owner of the eating house came in from the street. He was a tall, fat man with small feet who walked with the grace of a dancer. A curious sight. "A bad business,'' he said, shaking his head. "Very bad.''

"What did Brackban mean about Pasel being a free town?'' I asked him.

"When the war began, we refused to send men to serve against Edmund. As a reward, he declared Pasel a free borough. No man resident here with land pays tax. But trappers, hunters, and loggers all pay a portion of their profits to the king.''

"The gratitude of kings is short-lived,'' observed Mace.

"It would appear so. Can I fetch you more food, sirs?''

Mace asked for some toasted bread and cheese, while Ilka and I ordered hot oats and honey. We sat in silence while the owner prepared our second breakfast. When he returned, Mace bade him join us, and he poured himself a flagon of ale and sat with us.

"Brackban spoke well,'' said Mace.

"A good man,'' replied the owner. "He led a company of soldiers in the Oversea War—received a golden medal after the siege of Ancour. Little good it will do him now. We told him to order the nun from Pasel, but he refused. God's curse upon women with sharp tongues!''

"A pretty young piece,'' put in Mace.

"Pretty? I suppose so. But trouble! Spends her days begging for coin and then feeding the crippled and the useless. I ask you, what is the point of such actions? A man is useful only as long as he can contribute to the general good. To feed him thereafter is to waste good food and prolong his agony. Better that he die quietly with dignity.''

"Perhaps she believes all life is sacred,'' I said softly.

"Pah!" was his first response. Then: "Last autumn a tree fell upon the legs of a young logger, crushing the bones beyond repair. The man was finished and ready to die. But no! She takes him in, feeding him, reading to him. The pour soul lived another six months before gangrene finally took him. You think he thanked her for making him suffer?"

"Perhaps he did," I offered. Below the table Mace's boot cracked into my shin.

"Women," he said. "They all make us suffer one way or another. But tell me why Brackban refused to send her away. After all, he was the captain of militia."

"Besotted with her, I suppose," said the owner. "That's all I can think. Now he'll hang for it—or worse."

"Perhaps not," said Mace. "Perhaps he'll be rescued. Who knows? The Morningstar may come to his aid."

"Morningstar! Why would he care what happens in Pasel? This is a working town, full of working men. They say he is a rebel lord—another cursed Angostin. He'll end up as a duke or something, pardoned by the king. They look after their own. Bastards!"

"I've heard," whispered Mace, leaning in close, "that the Morningstar is of the line of Rabain."

"Would that were true! But it isn't, man. These stories are like children's tales. Men tell them to make us feel there is hope. There isn't hope for the likes of you and me. We just earn our bread and hope to stave off sickness and death long enough to sire a family. This is the world of the Angostins, and even if the Morningstar were Rabain himself, they would snuff him out like a candle." Pushing himself to his feet, he smiled ruefully. "Well, it was nice talking to you, but I've work to do."

Wulf returned after an hour or so and slid onto the bench alongside Mace. "Brackban is well liked, a regular hero."

"What about the woman?"

"Tolerated but not loved. She's an outsider, and she expects people to live up to the teaching of the church. Not just praying, mind, but actually doing. She's made a lot of enemies, most especially the local priest. Stood up in his church and pointed to his whore and his children, asked him where in the book it says a priest can behave like that!"

"In front of the congregation?" asked Mace, amazed.

"In the middle of his sermon. Called him a fornicator."

"She said that in church? For a nun she has little shame. Spirited, though. I don't suppose the priest is campaigning for her release."

Wulf chuckled. "Says she's demon-possessed and ought to burn."

"What about the meeting?"

"You were right. It is at a barn on the western side of the town. They'll be heading there now."

"Then let's join them," said Mace.

I was baffled by Mace's actions, but I said nothing as we walked through the town. The streets were empty, but there was blood upon the hard-baked clay of the town center.

The barn was tall, used to house all the winter feed for the local cattle, and it was situated in a wide meadow surrounded by trees. As we approached it, a militia soldier carrying a spear stepped out into our path.

"What's your business here?" he asked.

"We have come for the meeting," said Mace.

The soldier stared at him for a moment. "I don't know you," he said.

"Yes, you do, my friend," responded Mace with a broad smile. "For I am the Morningstar. And this is Wulf the hunchback and Owen Odell the bard." He did not introduce Ilka.

The man stepped back, mouth open. "If this is some kind of jest . . ."

"You think I would jest while my friend is a prisoner in the keep, while they prepare Brackban for hanging?"

The man was impressed, as well he might be. Mace was an inspiring figure, tall, handsome, and rakish, the very fabric of legend. The soldier hesitated. "I've been told to keep all strangers away. But not you, sir. They'd not want me to stop you, God bless you!"

Mace patted the man's shoulder, and we walked on. He turned to me. "Make my entrance dramatic, Owen."

Two more soldiers stood guard at the double doors of the barn, but they had watched us walk past the first sentry and therefore greeted us more warmly.

"You are a little late," said one. "The meeting has already started."

Mace said nothing but strode inside. Some forty men were present, seated on bales of hay, listening to a gray-headed elder who was talking of making an appeal to Azrek in Ziraccu. Mace walked to the front, while Wulf, Ilka, and I remained behind the listeners.

"Who are you, sir?" demanded the graybeard.

I let fly the spell, and golden light flared around Mace's head, rising to form an arched rainbow beneath the rafters.

"I am the Morningstar!" thundered Mace. He let the words hang in the air for several heartbeats. Then: "And I am here to see if you will allow the enemy to hang Brackban."

"No, we won't!" shouted one of the guards, but the assembled townsmen sat silently. These were hard-nosed men of business, traders, merchants, landowners. They might have been unhappy over the fate of Brackban, but they would sacrifice him in an instant to save their livelihoods.

Mace shook his head. "All over the north the banner of rebellion is being raised. The Angostins are finding that the Highlanders do not make willing slaves. They pay a toll now to travel our roads. They pay it in blood. They will go on paying it in blood until we are free of them.

"I know what you are thinking, each and every one of you. You do not want war to visit this town. You do not want to see your buildings burning, your wives raped, and your children murdered. You want life the way it was. There is nothing shameful in that, my friends; that is what we all want. But it is too late. In the south of the forest the Angostins have burned and pillaged the settlements. They are bringing in Ikenas to settle the land. Look at the events of today! You are a free town, yet foreign soldiers can ride in, arrest your captain of militia, and take their swords to innocent citizens. What will come next? Taxes will be doubled, tripled. They will take everything you have."

"And what do you suggest?" asked the elder who had been addressing the men when we arrived. "War? We have just lost a war, all our knights and nobles slain."

"Angostin knights!" stormed Mace. "Angostin nobles! North against south. Who cares what happens to Angostins? How many Highland knights were there? How many Highland nobles? But this war we will not lose. Even now I have an army building that will sweep the enemy from our lands. A Highland army!"

"Where is this army?" asked another man. "I see no warriors."

"You will see them, my friend. But they are not needed here, not where there are Pasel men of stout heart and great courage. Highlanders! Or has Angostin wealth eaten into your souls, turning your blood to water?"

"It hasn't turned mine to water!" shouted a stocky bearded man, rising to his feet. "What would you have us do?"

"Sit down, Jairn," ordered Graybeard. "No one here has given this man the right to speak for us."

"Yes, sit down, Jairn," said Jarek Mace. "Sit down for the injustice. Sit down while they slay your captain. Sit down while they break their promises and rape your wives. Sit down and listen to spineless old fools like this one."

"No!" roared Jairn. "I'll be damned if I will. When my leg was broken the fall before last, it was Brackban who came to my farm and brought in my crops. And you, Cerdic, who was it that gathered the men to help you rebuild when the fire gutted your home? It was Brackban! And when raiders took the prize cattle, who was it that hunted them down? Who was it that brought them back to their owners? Is there any man here who would sleep well at night knowing that he did nothing to help Brackban in his hour of peril?"

Several of the men shouted agreement, but the majority began to talk among themselves, arguing in loud voices. Mace raised his hands for silence, but he had lost the attention of the crowd.

I sent up a swift spell sphere, dark and small, that exploded like a thunderclap.

There was silence then, all right!

"Now there is no more time for talk," said Jarek Mace. "All those who will fight to see Brackban freed, walk to the left. Those with no stomach for justice can remain seated."

Jairn was the first to stride across the barn. Others followed until only seventeen were still seated. Mace called the sentries to him. "Make sure none of these cowards leave this barn until morning," he said.

"You can't imprison us!" a balding sandy-haired merchant complained.

Mace dragged the man to his feet. "I can do what I like with you, you gutless piece of horse dung! Be thankful I'm leaving you alive!" Hurling the man from him, he swung on the remaining sixteen. "There comes a time when a man has to choose sides," he told them. "When the day of freedom comes, the

Highlanders will know who fought for them—and who left them to rot. Then there will be a reckoning. Prepare yourselves for that day!''

I think he was unfair to them. Several were old, and as to the others—well, it is no crime for a man to know fear or to need time to reach weighty decisions. Some, no doubt, were family men concerned for wives, children, or infirm parents. But he left them feeling ashamed.

We walked into the sunlight, where Mace sat down with Jairn and the others. For some minutes I sat with them, but battle plans and strategies were of little interest to me then, and I wandered away with Ilka to sit on a stone wall and stare out over the mountains. I had no idea why Mace should suddenly become the hero, and it unsettled me. I felt I had missed something of import, as indeed I had.

Ilka sat beside me and pointed to the harp bag slung from my shoulder.

"I am in no mood for music," I told her. She looked crestfallen, and I relented. "What would you like to hear? A ballad? A dance melody?" She shook her head. "What, then? A marching tune? A battle song? No? Then I am at a loss, lady."

Leaning forward, she touched my chest just above the heart, then gestured toward the trees and the mountains and the sky.

"You would like to hear the music of the land?"

She nodded and smiled.

I tuned my harp and, closing my eyes, let my mind flow free, my fingers dancing upon the strings.

But it was not the music of the land or of the trees or mountains. It was the music of the birth of love as I felt it then on that summer's day on a stone wall, beneath a cloudless sky. After a while I opened my eyes, watching her as she listened, and I saw that her eyes were moist with tears, her cheeks flushed.

I know now that she understood my feelings, reading the message in my music from the first halting notes.

But I was younger then and not so wise.

The assembled men discussed plans for attacking the castle for almost an hour before Wulf, his face flushed and angry, heaved himself to his feet and stalked across to where we sat.

"How goes it?" I asked him.

He hawked and spit. "What if? That's all I'm hearing. Let's

storm the walls! What if they've hot oil? Let's burn the gates! What if they charge out at us? I shall go insane if it carries on much longer. Already some of them are losing the will to fight. They ask: 'What if we win? What then? More troops will be sent; the town will be put to the torch.' ''

"Surely the taking of such a small keep should pose little difficulty," I said.

"Really? Well, why don't you go and tell them, General? Mace is just about ready to crack skulls."

"Very well." Replacing my harp in its shoulder bag, I strolled back to where the group sat. Wulf followed me, his anger replaced, I think, by amusement. When I saw that expression, my doubts flared. Who was I to plan an attack? What experience could I offer? Mace glanced up as I approached. He, too, was looking angry, his face flushed. In that moment I realized it would be wrong to offer yet another opinion to the argument. It was time, as my father would have said, for decisive action. Yet even were my plan to be a good one—which I was beginning to doubt—then it would still take away from Mace the authority of the Morningstar, for it should have been he who thought it. "Could I speak with you for a moment?" I asked him. He nodded and stood, and we walked away from the debating townsmen.

"A gutless bunch of whoresons," he said as we moved out of earshot.

"They need leading," I told him.

"I am trying, damn you! I have never been an officer. And to be truthful, I don't know how to attack a castle, save to storm it!"

"There are fifty men at the keep," I said, keeping my voice low. "But they will need to sleep—no more than four or five will be on watch in the darkest hours of the night. But we do not have to storm them; we have already been invited in. Lykos has ordered the town leaders to attend him at dusk. We will just walk in."

"And then what?" he snapped.

"Once we are inside, we will take Lykos as a hostage. Then I will send a signal to Wulf and the others, and they can disable the sentries and take the keep." As I outlined my plan, I became more nervous, expecting its flaws to be brutally pointed out.

Instead Mace slapped me on the shoulder. "By God, it is worth a try!" he said. "I'll put it to them!"

"No!"

"Well, we cannot do it alone!"

"I know. That's what I meant by leadership. You have been a soldier. At what point in a battle did your officer say to you, 'Well, men, I'm thinking about signaling the charge; what do you think?' Now is the time to establish your authority. Think like a king, Jarek. Praise them for their courage and *tell* them what they are about to do."

His eyes narrowed, and he nodded solemnly, standing silently for a moment. "What if they laugh in my face? Or simply refuse?"

"Then you tell them they are not worthy of the Morningstar and we leave."

He swore then and rubbed at his chin. "By God," he hissed, "I'll not be thwarted by this miserable bunch! If it is a performance that's needed, then that's what they'll get!"

He grinned at me, then returned to the waiting group. But this time he did not sit among them; he stood with hands on hips, waiting. The conversations died down. "I have listened to all that has been said," he told them, speaking slowly and with great authority. "You are all Highlanders. You have courage. I am proud that you have chosen to stand beside me. Very proud. But the time for talking is done. Lykos has called for the town leaders to attend him at the keep. Ten of us will go. Wulf, you and the others will remain outside, hidden. Now, I have already commended your courage, but the eight men who walk into that keep beside Owen and me must be warriors, swordsmen, daggermen, men who know how to fight. I cannot judge which of you are the best; you must decide that. Do it now, while I explain to Wulf what needs to be done."

Signaling the hunchback to him, he turned his back on them and strolled away once more.

I watched the men, saw the change in them as fresh confidence filled them. For a moment only they were silent, then they began to talk of skills with the blade. Who should go, who should stay? From fear-born indecision they were now vying for the right to accompany the Morningstar.

I held the smile from my face and approached Mace and Wulf. "You have them," I told him. "That was well done."

"So easily swayed," he said, contempt in his voice.

"It is a valuable lesson to learn. Men will always follow confident leaders even if the way is fraught with peril."

"Well, it is that," said Wulf. "Ten men walking into the enemy's fortress. I think you are insane."

In that moment I felt the terrible weight of responsibility upon me. It was my plan, and on it rested Piercollo's chance of life. I cared little for Brackban or the woman, since I did not know them then, but the giant Tuscanian was my friend, and my fears for him were great.

All my nervousness returned with doubled force. I have said that I had little interest in matters of strategy, but that was because my father and brothers were masters of the art. Young Owen, on the other hand, was a simpleton in such matters. I thought of the plan again, imagining my father examining it. Its one strength was its simplicity, but the weaknesses were many. I tried not to think of all that could go wrong.

But if I was worried at that moment, it was as nothing compared with the nervousness I felt as we approached the keep. The sun had vanished behind the great peaks to the west, and the sky was the color of blood as we walked slowly up the hill. The round tower with its gates of oak was a simple structure, no more than 60 feet high and perhaps 150 feet in circumference. I had seen many such. On the ground floor would be the dining hall, on the first the sleeping area, with its double-tiered rows of pallet beds. On the third was situated the home hearth of the captain and his lady, usually two rooms—a small bedroom and a dining area. Above that was the roof, from which archers could send down arrows, spears, or hot pitch on any invading force. The small dungeons, perhaps two cells, would usually be dug into the hillside below the keep.

I guessed that Lykos would see us in his rooms on the third floor.

We could see a single sentry up on the roof, leaning over the battlements and looking down as we approached. He shouted an instruction to the gatekeeper; we heard the bar lift, and the gates opened.

Two armed men stood beyond them. "All weapons to be left here," said the first. We had expected this, and Mace unbuckled his sword belt, followed by Jairn and the other men, most of whom were Brackban's militia soldiers. None was wearing ar-

mor now, but loose-fitting tunics and leggings of wool. The
swords and knives were left on a bench inside the doorway. One
of the sentries moved forward to search Mace; as he did so, I
sent a tiny sound spell into the man's right ear, a buzzing like
an insect. He jumped and twisted, then the sound moved behind
him and he turned swiftly. "What's the matter with you?" the
second sentry asked.

"Cursed wasps!" said the first.

"Are we to stand here all night?" asked Mace. The man
swore, for the buzzing had sounded by his left ear now.

"Take them up!" he ordered the second man. Slowly we filed
after the sentry into the dining area, where several soldiers were
seated at a bench table, eating soup and bread, and on to a
winding stone stair that led up through the sleeping quarters,
where around twenty warriors were lounging on their beds.
Something about the scene aroused my fears, but there was
nothing overtly threatening, and I forced myself to stay calm.

At the next floor, to the right of the stair, was a door upon
which the sentry rapped his knuckles.

"Enter!" came a muffled voice from within. Just as the soldier laid his hand on the catch, Jairn slid a short iron bar from
his sleeve, cracking it down on the man's neck. The soldier fell
back without a sound, and Jairn caught him, lowering him to
the floor. Mace and the others drew the daggers they had hidden
within the folds of their tunics and prepared to enter the room.

"No!" I whispered suddenly. Mace froze.

"What is it?"

My mouth was dry, and I knew with sick certainty that we
had walked into a trap. But before I could explain, I heard the
stealthy sounds of footfalls on the stairs both above and below
us. Mace heard them, too. He cursed softly, then smiled. "It is
not over yet," he said grimly.

And hiding the dagger in his sleeve, he opened the door.

Slowly we filed inside. There were fifteen soldiers, armed
with swords and shields, waiting for us. Lykos was standing at
their center, his arms folded across his chest.

"Welcome, Morningstar," he said. "I shall do my best to
make your stay as unpleasant as possible."

"You are too kind," Mace told him. Then, his voice calm,
he spoke to me. "It is rather dark in here, Owen."

The room was lit by several lanterns, casting dancing shadows to the walls, but I knew instantly what Mace wanted. Soldiers were crowding behind us on the stairs now, pushing their way into the room. The men with us did not attempt to resist, for they were in a hopeless position. I closed my eyes, let the power swell, then sent a blast of white light up to the ceiling, adding a thunderclap in the process.

In that moment Mace leapt at Lykos, the black dagger sliding into his right hand, his left arm circling the officer's throat and dragging him back. The dagger point pricked into the skin of Lykos' neck.

"Tell your men to lay down their weapons," hissed Mace.

"No!"

"Then die," Mace did not drive the dagger home but slowly eased the point through the skin, slicing alongside the jugular. Blood spurted, but the wound was not yet lethal. The blade stopped. "Still just time to change your mind," said Mace, his voice pleasant, conversational, almost solicitous. It is one thing to face sudden death with courage, quite another to wait while a dagger slowly rips into your throat.

"Lay down your weapons!" ordered Lykos, and one by one the soldiers obeyed him, their swords clattering to the floor.

"Would someone be so kind as to free the prisoners from the dungeon?" asked Mace. A tall warrior with a thin wedge-shaped face moved slowly toward the door. "Go with him, Jairn. You, too, Owen. I'll just stay here and become better acquainted with Captain Pig Breath."

When the dungeon doors were opened, we found Piercollo unconscious, his face bloody and bruised, his right eye swollen to the size of a small apple, blood seeping from below the lids.

Beside him the Pasel captain Brackban was chained to the wall. He was unhurt. "You are free, Captain," I told him, "but I would appreciate your help in carrying our friend here."

Brackban asked no questions and, when his chains were loosed, moved to kneel beside Piercollo.

"They burned out his right eye with a hot poker," he said. "Lykos did it for pleasure, for he told us the Morningstar was sure to attempt a rescue, and he asked no questions of the big man."

Gently he turned Piercollo to his back. The giant groaned in pain, then struggled to rise. Jairn and Brackban helped him to his feet.

We found Astiana in the next cell, and she followed Brackban and Jairn out of the keep onto the hillside. I ran back up the stairs to where Mace still waited, his knife at Lykos' throat.

"They are clear," I told him. He nodded and backed toward the door, pulling the bleeding officer with him.

At the gates we gathered our weapons and ordered the soldiers to wait within the keep while we took Lykos out onto the moonlit hillside.

Wulf ran up to us, bow in hand. "What went wrong?" he asked.

"Everything," replied Mace.

We reached the safety of the tree line, where Brackban was sitting with the injured Piercollo. When Mace saw the blinded eye, he dragged Lykos to a nearby tree, pushing him against the trunk. "Now you will die!" he snarled.

"Don't do it, Jarek! He is a hostage!" I shouted. "The rules of war state—"

"I do not play by their rules," said Mace. But the dagger did not plunge into Lykos' heart; instead, Mace lanced the point into the Angostin's right eye, the blade twisting. The officer's scream was awful to hear. Mace dragged the dagger back, then moved in close to the half-blinded man. "I'm going to let you live for a little while, you worm, so that you can suffer as he is going to suffer. But when you are healed, I'll come back for you. You hear me? The Morningstar will come back for you!"

Hurling the whimpering man from him, he stalked away into the forest.

I ran after him, grabbing his arm. "Why are you so angry?" I asked him. "You won! You rescued Piercollo and the others."

"You fool, Owen! You heard Brackban back in the market-place. They have all the tax money there in that damned keep. I could have been rich—and clear of this cursed forest. Now they'll be hunting me even harder. A pox on your Morningstar!"

I felt confusion in my soul as we made our way deeper into the forest, in turn both elated and depressed. My elation came from recognizing the trap before it was sprung, the depression from walking into it in the first place. It made my plan seem naïve and stupid, for I had been outthought by Lykos, and only Mace's speed of action had saved us.

How had I known of the trap? I wondered at this for some

time and realized it was the soldiers in the sleeping area who had alerted my subconscious. As we had walked into the keep and up the long winding stair, I had seen soldiers lounging on their pallet beds. But the men had been wearing breastplates and boots. No warrior, save one expecting trouble, rests in this way. I should have seen it more swiftly, I know, but it was pleasing even so to realize that the weakest son of the great Aubertain could at times think like a fighter.

And was my plan so naïve? No. What I had not considered was how the legend of the Morningstar would be interpreted by Lykos. Had he known the real Mace, Lykos would never have expected a rescue attempt. But he didn't; he knew only the legend. And such a hero would surely die of shame if he did not attempt to aid his friends.

We made camp in a deep cave high up on the flanks of a tall mountain. From the entrance we could see the land around for miles, and there was no obvious possibility of a surprise attack.

On the walk to the mountain each of the twenty-strong party—save Piercollo, who was in great pain—collected wood and tinder for the night fire. On Wulf's instruction I lit the fire close to the back wall of the cave. In this way the breeze from the entrance forced the smoke up against the rear wall and out of the cave overhead, leaving the air below pure and clean. The wood was dry, for it had been gathered above ground, snapped from dead trees. Branches left on grass or moss or earth tend to soak in water and make poor fuel.

Astiana tended to Piercollo's ruined eye, making a compress of herbs, which she bound over the wound. Brackban, Jairn, Wulf, and Mace sat together at the cave mouth, discussing, no doubt, the events of the evening. The other men, mostly militia soldiers who had served with Brackban, stretched themselves out near the fire and slept.

Ilka approached me, taking my hand and pointing to Piercollo. "I am not a healer," I said gently. Lifting her right hand, she waved it, stretched fingers miming the actions of a magicker. "That is not my skill, Ilka," I told her, but she continued to tug, and I moved alongside the wounded man.

Astiana looked up but did not smile. "It could become infected," she said. "It was not a clean wound."

"No infection," mumbled Piercollo. "They used hot metal . . . very hot. Very red. The eye is gone, I think."

Taking a deep breath, I placed my hand upon the compress. "Tell me if this helps or hinders," I said, casting a cooling spell over the area.

Piercollo lay back, his good eye closing. "Better," he whispered. "Much better." I deepened the spell, my hand trembling with the cold. His breathing slowed, and he slept.

I left the women tending him and joined Mace and the others. Brackban thrust out a meaty hand and grinned. "My thanks to you, sorcerer."

I shook my head. "Sorcery is, thankfully, not my area of expertise, sir. But I was pleased to assist in your rescue."

"Talks prettily, doesn't he?" put in Wulf.

"I don't judge a man by how he talks," said Brackban, "but by how he acts. I know you did not enter that keep to rescue me; you were looking for your friend. But even so I am now in your debt, and I always repay."

"You have nothing to repay," Mace said easily.

"I disagree, Morningstar. Jairn says you have an army in the south of the forest. I would be honored to join it. I have some experience with soldiering; I have trained men for battle."

As clearly as the sun shining through a break in a storm cloud, I saw then what needed to be done. When I had sent Corlan and his men south, it had been to eliminate a danger to us, to put distance between us. But now Owen Odell, the son of Aubertain, knew without doubt what action was called for. The reign of Azrek in this land was evil, and evil must be countered wherever it is met. Mace had no understanding of this, but then, Mace was no longer in control.

Before he could answer, I spoke up. "The army is not yet gathered, Brackban. When the Morningstar spoke of it, he meant the men of the Highlands, who even now are tending farms or raising cattle."

"I don't understand," he said, tugging at a blond braid of hair that hung from his temple.

I looked into his clear blue eyes. "There is no army—not yet. The time is not right. The war between north and south is barely over; the southern Angostins control all the major cities. To begin an uprising now would be futile. But soon the majority of their forces will travel back to the south, leaving garrisons to control the Highlands. Then we will gather the men; then we will cast the Angostins from among us."

"What then can I do?" he asked.

"You can recruit the iron core. Find men of courage, men with ability. Old soldiers, veterans. Then we can call the men of the Highlands to arms. We can train them, arm them."

"What about coin? Arms cost money."

"Go south and seek out a man named Corlan. He will supply coin. Tell him you are sent by Jarek Mace. Corlan leads the men of the Morningstar. You will aid him where you can, but your responsibility will be the gathering of officers. The heart of the army."

"Is this the same Corlan who has brought murder and savagery to the forest for the last five years?"

"It is. But he fights now for the Highlands."

"And you trust him?" The question was asked softly, but Brackban's eyes had hardened, and I knew he was skeptical.

Mace leaned forward. "He has sworn the soul oath," he said. "As you will—as will every man here. If he betrays us, he will die horribly. Is that not so, Owen?"

"Yes. But it is not necessary for Brackban to swear. I can read his heart, and he is a true man."

"I will swear it anyway," said Brackban.

Once again I conjured the dancing flame and watched as it glided along Brackban's arm, disappearing into his chest.

"Do you swear to follow the Morningstar unto the ends of life and to give your life in order to free the Highlands?"

"I do."

"So be it. The soul fire now burns inside you. It will strengthen your resolve and aid your courage. But should you ever betray the cause, it will rot your body from within and you will die. You understand?"

"I understand." He reached out his hand to Mace, who took it in the warrior's grip, wrist to wrist. "Until death, Morningstar," he said.

"Until death," agreed Jarek Mace.

After banking up the fire, I slept, a thin blanket around my shoulders, my head pillowed on my arm. I could feel the warmth of the flames on my back, and my thoughts were mellow. Piercollo, though grievously hurt, was alive and free, owing in no small measure to my talents. I felt relaxed and free of care.

* * *

I drifted into sleep and awoke by another fire, beneath a sky shining with the light of two moons, one a crescent, the other full and huge, its surface scarred and pitted like a silver plate engraved with black ink.

I sat up and stared around me. The landscape was flat, but the small blaze had been set on the brow of the only hill for miles. It was a poor place for a fire, with nothing to reflect the heat. And yet the setting was somehow perfect. I became aware—as dreamers do—that I was not alone; three other men sat close by, hooded and silent. I looked at the first man, and his head came up. He was not unhandsome, the face slender, the eyes dark, the skin swarthy. He pushed back his hood, and I saw that he was wearing a black helm upon his long hair; he was not old, yet his hair was already silver.

"You wear the ring," he said. The other two men had not moved, and I switched my gaze to them. They shimmered and faded in the moonlight, and their heads remained shadowed within the hoods. "I am Gareth," said the first man, lifting his hand. I saw his ring then, the twin of the one I now wore, the white stone shining like a tiny moon.

"I found it," I told him.

"I know. It was at the gray keep."

"My ring," came a hoarse whisper from my left. The shimmering figure raised its head, and the moonlight fell upon a translucent face, the image drifting between flesh and bone. One moment his features were clear and human; the next, as he moved, the skull shone through. "My ring," he repeated.

"It was not my intention to steal it," I said.

"Yet you have it," said Gareth.

"It was upon the hand of a dead man. Is that theft?"

"You took what was not yours."

I could not argue against such logic, and I shrugged. "I will return it if you wish."

"You read the inscription?"

"Yes. Guard am I, sword pure, heart strong."

"Did you understand it?"

"No."

Gareth nodded. "I thought not. The sorcerer who attacked you—he would have understood. Not enough to be fearful but enough to wreak chaos. What do we guard, Owen?"

"I don't know. Some hidden treasure? A holy relic?"

"We guarded the Three, lest the evil should come again. Now two have been found, and the third is sought. Where do you stand in this?"

"How can I answer? I do not know of what you speak."

"The skulls, Owen."

Once when I was a small child I was playing on a frozen lake, when the ice gave way beneath me. The shock of the icy water to my system was terrifying. Such was the feeling of dread that touched me now when Gareth spoke.

The skull at the keep. One of the Three. One of the Vampyre kings.

"Why do you guard them?" I asked at last.

"On the orders of Rabain and Horga," he answered. "When the kings were slain, it was found that the skulls could not be destroyed. Horga took them and kept them apart. She tried to burn them in fierce furnaces. They were struck repeatedly by iron mallets. They were dropped from high cliff tops, but they did not shatter on the rocks below, nor were they even marked. At last, defeated by them, Horga and Rabain ordered them to be taken to three secret locations, there to be guarded for eternity by the Ringwearers."

"You are a thousand years old?" I asked him.

He smiled then and shook his head. "No. Three families were chosen from among Rabain's knights. From father to son they passed the rings and the secret. It was never to be spoken of, but the head of the family was pledged to guard the resting place of the skulls so that they would never again be brought together."

"Why? What peril can come from old bones?"

He shrugged and spread his hands. "I cannot say. I do not know. But Horga claimed that if ever they were to be gathered in one place, then a great evil would live again. The families were true to the promise of their ancestors. We lived our lives chained to the past, the Ringwearers . . . until ten years ago." He pointed to the farthest figure, who still had not moved. "Lorin spoke of the skull, and the word reached Azrek. You know of him, I believe."

"Yes."

"He sent men to the forest, hunters, killers. Lorin fought them off, slaying four of them, but they returned with Cataplas, and Lorin died. But first they tortured him until finally he broke and talked of the gray keep.

"Cataplas journeyed there with his killers. Kircaldy was there. He fought also, then barricaded himself in the tower. Cataplas sent a spell of fire that burned the flesh from his bones, but Cataplas did not find the skull—not until you came and unwittingly made him a gift of it.

"Now there is only one: the skull of Golgoleth, the greatest of the Vampyre kings. Cataplas seeks it. Azrek desires it. It must be denied to them."

"Do they know where to find it?"

"I think that they do."

"How?"

"The kings were joined by sorcery, and there are lines of power between the skulls. One was not enough to locate the others, but with two a skilled sorcerer will be drawn to the third."

"What would you have me do?"

"Kircaldy and Lorin both died before they sired sons. Lorin's ring was taken by Cataplas, but you have the ring of Kircaldy. Will you take on the responsibility of the promise? Will you become a Ringwearer?"

There was no need for me to consider my words. "I will," I said.

"You may die for that promise, Owen Odell."

"All men die, Gareth."

"Then journey to the troll reaches. Come as quickly as you can. I will find you—if I still live."

I noticed then that the spirit of Kircaldy was no longer present. "Where has he gone?" I asked.

"To a place of rest."

"And what of Lorin? He remains."

"Cataplas has his ring. Until another guardian is found, Lorin will know no peace."

When I awoke, the cave was dark, the fire merely embers casting soft shadows on the far wall. I rose silently and walked to the entrance. A cold wind was blowing across the mountainside, but I found Mace sitting with his back to a boulder, a cloak wrapped around his shoulders.

"You look lost in thought," I said, seating myself beside him.

"There is much to think about. Do you think Rabain was like me?"

"What do you mean?"

"An outlaw, a mercenary. Was he trapped into becoming the hero, or was he truly your Morningstar?"

"I don't know, Jarek. Once I would have said he was everything the stories claim. But now I have seen the birth of a legend."

"And you are disappointed."

"Not exactly," I told him. "You did stand upon the road alone and defy the Angostins, and you did fight your way clear on the day of the burning. Because of that Megan was freed. You faced the Shadows of Satan, and you rescued Piercollo. You have courage. No man can take that from you."

"Perhaps," he said, staring away over the mountains.

"What is troubling you?"

"Brackban swearing to follow me unto death. I don't want that sort of devotion; it makes me uneasy."

"I now understand the mystery of Cataplas and the Three," I said, seeking to change the subject. He was at once interested, and I told him of the dream meeting with Gareth and the ghosts.

"You believe it was a true vision?"

"I do."

"And you intend to find this Gareth in the troll reaches?"

"I must. I am now a Ringwearer."

He chuckled and shook his head. "Oh, Owen, what a wondrous fool you are. What help will you give Gareth? How will you stop Cataplas and his killers? Sing them to death, perhaps?" He laughed, and I felt foolish.

"You could come with me," I pointed out.

"Why would I wish to?"

"You are a hunted man, Jarek Mace. Cataplas will find you one day, and with the third skull perhaps his powers would double. Then where would you be, lord of the forest? How will you battle the demons who will stalk you in these dark woods?"

Still good-humored, he thumped my shoulder. "Good, Owen! You do not appeal to my fine nature or mention friendship and loyalty. You send your shaft straight to the gold. I like that!"

"Then you will come with me? Gareth is in peril. He urged me to travel with all speed."

"I'll think on it."

◇ 9 ◇

Brackban, Jairn, and the militia soldiers left soon after dawn, heading south, but Piercollo had developed a fever in the night, and Astiana remained behind to care for him. There was no way the giant would be fit to travel for several days, and though Mace wanted to leave him behind, Wulf and I refused. Ilka, though incapable of speech, made it plain she felt the same, sitting beside the wounded man and glaring up at Mace.

Jarek took his bow and quiver and left the cave without a word.

I banked up the fire with the last of the fuel and sat watching him stride out toward the forest.

Astiana moved alongside me. "Is he truly the Morningstar?" she asked.

"He is," I told her.

"He is a callous man, hard and bitter."

"That also," I agreed.

She asked how we had met, and I told her of the rescue back in Ziraccu, though I left out small details such as Mace's adulterous adventures with the noble lady and his return for a share of the reward. I spoke also of how we saved Megan from the fire and of the fight with the beasts in the forest.

"They say he is Rabain come again," said Astiana, her gaze locked to mine. "Would you agree with such sentiments?"

"Who am I to agree or disagree? I am but a bard. Who was Rabain? What do we know of him save that he fought the Vampyre kings and was made king himself? Mace was talking of him earlier. Was he a wolfshead or a rebel knight? A prince or a peasant?"

"You are cynical, Owen," she said. "I thought all bards were romantics, singing of chivalry and honor."

"I sing of those things. I dream. But here there is a grim reality. Death is sudden, brutal. Men are cruel, mindlessly vicious. Why did Lykos blind Piercollo? Why did they tie Megan to the burning stake? Why do the Angostins glory in war?" I glanced back to where Wulf was sitting with Ilka beside the fire. "The hunchback is my friend, brave and steadfast. Yet when first I saw him he was kneeling over the body of a traveler he had slain; he was cutting the rings from the dead man's fingers. And Ilka—sweet Ilka—was raped as a child and had her tongue torn from her mouth. Where is chivalry in this? A man who taught me to create illusions of light, sweet and beautiful, now transforms men and animals into demonic creatures filled only with the lust to kill. Where is honor in this?"

"Honor is here," she whispered, placing her hand over my heart. "Or do you believe that good can exist only in pure surroundings, untouched by the world's darkness? What value would there be in that? Virtue is like a ring of gold. It does not matter where you place it, in a swamp or a cowpat; it will remain gold, untarnished. Lesser metals are corroded, ruined, corrupted. Not gold. The true heart remains true."

"Just words," I snapped more brutally than I had intended. "The evil triumph always, for they are strong and merciless. Good men are hampered, chained by their honor. They cannot compete, for they play by different rules."

For a while she was silent, and we sat in the new sunshine, both lost within our own thoughts. I think I almost hated myself for voicing such a philosophy of despair, and my heart was heavy. But after some minutes had passed, she spoke again.

"I do not agree with you. A thousand years ago the Vampyre kings ruled this land. They were brought down and destroyed. There evil was colossal, yet a good man destroyed them. The battle between good and evil is circular. Good wins, evil wins, good again. The rules are immaterial."

"How is your philosophy different from mine, Sister?" I countered. "If such a circle exists, then there can never be a true victor."

"I know," she whispered. "But then, victory is not the prize; it is the battle itself. You are part of that battle, Owen. You and

Wulf and Piercollo. Yes, even Jarek Mace, though he knows it not.''

"Oh, he is a warrior, no doubt of that,'' I agreed. "But which side does he fight for? I don't think he cares about good or evil. He cares only for Jarek Mace.''

Piercollo awoke and groaned in pain, and Astiana rose and moved to where he lay. I stood and walked out into the sunlight.

The ring, with its pale stone, felt heavy on my hand.

In that moment I felt like pulling it clear and throwing it high over the hillside. I would be free. I could walk from the forest and head south, all the way to the coast and my father's estates, far from war and brutality. I could sit by a warm fire in the evenings, my belly full, and I could play my harp and sing my songs without fearing a dagger in my ribs or a demon at my soul. It was tempting.

But at that moment—perhaps because I was thinking of home—I saw again my father sitting in the high-backed chair, his children at his feet, his warhounds close by. And I could hear his voice, deep and slow, as he told us stories of manhood or set us riddles to solve:

> *"There were once three men, proud and strong, the best mountain climbers in all the land. In every city tavern people would gather and wonder which man was greatest. Finally they agreed to meet to decide the issue once and for all. There was a peak of sheer granite, three thousand feet high, which men called Rasboreth. No one had ever conquered Rasboreth, though many had tried, and many had died or been crippled in the attempt. Just as they were about to begin the climb, an angel appeared and told them all that their deaths were but one day distant. The first man said, 'I shall go home and fill my belly with wine until the time of my death.' The second man said, 'I shall find a woman with a soft body and welcoming eyes, and I shall lie with her until the time of my death.' Both turned to the third man. 'And what of you?' they asked him.*
>
> *'Me? Why I shall climb the mountain.' "*

He had laughed at our noncomprehension, and we had gone to our beds none the wiser. But now I knew what he meant. A man must finish what he starts, allowing no threat or fear to stand in his way.

I had made a promise to Gareth, and I would keep it. Mace was dismissive of my talents as a warrior, but my skills lay in other directions. I did not see myself as essentially heroic. My fears were very great. But I learned at my father's knee that a man is judged not by his words or by his principles or even by his wit. He is judged by his actions.

How could I, Owen Odell the Angostin, speak out against evil if I did not stand against darkness?

A hand touched my shoulder, and I turned to see Piercollo beside me. His face was gray, the bandage over his eye bloody.

"I am sorry," I told him. "You have suffered terribly."

"But I am alive, my friend, thanks to you. I will repay. Piercollo will stand with you and with the Morningstar. We will make war upon these men of evil."

I seem to remember a cloud passing across the face of the sun at that moment, but probably it did not. The weight of that memory, even after all these years, is still great. For I knew that something of beauty had been lost to the world, and I grieved for it.

From that day to the last battle I never heard Piercollo sing again.

Mace returned toward dusk with fresh cuts of venison, and we spent a second night in the cave. Piercollo's fever had begun to pass, but he was still too weak to travel far.

We broiled the venison and ate well that night. Mace was in better humor and told us that he had seen hunting parties of soldiers scouring the woods and forest tracks, but none had chanced upon our trail. "There's not a woodsman among them," he said.

Even so we kept watch that night, taking it in turns to sit just inside the cave mouth watching the moonlit hills.

I took the last watch, relieving Wulf at around midnight, and sat wrapped in a blanket beneath the stars. It was a clear night, soundless, a cool breeze whispering across the cave entrance. The smell of damp grass was in the air, and bats flew above me. An old badger with a twisted front paw moved out onto the hillside, his fur like silver thread, his gait clumsy. Yet he had great dignity as he slowly made his way down the slope.

At the bottom he paused, his snout lifting to scent the air. Suddenly his dignity fled, and he scurried into the undergrowth. I was immediately tense, narrowing my eyes to scour the tree line.

But I could see nothing.

Then a huge gray wolf came into sight, padding across the grass. He was followed by six more. Something small caught my eye, and I swung my gaze to see several rabbits near a half-buried boulder. The wolves ignored them.

This struck me as curious but not threatening. Perhaps they had recently fed. Perhaps they had discovered the carcass of the deer slain by Mace.

On they came, straight toward the cave.

"Mace!" I called, and he came awake instantly, as did Wulf. Both men gathered their bows and moved alongside me. I pointed to the pack no more than a hundred paces distant.

"You woke me for wolves?" snapped Mace.

"Look at them," I said. "They are coming straight at us. No turning of heads, no interest in the rabbits."

Mace muttered some obscenity and moved back to the fire, blowing it to life and adding a thick, dry branch. The dead leaves caught instantly, flaring to life. Mace ran back to the entrance and stepped out onto the hillside. The wolves saw him and increased their speed.

Wulf notched an arrow to his bow. In the pale moonlight it shone like silver.

"Get back, Mace!" I yelled. "They are possessed!"

Mace hurled the burning branch at the first gray beast. The brand hit the wolf in the face, the flames singeing the fur of its back, yet it ignored the fire and ran straight at him, leaping for his throat. An arrow from Wulf lanced into the beast's chest, and it slumped to the earth.

Mace drew his sword, cleaving the neck of a second wolf, but the remaining five were all around him now. Wulf killed another, then threw aside his bow and ran at the creatures. Pulling an arrow from the quiver he had left behind, I followed him. A huge wolf hurled itself at Mace, knocking him from his feet. Losing his grip on the sword, he made a grab for his dagger; he would have been too late, but I arrived alongside him and tapped the wolf with the shining arrow. It froze momentarily, then ran away across the hillside with its tail between its legs. Two more charged in. Mace rolled to his knees to drive his dagger into the throat of the first, and I threw the arrow at the second. The point barely broke the skin of the beast, but still the wolf, freed from the spell, loped away from us. The last of the creatures leapt at Wulf, sinking its fangs into his forearm. His short sword plunged into the creature's side, the blade piercing the heart. Its forelegs folded beneath it, and it sank to the earth without a sound. Wulf tried to pull the jaws apart, but they were locked to his forearm. Mace and I managed to prize them clear. Wulf pushed back his torn sleeve, and blood gushed from the puncture wounds above and below his left wrist.

The hunchback swore loudly. "Were they rabid, do you think?" he asked.

"No," I assured him. "Cataplas cast a spell on them. As soon as we touched them with our weapons, the spell was leached away. Had they been rabid, they would have continued their attack." I was not sure that this was true, but my words comforted Wulf.

"Why me?" muttered Wulf, trying to staunch the flow of blood. "They were all around you, Mace, and you haven't a scratch!"

"The gods favor the handsome, Wulf—you should know that. And you should have known better than to run at wolves."

"I saved your life, you bastard!"

"True," Mace agreed, grinning. "Which is the second thing to remember about gods: they rarely aid the stupid."

"It's not a mistake I'll make again!" responded the hunchback, turning back toward the cave. Astiana bound his wounds, but Wulf was still complaining as the dawn came up.

"We must move," said Mace, kneeling beside Piercollo. "Can you keep up with us?"

"We should stay for at least another two days," put in Astiana.

"Perhaps we should. But who knows what the sorcerer will send against us next time. Tell me, Owen," he said, turning to me, "does Cataplas know where we are?"

"I believe so. He would have been linked to the wolves."

"Then we have no choice," said Mace.

The giant pushed himself to his feet. "I will be with you, Morningstar. Do not concern yourself. Piercollo is strong."

"What about you, Sister? Where will you go?"

"I will travel with you as far as the village of Willow. It is close to the troll reaches, and I have friends there."

Mace smiled. "I always like the company of attractive women."

"And I like attractive men," she told him icily. "It's a shame there are none close by."

"I think she loves me," Mace told me as we set off toward the north.

We traveled toward the northwest, moving with care, listening for sounds from the soldiers hunting us. Twice we saw mounted warriors, but they were far off and we passed by unseen.

Piercollo walked in silence, uncomplaining, though the pain from his eye must have been great. We halted at midday in a sheltered hollow, where Wulf built a fire beneath the spreading branches of a tall pine. The wood he used was dry, and what little smoke it made was dissipated as it passed through the thick branches overhead. We cooked a little of the venison and sat quietly, each with his own thoughts. Wulf's arm was paining him, but the hunchback had been lucky; the bite had been partly blocked by his leather wrist guard, and the wounds were not deep.

Ilka came to sit beside me, and for the first time I took her hand, raising it to my lips and kissing the fingers. It was as if I had struck her, and she jerked her hand from mine, her eyes angry.

"I am sorry," I told her. "I did not mean to offend you."

But she stood and walked away from me, sitting beside Piercollo and Astiana. It had been an unconscious gesture and one of love, yet I had forgotten the reality of her life. Because she had been raped, tortured, and forced to become a whore, such a kiss for her was simply a request for carnality. I felt clumsy and stupid.

That night, after another seven or eight miles of travel, we found shelter under an overhang of rock. Mace gestured to Ilka, summoning her. When she shook her head and turned away, he stood and walked around the small fire to where she sat.

"Is it that time of the month?" he asked her. Once more she shook her head.

"Then come with me." Ilka rose and stood before him, her hand on her scabbarded saber. Then she pointed first at Piercollo, then at Wulf, and finally at me. I didn't understand what was happening, though I was glad she had refused him. "What is happening here?" asked Mace, becoming irritated.

Ilka was agitated now, but she could not make herself understood. It was Piercollo who finally saw what she was trying to say.

"She is one of us now, Mace," he said. "She is no longer a whore."

"But she *is* a whore," Mace pointed out. "It's what she's good at, and it's what I need!"

"Leave her be, Jarek," I said. "She was forced into the life, and now she has chosen to forsake it."

"There's nothing wrong with being a whore," Mace snapped.

"Nor with not being one," put in Astiana.

"I don't need a nun to advise me about whores," Mace replied, angry now.

"No, I would imagine you are expert enough in that area. After all, why would any woman sleep with you but for money?"

"They don't do much sleeping, Sister. But since Ilka has discovered purity, perhaps you would like to take her place. I'll give you a silver penny for the poor." Astiana's hand streaked for his face, but he caught her wrist and pulled her in close. "I like passion in a woman," he said, lifting her from her feet.

"Let her go, Mace," said Piercollo, his voice dangerously low. The giant climbed to his feet, his huge hands clenched into fists.

Mace glanced at him and smiled, but there was no trace of humor in his eyes. "I'll not harm her," he told him, releasing the woman and stepping back.

Astiana's face was flushed, her anger barely controlled. "To think," she said, "that I glorified your name to the people. You are no better than those you fight. You are a disgusting animal."

"I never claimed to be otherwise," he responded. "Not once. But I am not here to live your dreams, and I am not responsible for them. I am a man trying to stay alive and enjoy myself while doing it. Is that so wrong? And as for disgusting animals, well, I never saw an animal to fit that description. Plenty of men, yes, and a few women. But never an animal. And do not fear for your virtue with me, Sister. I'll not trouble you."

Turning away from her, he approached Piercollo. "Anything else you wish to say?" he asked.

"Nothing," the giant told him.

"Don't ever threaten me," Mace warned him. "Not ever!"

"She is of the church," said Piercollo. "It is not right to treat her with disrespect."

"A black dress does not command respect," hissed Mace. "I've known churchmen who were adulterers, torturers, killers. And I've shared the beds of a nun or two. They are just people like you and me, only they are mostly weaker, clinging to superstition, hiding behind convent walls because they haven't the courage to face real lives. Respect? I'll tell you what I respect. Gold. It asks nothing and gives everything. It keeps you warm, and it buys you pleasure. And there's not a man alive who won't sell his soul for the right amount of it."

"Spoken like the hero you are!" stormed Astiana.

"Hero?" responded Mace. "Where are the heroes? The Angostins have slaughtered them all. There are no more heroes, Sister. They lie upon the fields of battle, the crows feasting upon their eyes. They went into battle with clubs and staves, told they could defeat armored knights and seasoned troops. And they believed it! Well, they had no chance, but they were heroes. That's what heroes do, isn't it? They tackle impossible odds and laugh in the face of death. Well, I saw no laughter. Only terror as the first charge cleared their ranks and the swords and maces and spears and lances tore into their flesh. I am not a hero, Astiana. But I am alive."

The conversation died there. Wulf banked up the fire, and Piercollo sat silently staring into the flames, while Astiana turned away from us and settled down to sleep with her back to the fire.

I felt low then, a deep depression hanging over me. We tend to think of heroes as men apart—their angers are always colossal, but they rage only against the foe. We rarely see them in a damp forest, complaining about the cold, and never think of them urinating against a tree. They never suffer toothache; their noses are never red from sneezing in the winter. Thus we strip away the reality.

In tales of old the sun shines brighter, the winter snow becomes beautiful, an elven cloak upon the land. And the hero rides a white stallion and searches for the monster who has kidnapped the princess. Always he finds her, slaying the beast who took her.

Still angry, Mace wandered away from the campsite. I followed and found him sitting upon a ledge of rock. "Do not lecture me, Owen," he warned.

"I am not here to lecture. She was wrong, and you were quite right."

"You don't believe that; you are merely trying to ease my irritation. I saw your eyes when I told you of the gold in the keep. You were disappointed. Just as when I refused to fight fifty soldiers to save Megan."

"Perhaps I was," I agreed, "but that does not make me right. You are not responsible for the dreams of others. Yet you did take the name, and it is the name that haunts you."

"I know. And you would like me to live up to it. I can't, Owen. Not even if I tried. It is not in my nature, my friend. Can you understand that? I know what I am. When I was a child I longed for friendship. But I was the son of a whore, and no one wanted me to join their games. I learned to live without them. I joined the circus when I was little more than twelve. The master there beat me ceaselessly, using pain to teach me. I walked the high wire, I swung upon the flying bar, I danced with the bear. I learned to juggle and to tumble, but always he was there with his crop or his cane. I learned then, Owen, that a man stands alone in this world. He does not ask to enter it, and he begs not to be taken from it. In between there is fear, hardship, and a little pleasure. I choose to seek pleasure." He lapsed into silence for a moment, his eyes distant. "Why did the whore refuse me, Owen? I have never been unkind to her."

"She does not wish to remain a whore," I told him.

"Why? What else is there for her?"

"She will be my wife," I said, speaking the words before I even realized they were there.

Where I expected a sneering comment or, worse, a scornful laugh, he merely nodded sagely. "You could do worse," he said with a shrug.

"How long before we reach the Ringwearer?" I asked, changing the subject and suppressing my anger.

"Maybe too long," he replied. "We can travel no faster."

"What about horses? We could buy them in Willow."

He shook his head. "We can move faster without them. Trust me. I just hope that this Gareth is a canny fighter, for there is no doubt the enemy will be upon him before we arrive."

I tried not to think about the perils facing Gareth: the killers, the sorcery of Cataplas, the demons he could summon.

I could only hope we would be in time.

The weather was kind for most of the journey to Willow, the sun shining, and the only hours of rainfall coming during the fifth night, when we were sheltered in a deep cave with a fine fire to keep the chill from our bones. Piercollo's wound was healing well, though I must admit that I shuddered when I saw Astiana remove the bandage and bathe the ruined eye. The red-hot iron had destroyed the muscles around the now-empty socket, and crimson scars radiated out from the wound. Mace cut an eye patch from a piece of black leather, and this held in place a poultice of herbs prepared by Astiana. Piercollo bore his pain with dignity and courage and on the fourth day even re-sumed cooking for the company. It was a welcome relief, for Wulf was perhaps the worst cook I can remember. According to Mace, he could make fresh rabbit taste like goats' droppings.

We ate well for the next three days, Piercollo gathering herbs and wild onions and Wulf snaring rabbits and a hedgehog or two. One morning we even dined on a fungus growing from the side of a tree. Ox heart, Piercollo called it, and indeed it dripped red when torn from the bark. It had a savory taste and, when cooked with sliced onions, was most welcome to the palate.

On the morning of the eighth day of travel we climbed to a hilltop overlooking the village of Willow. There were some thirty houses there and no sign of a keep or tower. The largest building was a church situated at the village center. For some time we sat looking down at the settlement, watching for soldiers, but seeing none, we ventured in.

There was a tavern on the eastern side of Willow, and bidding farewell to Astiana, who headed for the church, we entered the building, taking a table near a shuttered window and ordering meat, bread, and ale. There was no ale to be had, we were told, but the village was renowned, said the innkeeper, for its cider. It was indeed very fine, and after several tankards I felt a great warmth for Willow growing inside me.

Mace called the innkeeper to our table and bade him sit with us. There were no other customers, and the man, a round-faced Highlander named Scoris, eased himself down onto the bench alongside me. He smelled of apples and wood smoke, a most pleasing combination. I warmed to him instantly.

"We are seeking a man named Gareth," said Mace.

"By God, he is becoming popular," replied Scoris. "Has he discovered a gold mine?"

"I take it we are not the first to ask for him?" I asked.

"No. Two days ago—or was it three?—Kaygan the swordsman came here. Is he a friend of yours?"

"No. Who is he?" asked Mace.

"Mercenary soldier. It is said he's killed seventeen men in one-to-one combat. He's Azrek's champion now, so he says. He put on a show here. Never seen the like. Tossed an apple in the air and cut it into four slices before it fell. And sharp? His sword cut through two lit candles, sliced through them but left them standing."

"What kind of blade does he carry?" inquired Mace, his voice soft in tone but his eyes betraying his interest.

"Saber."

"What did he look like?"

"Tall man, much as yourself. Only slimmer. Golden hair and slanted eyes, like one of them foreigners in the old stories. Only he ain't no foreigner. Born in Ziraccu—almost a Highlander."

"What did he want with Gareth?" I asked Scoris.

"He didn't say, and I didn't ask. He was a showman, all right, but not a man to question, if you take my point. Friendly enough on the surface, but he has dead eyes. Never question a man with dead eyes."

"What did you tell him?" put in Wulf.

"Same as I'll tell you. Gareth is a hermit. Strange young man, white-haired, though 'e's no more than twenty-five, maybe thirty. Lives up in the hills somewhere. Comes to the village maybe twice a year for supplies—salt, sugar, and the like. He's no trouble to anyone, and he pays for his food in old coin. Some say he has a treasure hid in the mountains, and a few years back a group of ne'er-do-wells journeyed up into the high country to take it from him. They didn't come back, and they weren't missed, I can tell you. I expect Kaygan heard the treasure stories and wants it for himself."

"We seek no treasure," I told him, "though I think you are right about Kaygan. How shall we find Gareth?"

"Just head north. If he wants to be found, you'll see him."

"How many men were with the swordsman?" queried Mace.

"Seven. They had a tracker with them, Cheos. Local man. He's good. They say he could trail the north wind to its lair in the ice wastes."

"You have been very helpful," I said. "Many thanks."

"Ah, it was nothing," replied the innkeeper with a wave of his hand. Mace produced two silver pennies, which he laid before the man, but Scoris shook his head. "I'll not have it said," he told us, dropping his voice, "that I charged the Morningstar for breakfast."

With a broad smile and a wink he rose and returned to his kitchen. "How did he know you?" whispered Wulf.

Mace chuckled. "It is not me he recognized, half-wit! How many men travel the forest in the company of a giant and a hunchback?"

He was just downing the last of his cider when Astiana ran into the tavern. "Lykos!" she shouted. "He's here!" Wulf leapt to his feet, grabbing for his bow. Mace and I rose. Piercollo curled his hand around the haft of a long bread knife.

"Time to leave!" said Mace softly.

"Show yourself, wolfshead!" came the shout from beyond the tavern. Mace swore and moved to the shuttered window, peering through the crack.

"There must be twenty men out there," he said.

"There are a dozen more beyond the back door," Scoris informed us, his face red and his eyes showing his fear.

"They were hidden in the church," said Astiana. "The priest warned me, and I came as fast as I could."

I moved to the window. Lykos, in full armor and helm, a sword in his hand, sat upon a gray gelding. The helm's visor was partly open, and I could see that his eye was bandaged, the wound seeping blood, which had stained the cloth. Around him were men-at-arms, several with crossbows aimed at the door but most armed with swords.

"I have a cellar," said Scoris. "There is a tunnel that leads out into the storehouse and barn. Use it quickly!"

Mace took his bow and notched an arrow to the string. "Not yet!" he said grimly. Drawing back on the string, he gave a swift instruction to Wulf. The hunchback moved behind the door and suddenly wrenched it open. Three crossbow shafts hammered into the wood, a fourth slashing through the doorway to punch home into the wall.

Mace stepped into the doorway. "I told you what would happen, Lykos, when next we met." The crossbowmen were frantically seeking to reload, the swordsmen standing by uselessly. Mace raised his bow, the arrow flashing through the air to lance between visor and helm, and Lykos reeled back in the saddle, the shaft piercing his brain. For a moment he sat stock-still, then his body fell, his foot catching in the stirrup. Such was the clang of the armor as it struck the ground that the gelding reared and fled in panic, the armored corpse with foot caught dragging behind. Several men ran after the beast; the others charged the tavern.

Mace leapt back inside, slamming shut the door. Wulf lowered the guard bar into place. Scoris waved us out into the kitchen, lifting a trapdoor; there was a narrow flight of stairs leading down into darkness.

"Go quickly!" said Scoris, handing Piercollo a lit lantern.

"You will be in great trouble for this," I said.

"No matter!"

Mace was behind him. I saw his hand come up, heard the thud of the blow on the man's neck, then Scoris fell forward upon me. Lowering his unconscious body to the ground, I rounded on Mace. "What have you done?"

"Protected him as best I can. Now move!"

Piercollo went first, followed by Ilka, Astiana, Wulf, and myself. Mace pulled shut the trapdoor behind us and brought up the rear. The cellar was dank but filled with the sweet smell of cider casks. Swiftly we crossed it, coming to a tunnel that sloped upward. At the far end, some twenty paces distant, we could see a thin shaft of light. Piercollo doused the lantern, and we silently approached the storehouse. Sliding back the bolts on the hinged trapdoors, we emerged into the building. All was silent inside, but we could hear the distant shouts of the disappointed soldiers back at the tavern.

The store was filled with hanging carcasses of salted meats, barrels of apples and other fruit, sacks of flour and sugar, oats and wheat. There were two great doors, wide enough to allow the passage of wagons, and a side exit leading to the north.

Wulf opened the side door, peering out. There was no one in sight.

And the trees were but a few hundred feet away.

We ran across the open ground, every moment fearing the sound of pursuit. But we passed unseen from Willow and once more entered the forest.

The songs talk of the fight with Lykos, telling us that Mace met him in single combat while Astiana stood on a scaffold with a rope around her neck. But life is rarely like the songs, my dear ghost.

That is a sorry fact for a bard to learn. For we like our heroes pure, you see—golden men, demigods without flaw. Just as we like our villains to be black-hearted and vile. When men sit in taverns, supping their ale and listening to poets regaling them with epic stories, they cannot be bothered to think. They do not wish their enjoyment to be sullied by shades of gray. No, they desire only sinister black and spotless white. And are women any different? No, again. Forced by their fathers—yes, even sold by them—into a life of servitude and drudgery, they *need* to believe there are heroes. They look at the dull, flat features of their husbands and dream of golden-haired men who would slay dragons for them.

We even follow this practice in life itself. The enemy is always reviled, pictured as the despoiler of women, the eater of babies, a living plague upon the earth, a servant of Satan. Wars are never fought for plunder or gain. Oh, no, they are always depicted as ultimate battles between good and evil. But then, looking at the nature of man, that is understandable. Can you imagine the scene, the great king gathering his troops before an epic battle. "Right, my lads," he says as he sits upon his great black stallion, "today we fight for my right to steal gold from whomever I choose. The enemy are men much the same as yourselves. A good bunch, probably, with wives and children back home. And at the end of the battle, when I have more riches than I'll ever spend in a lifetime, many of them—and indeed, many of you—will be worm food or crippled. Better to be dead, really, because I'll have no use for you once you can no longer wield a sword. All right, lads. Let's be at them!"

No. Far better for the poor foot soldier to be told that he is fighting for God, and right, and justice in the world against an enemy spawned from darkness.

But where was I? Ah, yes, Lykos was dead, as Mace had promised he would be. And thus the legend grew.

Word flew through the forest faster than a raven's flight, the story growing, adding to the myth of the Morningstar. The townsmen of Pasel, learning of the killing, rose up and retook the keep. The revolt spread, and Rualis rebelled against the Angostins, slaughtering the soldiers and the noble families who had ruled there for three centuries. Farther south Brackban was gathering men to the Morningstar's cause.

Corlan the outlaw had attacked three convoys, and his men of the Morningstar were heroes now, carrying a sacred flame in their hearts.

You have never seen a forest fire, ghost. It is a fearsome thing. One moment all is silent, dry, and hot; the next, a tiny flicker of flame dances upon dead leaves. Other dancers join it, and they run across the ground, flaring up against dead wood. A breeze fans them, and they scatter until it is a dance no longer. Flames roar high into the sky, great oaks burn like tinder, and the dancers become a ravening monster propelled by the wind.

Such was the rebellion.

When I had sent Corlan south, it had merely been to separate him and his men from us, to put distance between us. I do not believe—though I would like to—that I planned the rebellion from the start. But I will say with all honesty that the seed of the idea was growing when I gave Brackban his orders. Why should the Highlanders not control their own destiny? By what right, save that of conquest, did the Angostins rule?

But this was not in my mind as we walked toward the troll reaches, seeking the Ringwearer, Gareth.

I was more concerned with our safety, for ahead of us were stretches of forest and mountain inhabited by creatures many times stronger than men. Here was the last refuge of the trolls and, according to fable, many other ancient races, dread beasts and sorcerous evil.

But more immediate was the threat of Kaygan the swordsman and his seven killers, and worse than these the ever-present fear of Cataplas and his sorcery. None of which seemed to bother Mace as we walked. He was in high good humor.

"All that armor plate," he said, "breastplate, shoulder guards, greaves, thigh protectors, gauntlets, helm. Must have cost at least thirty gold pieces. And one arrow ends his miserable existence. By God, isn't life wonderful?''

"There is nothing wonderful about the taking of a life," put in Astiana, "though I grant that Lykos deserved death."

"It shouldn't have been as quick," said Wulf. "I'd like to have had an evening in his company with some hot irons and a blazing fire."

"To achieve what?" asked the sister stonily.

"Achieve?" responded Wulf. "Why, I would have enjoyed it."

"I can see no pleasure in such torture," muttered Piercollo. "He is dead, and that is an end to it."

The clouds gathered, and the sky darkened. We sheltered from the coming storm in an old log dwelling, long deserted. The west wall had collapsed, the cabin was open to the elements, but there was enough of a roof left on the east and north walls to protect us from the rain and the gathering storm.

As we sat around the fire blazing in the stone-built hearth, I entertained the company with the tale of Arian and Llaw and the return of the Gabala knights. But after this, following requests from Wulf and Mace, I performed once more Rabain's battles with the Vampyre assassins.

The magick was as usual greeted by warm applause, save from Astiana, who as a sister of God frowned upon the talent.

"Did Rabain's son actually kill him?" asked Mace suddenly as the figures faded away. "In life, I mean."

I shrugged. "I don't know. All we know of Rabain comes from legend, word of mouth. In some tales it is his son who slays him. In others he journeyed across the Far Sea. In at least one he climbed into a chariot of fire and journeyed to join the gods."

"There are other legends of Rabain," said Astiana, "older, darker. In these, he has no son."

This aroused my interest, and I questioned her further. "When I was first a novice," she explained, "there was an old monk who gathered such stories, writing them in a great book. He said that the first tales of Rabain were of a demon summoned from hell, Ra-he-borain—the Summoned One. The Vampyre kings had destroyed the armies of light and Horga the sorceress, in desperation, called upon a prince of blood. He was a killer, damned to an eternity of torment, burning in lakes of fire. She drew him back, and he slew Golgoleth. All the Vampyre armies fell to ash in that moment, for as the old tales have it, when the lord of Vampyres dies, his legions die with him.''

"What happened to Rabain?" asked Mace.

"He was returned to the pit."

"That's hardly fair," Wulf complained.

"Life isn't fair," said Mace, chuckling, "but I like the tale. At least his son doesn't betray him in this one. Did he get a chance to enjoy a parade?"

"He enjoyed Horga, I understand," said Astiana primly. "That was his price for doing what was right. She was the most beautiful woman in the world, and he demanded her body. It was that act which meant he would be returned to the pit. He knew this, but such was his desire that he suffered the fires of eternity to have her."

"Must have been some woman," said Mace with a broad grin. "Though I can't say as I would ever strike such a bargain. So, poor Rabain still sits in his lake of fire. I wonder if he thinks it was worth it?"

"According to legend," Astiana continued, "Ra-he-borain merely waits to be called again, his pain as nothing compared with his memories of Horga."

"That is a tale invented by a woman," said Mace scornfully. "You all think too much of yourselves."

"And you think too little," she snapped.

"You are wrong, Sister. There are parts of a woman that I revere."

The threatened row did not materialize, for at that moment the storm winds died down and we heard a terrible scream echo through the forest.

"By God's holy tears!" whispered Wulf. "That chills the blood!"

Mace rose. "I think the Ringwearer has made contact with Kaygan and his men," he said.

"We must help him," I cried, the scream still echoing in my head.

"We can't," Mace told me. "Not yet. There is a storm raging over the forest. What good could we do, blundering around in the dark and the wet?"

"But it is one man against seven!" I protested.

"It's better that way," muttered Wulf. "At least he knows that every man he sees is an enemy."

"But the scream . . . it could have been Gareth. They may already have him!"

"That is unlikely," put in Mace. "They will be sheltering from the rain, just like us. This is no weather to be hunting a man."

Thunder rolled across the sky, lightning following instantly, and the rain fell with great force. Wulf banked up the fire, and we sat in silence for a while.

"What will we do tomorrow?" I asked at last.

"You and the women will wait here," said Mace. "Wulf and I will find Gareth."

"And then?"

"We'll see. Take the first watch, Owen, and wake me in about four hours." Wrapping himself in his cloak, Mace settled down, falling asleep almost instantly.

The fire was warm and comforting, making me sleepy, so I moved away from it to sit below the edge of the broken roof, the dripping water splashing my boots. The forest beyond was cold and uninviting, gleaming with dark light. Somewhere out there, beneath the wind-whipped trees, a man was fighting for his life . . . a man alone.

I shivered and pulled my cloak tight around my shoulders. Astiana moved alongside me. "Can you not sleep?" I asked, keeping my voice low.

"No. Who is this man you are trying to aid?"

"His name is Gareth." I told her then of the skulls and of my dream, and I spoke of Cataplas and his yearning for knowledge. She listened intently.

"I have not heard this legend of the skulls, but the oldest of the stories says that upon his death, Golgoleth pledged to return. The bodies of the Vampyre kings were burned, but the skulls remained untouched by the flames. They were said to have been hurled into the sea from a ship that sailed to the edge of the world."

"There are many stories of Rabain," I said, "but the heart of them remains constant. He fought the evil of the kings, destroying them—he and Horga."

"I wonder what happened to her," said Astiana.

I shrugged. "She married a farmer and raised strong sons.

She became an abbess, a sister of mercy. She walked into the forest and became an oak, tall and commanding. She transformed herself into a dove and flew across the Gray Sea. Perhaps she did all of these and more. But I expect she just got old and died like everyone else.''

Astiana took my hand, lifting it to peer at the moonstone ring. "Why did you agree to wear it?" she asked softly.

"I cannot say. But it was right that I did.''

"You are not a warrior, Owen. How can you fight men like Kaygan?''

"I will do the best I can, sister. I was not the greatest of my father's sons, and my skill with weapons is poor. But still the blood of Aubertain is in my veins. And he is a man who would never step aside for evil. Nor will Owen Odell.''

"You are very brave, Owen," she said, releasing my hand.

Direct compliments always make me feel uncomfortable, and I changed the subject. "Why are you still with us, lady? You have no love for Mace, and you do not like violence.''

"You are wrong, Owen, on both counts. I knew it when I left you all in Willow.''

"Sweet heaven!" I whispered. "You can't be in love with Mace!''

"I did not say I was in love," she snapped. "Why is it that men always reduce things to the carnal?" But her face was flushed, and I believed then and believe now that my arrow was close to the mark. For some reason the knowledge depressed me. Why was it, I wondered, that so many women fell for the charm of rogues, offering their love to men who would drink it like wine and then cast them aside like empty bottles?

"He is a powerful man," she said at last, her voice low.

"Yes," I agreed, "and the world is filled with men of such power. They cheat, they wound, they lust, and they kill. We are sitting in this desolate place because of men of power, and we are being hunted by men of power.''

My voice was harsh, the bitterness spilling like acid. Astiana said no more and backed away from me, returning to the fire.

The rain began to ease, and the moon shone bright through broken clouds. I sat alone through the night, lost in memories, walking the gardens of vanished dreams.

As a child I had so wanted to be like my father, another man of power, tall and strong, a fearless knight. It was not in me, for I never learned to like causing pain and gained no pleasure from success in competition. When I was thirteen—just before my fourteenth birthday, in fact—I remember Aubertain responding to a challenge at a tournament. In full armor, with sword and mace, he fought his opponent, hacking and hammering until the man's helm had burst its rivets. Then the bloody mace had crashed through the skull, and the knight had fallen. Aubertain had raised his mace and sent forth a scream of victory that clawed into my heart with talons of fire. I felt his surging exhilaration, sensed the ecstasy that certain men gain from combat. My dreams of being a knight died on that day, and I saw other things. I saw the knight's widow being helped from the viewing dais. I saw her ashen face and her wide, disbelieving eyes. And I watched his sons run to the broken body, passing through the shadow of the triumphant Aubertain.

I was glad that my father was alive, but I never, ever desired to be a warrior after that.

The rain came again just before dawn, then faded away, leaving the forest washed clean and ready for the new sun. Mace awoke with the first rays of morning and moved across to me. "Good man. We needed our sleep," he said, patting my shoulder. "We may have to fight today."

"Will you challenge Kaygan?"

"God, no! If I see him, I'll send a shaft through his back. You stay here. Wulf and I will scout around for a while."

Armed with their longbows, they set off through the forest—Mace tall and powerful, Wulf shorter and stockier, yet both men moving with animal grace, entirely at home in their surroundings.

A short time later Piercollo decided to explore for herbs and wild onions. His eye was still paining him, and he rarely spoke. His presence, once so vibrant with love of life, was now brooding and dangerously quiet.

"Be careful," I said. "There may be enemies close by."

"Good for them if they don't find me," he grunted.

I boiled some oats and shared them with Ilka and Astiana. The two women sat close together, and every once in a while Astiana would look at Ilka and nod or shake her head. For some minutes I watched.

"You are communicating," I said at last. Astiana waved me

to silence, and the two of them sat staring at one another, the breakfast forgotten. Suddenly Ilka nodded and smiled, reaching out to take Astiana's hands in hers.

"Yes," said Astiana, "I hear you."

Tears welled in Ilka's eyes, and the two women embraced.

"You are a mystic," I said, moving in close.

Astiana shrugged. "I have a gift from God. It is not the same."

"What does she say?"

"Be patient, Owen," she advised me. "We are almost there."

I wandered away from them to sit by the ruined wall. It was there that I caught sight of armed men moving from the undergrowth, and my heart began to beat faster. Three of the men carried longbows; the remaining two wielded barbed spears. I stood and waited as they approached. One of the spearmen grinned as he saw me. He was a handsome, golden-haired fellow with eyes the color of a winter sky, blue and chilling.

"God's greeting, Brother," he said, his voice mellow.

"And to you," I responded. I saw them relax as they neared. The golden-haired stranger let fall a canvas sack from his shoulder and thrust his spear into the earth beside it. Stepping into the shelter, he saw Astiana and bowed low.

"Well, this is pleasant," he said, turning to me. "Two lovely women and a young man together in the forest. How sweet! How inviting!"

There was an edge to his voice that left me tense and apprehensive. I glanced at his companions; they were hard-faced men, grim and tough, and I saw that their gazes lingered upon the women. All color fled from Ilka's face, and her eyes were wide and fearful. She had lived this scene once before, the horror of it never leaving her. Now she was facing her nightmare again. Astiana smoothly rose to her feet, her expression serene.

"Who might you be, sir?" I asked the leader, though I knew the answer, having seen the curved saber at his side. But I wanted to divert him, to take his attention from the women.

"I am Kaygan," he said.

"Not the great swordsman, the champion of Azrek?"

"You have heard of me?"

"Who has not, sir?" I said, hoping that flattery would win him over. "It is an honor and a privilege to meet you. Why, only a few days ago we heard of a display you gave in the town of Willow. Men were still talking of it.''

"How gratifying," he said. "And you, what is your name?"

"Graeme," I lied. "Graeme of Ebracum. I am a bard, sir, and would welcome an opportunity to talk with you of your exploits. Perhaps I could compose a saga poem based upon them.''

"You seem right friendly, Master Graeme. But we have other thoughts on our minds, do we not, lads? Last night we lost two of our men, but we captured and killed our enemy. So today we are in the mood to celebrate our victory. What better way is known to man than to enjoy the soft bodies of women? You, Sister, remove your garments, if you please. It has been a long time since I've heard a nun screaming with pleasure.''

"I doubt it was pleasure," Astiana told him.

"Surely a hero would not stoop to actions so base," I said swiftly.

He laughed and shook his head. "Base? There is nothing base in rutting with women. It is what they were created for—to pleasure men. Now, Sister, the garments. I wish to see those hidden breasts.''

Ilka scrambled to her feet, drawing her saber. Kaygan stepped back, his smile in place. "Such spirit!" he whispered. "Perhaps I should have you first, my pretty! Cheos, you and Symen take the nun! This one wishes to see my skill with a saber.''

Two of the bowmen put down their weapons and advanced on Astiana. "Never had a nun," said the first, a thin bearded woodsman in brown leather leggings and a deerskin jerkin.

"Then it's time you widened your education, Cheos," said Kaygan. "You will find the experience most satisfying." He drew his own weapon and extended the point, tapping it against Ilka's blade.

"No!" I shouted, drawing my dagger.

"Oh, and kill the bard," he said, not even looking at me.

I am not quick to anger, but the contempt with which he treated me fired my blood. One of the men drew his knife and advanced upon me. So great was my fury that instead of retreating or begging for life, I threw myself at him. His eyes widened in shock, and he tried to stab at me. With my left hand I thrust aside his arm, my dagger slicing into his belly and up into the lungs above. He sagged against me and gave out with a low groan. Wrenching the blade clear, I let him fall. Kaygan turned and glazed at me with new eyes. "You will die slowly for that," he promised.

"Show me!" I snarled.

An arrow slashed through the air to punch through the temple of the man Cheos. He staggered to the left and then fell across the fire, flames searing up around his clothing. Another arrow slammed into the chest of the second man, Symen; he grunted and fell back against the wall, vainly trying to pull the shaft loose. Kaygan leapt to where Astiana stood at the far wall, seizing her habit and dragging her in front of him.

"Let her go!" I ordered him. He replied with an obscenity, lifting his saber and holding the blade at Astiana's throat.

"Who is out there?" he demanded of me.

"The Morningstar," I told him. "And you are about to die!"

"Jernais, get the other woman!" The last of his men ran at Ilka, but an arrow punched through his back, high on the shoulder, just as he reached her. As he arched back, screaming, Ilka stepped forward to slash her saber through his throat.

"You are alone, Kaygan," I said softly. "Or do you think to spend the rest of your life hiding behind the sister?"

"Call him in!" he ordered me. "I wish to see his face."

I walked out into the open. "Only one is left alive," I called, "and he is holding Astiana hostage." Mace and Wulf stepped into sight, arrows notched and bows bent. "He wants to see the Morningstar."

Mace tossed his bow to Wulf and strode into the ruined building.

"You don't look so formidable," sneered Kaygan.

"Are you going to kill her or stand there talking all day?"

"I will kill her unless you agree to meet me in single combat, sword to sword."

"All right," said Mace suddenly, "let her go and we will duel." Drawing his sword, he stepped out into the open, turning to see Kaygan hurl Astiana aside.

"Now, Wulf!" snapped Mace. The hunchback sent his shaft straight at Kaygan's chest, but the man's saber flashed through the air, cutting the arrow in two. Mace swore, and Kaygan ran forward and leapt into the clearing, a wide grin on his face.

"Now you'll die, you whoreson!" he shouted.

◇ **10** ◇

MACE'S BLACK BLADE parried swiftly as Kaygan launched an attack of blistering speed, the saber clanging against the longsword with a sound like a ringing bell. Kaygan was lithe and fast, supple and agile, while Mace, normally so catlike and graceful, seemed clumsy by comparison. The clashing of blades continued while Wulf circled the fighters, bowstring drawn back, seeking a chance to kill Kaygan.

No duelist myself, still I could recognize quality in a swordsman, and these two were of the finest. Both were cool, their concentration finely honed, each parry followed by a deadly riposte in a game of cut and block, thrust and counter. But Kaygan was the better.

They fought for some minutes, their blades crashing together, before the first blood was spilt, Kaygan's saber sliding along Mace's sword and opening a shallow wound in the taller man's shoulder. Mace leapt back, and Kaygan followed in swiftly, the point of the saber lancing toward his opponent's belly. Mace swayed to the left, his sword arcing toward Kaygan's face. Off balance, Kaygan hurled himself to the ground, rolling to his feet in one easy movement, but blood was flowing from a gash in his cheek.

Both men circled warily now, and it was Kaygan who spoke first. "You do not have my skill, Morningstar. You know it! How does it feel to be about to die?"

Mace laughed aloud. Kaygan swore and attacked again. Mace blocked the cut and then kicked out, his boot thudding into Kaygan's groin. But the man twisted at the last moment, taking the weight of the blow on his thigh. Even so, he was forced back, and Mace counterattacked, the black sword hammering down against the slender saber and pushing it back. A long cut appeared on Kaygan's head, bright blood drenching the golden hair.

Once again both men moved apart, circling. "I hear you're good with apples," said Mace. "Fight back often, do they?"

With a snarl of fury Kaygan leapt into the attack, his sword a flashing blur of white light. Mace fell back against the ferocious onslaught, his jerkin sliced, a thin line of blood across his chest. There was no respite now, both men fighting to the limits of power and endurance.

At first I thought Kaygan would win it, but as time passed he seemed more desperate, less sure of his skill.

Finally, as he launched yet another attack, he stumbled. Mace's blade flashed over the saber, sweeping down into Kaygan's neck, cleaving the collarbone and rib cage to exit in a bloody spray from his chest.

Azrek's champion died without a sound, his body slumping to the earth. Mace staggered back, then turned on me, his eyes angry. "Why didn't you cast a spell or something? You could have blinded him with a flash of light!"

"You didn't need me," I said. "And such a light might have blinded *you!*"

"By God, he was skillful," said Mace. "I never want to fight his like again."

Moving away from us, he sat by the stream, cupping water in his hands and drinking his fill. His face was bathed in sweat, and he stripped his clothes from himself and splashed naked into the stream, lying down on the cold stones and allowing the water to run over his body. Both cuts were shallow and needed no stitches, but they bled profusely as soon as he left the water to sit in the sunshine with his back against a tree.

"I'll get some cloth for bandages," I told him.

"No. The blood will clot of its own accord. I saw you kill a man today, Owen. How did it feel?"

"Awful. I never want to do it again."

"The next one will be easier. Why did you do it?"

"They were going to rape the women."

"And you thought to stop five of them?"

"I thought I would do *something*. A man cannot stand by at such a time."

He chuckled. "Of course a man can, but that is beside the point. You did well. What a hero you are, Owen Odell! A rescuer of maidens. A fit companion for the Morningstar, wouldn't you think?"

"I thought Kaygan would kill you," I told him, changing the subject. "He was better than you—faster, more skillful. You knew that."

"So did he," he replied, his expression becoming serious. "But there are two kinds of warrior: the one who likes to win and the one who fears to lose. Both can be good. Both can be exceptional. But in a contest between the two there can be only one victor. Fear has no place in combat, Owen. Before, yes. After, often. But not during."

"How did you know that he feared to lose?"

"When he asked me how it felt to know I was going to die."

"I don't understand."

"The nature of combat, Owen. We threaten our opponents in order to inspire fear. Yet how do we decide what will frighten them? How? We think of what terrifies us, and we try to use it against our enemy. He asked me how it felt to face death. That, then, was his greatest fear. That's why I laughed at him."

"And that's why you knew you'd win?"

"That and one other small point," said Mace with a grin.

"And what was that?"

"He couldn't position himself for the kill because he knew that if he moved an inch the wrong way, then Wulf would put an arrow through his heart." Mace laughed aloud. "Life just isn't fair, is it, Owen?"

"Could you have beaten him without that advantage?"

"I think so. But why should I?"

"It would have been more honorable."

He shrugged. "Such honor is for your songs, my friend. When an eagle sees a rabbit on open ground, he does not think, Poor creature. I will wait for him to move closer to his burrow. Life is a dangerous game, Owen. It is deadly serious. And the difference between life and death is like this!" Holding up one hand, he snapped his fingers. "One thrust! One cut! A fall from a horse. The touch of a plague wind. If I could, I would have cut Kaygan's throat in his sleep."

"Do you even understand the concept of honor?" I asked him.

"Obviously not," he replied. His gaze flickered past me, and I turned to watch Astiana approach. "Ah," whispered Mace, "the grateful thanks of the rescued maiden!"

"Why don't you clothe yourself?" she demanded. "Such displays of nakedness are obscene."

Mace climbed to his feet and stood before her with hands on hips. "There are women who have paid to see me thus," he said softly. "But I wouldn't expect a dried-up, passionless piece of baggage to understand that. And so, Sister—and I say this with all the respect you deserve—kiss my buttocks!"

I tensed myself for the exchange I felt was sure to follow, but Astiana laughed, a rich, merry sound that made us all smile. All, that is, save Mace. "I would sooner kiss your buttocks than your face," she told him. Then she glanced down, studying his lower body. "And as for paying to see it, I wonder how many asked for their money back when they saw how little they were getting."

Wulf guffawed, and Ilka smiled. Mace reddened, then he, too, grinned. "What does one expect after a cold bath?" he asked me.

Gathering his green woolen leggings, I tossed them to him. "Sharper than a serpent's bite is the tongue of a righteous woman," I quoted.

"Amen to that!" he agreed, dressing swiftly.

Piercollo walked into the clearing, gazed at the bodies, and then approached us.

"They found their man," he said, his voice low. "They nailed him to a tree. It is not a pretty sight."

"We'll find him," said Mace. "Stay here with the women." Calling Wulf to him, they backtracked the giant. I followed them, but I soon wished I hadn't.

Gareth had been tortured in ways I will not describe. Let it be sufficient to say that there was no way to recognize the man I had seen in my dream save by the blood-drenched white hair. He had been blinded and cut, burned and gouged.

Wulf knelt by the man, then looked up at Mace. "They continued long after he told them everything," he said. "By God, I'm glad we killed them!"

I felt a whisper of wind against my face and stood frozen in shock, for within that gentle breeze I heard words, soft, sibilant, like distant echoes. "Gareth?" I said, amazed. Wulf and Mace both turned to me, but I ignored them. "Speak slowly," I whispered. "I cannot . . . yes, yes, that's better. Yes, I can see it. Wait!" I walked to the edge of some bushes to the east and knelt, pushing apart the thick branches. There, nestling on the dark loam, was a moonstone set in a ring of gold. I lifted it and returned to the body, no longer averting my eyes from the wounds.

"I have found it, Gareth," I said. "And your killers are on the road to whatever hell they have earned."

The voice in the wind whispered again. I turned to Wulf. His dark eyes were staring at me, his ugly mouth open. Lifting the ring, I offered it to the hunchback. "For a thousand years," I told him, "the Ringwearers have pledged to protect the skulls. Will you take on this task now and allow our friend Gareth to find his rest?"

Wulf backed away. "I want nothing to do with it," he said. "You hear me?"

"Oh, the devil with it," said Mace. "I'll take it!" Scooping the ring from my hand, he tried to place it on his signet finger. But the ring was far too small. "It's made for a child," he complained.

"No," I said gently, not taking my gaze from Wulf. "It was made for a man. Take it, Wulf."

"Why me?"

"I don't know," I admitted, "but the spirit of this man is here with us. He chose you."

"My hands are bigger than Mace's. No way it will fit."

"Try!"

"I can't!" he screamed, backing away. "It'll be the death of me. I know that! I can feel it in my bones. And I hate sorcery!" For a moment only he was silent. "Why did he choose me? Ask him that? Why not Mace?"

"I don't need to. He told me. Because you have the heart, and when you give your word, it is like iron."

He swallowed hard. "He said that? Truly?"

"Truly."

Wulf stumbled forward and took the ring from Mace. It slid easily over his middle finger, sitting snug and tight. "Do I have to make an oath?" he asked.

"You already did," I told him, and the whisper in the wind became a fading sigh. "And he is at peace."

We prized loose the poniards with which Gareth's arms were nailed to the tree and buried his body in the shade of a spreading oak. We were silent as we returned to the ruined cabin, but as we came in sight of the building, Mace pulled me aside, leaving Wulf to walk on to where Piercollo and the women sat in the sunlight.

"What else did he say?" asked Mace.

"What makes you think there was anything else?"

"Ah, Owen! Some men are born to be liars. Others are like you. Now tell me."

"He said there were forces of evil gathering. Very powerful." I turned away, but Mace caught me by the shoulder, spinning me.

"And?"

"He said we couldn't stand against them. Is that what you wanted to hear? Are you satisfied now?"

He smiled grimly. "He said we were going to die, did he not?"

I looked away and nodded. "What now?" I asked him.

He hawked and spit. "We fight," he said. "Where can we run?"

"You will fight on even though you cannot win?"

"Of course I can win, Owen. Azrek is only a man, but I am the Morningstar!" He chuckled, then slapped me on the shoulder.

"You are mocking me," I said sternly.

"Just a little, Owen. Just a little."

The skull of Golgoleth was in the canvas sack where Kaygan had left it, his spear buried in the earth beside it. Wulf swung the sack over his shoulder and sat down away from the others, his face set, his eyes distant.

Mace wandered into the shelter, idly stirring the fire to life, adding wood though the day was warm. Piercollo approached me. "What happened, Owen?" I told him of the spirit conversation and of Wulf's decision. He nodded glumly. "I think the good God is having big joke on us."

"If he is, I fail to see the humor." I took out my harp and tuned the strings. I did not feel like playing, but I idly ran my fingers through the melody of Marchan, a light stream of high notes like the bird song of morning. Piercollo walked away toward Wulf, and Ilka came to sit upon my left, Astiana beside her.

"Ilka has a question for you," said the sister. I stopped playing and forced a smile. "She wishes to know why you kissed her hand."

It was the wrong time for such a conversation, for my heart was heavy and my mind filled with the death of Gareth. I looked into Ilka's sweet, blue eyes and sighed. What could I say? To talk of love at such a time was, I felt, beyond me. The silence grew, and I saw Ilka's eyes cloud with doubt, uncertainty, perhaps dismay. I tried to smile, then I reached out and took her hand once more, raising it to my lips and wishing that I could talk with her as Astiana did. But I could not.

I walked away from them to be by myself in the sunlit forest.

A few months before I had been but a bard, earning a poor living in the taverns and halls of Ziraccu. Now I was an outlaw, a wolfshead, a hunted man. And I walked in the company of a legend. Sitting down on a fallen log, I glanced around me and saw a leg close by, the body hidden by bushes. Rising, I walked toward the corpse; it was Kaygan, his dead eyes staring up at me, his men lying close by, heaped one upon another. Piercollo must have thrown them there while Mace, Wulf, and I were burying Gareth.

Tonight the foxes and carrion would feed; the crows would follow in the next few days, once the stench of decay carried to them.

I began to tremble and felt the beginnings of panic stirring in my belly. How could we stand against Azrek and Cataplas? And even if we were to succeed, we would only bring down upon the Highlands the wrath of Edmund, the Angostin battle king.

How easy it is to talk about standing against darkness. How bright and brave the words sound. But it is one matter to raise your courage like a banner on a single day of battle and quite another to endure day after day, week after week, with every moment promising the kind of death Gareth had suffered.

Birds fluttered from the trees to my left, and I heard the sound of walking horses. My throat was suddenly dry, my heart hammering. Spinning, I ran for the cabin. Wulf was still sitting alone, the sack in his lap.

"Riders!" I said as I ran past him and into the ruined building. Mace had heard me and was instantly on his feet, gathering his bow and notching an arrow to the string. Without a word he leapt past me and loped across the clearing. Piercollo threw his vast pack over his shoulder while Astiana and Ilka gathered their blankets. Only a few heartbeats had passed, but when we stepped back into the open, Wulf and Mace had vanished.

I stepped from the cabin just as a knight rode from the trees. Behind him were three men-at-arms dressed in tunics of gray wool, with leather helms upon their heads. The knight himself was in full armor of shining plate, his cylindrical helm embossed with gold and sporting an eagle with flared wings. His breastplate was plain, but gold had been worked into his shoulder guards and gauntlets, and the pommel of the sword at his side was a ruby as large as a baby's fist. His horse, a gray stallion of at least seventeen hands, was also armored, its chest and flanks protected by chain mail. The knight saw me and raised his arm.

"We seek the Morningstar," he said, his voice muffled by the helm.

I said nothing, and the knight swung his leg over the saddle and dismounted, his armor creaking. Raising his gauntleted hands, he lifted the helm from his head, laying it over the pommel of his saddle.

"We have come a long way, fellow, and would appreciate a little hospitality."

"Hospitality is in short supply," I told him. "What business have you with the Morningstar?"

"That is for he and I to discuss," answered the knight. One of the men-at-arms dismounted and moved alongside him, raising his shoulder guard and unhooking the curved pins that held it in place. This was repeated on the other side, and the plates were lifted clear. The knight himself removed his gauntlets and unhooked the forearm and bicep protectors, laying them across his saddle. Slowly and with care the man-at-arms unhooked the leg guards and greaves, lifting the soleless iron boots from around the knight's legs and feet. At last the nobleman was free of all the armor, and the man-at-arms spread the pieces on a blanket and sat cleaning them with a cloth, which he first dipped in a glass jar of grease.

The knight walked across to where we stood. He was a tall handsome man with dark hair, tightly curled, and fine, delicate features, his eyes deep brown and closely set on either side of a curved Angostin nose. Beardless, he was not much older than Mace or myself, in his early to middle twenties.

"I am Raul Raubert," he said, as if the name had a power. I had not heard it and said so. He shrugged and smiled. "My family has . . . had . . . estates in the north. And you must be Owen Odell, the bard."

"I am," I admitted. "How do you know of me?"

He smiled again. "Who does not know of you? The sorcerer who aids the Morningstar, who cast his spells to save a witch from burning? The tales of you all are spreading far, my friend. Even to Ebracum, I understand." Noticing Astiana and Ilka, he turned away from me and bowed smoothly. "Forgive my bad manners, ladies, but I have ridden far. Even so, that is no excuse for ignoring you. Raul Raubert, Earl of Arkney."

I stepped forward. "The sister is Astiana of the Gastoigne Order. And this is Ilka, one of our company."

"I am charmed," he said. "Your presence here gives grace to the setting." As he swung back to me, his smile faded. "Now to more pressing matters, if you please, Master Odell. Where is the Morningstar?"

"He will make his presence known when he is ready, my lord," I said smoothly. "Do you come to fight him or serve him?"

"Neither," snapped the nobleman. "I am an earl of the kingdom. I serve only the king."

"The Highland king is dead," I pointed out. "Slain by Edmund. If you wish to serve kings, I suggest you travel to Ebracum."

"By heavens, you are a provocative fellow! Beware, sir, lest I order my men to give you a thrashing."

I could not stop myself, and my laughter rang out. "You think me amusing?" stormed the young knight, his face reddening.

"No, I think you are an Angostin born and bred. You stand in a forest, virtually alone, and you think to threaten me. Does it not occur to you that within the next few minutes you might die? Can such a thought seep through the mass of bone between your ears? The Angostins are hated here, whether they be northerners or invaders. And should the Morningstar desire it, he will kill you without warning."

"You mean he is not Angostin?" said Raul, astonished.

"I mean exactly that."

"Then how has he raised a rebellion? Why would anyone follow him?"

"I see you have had a sheltered upbringing, Raul Raubert. And life is about to offer you a number of surprises. But let us begin with the simple observation that there were kings and princes long before the Angostins invaded this land."

His expression hardened. "Do not treat me like a dullard, sir. I am well aware of the kingdom's history. I had thought, however, that the Morningstar was a brother noble who had hidden in the forest following the defeats on the battlefield. Such is the story that is spreading through the land. And he cannot be just another robber—otherwise the angel would not have led me here."

Now it was my turn to be surprised. "Angel? I don't understand."

"I came into the forest three days ago. We camped by a small lake to the west. As I sat by the water's edge, a vision came to me of a beautiful angel floating just above the surface of the lake. She asked my name. I told her. She said I should seek the Morningstar and told me to ride east. Last night she appeared again as I lay beneath the stars. Now I am here, and you tell me the Morningstar is no nobleman. I do not believe it!"

I lifted my hand, palm upward. "Would this be the angel?" I asked him, shaping the sunlight into the image of the young Megan.

"Yes, by God's grace! Who is she?"

"A friend," I told him. "Come inside, my lord, and we shall wait for the Morningstar together."

Piercollo had rebuilt the fire and was setting a pot of broth above it. I introduced him to Raul, but the nobleman merely nodded his head in the giant's direction and then ignored him.

"How goes it beyond the forest?" I asked Raul.

"Badly," he answered, settling himself beside the fire. "We won one battle in the north, scattering the enemy. We felt the tide was turning and were jubilant. But then Edmund himself took the field, and three of our most senior nobles fled during the night with their men. We were crushed then, scattered. Men say that Edmund hanged every man he could catch. They herded the prisoners to a wood near Cousen, and there weren't enough branches for the ropes. So Edmund had gallows built. Six thousand men were slain there.

"Now the forest is the last refuge for men whom Edmund terms rebels. You know he captured Delain, the Earl of Postney, and tried him for treason? He was hanged, partly boiled, and dismembered. How can you try a man for treason when you are not his king?"

I shrugged. "The conquerors make the laws, my lord. Should they judge it treason for a Highlander to breathe mountain air, then it *is* treason."

"How great is the Morningstar's army?"

"It has not yet lost," I said carefully, "and therefore is in better order than the one you left."

"But can it stand against Edmund?"

"Time will answer that, my lord."

"You are being evasive. How many cavalry do you have? How many knights? Men-at-arms?"

"I am but a humble bard, Raul Raubert. These questions must wait until you meet the Morningstar. You have ridden far. Rest for a while." I cast a spell of drowsiness; it is not one of my better enchantments, being a variation on the spells of contentment and warmth, but Raul was already weary, and he yawned and stretched out on his side, his head pillowed on a rolled blanket.

"Wake me . . . when he returns," he said.

"Of course, my lord," I told him, my voice low and soothing.

I rose and moved outside where the men-at-arms were sitting together on the grass. One of them stood and approached me. He was a burly fellow with short-cropped, wispy black hair balding at the crown.

"Where is my lord?" he asked.

"Sleeping. Have you come far?"

"Far enough, by God! We've had our asses kicked from the northern sea to the edge of the forest."

"You took part in the battles?"

"Aye, for what it was worth. Is there any food here? We haven't eaten for three days."

"Of course. Wait here and I'll bring you some broth."

I ate with them, learning their names and their background. The man who had first spoken to me was called Scrymgeour.

He had served the Arkney family for twenty-two of his thirty-seven years, first as a stable boy and then as senior herdsman for their vast herds of cattle. The other two were Cearus and Ciarhan, brothers who had been part of the Arkney contingent. Two hundred men had marched from the north—these three remained.

"How did you escape?" I asked Scrymgeour.

"Blind luck. Lord Raul is not the brightest of men, but he's a bonny fighter. They hit us from both sides, having knights hidden in a wood on our flank. Lord Raul charged at them as they charged at us. We followed, and somehow we cut through them. Some of them swung their mounts to give chase, but as we entered the woods, a mist came up and they lost us. By the time it had cleared, the battle was over, if battle it could be called. God's teeth, you should have seen the bodies. As far as the eye could see! So we headed southwest. God knows why! But he has this dream now that the Morningstar will free the land."

"You don't think that he will?"

"Ain't likely. Look at the stories. He robs a tax column, rescues a witch. What else? I don't doubt he's a hero, but he's not an army, is he?"

"Not yet," I agreed.

He shook his head. "This Edmund is a great warlord, no question. His troops are well disciplined, his captains know their trade, and his tactics are brilliant: hit hard and fast. He's never lost. I've seen three battles now, and believe me, there's no stopping him."

"Why, then, do you stay with the earl?"

"His father asked me to look after him. A great man, he was, and good to me and mine. Fair, you know? Two years ago I was gored by our sire bull—laid up three months. My wage was paid, food was brought to my wife, and the old earl's own surgeon came to tend my wounds. You don't forget that."

"No, I imagine you wouldn't," I agreed. "He died, I take it?"

"He was hanged by Azrek. They had to carry the old man from his sickbed to do it." His face darkened, his eyes narrowing. "Doubt he knew what was going on. Paralyzed, he was. Couldn't speak."

"Why did they hang him?" I asked softly.

"Said he was supporting rebellion, we were told. The news only reached us a fortnight past. That Azrek is the worst kind of scum. The old earl was his uncle, you know. Many's the time he came north as a boy to play in the estates at Arkney. He virtually grew up with Raul. Twisted little swine he was then. I caught him once torturing a puppy. Said it bit him, lying little toad!" He cleared his throat and spit. "But he can fight, too. Good swordsman, best I ever saw. Gilbaud Azrek. I hope I live long enough to ram six inches of steel into his guts!"

It was coming on toward dusk when Mace and Wulf reappeared, their bows across their shoulders. The brothers, Cearus and Ciarhan, were asleep. Scrymgeour was sitting with whetstone in hand, his back to a tree, sharpening his sword with long sweeping strokes.

"What took you so long?" I asked Mace.

"Once we saw you were in no danger, we decided to backtrack them to see if they were alone."

"And they were?"

"Of course. You don't think we'd have come back if it was a trap."

"Nice to know," I told him.

Grinning, he walked past me and approached Scrymgeour. The man-at-arms stood and sheathed his knife.

"You know who I am?" Mace asked him.

"I'd guess you to be the man called Morningstar."

"And that doesn't impress you?"

"Should it?"

"No, it shouldn't, my friend," said Mace. "I don't want dreamers around me, men with their heads full of legends and fables. I want men who know how to keep their swords sharp and their wits sharper."

"Good enough," said Scrymgeour. "They say Azrek has offered two thousand gold pieces for your head."

"The price has some way to go, I think," Mace told him.

"You're not Angostin. You sound like one, but you're not, are you?"

"I am the Morningstar," said Mace. "I am the mountains and the forest. I am the voice and heart of the Highlands. With all of this, do I need to be Angostin?"

"I am not the man you have to convince," said Scrymgeour

at last. "My lord lies sleeping in the shelter. Convince him and you'll have me."

"I like loyalty in a man," said Mace easily, though I could sense his annoyance. He had turned his full power and charm on Scrymgeour, but to no avail, it seemed. He swung away, and we walked toward the shelter. In the few brief strides before we reached it I told him of Raul and the vision Megan had sent him. He nodded and asked no questions.

Inside the ruined cabin I awoke the nobleman. Seeing Mace, he scrambled to his feet, rubbing sleep from his eyes.

"Welcome to my camp, Raul Raubert," said Mace, his voice deepening, the accent sharpening and becoming more Angostin.

"You are . . ."

"I am the man the vision sent you to find."

"To which of the noble houses are you connected, sir?"

"All that is past, Raul. Dead. Burned to ashes. Here I make no distinction between Angostin and Highlander. You understand? Here we are all men, and we will be judged by our actions. Once you were the Earl of Arkney. Now you are a young man abroad in the forest with nothing more than your armor and your weapons. It matters nothing that you are Angostin. Out there you are less than nothing, for you cannot catch a rabbit for your supper, and if you could, I doubt you'd know how to prepare it. You would starve in the summer, freeze to death in the winter. How will being Angostin save you? From this moment you are a Highlander, nothing more and nothing less."

The young man blinked and swung his gaze first to me, then to Wulf and Piercollo, and finally back to Mace.

"I . . . don't know what to say. I am Angostin and proud of it. I don't know if I can put that aside."

"There is always more than one choice in life, Raul," said Mace sternly. "You can, if you wish, ride from here and seek a ship to take you across the sea. You can sign on as a mercenary knight in foreign wars. Or you could put aside your armor and seek employment in the south under another name. Perhaps you could be a scribe or join a monastery. But I hope you will stay here and fight for your country and your people."

"I want to fight," said Raul. "Gilbaud Azrek murdered my father, and I must avenge him. My soul will not rest until I do."

"Then what are you, Raul Raubert?"

"I am a warrior. A knight. What would you have me say?"

"What are you?" repeated Mace. I saw that Scrymgeour and the brothers had entered the shelter and were listening intently. Raul swallowed hard.

"I am a Highlander," he said.

He made as if to kneel, but Mace stepped forward, taking him by the arms and pulling him upright. "I don't want men on their knees," he said. "I want men who will bow the knee to no one."

It was a fine performance, and I could see that the newcomers were all impressed by it. Mace was the very picture of nobility. Astiana smiled softly and shook her head. I caught her eye, and we exchanged smiles.

Mace strode from the cabin, calling me to him. "Well?" he asked me as we moved out of earshot.

"You were very fine," I told him.

"Yes, I surprised myself. How simple it all is. How people long to be led. I wish I'd discovered it years ago."

"What do you plan?"

He turned to me, laying his hand on my shoulder. "You began it, Owen. Now I shall finish it. I will gather an army, and I will take Ziraccu. After that . . . who knows? There will be gold and plunder aplenty. I intend to be rich, Owen. Maybe I shall cross the sea to warmer climes, buy a palace. By God, why stop at a palace?"

"You are mightily pleased with yourself," I snapped, "but may I remind you that we are still a small band of outlaws and there is no army as yet."

"You don't see it, do you?" he responded. "The Earl of Arkney was ready to bend his knee to me—an Angostin prince! Oh, I shall raise an army. No doubt of that. Azrek can have no more than five hundred men at Ziraccu. There are ten times that many warriors in the forest. We will sack the city, and then I shall disappear."

"Why stop at Ziraccu?" I said, intending my voice to be mocking. But he did not notice the tone; instead he laughed aloud.

"One should not be too greedy, my friend. I can win that battle, but once I have, the rebellion will be over. Edmund will march his armies back to the north and crush any who stand in his way. But that will matter nothing, for the Morningstar will be long gone.''

"And leave behind all those who followed you? Yes, that sounds like you, Jarek Mace. You will not have to see the ropes hanging from every tree or the rotting corpses upon them.''

His smile faded. "I did not ask these people to make me their hero. I owe them nothing. I owe you nothing.''

"I agree. But what you said in there was wonderful. No more Angostin overlords, no more serfs and slaves. Merely Highlanders, men judged by their actions and not by their blood. That's worth fighting for, Jarek. That's worth dying for!''

"Nothing is worth dying for!'' he stormed. "And I'll tell you why: because nothing ever changes. There will always be kings, and there will always be serfs. Edmund has conquered the north, but he will die one day, and there will be other civil wars. And yes, the north will be free, because a Highland Edmund will arise. But nothing will change, Owen. Not for the likes of you and me. Not for Wulf or Ilka. The strongest conquer; the weak suffer. It is the world's way.''

"It is the coward's way!'' I stormed. "What man has made, man can change. Yes, there have always been despots and tyrants, but equally there have been benevolent rulers, strong men who cared for their people. But if men followed your philosophy of despair, they would build nothing. What would be the point of fashioning a home from timber and stone? One day the timbers will rot and the roof fall in. Why learn which herbs will conquer which diseases? We are all going to die, anyway. Why teach our children to read? They'll never be able to change anything!''

For a moment he seemed taken aback, but it was more as a response to the passion of my argument than a result of the argument itself. "By God,'' he said, "if you could fight like you can talk, you'd be a formidable opponent.''

"Go ahead, Jarek Mace, mock if you will. It is something you are good at.''

"I am good at many things, Owen,'' he replied. "Keeping myself alive during a bloody war is but one of my talents. Being a hard man to kill is another. Now I am playing this game of yours to the best of my ability. Do not ask for more, for there is no more to give. I care nothing for Angostins. And I am not even a Highlander, I am a lowborn Ikenas. They want to make me Rabain reborn, so be it! They want to follow me to the gates of hell, well, let them. All I want is to see Azrek dead and to have some gold to spend. Is that so bad?''

"You could be king," I said softly. "Can't you see that? The people will rise in their thousands.''

"And Edmund will crush them," he said, hammering his fist into the palm of his left hand for emphasis.

The light was beginning to fail, and we walked back toward the shelter.

I thought I saw a shadow move at the edge of my vision, but when I swung around, there was nothing to see. And night flowed over the clearing, the sky thick with clouds that covered the moon and stars.

I have discovered in my long life that there are many words and phrases that have more power than any spell of magick. The most well-known of these is, of course, *I love you*. But by far the most deadly is *if only*.

For these two words can strip a man's strength, his courage, and his confidence. They become the father of regret and anguish and pain. A man kneels by his dead children in a plague village and thinks, If only we had journeyed south in the summer. A farmer gazes at his rain-ruined crop and believes he would have been a rich man if only he had bred horses instead. Lives are ruled by *if only*.

I have my father to thank for being free of the spell cast by those two words.

"Foolish regret weighs more than iron," he would say. "Every man alive makes mistakes; that's how he learns. Only the weakling talks of life's unfairness or claims he is jinxed by bad luck. The strong man shrugs his shoulders and walks on.''

I remember one winter evening, as we were gathered around the fire, when one of my brothers, Braife, was crying because his favorite hound had been killed in a fight with wolves. He was weeping not just because of the loss but because he had chosen to carry a spear that day and not a bow. With the bow, he said, he might have driven the wolves back.

"Most likely," agreed Aubertain, "but you weren't carrying the bow. It was not even a mistake, nor yet an error of judgment. You were hunting boar, and for that a man needs a long spear. Everything you did was correct, but the dog died. When I was a young knight in the Oversea War, I had a friend called Ranuld, a bright, witty, shining man. We were riding together through a forest, hunting deer, when he suggested trying to the east. I maintained the deer would be in the west, and it was to the west that we rode. We had traveled no more than a mile when a band of robbers leapt from hiding in the undergrowth. We drove them off, of course, killing three, but when they had gone, Ranuld fell from his horse. He had a deep dagger wound in his chest, and it had pierced the lung. He died in my arms then. I screamed my bitterness to the heavens, and I regret his death to this day, but not with guilt. I chose the west because the forest was more dense there and the ground was low, indicating water and good feed for deer. It was not my fault that he died. Nor was it your fault, Braife, that the hound was slain.''

Forgive me, my ghostly friend, for this departure from the trail, but it has relevance.

I thought I saw a darting shadow in the trees, and I did not mention it to Mace or to Wulf. I wish I had, but in my mind at the time I dismissed it as a trick of the fading light or a fox moving stealthily.

But it was Cataplas . . . and I should have guessed it and warned Mace. We could have hunted him down and prevented so many tragedies. Yet I did not think of it. Perhaps Cataplas protected himself with a spell; perhaps I was tired. I do not know. And despite the whispering memory of my father's advice, I still regret that missed moment.

We moved into the shelter. Raul was talking to Astiana, while Piercollo and Ilka were preparing supper. The brothers and Scrymgeour were gambling, using bone dice, and Wulf was sitting by himself with the wrapped skull in his lap.

It was a warm evening with a gentle breeze blowing over the ruins, and I played my harp after supper, summoning sweet melodies of summer dances to entertain the company. Wulf did not join in with his flute, and Piercollo, despite my cajoling, declined to sing.

The hours flowed by. Wulf and Ilka were asleep, but Astiana was entertaining the others with tales of the Elder Days. At first I listened, for there were several I had not heard, but then she moved on to the stories of the Gabala knights, and I wandered away to sit facing the forest, staring out into the darkness.

The stars were bright, and there were few clouds. Wrapped

in a blanket, I sat for perhaps an hour before I felt the need to sleep. It was like warmth stealing over me, bringing with it the memories of childhood—fires in the hearth, my brothers nestling alongside me, the great warhound Nibal on the floor beside the bed, his huge head resting on his paws. I leaned my head to the wall beside me. But I could feel no rough stones; it was as if a feather pillow had been placed there. My body felt light, my mind drifting, and it seemed that I floated gently down through warm water into the mindless security of prebirth.

From far away I could hear a voice calling me. It was irritating, like the buzz of an angry insect. I tried to shut my mind to it, but already the warmth and comfort were drifting away. Angry now, I moved my head. The cold stone rasped against my ear. I groaned and awoke, but the voice remained.

"Beware, Owen! You are in peril!"

Opening my eyes, I saw the image of Megan's face floating before me, shimmering in the darkness. This was the Megan I knew, old and yet unbending. I blinked and yawned, my body slow to function. "Awake, Owen!" she ordered me. My mouth was dry, and I pushed myself to my knees, realizing that a powerful sleep spell had been laid upon me. Swinging my head, I saw that the others were sleeping heavily, sprawled by the dying fire.

Megan disappeared as I got to my feet. The stars were no longer shining, the sky was dark with clouds that sped by with unbelievable speed. I looked out into the night, but there were no trees, only a rolling mist that swirled around the cabin.

"Mace!" I shouted, stumbling toward him. "Wake up!" Grabbing his shoulder, I shook him savagely. His eyes opened dreamily, then shut again. Hauling him up, I slapped his face. Once. Twice. His eyes snapped open.

"What in the devil . . . ?"

"Sorcery! Wake the others!"

He rolled to his feet, snatching up his sword. As it slid from the scabbard, it was shining like moonlight trapped in crystal. I took a deep breath, gathering myself for the coming attack, trying to calm my mind, preparing it for whatever enchantment I could muster. Wulf awoke next, and then Piercollo, Raul, the brothers, and Scrymgeour.

But of Ilka and Astiana there was no sign.

The sound of chanting came from the mist, echoing around

the cabin. At first there seemed no meaning within the noise, but slowly a single word became clear within the chant.

"Golgoleth! Golgoleth! Golgoleth!"

Raul had his sword drawn, but I moved alongside him, saying, "That blade is useless against the foes we face." Wulf had drawn both his short swords, and I took one from him, handing the glittering weapon to the astonished earl. Mace tossed his spare knife to Scrymgeour, and we waited for the attack.

Black-cloaked shapes were moving in the mist, and the chanting continued, low and insistent, sinister and threatening.

"It is only noise," Mace pointed out. I nodded.

The mist slowly cleared. But there were no trees, no forest, no sky.

The ruined cabin stood now within a great gray hall.

A hooded figure was seated upon a white throne, which could have been of ivory but was more likely, I considered, to have been shaped and worked from bone. Around him stood many soldiers, their faces covered by dark helms, curved swords in their hands. One of the soldiers approached the cabin entrance and lifted clear his helm. His face was pale and bloodless, his eyes dark, and when he spoke, elongated canines gleamed white in his lipless mouth.

"Surrender the skull!" he said, his voice cold.

"This is a hall of the dead," I whispered to Mace. "He is—"

"I know what he is," snapped Mace, his gaze locked on the Vampyre's.

"Return it!" echoed the order.

"Come and take it!" Mace told him.

We were standing with our backs to the hearth, bright swords in our hands. But then the thought came. If we were truly in a hall of the dead, then we had been drawn from our bodies. We were souls, not flesh. And in that instant I realized something else.

The cabin could not exist here!

"Form a circle!" I shouted, spinning on my heel, my dagger ready.

The walls of the cabin dissolved, and a score of dark shapes rushed in. The brothers Ciarhan and Cearus had been placed behind us in what we had hoped was a position of safety. Dark blades plunged into them, and they fell. Wulf was the first to react; he charged at the attackers, his silver blade slashing through them. I leapt to join him with my dagger raised.

The Vampyres fell back, dismayed. I glanced down to see if the brothers were still alive, but there was no sign of them or of the slain Vampyres. The stone floor of the hall was bare.

We stood in a circle now, with the Vampyres all around us.

"We cannot fight them all," said Wulf. "What do you suggest, Mace?"

"Take my sword," Mace told Piercollo, then moved back to where Wulf's bow lay. Notching a gleaming arrow to the string, he stepped forward and aimed the shaft at the herald. "Send us back!" he ordered.

"I faced the first death like a man," the herald sneered. "I can face the second in the same way."

I moved alongside Mace and whispered, "Ignore him. Take the one on the throne!" Mace swayed to his right, the arrow flashing through the air, a gleam of silver light that sped toward the breast of the hooded figure. Just before it struck the figure disappeared, and the shaft hammered into the throne. The bones fell apart, crashing to the floor of the hall.

The world spun crazily, and I recall the sensation of falling, spinning through the air.

I awoke with a start to see Astiana leaning over me. As I opened my eyes, she whispered, "Thanks be to God!"

I sat up. Mace was on his knees, rubbing his eyes. Wulf was groaning. Piercollo was sitting by himself with his head in his hands. The earl was kneeling with Scrymgeour beside the bodies of the brothers. There were no marks upon them, but they were cold and dead.

"Where is it?" shouted Wulf suddenly, the sound making me jump. "Where is the skull?"

"The enemy has it," said Astiana softly.

"What are you talking about?" hissed Mace. "We fought them off."

She shook her head. "Last night a vision came to me, warning me of great danger. I tried to rouse you all, but only Ilka awoke. Then a man appeared from the forest, a tall, thin man with a straggly beard. Ilka had her saber ready, and he did not threaten us. He merely said that unless we gave him the skull, none of you would wake. At first I did not believe him, but then he told me to check the heartbeat of the earl's men. Two of them were already dead. Then I knew he spoke the truth.''

"You gave Cataplas the skull?" I said, astonished. "You have delivered a great weapon into the hands of evil men!"

"I did it to save you," she argued, tears in her eyes. "And I was right! You returned!"

I was furious. "We came back . . ." I began.

Mace grabbed my arm. "We returned," he said gently, "thanks to you, Astiana. Now, let us say no more about it."

The dawn was breaking, and the first rays of the morning sun shone down upon us.

"I did the right thing, Owen. I did!" said Astiana, moving alongside me.

My anger died down as swiftly as it had come. "Of course you did," I told her, smiling, and I glanced at Mace.

My father would have liked him. The spell of *if only* had no power over the Morningstar.

It took almost a month to reach the southeastern edges of the forest, where the distant towers of Ziraccu could be seen from the highest hills. All around us the world was changing. Corlan had intercepted five rich convoys and was becoming almost as great a legend as the Morningstar. Brackban had gathered a powerful force of some five hundred men and had fought two skirmishes with Ikenas soldiers, fighting them to a standstill in the first and routing them in the second.

Towns and villages had risen against the invader, and word of the rebellion had reached Ebracum, where Edmund the king was spending the summer and autumn. In one of the ransacked convoys Corlan had found correspondence from the king to Azrek demanding action against the Morningstar, allied to a promise of more troops in the spring.

But this we did not know as we began our journey.

For the first few days, as we traveled, Ilka stayed close beside Astiana, locked in the silent communion of spirit, and I found myself envying the Gastoigne sister her ability. Longing to share it, I became morose and distant. But after some ten days, as we camped in a shallow cave, Ilka came and sat beside me, reaching out and lightly touching my hand. I heard a whisper then, deep in my mind, like the memory of a lost song.

"Owen."

I shivered, and my hand trembled. "Owen," came the voice again, hesitant, lacking in confidence.

"I hear you," I whispered.

She smiled a wondrous smile, her blue eyes wide, tears glistening there. And she said no more for a little while. I took her hand in both of mine, stroking her skin.

"I love you," I told her, my voice breaking.

"Why?" whispered the voice in my mind.

At first I could say nothing. How does a man answer such a question? I rose, drawing her up with me, and we walked from the camp to sit beneath the bright stars. Her face was bathed in silver light, her blond hair shining almost white in the moonlight.

"When I first came to the village," I told her, holding gently to her hand, "I sat in despair by the lakeside. I could see only evil everywhere. And I played my harp—you remember?" She nodded. "And then you came to me, and you danced. You changed the music in my mind and my soul; you were a dancing flame in the winter of my heart. I think from that moment my love for you was born. You understand?"

"Owen Odell," came the voice in my mind, rippling like a song, making a gentle melody of the name. Moving close beside me, she kissed my cheek, and I drew her in to an embrace.

Ilka nestled beside me, and we sat in companionable silence, her head against my chest, but we did not make love that night or for many nights after. In truth I was afraid, for I was inexperienced, and I did not wish our love to be sullied by doing that which had brought her such pain in the past.

What foolishness. Love changes everything, and as a bard—if not as a man—I should have known that simple fact. When at last we lay together on a blanket spread beside a stream, I felt her joy, bright, unfettered, and free. That one fumbling and inexpert union was for her, she told me later, like a bridge of light across a dark stream.

From then on we were inseparable, and even Mace neither made jokes at our expense nor attempted to bed her again. I do not know to this day whether Ilka ever loved me with the same passion I felt for her. And it does not matter. She needed me, and she was happy. This was everything.

Piercollo understood it better than many men would, but he was a man of music and his soul was great. "I am happy for you, my friend," he said as we approached the end of our journey. "She is a good girl. And she deserves happiness—as do you."

"Have you ever been in love?"

For a moment he was silent, then he shook his head and his smile faded. "Only with the great song," he said, and walked on ahead.

My soul was light, my mood merry. Thoughts of Cataplas and Azrek were far from my mind, and the loss of the skull seemed a reason more for relief than for concern. It was a burden, and we were free of it. But Wulf did not see it this way; he had made a promise to Gareth's ghost and felt he had been shamed. No matter how many times Mace and I tried to reassure him, he remained sullen and withdrawn.

"I must get it back," he repeated. "I must."

Astiana was unrepentant about surrendering the skull, which irritated me somewhat. Had she accepted that there might be the slimmest of possibilities that she was wrong, then I would have been the first to say, "Well, what's done is done. Let us forget it." But she did not. Despite all her fine traits and her courage, she had one great failing—an inability to admit to error.

It is baffling to me why so many people find it difficult to say "I was wrong." The words, when spoken with repentance, always turn away wrath. But those who cling to their absolute rightness despite any evidence to the contrary will always arouse anger in their comrades or superiors.

Nonetheless we traveled on in relative good humor, coming at last to Corlan's camp in the village by the lake where I had first met Megan.

It was no surprise—indeed, it was a great joy—to see her sitting outside her cabin with a homespun dress of brown wool clinging to her bony frame, a faded red shawl around her shoulders.

"You took your time," she said as I approached her, smiling.

"Mace wanted to return to the ruined castle to find more weapons of enchantment."

"And he looks right pretty," she said as Mace, sporting a black raven-winged helm and cuirass, marched across the clearing to be greeted by the blond archer, Corlan. The two men embraced as a crowd of warriors looked on, cheering.

Megan ushered Ilka and myself into her cabin, and we sat by the fire in the easy silence only friends can create. Her scorched skin had healed remarkably, without scars or weals.

"It took time," she told me, "but Osian nursed me well. I am glad that you prospered, however. And Mace. He is important, you know—more than you would believe."

"To whom?" I asked, making light of her comment.

"To you. To us. To the future—and the past."

"He is what he always was, Megan—an outlaw, selfish, self-obsessed, and vain. The man will never be a saint."

She chuckled and shook her head. "You do not believe in redemption, Owen? How disappointing. Perhaps Mace will surprise you."

"You believe in him?" I asked, surprised.

"I saw him—a long time ago—produce heroism and courage in a situation of darkness and despair. There is more to him than you see. But that is because you cannot tear yourself from stories and legends. Heroes, in a bard's eyes at least, must be tall and fair, villains dark and terrible. Yet sometimes both can be fair and terrible, the roles shifting and changing. But we will see. All this is for another day. Now there is a more immediate problem, and I think Mace is just learning of it."

"What is that?"

"Ziraccu is a closed city. The gates have been barred for more than two weeks now. People go in—travelers, merchants—but none come out."

"They have the plague?" I whispered, making the sign of the protective cross.

"Worse. But we will wait for Mace. I do not want to have to tell the story twice."

"Does Cataplas have a part in this?"

"Do not concern yourself with him," she said wearily. "His evil is as nothing compared with what is awakening in Ziraccu."

"The skulls?"

"The evil of Golgoleth," she said, her face pale.

Just then we heard excited shouts from outside the cabin, and Mace loomed in the doorway. "Owen, get yourself out here."

Scrambling to my feet, I ran outside. A scouting party of Corlan's hunters had emerged from the forest, two of them holding the arms of a struggling man.

"Well, well," said Mace. "He does not appear so terrifying now, does he?"

I said nothing. For the prisoner was Cataplas . . .

His condition was a shock to me; his hair and beard were matted and filthy, his purple robes torn and mud-stained, the skin of his face loose and sagging, his eyes red-rimmed and bloodshot.

The hunters dragged him toward Mace, but he turned his head and saw me. He smiled wearily.

"Hello, Owen," he said. "How are you?"

A hunter cuffed him on the side of the face, then hissed, "Be silent until you're spoken to, wizard!"

"They are very ill mannered," said Cataplas, still speaking directly to me. The hunter raised his hand again, but Mace stopped him.

Megan walked from the cabin to stand beside me. She sighed as she saw the captive, and her eyes were sorrowful. "Bring him inside," she ordered the men, "and fetch the captains."

"Ah, Megan," said Cataplas sweetly, "how pleasant to see you again. Are you well?"

"That I am, Cataplas. But it is no thanks to you."

"I tried to learn, to follow your wisdom and your teachings. But . . . I am not in the best of health now."

"I see that," she told him. Approaching the guards, she spoke again. "Release his arms. He has no power to cause harm." They obeyed her, and she led the stooped old man into the cabin.

Wulf approached, his eyes angry, a sharp dagger in his hand. "He didn't look so pathetic when he sent the dead after us," he snapped. "Nor when he delivered our souls into hell. Let me cut his heart out, Mace!"

"Perhaps later," agreed Mace, patting the man's twisted shoulder, then following Megan into the cabin. I stood outside, still reeling from the ruin in the eyes of my old master. The man was a shell, his mind almost gone.

The powerful figure of Brackban moved past me. Then the outlaw Corlan approached the cabin, but instead of entering, he came alongside me. I looked up into his gray eyes. His pale hair was tied back in a long ponytail that accentuated the harshness of his features, the high cheekbones, and the cruel mouth.

"A word with you, sorcerer," he said, keeping his voice low. I nodded dumbly. The last thing I needed now was a conversation with a murderous outlaw whom I had tricked into becoming a soldier of the light. Yet I stood there, my face expressionless.

"We all swore an oath," said Corlan, "and I have done my part. You agree?"

"It would appear so," I answered him.

"Now I want to be released from it."

"Why?" I asked him, only half-interested.

He seemed confused, uncertain, and he licked his lips nervously. "I am not a good man," he said at last. "I blame no one for it save myself. And I joined this venture for gain, I admit it. But now . . ." His voice trailed off, and his face reddened. "Listen to what I say, sorcerer; I will have no part in betraying these people. You understand? They look up to me, they trust me. I want my soul released from the promise."

I stared at the man, disbelieving, and he misread my expression.

"I know you think me a fool, and Mace will laugh until his sides split. But there it is. And my men feel as I do—every one of them."

"You think it is any different with Mace?" I countered.

Now it was his turn to be shocked. "What? What do you mean?"

"It is not difficult, Corlan. Look at everything he has done. Where is the profit? What gain has he made, save to be hunted by men and demons? He is the Morningstar. And had we, when first you came to us, asked you to give up the outlaw life and fight for justice, would you have done it? No. You would have laughed at *us*! Can you not see it, my friend? You do not need to be released from the soul oath. You have freed yourselves."

He shook his head. "You mean you tricked me?"

"I would not say tricked. What I offered was to make you rich beyond the dreams of common men. Answer me this: What riches are greater than the love and admiration of your fellows, the trust you spoke of? Would you sell it for gold or gems? I kept my promise, Corlan. You are richer now than ever before. Is that not so?"

He took a deep breath, then nodded.

"Now let us hear what the wizard can tell us," I said, striding away and into the cabin.

There were around a dozen people inside, some of Brackban's new officers and several of Corlan's hunters. Mace was sitting between Raul and Wulf, and the men formed a half circle around Megan and Cataplas. The old seeress was speaking as we entered, and I bowed in apology for interrupting her.

Corlan and I edged our way into the circle, and Megan began again. "I believe I know what is happening in Ziraccu," she said, "but this man was there, and you must listen to what he says." Half turning, she touched Cataplas on the shoulder. "Can you hear me?" she asked him gently.

"You must let me go," he told her. "They will seek me out, you see, and my powers seem to have deserted me."

"First tell us what happened when you returned with the skull."

He began to tremble and blink rapidly, his skeletal frame convulsing. Megan reached out, laid her hand upon his head, and whispered words in a language I had never heard. His eyes closed, and his trembling ceased.

"Can you still hear me, Cataplas?" she whispered.

"I can, my lady." His voice was stronger now, though slow and halting.

"You are carrying the skull of Golgoleth, and you are back in Ziraccu. How do you feel?"

"Very fine. I have them all now. The secrets of the past will be mine. My quest for knowledge and wisdom is almost at an end."

"What do you do?"

"I run through the streets, my heart beating rapidly, and I mount the stairs to my rooms. But Azrek is waiting there. 'You have it?' he demands, stretching out his hand. 'Yes,' I tell him. He is pleased, but he does not smile. 'Show it to me.' The other two skulls are on my desk, and I hesitate. 'Surely we must take care,' I warn him. 'We do not yet understand the power that may be unleashed.'

"He waves his hand angrily, strides forward, and takes the velvet pouch from my hands, pulling it open. So hasty is he that one of the sharp canines pricks his finger, and blood flows from the wound. I feel a surge of force, dark and cold, and I try to raise a spell to protect myself. But it is too late. Azrek staggers back, the skull glowing like a lantern. He tries to drop it, but it holds to his hands. The hands . . . they are glowing, too, every vein shining. I watch as the force flows up his arms. 'Oh, God!' he shouts. 'Help me!' I should have run, but I could not. The light reaches his face—so bright. Then the skull fades and falls to ash. Azrek's head is down, and I cannot see him clearly. But now he looks up. Oh, dear God, he looks up!'' Cataplas said nothing for a moment, his mouth hanging open, a thin stream of spittle running to his chin.

''And then?'' prompted Megan.

''It is not Azrek. The man is tall, his eyes jet-black, his hair white and long. He gazes at me. 'You desire knowledge,' he says, his voice deep and melodious. 'And you shall have it. The wisdom of the universe will be yours. Now fetch me two men, strong men, for my brothers ache to live again.' I did as he bade me, and in the days that passed I watched more soldiers becoming Vampyres; I saw them move among the people of the city, I heard the screams, the begging, the cries of the damned. On the eighth—no, the ninth day—I tried to flee. Early in the morning, with the sun bright and the city apparently deserted. But as I reached the shadows of the postern gate, he was there. Golgoleth. I used all my power against him, but it was as nothing, and he reached out and gripped my face, his long nails piercing the skin. 'Foolish little man,' he said, and I felt the enchantment being drawn out of me. 'Go from here,' he told me. 'Go into the forest. There you will wander, lost and alone, tired and hungry. And I will find you. Just as your love of life reaches its highest point I will find you—and take your soul.' The gate opened, though no hand touched it, and he flung me out into the sunlight. I ran then . . . and ran . . . and ran. And now he is coming for me.'' He began to weep, but Megan whispered words of power, and his head sagged forward.

The men in the room were silent for a few moments, then Mace cleared his throat. ''It can't be true, Megan! His mind has gone, for God's sake.''

''It is true, Morningstar. The Vampyre kings have returned.''

◇ 11 ◇

"I DON'T BELIEVE it," said Brackban, breaking the stunned silence. "It is lunacy. His mind has obviously gone."

"Believe it!" said Megan. "It is true. It was always the fear, from the first moments of Rabain's victory. That is why the skulls were hidden far from each other, why three families took a blood oath to protect them for all time. The Vampyre kings have returned, and Ziraccu is a city in torment. But that is only the beginning. Soon there will be a Vampyre army swarming into the forest. And the defeated will not be allowed to die . . . with every victory Golgoleth's army will swell. And then it will be as it was in this land two thousand years ago, a time of darkness and despair."

"How can we stand against Vampyres?" asked Corlan. The man was visibly shaken, his eyes wide with fear.

"Only as they did then," said Megan softly. "As Rabain did."

"But he was an enchanted warrior," put in Astiana, "or a demon summoned from hell. He fought them with their own powers."

"He was no demon," said Megan. "He was a man, as were his companions. They did what true men always do: They stood against the dark and defied the might of Golgoleth."

She fell silent then, and her eyes sought out Jarek Mace. She was not alone in this. Everyone in the room turned to look at the outlaw warrior.

"I am not Rabain," he said, his jaw set, his expression grim.

"You are the Morningstar," said Megan.

Mace did not reply. Pushing himself to his feet, he left the cabin. I hurried after him, finding him at the lakeside leaning against the jetty rail. The sun was behind the mountains, the sky ablaze, great shafts of light piercing the clouds. The lake was the color of blood.

"What is happening to me?" he asked.

"I don't know," I answered truthfully.

"I am going to leave. I'll go south—right down to the coast. And I'll take a ship across the sea, all the way to Ventria, where the palaces are roofed with gold and the mountains sparkle with precious gems. That's what I'll do."

"And what will happen to the people here?"

He spun on me. "I am not responsible for them! I am not a king, nor would I want to be. For God's sake, Owen! It was all a jest! They took my money. I went after them. I couldn't go alone, so I talked the men of the village into fighting alongside me. And the name was yours, from that stupid conversation about heroes! And that is all it is—a name. I was prepared to lead a force against Azrek—you know that. But a city of Vampyres. Hell's teeth, Owen!"

"A rather apt description, I would have said."

But he did not smile. He shook his head. "Last night I actually prayed. I felt such a fool sending my words up into the night sky. But there was no answer."

"What did you ask?"

"I asked for a way out—and a castle by the sea. What do you think I asked for? I needed guidance. And what do I get? A city full of the undead."

"Corlan came to me earlier," I told him. "He asked to be released from the soul oath."

"You see, he's no fool! He knows when the game is over."

"He told me he did not want any part in trickery or robbery or gain. He and his men have decided not to play the game but to live it. He is fighting now for the people, for the land. For justice, if you will."

"Then I take it back. He is a fool. God's blood!" Suddenly he smashed his fist down on the jetty rail, which shivered under the blow, the wood cracking. Then he sighed and glanced up at the sky. "He must be laughing now," he said.

"Who?"

"God, the devil, whoever was listening when Jarek Mace resorted to prayer. I feel like a pawn in someone else's game.

Whatever I do enhances the legend. If I was to piss in public, someone would swear a golden tree had grown from the spot.''

''And yet you survive, Jarek. Have you considered this? Gareth and the Ringwearers are dead. Demons have been sent against you, sorcerous beasts have hunted you, a host of the dead have come for you. Yet you live! Have you thought of that? I am not a religious man, Jarek. I don't know if there is a God or many gods. But I have seen the halls of hell, and I know there is a power granted to those who wish to do evil. Yet here in this land, because of you, a man like Corlan will forsake his outlaw ways and be prepared to die for the cause. All over the forest men have been lifted by your deeds.''

''My deeds?'' he stormed. ''What have I done save try to stay alive? You know I was merely trying to recover my money in that first attack. And you know also that I had no part in trying to save Megan. And as for Piercollo . . . I wanted the tax money. You think they would sing about me if they knew?''

''You still don't see it, do you?'' I told him. ''There is a power granted to the evil. But in balance there must also be powers given to the good. My father used to study history. He sat us down one evening and told us many stories. But each had a common theme. In the darkest hour of any nation there will always come a man to fit the moment. Here and now, you are that man.''

''I don't want to be. Have I no say in it?''

''I do not believe that you have.''

''I am heading south in the morning. You can believe that!''

We stood then in the gathering darkness, but there was no comfort in the silence. I could feel the tension radiating from him, the bitterness and the frustration. But I knew that he would not leave. He was chained to a destiny he did not desire, and though he would rail against it, he was powerless to change it. On my travels I have met many actors and performers. There was a man once called Habkins, who played out the great dramas—the fall of the king, Caracaun, the dream of lances. One evening before a performance I saw him sitting ashen-faced in the wings. We spoke at some length, and he explained that he hated performing: It always made him nauseous. ''Why, then, do you do it?'' I asked him. He looked at me as if I had asked the most ludicrous question. ''The applause,'' he answered.

I think that was how it was for Jarek Mace. He was a hero in the eyes of the people. They cheered when he approached; they gazed at him with awe and adoration. Were he to turn his back on them, that love would become hate and they would despise him.

We stood for a while, then I returned to the cabin. Cataplas remained in his enchanted sleep, but Megan was sitting beside the fire, idly tossing twigs to the coals and watching them flare into dancing life. Ilka and Astiana were asleep, Wulf and Piercollo sitting at the table quietly throwing dice.

I moved alongside Megan. "You lied to me, lady," I said, keeping my voice barely above a whisper.

"I lie to a lot of people," she answered.

"You told me Cataplas was your teacher when he was your pupil."

She nodded. "I had my reasons, Owen. And they were not evil."

"Who are you?"

She laughed then. "Are you still seeking a princess for your song? I am what you see, an old woman who has lived too long and seen too much. Will Mace stay?"

"I think so. But can we defeat Golgoleth?"

"Rabain did."

"You said that before, but it is no answer."

She sighed. "What answer would you have me give you, Owen?"

I thought about it for a moment, then smiled ruefully. "You have a point."

Suddenly her back stiffened, and she cried out. "What is wrong?" I asked her.

"We must get Cataplas out of here," she shouted, pushing herself to her feet and stumbling to where the sorcerer lay. Shaking his shoulder, she woke him.

"I am tired," he complained. Megan dragged on his arm.

"Golgoleth is coming for you!" she said. His eyes widened, and he scrambled to his feet.

"No!" screamed Megan. "Don't run! I can help you!"

But Cataplas darted through the doorway and into the night. Faster than Megan, I sprinted after him. The moon was shining now, and there was a sound in the air, a beating of invisible wings, a hissing of breath.

The trees to the south began to sway as if a great wind were rushing through them. I saw Mace, still by the rail. He drew his sword, and it shone with a blinding light.

Cataplas stopped, turned, and looked to the south. He did not scream or cry out. Instead he fell to his knees, hands clasped as if in prayer.

The beating of wings grew louder, but there was nothing to be seen. An empty barrel rolled to its side; a shutter snapped away from a window. Thatch from rooftops was torn loose and swirled like snowflakes over the clearing. Men and women ran from their homes, twisting and turning, straining to see the monster that was almost upon them.

Then Cataplas screamed and rose into the air, great wounds appearing on his chest and back. Slowly and with infinite cruelty the invisible demon tore the wizard apart.

Megan ran to the spot below where the dismembered corpse hung in the night sky, some thirty feet in the air. Blood was splashing to the ground around her. Raising her hands, she pointed at the demon, and I saw her lips move, though no sound could be heard above the slow beating of the wings.

A shaft of light flashed from Megan's hand, and for a single terrible moment we saw the demon. It was a creature of bone, no skin, no vital organs, no feathers or fur. Merely white, bleached bones and eyes that burned with dark fire. Its neck was curved, the head round like that of a giant eagle, and its beak was long and hooked. The light blazed around it as it hovered there, and the dark, smoky eyes gazed down at the old woman below. The talons that held the ghastly corpse opened, and the bloody remains fell to the ground. Then the demon swooped.

An arrow of blinding light leapt from the bow of Jarek Mace, lancing upward, the point hammering into the segmented neck. As the demon reared up once more, a second arrow from Wulf struck one of the great wings, snapping a slender bone.

And the creature disappeared.

Megan fell to her knees. Mace and I ran to her side.

The blood on the ground floated up in a red mist before us, forming into a crimson face, the eyes glaring at Mace.

"I let Cataplas find you, Morningstar," came a cold voice. "I wanted you to know your enemy and see your own fate. You cannot hide from me. I know your true name. I can find you wherever you go. There is no hiding place for the enemies of Golgoleth."

Mace said nothing . . . and the face disappeared, blood splashing to the earth.

"Don't ask me why, Mace," said Wulf, "but I get the feeling he doesn't like you."

Mace forced a tight smile and helped Megan to her feet. Men began to gather around, their faces white and fearful in the moonlight.

"What will we do, Morningstar?" asked one.

"Get some sleep," Mace told them, striding away.

Corlan approached me. "The wizard spoke the truth. We are dealing with the powers of hell. Can your enchantment protect us?"

"No, but the arrows Mace gave you can. You saw the shafts shining as they struck the demon. They are crafted with old magick, Corlan."

"We need more than arrows," he said.

"I know."

"I'll fight any man alive, any ten men. What I said today, I meant. I would take on the battle king himself. But . . . God in heaven!"

"Stay calm," I advised him. "We'll talk in the morning." There was nothing else I could say. The evil was growing within the walls of Ziraccu, and I could think of no way to combat it. Megan was a powerful enchanter, but her spell of light had merely irritated the demon. And yet the strength in that spell was ten times, twenty perhaps, greater than anything I could create.

I strode into the cabin where Mace was sitting with Megan and Astiana. She looked old now and very frail. Pulling up a chair, I joined them.

"You can't," I heard Astiana say. "It would be madness."

"Give me another choice," Mace snapped, "and I'll gladly take it." Astiana shook her head and rose. Silently she left the cabin.

"What are you planning?" I asked him.

He ignored me, his gaze switching to Megan. "Well, can *you* help me?" he demanded.

"I will do what I can, Jarek. But you must understand that my strength is not what it was. I am like a child compared with Golgoleth."

"Will you tell me what is going on?" I asked again.

"He is planning to enter Ziraccu," answered Megan.

"It is a city of Vampyres," I said. "You can't mean it."

"As I've just said to Astiana, if you could find another choice, I'd be willing to listen," he answered.

"But what is your plan?"

"I'll scale the walls, find Golgoleth, and cut his bastard head off!"

"Just like that?" I asked him, unable to keep the sarcasm from my voice.

He swore then, and for a moment I thought he would strike me. Instead he turned his head and took a deep breath. Then he spoke. "Do you think I want to do this, Owen?" he said, not looking at me. "But you heard him. He says he can find me anywhere, and Megan tells me that is true. So what do I do? Wait until his Vampyre army enters the forest? Wait until the entire land is peopled by the undead? No."

"Have you considered the possibility that he wants you to come to him? That it was why he appeared to you?"

"Yes, I have."

"And how do you intend fighting off a hundred Vampyres, a thousand?"

"I shall enter the city in sunlight and find him before dark."

"That will not help you greatly," said Megan. "Forget the legends, Jarek. Vampyres do not like sunlight, but they can bear it. There will be sentries, hooded against the glare of the sun. And there will be men who have been spared—evil men, who are now servants of Golgoleth. They also will patrol the walls."

"Then offer me a different plan!" he stormed.

"I cannot," admitted Megan.

"Then it is settled. I'll leave at dawn."

"Alone?" I asked him.

He laughed then, the sound harsh and bitter. "No, I'll ask for volunteers to accompany me, Owen." He sneered. "Everyone loves the Morningstar. I'm sure they'll all want to come."

I wanted to offer, I desperately desired to find the strength to stand beside him. But at that moment I could not. My mouth was dry, my hands trembling. I looked away then.

"I'm going to get a couple of hours sleep," said Mace, rising from the chair and moving to the pallet bed in the corner of the room. Megan did not move; she sat staring into the dying fire, lost in thought.

I needed fresh air, for my stomach felt queasy. I walked outside to find Wulf, Piercollo, Astiana, and Ilka all sitting together in the moonlight. Silently I joined them.

"Did she talk him out of it?" asked Wulf.

"No."

"It's all over, then," said the hunchback, staring down at the ground.

"It is so foolish," put in Astiana. "He is throwing his life away."

Ilka's sweet voice whispered into my mind. *"What will you do, Owen?"*

I looked across at her and swallowed hard. I'd had time to gather my thoughts and my courage. "I'll go with him," I said aloud.

She smiled and nodded. *"As will I."*

"I can't do it," said Wulf. "I want to, mind. Truly I do, but I can't."

"I will come also," said Piercollo. "He rescued me from the torture. I owe him."

Corlan approached with Brackban, Raul Raubert, and Scrymgeour. I stood and waited for them. It was Brackban who spoke first.

"We need to see the Morningstar," he said.

"He is resting. Can it wait?"

"No. Everyone is terrified, on the verge of panic. Already we've lost fifty men. They just packed their belongings and fled into the forest."

"What do you expect Mace to do?"

"Talk to them," said Raul. "Inspire them with a strong speech—give them back their courage."

"It is the wrong time, my friends," I told them softly. "Mace is resting. And he needs that rest. Tomorrow he intends to enter the city and slay the Vampyre kings."

"May God preserve us!" said Corlan, amazed. "Has he lost his mind?"

"No."

"Does he . . . intend to go alone?"

"Yes." I could see the relief in the outlaw's face, and he read my thoughts.

"Do you think me a coward?" he asked.

"Far from it," I said swiftly. "No man would relish the thought of entering Ziraccu. But I have spoken to Mace, and I think he is right. What else can we do? We could run, but they will come after us. We could hide, but they would find us."

"He is a man of courage," said Brackban, "but answer me this: Even if you get into the city and kill the kings, what then? How do you get out?"

"I don't think Mace is concerned with getting out."

We stood in silence then, and I watched their faces: Corlan, hawklike yet fearful; Brackban, strong, deep in thought; Raul Raubert, the nobleman, young and naïve, his expression troubled; and Scrymgeour, his feelings masked.

It was Raul Raubert who broke the silence. "I shall accompany him," he said, his voice shaking.

"Why?" I asked.

"I am a knight," he answered.

"What in hell's name does that mean?" roared Corlan.

Raul was taken aback by the force of the words. "I . . . I don't understand you."

"You're no better than me—just because you were born on silk sheets. A knight, you say? So you've had your shoulder tapped with a king's sword. So what? You're only a man like me."

"I know that," said Raul gently, "but there are vows that a knight makes on the eve of the king's blessing. You know what I am saying, Owen. Can you explain it?"

I sighed. "A knight pledges to support the king and to defend the weak against the strength of evil. It was a vow laid down in law after Rabain destroyed Golgoleth."

"Rabain and the knights," corrected Raul.

"Yes, exactly. Rabain was said to have stormed the gray keep, leading the knights of the White Order."

"So you see," said Raul to Corlan, "I have to go. I don't want to. But I have to."

I could see the torment in Corlan's eyes, and I knew what he was going through. He longed to make the same offer, but like myself in the cabin with Mace, he could not find the courage.

"I know what you are thinking," I said to the outlaw. "You would like to go. But bear this in mind. Some of the leaders must stay or all the men will drift away."

I saw him relax, and he smiled his thanks. Then he shook his head. "Brackban will stay. He is a leader of men. Me? I'm just a . . . a soldier. But I also made an oath. I took the soul fire into my veins. I swore to follow the Morningstar. And I'll do it. By God, I'll do it!"

When Mace emerged, the dawn light was seeping over the forest and the air was rich and fresh, the sky bright and cloudless, the last stars fading against the brightness of the sun. He moved into the doorway, tall and impressive, longbow in hand. He was wearing a dark brown leather jerkin over a shirt of white wool, leaf-green leggings, and knee-length doehide moccasins. He saw us and moved forward, his face expressionless.

"Come to bid me good luck?" he inquired.

"We're coming with you," I said.

"All the way?" he asked, a cynical smile accompanying the words.

"All the way," agreed Corlan. "To the gates of hell and beyond."

Mace said nothing, but his eyes raked the group, pausing on Raul Raubert, then sweeping onto Piercollo, Ilka, and myself. "A motley group of heroes," said Mace, but the smile now was genuine. "Well, let us be on our way."

We set off across the village toward the south and found Megan waiting at the edge of the trees. Mace halted before her. "I could do with a blessing," he said softly.

"For what is worth, you have it," she said, stepping forward and resting her hands on his shoulders. "I will be with you—not in the flesh but close by in the spirit. I cannot fight Golgoleth, but I can guide you and warn you of enemies close by. Now be warned—the Vampyres are fast and strong. They cannot be slain by iron or steel. The enchanted blades will destroy them. Or fire. Nothing else." Turning to Piercollo, she smiled. "Your great strength will avail you nothing, Tuscanian. You must carry a weapon."

"I will find something," he said.

Megan swung to face the rest of us. "You are about to confront enemies of supernatural powers. They are cunning, powerful, and infinitely evil. All goodness is gone from the Vampyres. They live only to feed, and they strike faster than you would believe possible. But they can do more. They can enter your hearts and make you fear them, and with that fear comes a slowing of the reflexes, a dulling of the mind. Do not engage in conversation with any of them. Faced with a Vampyre, you must kill it quickly. This may seem obvious to you now, but hold the thought in your minds. With the Vampyre kings it is even more necessary. They are also sorcerers of great power; they can be slain only by decapitation.''

"That's an inspiring little speech," said Mace.

"I am sorry," Megan told him, "but it is better to know what you face."

Mace sighed but said nothing more. Raul Raubert stepped forward.

"I think we should begin this . . . quest . . . with a prayer," he said. "Let us kneel."

I knew Mace had little faith in any god, yet he was the first to drop to one knee. The others followed until only I remained standing. Raul looked up at me. I felt foolish standing there and joined them. "Lord of all things," said Raul, his voice deep and solemn, "be with your servants this day. Make our hearts pure as we face evil. Make our limbs strong as we fight your enemies. And deliver us from the power of the dark. Amen."

As we rose, Brackban and several of the officers approached us, Astiana with them. She moved alongside Mace. "May God be with you," she said.

"There is a first time for everything," he replied, forcing a smile.

Brackban reached out and took Mace's hand. "Good luck to you, Morningstar," he whispered.

"Don't look so solemn," Mace told him. "We'll be back."

Wulf came running across the clearing, longbow in hand.

"Where do you think you are going, little man?" Mace asked him.

"To Ziraccu," answered the hunchback, scowling. "And don't ask me why, because I don't know."

"The possibility of stupidity should not be ruled out," quoted Mace.

Wulf grunted an obscenity that made us smile, and then Mace led us off toward the southeast.

The day was bright, but the clouds were gathering to the north, dark and gloomy. In the distance we could hear the far-off rumble of thunder. I walked alongside Ilka, holding to her hand. I had tried to dissuade her from accompanying us, but she had been adamant.

"I would worry about you," I told her.

"*And I, you,*" came her voice in my mind. "*But let us face it, Owen, I am a better fighter than you. At least with me there, you'll have someone to protect you.*"

It was a compelling argument, and I felt a little ashamed for accepting it. But in all honesty I was pleased she was there, and with the threat of death so close, I did not want to miss a single moment of her company.

We walked through most of the morning, halting for a brief lunch just after noon. Then we were on our way again, coming in sight of Ziraccu at dusk. The city was silent, the gates locked. But we could see sentries upon the walls, and I wondered what manner of men could agree so readily to serve the needs of the undead. Had they no heart, no conscience? What could they have been offered to make them become servants of evil?

But there was no answer to such a question. There never is. The workings of an evil mind cannot be gauged.

We made camp in a hollow and lit a small fire against a south-facing rock wall where the light could not be seen from the city. There was little conversation at first, for we all faced our fears in our own way. Ilka, whose talent was growing, could touch the minds of all the company, feeling their thoughts. Raul was thinking about his family and brighter, happier days in the north country. Corlan's mind was roaming back over all the dark deeds he had committed, while Wulf was remembering his wife and lost children. Piercollo was recalling days of sunshine and grape harvesting in Tuscania, while Mace was quietly planning his route to the central palace.

"*Why do you love me?*" asked Ilka suddenly.

"You make my soul complete," I whispered, drawing her in close to me, feeling her head resting on my shoulder, her lips against the skin of my neck.

"*You are a romantic, Owen Odell. How will you feel when I am old, wrinkled, and white-haired?*"

"To arrive at that point will mean that we have walked life together, and I will be content. I will have watched each white hair arrive. That will be enough for me."

And we talked long into the night. I told her of my father and brothers and of our estates by the south coast. She in turn spoke of her life. Her mother had died when Ilka was six, and she had been raised by Wulf's older brother and his wife. He had died in a hunting accident, gored to death by a wild bull. After that Wulf had supplied food for the family. Of her rape and mutilation she said nothing, and I did not press her. Better by far, I thought, for those memories to be buried deep, covered by layer after layer of love and friendship.

At last we slept, all save Mace, who sat by the fire deep in thought.

Two hours before dawn he woke me, and I rose silently, not disturbing Ilka. Mace walked away from the campsite, climbing a hill and sitting upon a fallen tree, staring out over the walls of the distant city.

"It will be simple to get in," he said. "Getting out is an altogether different question."

"Let's worry about that when we've killed the kings," I suggested.

He chuckled. "You have great faith in our abilities, bard."

"Well, I don't think this is the time to concern ourselves with failure."

"True." He glanced back toward the campsite. "Why did they come?"

"I can't answer for them all. Raul is here because he is a knight and is sworn to fight against evil; also, he made an oath to you. Corlan is here because he would not allow Raul to appear superior to him. Ilka came because of me. Piercollo owes you his life, and Wulf loves you like a brother. As for me, why, I also came because of you."

"Me? Why?"

"This may sound trite, Jarek, but I believe in the Morningstar. I always did. It doesn't matter that you do not. What is important is what they believe," I said, my arm sweeping out to encompass the forest. "All those people in need of a hero. You are that man; they will remember you all their lives. And in a thousand years they will speak of you as they speak now of Rabain. Who knows, one day perhaps there will be an outlaw standing in this forest who will wonder if he is like the Morningstar."

"This isn't a song, Owen. In all probability we'll die today."

"It will still be a song, Jarek. A great song."

"I hope you are here to sing it," he said, the smile returning.

"But more important than that, I want to be around to hear it, too."

Back at the camp the others were awake, sitting silently waiting for Mace.

"Well," said Wulf as we approached, "what is the plan?"

"There is a storm outfall by the south wall. It branches off through the city sewers, and there are three exits close to the palace. We'll make our way to the first, find the kings, kill them, then get out the same way."

None of us believed it would be that simple, but only Raul Raubert spoke. "There are portcullis gates across the outfall," he said, "and the entrance is sure to be guarded."

"Then keep your hand upon your blade," answered Mace.

A figure moved from the undergrowth, and Mace leapt to his feet with sword in hand, only to relax as he saw that it was Megan. The old woman was wearing a hooded cloak of soft gray wool and carried a long staff of knobbed oak.

"I thought you were remaining in the village," said Mace, sheathing his blade and leading her to the fireside.

"So did I," she answered "but I need to be closer to the city. My powers are weaker than I realized."

None of us spoke for a while, and I sat beside Megan and looked into her face. She was tired—bone-weary. I laid my hand upon her arm. "I want to thank you," I said softly, "for all you have done for me."

She nodded absently, then took a deep breath. "Gather around," she ordered us. One by one we sat before her, all except Mace, who stood back with hand on sword hilt. "When we talk of good or evil in a man," she began, "we do not think of the flesh or the muscle. We speak of the soul. And every man living is capable of both great evil and great good. The soul is like a fire with two colors of flame, white and red. The holy man will build the white. But the red is always there, waiting."

"We have no time for this," said Mace.

"Be patient, Morningstar," she chided him. "Now, the Vampyre is a changed being; he has had the white drawn out of him, and he burns with the red. There is nothing of the white fire within him, nothing that can give birth to kindness, love, or caring. He exists only for himself, only to gratify his appetites. You all know that Vampyres feed on blood. That is not quite true. Blood is life. They feed on the white, and the more they feed, the stronger they become. It is not that they have no souls, but they burn with a different light; they feed on innocence and purity. That is why there will be evil men within that city untouched by the Vampyres, working alongside them. There is so little of the pure spirit within them that there is nothing for the Vampyres to feed on.

"I know you all, your strengths and weaknesses. But know this: The fires in your souls will draw them to you. They will sense your presence, they will feel you close. Whatever you do must be done swiftly. You will have no time to hide and wait—once inside the city, you must strike fast and hard. And if a Vampyre is close, kill it. Remember what I told you: The enchanted blades will cut them down, or fire will consume them. Not so the kings; they must be beheaded.

"I will be with you. But as I said, I have few powers left. Once inside the walls, you will rely only on each other."

"God will be with us," said Raul. "I'm sure of that."

Megan said nothing.

We crouched down in the undergrowth at the edge of the tree line, watching the sentries prowling the battlements.

"Why wait for the dawn?" whispered Wulf. "Surely it would be better to creep down under cover of darkness."

"Look at them," answered Mace, pointing at the sentries. "Hooded and cowled against the coming light. They are Vampyres, and they can see in the dark better than you in bright sunlight. No, we wait. They will leave before the dawn, and then men will replace them. Still sleepy-eyed and half dreaming of warm beds. That's when we move."

"It is a great risk," muttered Corlan.

Mace chuckled. "Seven swords against a Vampyre city, and you talk of risks?"

Corlan grinned. "I think we are all insane."

The sun slowly crept above the eastern mountains, and the sentries disappeared from sight. "Now!" ordered Mace and we left the shelter of the trees and ran down the slope toward the walls. I kept my eyes fixed to the battlements, expecting at any moment to see a line of archers appear with bows bent, arrows aimed at our hearts.

But there was nothing, and we arrived at the cold stone wall apparently undetected. Slowly we traversed the city until we reached the floodgates set below the southern wall. The portcullis was old and rusted, debris clinging to the iron spikes.

"What now?" asked Raul Raubert. "It must be years since this gate was raised. It is rusted solid."

Mace splashed into the murky water and moved closer, examining the latticed iron. Piercollo joined him. The giant reached out and took hold of a vertical bar, his huge hands closing around the rotted iron. The muscles of his arms swelled out and his face reddened with the effort, but slowly the iron twisted in his grip. Flakes of rust fell to the water, then two rivets snapped clear. Transferring his grip, Piercollo began to work on a second vertical bar, then a horizontal. Within minutes he had opened a gap wide enough to allow entry.

Handing his longbow and sword to me, Mace clambered through. I passed his weapons to him and followed. One by one the others joined us until only Piercollo was left on the outside. "I cannot make it larger," he said, and only then did we realize that he could not join us. His massive bulk would never squeeze through so small a gap.

"Wait here for us," said Mace, and without a backward glance headed off into the dark depths of the city sewers.

The stench was nauseatingly strong, and I did not look down at the water swirling around my boots. We heard the skittering of rats, the scratch of tiny talons upon stone, but we waded on into the darkness. When Mace drew his sword, it blazed bright, casting huge shadows on the gleaming walls.

None of us spoke as we moved on. Such was my fear that I do not believe I could have forced words from my mouth.

The tunnel branched to the left, and we followed its winding course. A swimming rat brushed against my shin . . . then another. I drew my dagger and in the ghostly light saw hundreds of the black shapes swimming around me.

I almost panicked then and began to thrash about, kicking out at the rats. Mace waded back to me, grabbing my arms. "Keep calm!" he hissed.

"I can't stand them!"

"They are not harming you, but you are making too much noise!"

I took a deep, shuddering breath, fighting for control. Ilka's voice whispered into my mind: *"I am with you, Owen."* I nodded and swallowed hard, tasting the bile in my mouth.

"I am fine. Lead on, Jarek."

As we rounded yet another bend, I saw a corpse floating face-down in the filthy water. It was bloated, and the stink of corruption was lost amid the foulness of the sewer; the clothes had snagged on a jutting stone. Two rats were sitting on the dead man's back. What a place to die, I thought. What an awful resting place. There were more corpses farther on, some in the water, some on the narrow stone banks. The light of Mace's sword sent shadows across the dead faces, giving the appearance of life and movement. I could not look and fixed my gaze to Corlan's back.

Suddenly Mace halted and glanced to his right. There was an alcove there, deep and shadowed. He stepped toward it, and I saw a child huddled against the stone.

"Don't hurt me!" she pleaded.

"No one will hurt you, little one," I said, moving toward her, but she shrank away, her eyes wide and terrified. Wulf stepped in quickly, gathering a rag doll that lay beside the child and holding it out to her.

"Is this your friend?" he asked, his voice gentle.

"It's Mira," she told him.

"Well, you hold Mira tight because she must be frightened. And I'll carry you. Come on. Otherwise you'll get wet and cold."

"We are cold," she said. Wulf reached for her, and she moved into his embrace, her head resting on his neck.

Mace's sword slashed down, cutting through her back. She made no sound but slid from Wulf's grasp.

"You bastard!" roared Wulf.

"Look at her!" responded Mace. "And feel your neck!"

I came alongside Wulf, saw the tiny puncture wounds in his throat, and glanced down at the child, seeing for the first time the elongated canines and blood upon her lips.

The tiny rag doll floated away.

"Who would make a Vampyre of a child?" asked Raul Raubert.

"How did you know?" I asked Mace.

"Megan told me. She is here with us. Now, let's move on."

Wulf remained staring down at the corpse. "I will avenge you," he promised.

It was difficult to gauge time within the Stygian gloom of the sewers, but it must have been several hours before we finally reached a set of iron steps set into the wall. Far above we could see daylight spearing through a metal grille. Mace sheathed his sword and began to climb. I followed him, anxious to be out in the open air no matter what perils might await us there.

Mace eased the grille clear and clambered swiftly to the cobbled alleyway beyond. One by one we followed him.

The alley was deserted, and I glanced around, trying to get my bearings. To the right was the spire of the Church of Saint Sophas. To the left I could see the tall crenellated keep that was now a museum.

"We are in the merchants' quarter," I said. "The Street of Silk is down there, and that leads to the palace."

Mace nodded and gazed at the sky. The sun was already past its zenith.

"We don't have long," he said grimly.

Sunlight was bright and warm upon their backs as we moved off through the city. Everywhere windows were shuttered, doors bolted. And beyond those whitewashed walls, within the silent buildings, were hundreds of Vampyres awaiting only the night.

"Don't think of that!" warned Ilka.

But I could think of nothing else as we headed for the palace.

As far as we could, we kept to the alleyways and narrow streets, moving silently through the city past deserted market stalls and shops. Mace was in the lead, an arrow notched to his bow. Wulf came next, then Raul, Ilka, and myself. Corlan followed behind, his pale eyes watching every building, every shadowed entrance.

But we saw no living creature. Bodies lay everywhere: livestock, horses, dogs. All drained of blood.

At last we came in sight of the palace, and Mace ducked behind a high wall, beckoning us to follow him. There were two sentries, hooded and cowled, standing in the shadows beneath the arched double doors of the governor's residence. They were some fifty paces distant, and they had not seen us.

"What now?" asked Raul.

Mace leaned in close to Wulf. "Do you think you could hit the man on the left?" he asked.

The hunchback glanced around the wall and sniffed loudly. "As long as he stands still. We need to loose our shafts together.

Either one of them could raise an alarm. You take the one on the right.''

Mace took several deep breaths, then looked at Wulf again. "Ready?''

"Aye.''

The two bowmen stepped out into the street, drawing smoothly back on their bowstrings. "Now!'' ordered Mace. The silver shafts flashed through the air, arcing high and then dropping. Mace's arrow thudded into the chest of the man on the right, who stumbled back. His companion turned, and Wulf's shaft plunged into his neck. "Let's go!'' snapped Mace, sprinting across the open ground toward the palace.

The first guard had fallen to his knees, but now he struggled to rise and began to crawl up the stairs toward the double doors. Corlan pulled up and loosed an arrow that took the man low in the back. He reared upright, them tumbled back down the stairs.

We reached the doors and pushed them open.

The hall inside was deserted, dark hangings blocking the sunlight from the six arched windows within. The smell that greeted us was musty and unpleasant, part mildew, part corruption.

We moved inside, closing the doors behind us. Corridors led off to left and right, and a long staircase lay before us, the carved handrails gleaming with gold leaf.

"Now what?'' whispered Wulf.

"Find the bastards and kill them,'' said Mace, but there was uncertainty in his voice. The hall was huge, the corridors dark and forbidding. Where would we find the kings? Above, below, left, or right? And how long did we have before dark?

"Owen, you and Wulf take the corridor to the left,'' said Mace. "Corlan, you and Ilka go to the right. I'll take the upstairs. Raul, you come with me.''

"You think this is wise?'' I asked him. "Splitting our force this way? Can the spirit of Megan not guide us?''

"She is gone,'' he said softly. "And if we were wise, Owen, we'd follow her lead. Let's move!'' Without another word he ran for the stairs, Raul following.

Wulf swore and laid aside his longbow and quiver. "It will be no use in there,'' he said, drawing his two short swords. The blades were so bright, the eye could not focus upon them. I drew my dagger, and we moved to the left. Within a few paces we found the entrance to a stairwell, winding down below the palace. Wulf swore again, keeping his voice low. "I must be insane," he hissed as he descended the first few stairs. I followed.

For some time we moved through deserted corridors, down stairways. All around us was an eerie silence, and I could hear the ragged, frightened rasp of Wulf's breathing and feel the pounding of my own terrified heart.

The only light was cast by our flickering blades, and all the doorways we came upon were locked from within.

I tapped Wulf on the shoulder. "This is pointless," I whispered. He nodded, and we began to retrace our steps.

"Beware, Owen," hissed the voice of Megan in my mind.

A whisper of movement came from behind me like a breath of cold winter air. I spun and lost my footing—it was that which saved me. Cold, cold hands touched my throat, but I was falling and the grip failed to take. I slashed upward with my dagger, which tore through the black cloak, thudding into flesh beneath. The Vampyre screamed then, a high-pitched awful sound that filled the ears and stunned the mind. My hand froze. But Wulf leapt forward to ram his sword into the creature's mouth, lancing it up through the brain. So great was the light from the blade that the Vampyre's skull glowed red. Pushing myself to my feet, I plunged my dagger into the point where I felt the heart should be. But the blade merely rang against the stone of the wall, numbing my arm, and the creature's cloak and tunic fell to the stairs. Of the Vampyre there was no sign.

From below we heard sounds of movement, and dark shadows played against the wall of the winding stair. "Back!" yelled Wulf.

I stumbled back up the stairs. A dark-cloaked figure moving with awesome speed, faster than a striking snake, grabbed at Wulf's ankle, dragging him down. Without thinking I hurled myself at the creature and sliced the dagger across its face, opening a jagged wound that did not bleed. Wulf stabbed upward, and once more the creature disappeared. But more of them were coming from below, and we turned tail, racing up the stairs and into the hall.

A woman grabbed me, lifting me from my feet, but Wulf stabbed her in the back, and she slumped forward, dropping me to the flagstones and falling across me. As she, too, disappeared, I felt what seemed to be a fine powder settling on my face and into my mouth. It tasted of ash. I retched and spit it out. Wulf spun on his heel and attacked the creatures storming the stairwell, but there were dozens of them, and they forced him back. A dark sword plunged into his chest, and the hunchback roared with pain, then sent a backhand cut that half severed the head of his attacker.

An arrow slammed into the forehead of the leading Vampyre, and he fell. Wulf scrambled back, the black sword still jutting from high in his chest. A second arrow hammered into the throat of an advancing creature, and I saw Corlan throw aside his bow and charge, his silver sword a blur of white light in the gloom of the hall. For a moment only I thought he would kill them all, such was the ferocity of his assault. But a jagged blade ripped into his belly, and he fell into their midst. Wulf's legs gave way, and he slid down the wall, dropping his swords. I ran forward, scooping one from the flagstones just as two of the demonic warriors attacked. I tried to block a thrust, but the speed of the blow dazzled me, and the sword moved past my guard, the blade missing me but the hilt cracking against my shoulder. Pain burst through me in a wave of fire. My arm was useless, and the sword fell from nerveless fingers. Death was before me. I looked into the bone-white face of my opponent, the white-gray eyes, the pallid skin, and the elongated canines. He lowered his sword and grasped my jerkin, dragging me forward as his mouth moved toward my neck.

Just then Ilka appeared, her saber ripping into his throat. Raul Raubert, yelling an ancient battle cry, joined the attack. And Wulf, brave Wulf, gathered his swords and heaved himself to his feet, half stumbling into the attack.

The Vampyres fell back, and at the rear of the group I saw a creature taller than the rest, face long and fine-boned, eyes slanted and dark. It was not the face I had seen formed from the blood of Cataplas, but the features were similar, and I knew that this was one of the Vampyre kings. My right arm was still numb, but drawing my dagger left-handed, I hurled it with all my strength. I am not and never have been skilled with weapons, but the blade flew to its target as if guided by the hand of destiny. It entered the creature's right eye and buried itself all the way to the hilt. He screamed, and his slender hands reached up, grabbing the hilt. But then he sagged and slid to the floor.

He did not disappear, but vainly sought to pluck the weapon loose.

"Raul!" I shouted. "The head! The head!" And I pointed at the struggling Vampyre king. Raul Raubert raced forward, his sword hissing through the air. It cleaved the creature's neck, and the head tilted. Yet still the hands scrabbled at the hilt. Raul struck again, and now the head came loose, rolling to the flagstones.

In that moment every Vampyre in the hall disappeared, and the flesh vanished from the corpse of the king. Close to the skeleton lay a skull seemingly carved from ivory, and in the empty eyesocket was my dagger.

I stumbled toward it, retrieving the weapon.

"Was that Golgoleth?" asked Raul. I shook my head. Corlan groaned, and I made my way to him, kneeling at his side. Blood was staining his chin, and his eyes had the faraway look of the dying.

"Is . . . Ilka safe?" he whispered.

"Yes."

His eyes closed. "They . . . took her. I'm . . . glad . . . she escaped."

"Lie still. Rest." I wanted to say words of comfort, but I had none. What could I promise this man, this killer, this hero? Redemption? Forgiveness and the promise of eternal life? I did not believe in those things. But I needed to say no more, for he died there without another word.

Raul had moved to the open doors. "God's teeth!" he said. I ran to the sunlit entrance. Outside, hooded against the sunshine, hundreds more of the creatures were swarming across the market square. Raul and I slammed shut the doors, lifting the bronze reinforced bar into place to secure them.

"It is not going to hold them for long," he warned. A great hammering started on the doors, the wood shivering.

"We've got to find Mace," I said.

Wulf was sitting with his back to the wall, the skull in his lap. His face was gray, and blood was seeping from the wound in his chest. The sword was still jutting there; it was high, just under the collarbone. "Can you walk?" I asked the hunchback.

He shook his head. "You go on," he said.

"There is danger close by," came Megan's voice. I spun, but the hall was empty.

"You are wrong, lady," I said aloud.

"I can feel it, moving closer to you. Deadly. Closer."

I swung again, but there was nothing save the creatures beyond the gates, and they could not effect a swift entry.

Something moved behind me, and I turned and saw Ilka approaching. Opening my arms, I took her into an embrace. My hands stroked the skin of her back, feeling the flesh beneath the thin tunic. "You are very cold," I said, rubbing her harder. Her head was resting on my shoulder, and I felt the chill of her face against my neck.

And in that instant I knew.

"Oh, dear God," I whispered, holding her close to me, waiting for the fangs to open my throat.

I felt her hand move to my side, but there was no sharp bite to my jugular. Instead she slumped into me, and I heard her sweet voice echo in my mind for the last time. Her head fell back. Her eyes were still beautiful, and I did not look at her mouth, not wishing to see the Vampyre canines.

I glanced down to see that she had taken my dagger and plunged it into her breast. I lowered her to the flagstones, tears blurring my vision, seeing not the Vampyre but the lover I would never hold again.

She died there, and her body did not disappear.

Raul laid his hand on my shoulder. "She saved you," he said, his voice low. "She was a Vampyre, and yet she saved you."

"It is almost upon you, Owen," Megan's voice screamed inside my skull. *"Run!"*

"The danger is past," I whispered, still cradling Ilka's body in my arms.

"No! I can feel it!"

Even through my grief I felt the sudden chill of understanding. "Megan!" I cried. "It is not here. The danger is with you. It is coming for you!"

But there was no answer. No link.

The numbness had faded from my shoulder, and I laid Ilka's body down and took up her silver saber.

Somewhere within this Vampyre-haunted palace was Golgoleth.

And I would find him.

Astiana awoke in the night, a dark dream hovering at the edge of memory yet slipping away before she could fasten to it. She sat up; the cabin was empty and cold, and she rose from the bed.

Mace and the others had gone, and she felt alone.

No, she realized, not just alone. Desolate. Empty.

You fool, she told herself, remembering again that night on the journey from the ruined cabin. Everyone had been asleep, save Piercollo, who was on watch. Astiana had felt the need for solitude and had wandered away into the forest to sit beside a silver stream. Swiftly she had disrobed, putting aside the thick woolen habit and her underclothes of cotton. The stream was icy cold, but she enjoyed the silky flow of the water over her skin.

Mace had found her there.

"You should not stray from the camp," he had said. "There are still robbers in these woods."

"I have the Morningstar to protect me," she had snapped, angry to be disturbed and sitting up with her arms across her chest.

"No need to be frightened, Sister," he had said. "I'll not molest you."

"I do not fear you," she had told him.

"You've a good body. Shame you've decided to waste it."

"How dare you!" she had stormed, rising from the water. "You speak of waste? I have spent my life helping others, healing the sick, giving hope to those who have no dreams. What right have you to speak to me of waste? What have you ever done save gratify your lust?"

"Not much," he had admitted. "And you are quite correct; it was a stupid thing to say." He had smiled suddenly and removed his shirt, tossing it to her. "Here! Dry yourself. You'll catch cold."

The shirt smelled of wood smoke and sweat, but she had used it anyway, then clothed herself.

"Thank you," she had told him. "Both for the shirt and for your courtesy." She was angry still but struggled to mask it. Although she would never have contemplated allowing Mace to make love to her, nevertheless she was irritated that despite finding her naked, he had made no attempt to seduce her.

"What will you do," she had asked him, "when the people

finally realize what you are, when they see you are not a legend?''

"I won't be there to suffer it, lady," he had told her.

The sharp retort died in her throat, for at first she thought he meant he would flee and then she realized what he was saying. Her resentment of him vanished like a spent candle.

"I'm sorry I said that," she whispered. "The words were born of anger."

He had shrugged and grinned. "The truth mostly is, I find."

"I don't want you to die, Jarek."

"Why should you care?" he had asked, pushing himself to his feet. "You don't even like me."

"No, I don't. But I love you." The words had rushed out before she could stop them, and strangely, she was not surprised. It was as if Mace's readiness to die for the cause had breached the wall between them.

"Oh, I know that," he had said. "Most women do."

Then he had walked away.

She had scarcely spoken to him after that.

Now he was gone. They were all gone.

Astiana sighed. I should be with them, she thought. I am a Gastoigne sister and pledged to stand for the light against the gathering dark.

Silently she left the cabin and walked across the clearing toward the night-dark forest.

She traveled for hours, long past the dawn, arriving in mid-afternoon at the remains of their camp fire. Wearily she sat by the ashes, her thoughts once more on the night by the stream.

Her limbs felt heavy, drained of energy, and she lay back on the soft ground with her head pillowed on her arm. Almost at once she fell asleep and dreamed she was floating beneath the stars in a jet-black sky. There was comfort in the dream, freedom from care and fear, and she soared through the night unfettered.

Below her lay Ziraccu, dark and gloomy, a black crown upon a hill. She flew closer, seeing the Vampyre mob beating on the gates of the palace. Such was the power of the evil emanating from the scene that it pushed her back, as if she had been touched by hellfire. She fled the city and found herself hovering above a hillside where a gray hooded figure was kneeling with head bowed.

Movement caught her eye. A man was creeping toward the gray-cloaked Megan, and in his hand was a dark-bladed knife.

"Megan!" screamed Astiana.

The hooded head came up, but the man sprang forward to bury his knife into her back. Megan fell and twisted, her hand pointing up at the assassin. Light blazed from her fingers, enveloping him.

And his screams were terrible to hear.

His flesh bubbled and burned, fire blazing from his eyes. The body collapsed, searing flames bursting through his clothes. Within seconds there was nothing on the hillside save a severed foot and half a hand.

Megan struggled to her knees, her bony fingers trying to reach the knife at her back.

Astiana's spirit sped back to her sleeping body, and her eyes opened. Rolling to her feet, she ran for the hillside.

Megan had fallen once more and was lying facedown on the grass. Astiana gently turned her, cradling the old woman's head. "Megan! Megan!"

"I . . . am . . . alive," whispered Megan.

A dark moon shadow feel across them. Astiana glanced up— and her blood froze.

Silhouetted against the moonlight was a tall, wide-shouldered man with a face as pale as ivory and eyes the color of blood. Upon his long white hair sat a thin crown of silver, inset with pale gems.

"Carleth!" hissed Megan, struggling to rise. The man smiled, and the elongated canines gleamed in the moonlight. Astiana could not move even when he bent and reached for her, his fingers curling into the folds of her habit. Slowly he drew her to her feet.

"I will give you immortality," he said, his voice low and seductive. "And you will serve me until the world ends."

"Let her go, demon!"

Carleth's head turned slowly, and Astiana saw Piercollo standing close by. The giant was unarmed, and Carleth gave a soft laugh. "You wish to stop me, human? Come, then. Come to Carleth."

"No!" shouted Astiana. "Run!"

The Vampyre king hurled her aside and advanced on Piercollo.

"My, but you are a strong fellow," said Carleth. "I can see that you have great power in those limbs. But you have a lesson to learn. This is real strength!" With stunning speed he launched himself at the Tuscanian, his fist cracking against the giant's chin. Piercollo was lifted from his feet and sent spinning to the grass.

"Astiana!" called Megan weakly.

Astiana, still half-stunned, crawled to her. Megan drew her dagger from the sheath at her side and pushed it into Astiana's hand. The blade was shining brightly. "Kill it!" Megan ordered.

Piercollo rolled to his knees, then staggered upright. Once more the Vampyre attacked, but this time Piercollo's huge hands closed upon its throat, squeezing tight.

"I do not need to breathe," said Carleth, untroubled by the pressure. His arms lashed up and out, breaking the giant's grip with ease. Piercollo launched a fist, but Carleth swayed aside and laughed aloud. "How pitiful you are." He struck Piercollo in the face, and Astiana heard the breaking of bone.

Rising to her feet, she ran behind the Vampyre king, plunging the enchanted blade deep into his back. Carleth screamed and swung toward her. Piercollo leapt forward, his right arm snaking around Carleth's neck and his left hand pushing down on the creature's shoulder. The giant's attack forced Carleth to his knees; then, with a titanic heave, Piercollo threw his weight back while pushing forward and down with his left arm. Carleth's neck stretched and snapped, the skin of the throat ripping and exposing the bone. Still the Vampyre struggled, and Piercollo was almost thrown clear. But with one more awesome effort he ripped the head from the shoulders.

Carleth's body fell to the ground, the head falling from Piercollo's grip.

The giant took a deep breath and rose, moving toward Astiana. "He did not hurt you?" he asked.

"No. Where are the others?"

"Inside," he said. "I think all is not well."

That is the story as Astiana told it to me. And Piercollo's words were uncannily accurate.

I took the stairs two at a time, Raul following me. I cared nothing now for life, for in my despair I thought nothing of a future without Ilka. All that drove me was the desire to see Golgoleth die. For with his death, the city would be free.

At the top of the stairs I halted. Ahead of me was a warren of corridors, and I swung to Raul. "Where did you last see Mace?" I asked him.

"We came up here and separated. I went left, but the doors were all bolted. There's a second stair leading up to the next level. I think Mace must have taken it."

I had never been in the governor's palace, and I struggled to remember all I had heard of it. Built some two hundred years before by one of the Highland Angostin kings, it now housed works of art, sculptures and paintings plundered from the continent during the Oversea War. There was a hall containing almost two thousand paintings, some of them hundreds of years old; that was on the third level. There was a window to my left, covered by a velvet hanging. Running to it, I tore the cloth loose, allowing light to spear into the gloom of the corridors.

But it was moonlight.

I moved forward toward the rising stairs. A black cloak was draped across the banister rail at the top, all that remained of a Vampyre warrior. "You were right," I told Raul. "Mace went this way." The saber hilt was slippery with sweat, and I wiped it dry on my tunic. Then I mounted the stairs. From below we could hear the relentless hammering on the doors, the creaking and the groaning of the wood.

We came to the top of the stairs, and I saw Mace's bow and quiver lying in the hallway. More than this, we heard the clash of sword blades coming from beyond an open doorway. Before I could stop him, Raul had leapt ahead of me, running to aid Mace.

But my mind was cool, my thoughts clear as ice crystals. I ran to where Mace's bow lay and looped the quiver over my shoulder. Then, taking up the bow, I moved to the left of the doorway, peering around the frame. The room beyond was full of dark-cloaked warriors forming a great circle around two swordsmen. I saw Raul overpowered and dragged forward, his arms pinned behind him, and then I watched as Mace and Golgoleth circled one another. The Vampyre king was tall, wide-shouldered, and powerful, moving with a speed both unnatural and chilling. For all his great skill, Mace looked like a clumsy farmhand, his sword flailing ineffectually.

Golgoleth was toying with him, taunting him. "You pitiful creature. Where has your skill gone? I expected more from you." The hall was lit by scores of red-glassed lanterns whose light made the scene glow like a vision of hell.

Mace was bleeding from many cuts to his face, arms, and body, but still he stood, moving warily, sword raised. I glanced up. All around the hall was a balcony, and many more Vampyres were crowded there, looking down on the battle. Golgoleth attacked once more, his body a blur, his black sword lancing out like a serpent's tongue. Mace threw himself to his right, rolling to his feet, but a fresh cut had appeared on his right cheek, and the skin was flapping, blood gushing to his jerkin.

"You worm!" roared Golgoleth. "For all that you have cost me I will make you suffer. There will be no eternity in the darkside for you. I will not make you one of us. You will know pain no mortal has ever experienced, and I will not let you die."

"Talk is cheap, you ugly whoreson!" snarled Mace, but it was a defiance born more of courage than of hope.

Laying down the saber, I notched an arrow to Mace's bow. Drawing back on the string, I aimed the shaft.

Just then something struck me from behind, hurling me to the floor, and I felt a weight upon my back and fangs ripping at my throat. I tried to roll, to twist my head, but the pain was excruciating. My face was pressed to the wooden floorboards; my hands scrabbled toward the saber lying closeby, but the Vampyre's fingers locked to my wrist.

I heard a hissing sound, then a crunching thud accompanied by the splintering of bone, and the weight vanished. I rolled to see Wulf on his knees at the far end of the corridor, his bow in his hands. A dark cloak was draped across me, a silver arrow upon it. I pushed myself to my feet.

The Vampyres within the hall had turned and were advancing toward me. Beyond them Mace had been disarmed, and Golgoleth was holding him aloft by the throat, shaking him like a trapped rat.

Swiftly I gathered the bow, notched an arrow, and loosed it at the broad back of the Vampyre lord. The shaft slashed through the air. As soon as it was loosed, I knew I had missed the killing shot, but the arrow plunged through Golgoleth's forearm. He did not even seem to notice it, nor did he loosen his hold on the dangling figure of Jarek Mace.

But just as the Vampyres reached me, I caught a glimpse of Mace reaching out and grabbing the jutting shaft, tearing it loose, and plunging it into Golgoleth's throat. A terrible scream rent the air, and the Vampyres advancing on me halted and spun. Releasing his hold on Mace, Golgoleth staggered back. Mace fell to the floor, but as Vampyres swarmed toward him, he gathered his sword and leapt forward, the blade of light sweeping in a vicious horizontal cut that hacked through Golgoleth's neck in one awesome stroke.

Within a single heartbeat the entire hall was empty and silent save for Raul Raubert and the bloody but triumphant Jarek Mace.

The Morningstar fell to his knees. I sank to the floor, my back to the wall, and saw again my lovely Ilka. Emptiness flooded my soul.

And I began to weep.

Raul approached, putting his arms around me. Thankfully he said nothing, and I was comforted by his presence. After a while Mace, carrying the skull of Golgoleth, joined us. Raul explained about Ilka and the others, and Mace patted my shoulder and walked out into the corridor.

Raul helped me to my feet, and we followed the Morningstar. He was sitting beside the ashen-faced hunchback. "All this for a few skulls," said Mace with a forced grin.

"You ain't so . . . handsome now," offered Wulf.

"Women love scars," countered Mace. Slowly we made our way down to the lower hall, Raul half carrying Wulf, and I supporting the Morningstar.

Night had fallen, but the city was empty and silent, and we sat on the steps of the palace and felt the cool night breeze upon our faces. The wound in my throat was stinging, but I scarcely felt it.

After a while we heard the sound of marching men and saw Brackban, Piercollo, and hundreds of warriors come into sight. Brackban ran to us, kneeling before Mace.

"By God, you did it!" he cried.

Mace was too weary to respond. "There is still one more king," I said.

Brackban shook his head and told me of Piercollo's battle with Carleth. "How is Megan?" I asked.

His face was solemn as he answered me. "She is alive, but

she has a knife wound in her back—deep and, I fear, mortal."
I closed my eyes, a great weariness settling over me. "You
won," I heard him say.

"I lost something more valuable, something more precious . . ." I could say no more. Pushing myself to my feet,
I wandered away into the deserted city.

◇ 12 ◇

MOONLIGHT BATHED THE silent city as I walked. I had no feeling for direction and was moving aimlessly. In the distance I could hear Brackban's men singing of the victory, their laughter echoing in the narrow streets.

I turned a corner and found myself standing in the same alleyway where I had first seen Jarek Mace leap from the balcony. It seemed as if centuries had passed since then . . . a different world. I sat down on the cobbles and wished that I had my harp. I could not even remember the name of the girl we had rescued. There were no more tears inside me at that time. Ilka was gone, and I felt the emptiness that comes with the cleaving of shared memories. Part of the joy of life is to sit with a loved one and say, "Do you remember that day on the mountain?" Or perhaps a walk by a stream or a dance at midsummer, when the rains come. Joys continually given the breath of life by the speaking of them.

We had made love only nine times. And I recall every precious moment, every touch and kiss, the sweetness of her breath, the smell of her hair.

I sat alone, my mind floating back through the days in the forest. A door creaked, and I looked up to see an elderly woman and a small child emerging into the night. The woman was skeletally thin, her shoulders bowed. The child was standing, clinging to her hand, her eyes wide and frightened.

"It is safe," I said. "They are all dead."

"I heard the singing," said the old woman. "The . . . creatures did not sing."

I stood then and approached them, but the child shrank back

against the woman's skirts. "How did you escape them?" I asked.

"We hid in the attic," she told me. "We have been there for . . . the lord knows how long."

I took her by the arm and led her back toward the palace. She was weak, as was the child. They had eaten nothing in all that time and had survived only on the rainwater that flowed down through a crack in the roof. At first the child would not suffer me to carry her, but her tiny body had no strength in it and she began to cry. I lifted her then, hugging her to me, and her head fell to my shoulder and she slept.

As we made our slow way through the city, other survivors crept out from their hiding places, drawn by the songs and laughter from the palace. Man is a great survivor. Floods, famine, drought, war, and pestilence—he will defeat them all. Even in Ziraccu, in a city of Vampyres, there were those who had found sanctuary, surviving against all odds.

But of the eighteen thousand original inhabitants, no more than six hundred remained.

By morning we had gathered them all. I walked among them and will never forget their eyes. All had that haunted look. None would ever come close to forgetting the terror, for many had been hunted by their own loved ones, friends, and brothers. Husbands had made prey of their wives; children, their parents.

Oh, Cataplas, how great an evil you unleashed upon the world! And it was an evil of the most vile kind—men, women, and children turned into Vampyres against their will, becoming creatures of vileness themselves. Men talk of the judgment of God. What did you say, Cataplas, when—if—you faced that inquisition? "It was not my fault? I didn't know?" Will that be considered a defense? I think not. What evil is greater than to force others to walk the path of darkness?

Of the six hundred survivors, some seventeen died within the next three days, some because they were malnourished, others because they were old and frail. But most, I think, merely gave up, having nothing to live for.

Brackban organized teams of helpers, and people from the surrounding areas moved into the city, taking over shops and stores, taverns and houses. I could not stay there. Neither could the Morningstar, and we walked together back into the forest.

But not before we had once more dealt with the skulls. Brack-

ban took the first and hid it somewhere in the city. Wulf took
the second, and I the third. I buried mine beneath the roots of
a huge oak. What Wulf did with his I never asked.

Jarek Mace said little as we walked on that first day. His
wounds were troubling him, but there was more on his mind
than merely pain.

We built a fire in a shallow cave and boiled some oats in a
makeshift bowl of bark. I sat and watched the flames licking at
the wood yet unable to burn through because the water within
the bowl was absorbing the heat. We shared the porridge and
then placed the empty bowl back on the fire. It was consumed
almost instantly, as if the blaze were exacting its revenge for
being thwarted.

"He died well then, Corlan?" asked Mace, breaking the long
silence.

"Yes. He charged them all fearlessly."

He shook his head. "Who would have thought it? Is he in
heaven, do you think?"

I shrugged. "I have never believed in paradise. But we have
seen hell, Jarek. So who knows?"

"I like to think he might be. But then, how would they weigh
the balances? He was a robber and a killer. Did this one act of
courage eclipse the rest of his deeds?" He sighed and forced a
smile. "Listen to me! Jarek Mace talking of paradise."

"I think you are talking of redemption, and yes, I believe no
man is so evil that he cannot redeem himself. He saved my life.
No question of that. He acted with great heroism—as did you."

"Nonsense! I went there because the bastard was hunting me.
I was looking out for myself."

"There is no one else here, Jarek," I said wearily. "Just you
and I. So let us drop the pretense. You are the Morningstar. It
is your destiny. You know it, and I know it. And you journeyed
to the heart of the evil because you had to, because that is what
being the Morningstar is all about. You are no longer Jarek Mace
the outlaw, the man of bitterness. You are the lord of the forest,
and the people worship you. In a thousand years they will speak
of you. You have changed, my friend. Why not admit it?"

"Still the romantic, Owen? I have not changed."

"You are wrong. You once told me that friendship was merely
a word used to describe one man needing some service from
another. You said it did not exist in the form bards use. But

Corlan died for you and the people of this land. You know that is true. And when you were ready to tackle Golgoleth alone, you did not expect anyone to accompany you. But we did. And something else—though you will not admit it—if I or Wulf had been in your place and set off alone to the Vampyre city, you would have accompanied us even if Golgoleth had never heard your name.''

"Pah! Dream on, bard! You do not know me at all, and I will not have you force your heroic images onto me. I like you, Owen. I like Wulf, and yes, I would risk much for you both. That much I have learned. But I will always look after my own interest first. Always! And I will give my life for no man.''

His face was flushed and angry, his eyes bright with a kind of fear. I was about to speak, but I saw in him then a secret terror, and I knew with great certainty that he understood the inevitability of his destiny. I felt cold suddenly, and into my mind came the image of the garlanded bull being led through the streets, with the people cheering and throwing flowers beneath its feet. But at the top of the hill, in the bright sunshine, waited the priest with the curved knife and the altar upon which the blood would run.

Our eyes held, and I knew that similar thoughts were filling the mind of Jarek Mace. He licked his lips and tried to smile, and I knew what he would say, what, indeed, he *had* to say, the words like a charm to ward off the evil of that final day in the sun.

"I am not the Morningstar, Owen. I am not.''

But we both knew. He was watching my face intently. "Well, say something, Owen, even if it is to disagree.''

I looked away. "I don't know what the future holds," I said, "but we are friends, and I will stand beside you.''

"That may not be a safe place to be," he whispered.

"I would have it no other way.''

The village was almost unrecognizable from the sleepy hamlet where I had first seen Ilka and Megan, where I had learned to cure meats and had filled my days with the splitting of logs and the playing of the harp. There were canvas tents pitched all along the lakeside, makeshift shelters erected close to the trees. Hundreds of people had moved down from the mountains as word of the fall of Ziraccu had spread through the forest.

Even as Mace and I emerged from the woods we could see a line of wagons on the far hills, wending its way down to the settlement.

People were milling around in the town center, and such was the crush that Mace passed unrecognized within it until we reached the calm of Megan's cabin.

The old woman was lying on her back, apparently asleep, an elderly man sitting beside her. It was the same man who had tended her in the village of Ocrey when she had been burned by Cataplas' spell.

"How is she, Osian?" I asked him. He looked up, his pale blue eyes cold and unwelcoming.

"She is preparing for the journey," he said, the words harsh, his bitterness plain.

Megan opened her eyes, her head tilting on the pillow. "The conquering heroes return," she whispered.

The room smelled of stale sweat and the sickly sweet aroma of rotting flesh. Her face was gray, the skin beneath the eyes and beside the mouth tinged with blue. I swallowed hard, trying to compose my features so that the shock of her condition would not register. It was futile. My face was an open window, and the clouds of my sorrow were plain for her to see. "I am dying, Owen," she said. "Come, sit beside me."

Osian rose, his old joints creaking, and slowly made his way out into the sunlight. I sat on the bed and took hold of Megan's hand. The skin was hot and dry, and absence of flesh making talons of her fingers.

"I am so sorry," I said.

"Carleth's assassin had poison upon his blade," she told me. "Help me upright!"

Mace fetched a second pillow, and I lifted her into position. She weighed next to nothing, and her head sagged back on a neck too thin to support it. "I should be dead by now," she said, "but my talent keeps my soul caged in this rotting shell." She smiled weakly at Mace. "Go out into the sun, Morningstar," she ordered him. He backed away swiftly, gratefully, without a word, and Megan and I were alone. "Like many strong men he cannot stand the sight of sickness," she said. Her head rolled on the pillow, and her gaze fastened to mine. "Such heartache you have suffered, Owen. Such pain."

I nodded but did not speak. "She was a good girl, bonny and brave," she continued.

"Don't say any more," I pleaded, for I could feel myself losing control. I took a deep breath. "Let us talk of other things."

"Do not let your grief make you push her away," she warned me, "for then she would be truly dead."

"I think of her all the time, Megan. I just cannot speak of her."

"You won, poet. You destroyed the evil; you made the land safe. But it is not over."

"The Vampyre kings will not return," I told her. "They are gone, and we have the skulls."

"And yet Mace will face Golgoleth again," she whispered. I shivered and drew back.

"What do you mean?"

"Exactly what I say. With sword in hand he must cross the walls of the castle and challenge the lord of the Vampyres. And next time he will not have you to send a shining shaft to his rescue. But he will have me."

Her eyes were distant, unfocused, and I could see that she was becoming delirious. I held to her hand, stroking the dry skin. "He will be gone from you, but he will return. I waited so long. So long . . . The circle of time spins . . . spins." She was silent for a little while, staring at some point in the past, some ancient memory that brought a smile to her face.

"Megan!" I called. But she did not hear me.

"I love you," she told the ghost of her memory. "Why did you leave me?"

Unconsciously her power flared, bathing her face with youth and beauty. "How could you leave me?" she asked.

I remained silent, for my voice could no longer reach her. But as I gazed on the glory of what was, I found myself echoing her thoughts. How could any man leave such a woman?

"You had it all," she said, bright tears forming and flowing to her cheeks. "You were the king. Everything you ever wanted!"

I called to her again, but there was no response. And in that moment I knew. From the first day, when she had known my name and we had sat talking about magick and life, I had yearned to know the mystery of Megan. Now it was all clear. Here she lay, weak and dying, yet even delirious she could still cast one of the seven great spells. My mouth was dry, my heartbeat irregular with the shock.

And I called her name—her true name. "Horga!"

The word was a whisper, but it flowed through her delirium. The spell of beauty faded, and she blinked and returned to me.

"I'm sorry, Owen. Was I drifting?"

"Yes."

"How did you know what to call me?"

I shrugged and smiled. "I also have talent, lady. When first I created the image of Horga, I used the beauty that you showed me from your youth. It seemed right. And I have always known there was something special about you—from that first day. And when Cataplas admitted you were his teacher, I knew you must have powers I could not even guess at. How have you lived so long? And why have you waited here, in this forest? Why? Did you know Golgoleth would come again?"

She nodded. "You will have all your answers, my boy. But not all of them now. I will set you a riddle, Owen. When did *you* first meet *me*?"

"It was here by this lakeside in winter."

"Indeed it was, but *I* first met *you* in the springtime, and you warned me not to read your mind, for there were memories there that were not for me."

"You have lost me, lady. We had no such conversation."

"Oh, Owen, that conversation is yet to be, and this meeting now is the memory from which you will protect me. The circle of time . . ." She fell silent again, and I could only guess at the effort of will that kept her alive. I felt her fingers press against mine. "I wanted . . . needed to live for just a little while longer," she said. "One question has kept me alive. And the answer is but a few months away. Now I will never know."

"Who was the man you loved?" I asked her as her tears began to flow again.

"Who do you think?"

"Rabain."

"Very good, Owen. Yes, it was Rabain. He was a great king, loved, perhaps even adored. He slew the Vampyre lords and created an order of knights pledged to combat evil. And he loved me. I know that he loved me! But he left me, Owen . . . he mounted his horse and rode from me. I have never forgotten that day. How could I? His armor was golden, and a white cloak was draped across his shoulders. He had no shield or helm. The horse was a stallion—huge, maybe eighteen hands, white as a summer cloud. And that was my last sight of him. I had begged him to stay. I offered him immortality. Such was my power then that I thought I could keep us both young forever. I even fell to my knees before him. Can you imagine that? I could have cast a spell to stop him, of course. I considered it, Owen. I could have made him love me more; I know I could. But that would not have been real. And it would have eaten away at me, as this poison is doing now. So I let him go.''

''Why did he leave?'' I asked her.

She tried to smile. ''An old man whom he loved came to him. A poet. He told him the future. Such a kind old man. But I think he was closer to Rabain that I could ever have been. And because Rabain needed him, I journeyed to fetch him. It needed mighty spells and great concentration. I wish now that I had refused.''

''What did he tell him?''

''I don't know, Owen. That's what I have waited all these years to find out. All these years . . . lonely years.''

''And you found no other lovers?''

A sound came from her then, a dry chuckle, and her eyes glinted. ''Hundreds,'' she said. ''As the centuries passed, I whiled away many a year with handsome men. Some gave me real pleasure, some even happiness. But none was Rabain . . . none was Rabain.''

''What happened to him?''

''I don't know. That's what was . . . is . . . so painful. He knew he was riding into great danger, as did I. But neither of us spoke of death. He told me he would come back, and I said I believed him. And I dressed him in his armor, fastening every hook, greasing the shoulder plates. Every hook. And at last I stood before him, and he leaned down and kissed me. And the armor was cold, so cold.''

''How long were you together?''

''Ten years. The merest fraction of my lifetime. I bore him a son, a fine boy who became a good man. He in turn had many sons and the line grew. I tried to keep them all in my mind, but it was not possible, save for one line that held true: the Arkneys. They are the blood of Rabain. When the Angostins first invaded the north, the Earl of Arkney married a Highland princess and

the line continued. That was what pleased me so much when
Raul Raubert stood tall alongside the Morningstar. He is the last
of that line, and the blood is still true.''

Once more she fell silent, then she smiled again, her eyes
sorrowful. ''But the line also produced Gilbaud Azrek.'' She
sighed. ''I have lived too long and seen too much.''

Her voice faded away, and I called her name. Her eyes flickered, and her voice whispered into my mind.

''You will see me again, Owen, but I will not know you.''

And she died there, slipping away without pain.

I held her hand for a little while. Then I covered her face and
left the cabin.

I found Mace sitting by the lakeside, skimming flat pebbles
across the surface of the water. I sat beside him, but he did not
look at me.

''Bastard life!'' he said, hurling yet another stone, which
bounced six times before disappearing below the water.

''You liked the old woman, didn't you?''

''Don't try to climb inside my head!'' he stormed.

''I do not wish to be intrusive. But she is gone, Jarek; she
passed away without pain.''

He said nothing but turned his face from me.

''How did you meet her?'' I asked him.

He shrugged. ''I was sitting by a camp fire, when she just
walked from the trees. She sat down as if I was an old friend
and began to talk. You know? The weather, the crops, the fishing. Just talk. I shared my meal with her. It was cold, and around
dusk she stood and said she had a spare bed in her cabin. So I
went with her.''

''Have you known her long?''

''No, maybe a month before I saw you in the forest. But she
was good to talk to. She didn't ask for anything. And she liked
me, Owen . . . for myself. You understand? Just for me—Jarek
Mace.''

''Like a mother?''

''I told you not to get inside my head! She was just an old
woman. But I was comfortable with her. I didn't have to think
about bedding her; I didn't have to woo her. You can have no
idea how good that is sometimes. Just to talk to a woman and
to listen. No seductive voice, no easy charm. And she was a

good woman, Owen. Back there when she faced the burning, I did want to help. I wanted . . . ah, what does it matter? Everything dies. Gods, you should know that by now.''

It was as if he had slapped me, for Ilka's face flashed into my mind and I felt the weight of grief.

"I'm sorry, Owen," he said swiftly, reaching out and gripping my arm. "I didn't mean to hurt you. She was a good girl; she deserved more."

"Well," I said, unable to keep the bitterness from my voice, "she was bedded by the Morningstar, so her life wasn't a complete waste."

"Don't say that!"

"What would you have me say? She was barely eighteen, and she's dead. I made love to her nine times; we had merely days."

"That's all any of us has, Owen. Just days. A few moments in the sun. Yours were shorter than most, but you had them. My mother gave me very little, but she offered one piece of advice I have long treasured. She used to say, 'What you have can be taken from you, but no one can take what you have already enjoyed.' You understand?"

"I wish I had never met her," I said, and at that moment I meant it. The sharpness of my sorrow seemed immensely more powerful than the love we had experienced.

"No, you don't," he assured me. "Not even close. You said it yourself: Her life was one of tragedy. But you supplied something pure, something joyful. You gave her a reason for being. Be proud of that!"

I looked at him with new eyes. "Is this the Jarek Mace who led a woman to suicide? Is this the robber who cares only for gold?"

He struck me then, a sharp blow with the back of his hand that made my head spin, and pushed himself to his feet. "Wallow in self-pity if you must," he said coldly. "I have more important matters to attend to."

We buried Megan in a meadow beneath the branches of a willow, an open spot overlooked by the mountains, with a stream close by. We made no headstone and did not even mark the spot. Such was the way of death in the forest at that time.

No prayers were spoken by any, but when the grave diggers had moved away and I stood alone by the small mound of earth,

I said my farewells, allowing the wind to carry my words wherever it traveled.

Horga the enchantress was gone from the world to whatever oblivion or paradise existed beyond the veils of life. As a bard I could hope that Rabain was waiting for her somewhere between worlds, but as a man I could feel only sadness at her passing.

The next few months were both chaotic and memorable. Angostin citadels were overthrown throughout the land, and the people were filled with the spirit of freedom. Yet these were not easy times. For despite the tyranny of Angostin rule, they still supplied law of a kind. Without them arnarcy beckoned, and Brackban was forced to become a judge as well as a general. Units were sent to police towns and cities; new laws were struck in the name of the Morningstar. Disputes needed to be settled, the rights to land established.

I remember well one case in which five families laid claim to a tavern in Ziraccu. The first maintained that it had ownership rights stolen during the days before the Angostin invasion; the second claimed to have bought the rights from Azrek; the third had an earlier claim, based on a deed signed by the Highland king some sixty years previously. The fourth swore that the most recent owner had willed it to them and produced documents to support its story. As to the fifth, well, it was in possession, having moved in following the slaying of the Vampyre kings. Their claim was that they had taken over a shell with no stock and had built up the custom, investing their own capital.

There were scores of cases like these, some judged by Mace, others by Brackban or Raul Raubert. But the lists grew, and other judges were appointed. Most came from the church, bishops and priests—even an abbess, though having a woman as a judge proved unpopular at first. Others were clerks or lawyers from freed cities.

Slowly, as autumn moved into winter, some degree of order was established.

The outlaws of Corlan now followed Mace like an elite royal guard, and Brackban continued his training of recruits and officers. The pace of revolution slowed, but despite the many irritations, the mood remained optimistic. Even when travelers, merchants, and tinkers moved up from the south with news of

Edmund's gathering army, there was little gloom. "We have the Morningstar," said the people. "Nothing can defeat him."

During those months I saw little of Mace. He rode through the land with Raul gathering men, giving speeches, collecting coin to pay for the weapons the new army would need. There was no line of credit offered by merchants, for they did not believe in the Morningstar. All they knew was that the Angostin battle king was preparing to march north in the spring, and where he marched, death and destruction followed.

Desperation makes for cost, my dear ghost. Our army was in dire need of weapons, and the iron for those was found only in the south. Therefore, we needed to pay men who were willing to smuggle them across to us. An iron-tipped spear that should have cost as little as two pennies now sold for twenty. Swords and halberds were seven, eight times the price. And armor? No matter how much coin we raised, the cost was prohibitive.

Edmund had closed off the southern borders, and merchants found with wagons loaded with weapons were hanged, drawn, and quartered. The ports were sealed also, and Ikenas galleons were anchored offshore, ready with the grappling irons to storm any ship that tried to sail past.

Our biggest fear was starvation, for a great deal of the food consumed in the north was imported from the richer, more fertile southlands.

Wulf and Piercollo were placed in charge of supplies for the army, but their roles widened as winter took hold. The movement of food to villages and towns cut off by snow, the filling of storehouses in cities, the distribution of supplies throughout the north—this consumed all their time. The winter months were fraught with peril, but save for isolated cases, there was no starvation. In the northern city of Callias a mob looted the storehouse, but Brackban's militia routed them, hanging twenty of the ringleaders as an example to others. It was the only serious incident of that long, bitter winter.

And what of Owen Odell during this period? I had no place in the new government, and Mace did not speak to me for weeks after the incident by the lakeside. I had no niche, no specific role. I helped Wulf and Piercollo with the organization of food, and I worked alongside Astiana in caring for the sick; the Gastoigne sister had moved into Ziraccu to help the survivors of Golgoleth's brief reign. There were orphans to be cared for, families to be found who would take in an extra child during the harsh winter months. And she founded a school where each day she taught unwilling youngsters the principles of letters and arithmetic.

· But for the most part I idled away my days thinking of Ilka and playing my harp. I lived then in Megan's cabin and continued her work of curing meats, preparing geese and poultry for the table, and gathering the herbs that Astiana used to draw out infections and fevers.

With the coming of spring, however, the mood of the people began to change. The talk was all of the coming war and the ferocious reputation of the battle king.

One bright morning, as I sat on a hillside overlooking the lake, I saw a rider gallop his horse into the settlement square. People swarmed around him as he sought out Brackban, who was visiting the town. I did not go down; I knew by the chill in my blood the news the rider carried.

The battle king was coming.

The snows were melting on the hillsides when I was summoned to Ziraccu. And as the riders came, bringing a spare horse, I was sure that Mace needed my counsel. I had felt somewhat aggrieved during the winter when he did not call upon me or seek my advice. And now, as I rode a tall stallion, I practiced in my mind the manner of my rebuke to him for his lack of courtesy. I would be gentle and ultimately forgiving but nonetheless send a shaft that would strike home.

Mace had not taken up residence in the palace; it was closed now, and none ventured into it. The Vampyres had gone, but the memory lingered and the evil done there had, according to local legend, seeped into the walls. Instead the Morningstar had taken over a house in the rich merchants' quarter. There were fine gardens around it, hemmed in by high walls. I rode with my escort to the front gates, where grooms led our horses away and servants ushered us into the main hall. The two riders who had accompanied me bowed and left me there, and it was Brackban, not Mace, who moved out to greet me. He led me through to a small library, and we sat in comfortable chairs of padded leather set beside a fireplace. The sun was hot outside, yet here in this room of stone it was cool, and a fire had been lit.

"Take off your boots and relax," said Brackban, moving to

a wide table of oak on which were scattered documents, scrolls, letters, wax, and a seal bearing the mark of the Morningstar. He looked tired, I thought, and thinner, and his long blond hair had been harshly cut close to his head. Wearing a long robe of dark green, he looked more a cleric than a warrior. There was a jug of wine on the table, and Brackban filled two silver goblets, passing one to me. Then he sat opposite and quietly drained his drink.

"Where is Mace?" I asked him.

He said nothing for a moment, then sighed. "He is gone, Owen. I don't know where."

"Gone?" I echoed, mystified.

"Three days ago he was reported to be heading for Ziraccu. He should have been here late yesterday. I can only think that he has been waylaid or taken by agents of the king. God alone knows where he is now."

I looked away from him. I knew instinctively that Mace had not been waylaid or captured; he had done what he always promised—he had cut and run now that the end was in sight. But what could I say to this strong, loyal man who had been left to pick up the pieces?

"Without him we are finished," continued Brackban. "We have a fledgling army, maybe three thousand men. They are good men for the most part, and brave. Edmund will have three, four times as many, and they are seasoned warriors. We have archers and foot soldiers, but he has cavalry, heavily armored knights who can strike fast and hard." He rubbed at his tired eyes. "What can we do, Owen? I am at the end of my strength. When word reaches the men that Mace is taken—or lost—then the desertions will begin. The lands will be open to Edmund. Have we done all this for nothing?"

"I will do my best to find him," I promised.

He nodded. "You do not think he was captured, then?"

"I don't know for certain what happened," I hedged, "but I will send a search spell. In the meantime, don't say anything about his disappearance. Where was he last seen?"

There was a map on the wall, black ink etched on pale leather. Brackban rose and walked to where it hung, stabbing his finger at an ornate triangle: the Angostin symbol for a city with a university. "He went to see the Bishop of Lowis; he is the senior tutor at the school there."

"Why should Mace want to see a teacher?"

Brackban shrugged. "The man sent him a letter. Mace seemed intrigued by it."

"Where is this letter?"

"I have no idea."

"Did you see it?"

"No. Mace merely said it had to do with some legend, some ancient artifact. I took little notice. God knows I have no time to study history, Owen. But I don't think it was important; it was just a whim."

"What do they study at the university?"

"Medicine, law, and history. But do not concern yourself with that. We have maybe two weeks; then two armies will face one another. If Mace does not arrive before then . . ." He spread his hands.

"What will you do if he has been taken or cannot be found?"

"What can I do? This is my land; they are my people. You think I will run away into the forest and leave them to their fate? I couldn't do that, Owen. Death would be preferable. No, I shall take my men and confront the battle king. Who knows, maybe God will favor us."

He spoke with little confidence, for he knew, as did I, that where battles were concerned, God tended to favor the army with the most lances. I left the house with a heavy heart and rode back to the village, seeking out Wulf and Piercollo. When I told them of Mace's disappearance, Wulf was not surprised.

"I've known him longer than any of the others," he said. "He's a solitary man, is Mace. And he looks out for himself. He's got courage, right enough, but it's not the enduring kind. You understand me? It's like the farmer who strives year in and year out. Come plague, pestilence, drought, famine, or locusts, he digs in and weathers the years. That's real strength. Mace can fight, probably better than any man I ever knew. But he doesn't have that strength. It was that way with Golgoleth. He went into the city because he couldn't have borne waiting for Golgoleth to come for him."

There was no anger in the hunchback's voice, no edge of bitterness.

"I shall try to find him," I said.

"Won't do no good, Owen," said Wulf. "He's turned his back on us; that's all there is to it."

"Even so, I shall try. Will you come with me?"

"Of course I will."

"As will Piercollo," said the giant, smiling. "I am tired of these people around me, the noise and the chatter. It will be good to hear the music of the forest. Where do we begin, Owen?"

"Tonight I will send out three search spells—north, west, and east. By dawn I will at least know which direction to travel. As we move, I shall send out other spells. Eventually we'll find him."

"How long is eventually?" Wulf asked.

"It could take weeks—months," I admitted.

"Well," he said grimly, "I'll be with you for six days. After that I'll make my way back here to join Brackban. I'll not have it said that Wulf was afraid of the fight."

We set off to the northwest two hours after dawn. I was tired, for I had been awake all night, holding to the search spells and focusing on the enchantment. The spell to the east showed nothing, but both north and west gave a glimmer of hope. I have already explained the nature of search globes, but when one casts such magick across large distances, there is no immediate, visible sign of success. The magicker must attune himself to the spell and rely on his instincts. When I held to the eastern globe, I felt only emptiness; this, then, was a cold route. At first the northern spell gave me a sense of warmth, but gradually this shifted to the western globe, thus giving me Mace's direction of travel.

"Where would he be heading?" I asked Wulf.

"There is a port, Barulis, at the Deeway estuary, northwest of here. If Edmund's fleet hasn't yet blocked it, maybe he is planning to take a sea voyage. Or he may just lie low in Barulis. But whatever his plan, it will take him some days to reach the city. I think I can cut his trail before then. We'll find him, Owen."

As we walked, I reached out with my talent, sending a new search globe to the northwest. As I concentrated my mind, honing my powers, I became aware, as magickers will, of an enchanter close by. I stopped, closed my eyes, and linked my thoughts to the globe. I became one with the spell, and my soul floated high above the forest in a circle of light. I had not the physical strength or the mental strength to hold myself for long in this spirit form, but it was long enough to see what I had both sensed and feared.

A second search spell was floating above the trees.

The enemy was also seeking the Morningstar.

There was much on my mind as we traveled. Ilka's death was still an open wound, and still I could not bring myself to talk to anyone about her. But I thought of her constantly. And Megan's dying words continued to haunt me. She had lived for two thousand years, waiting for the answer to a question. What question? And who could have answered it? And what did she mean when she told me that she would see me again but that she would not know me? Was she delirious then? Was it a kind of madness that precedes death?

But more than anything I thought of Jarek Mace and the confusion he must have felt at being a hero to so many. There is a legend of a giant called Parmeus who stole the book of knowledge from the gods. Every step he took with it saw the weight grow, until he felt he was carrying a mountain. At last he fell, and the weight pushed him far below the earth, where he still tries to carry his burden. Earthquakes and volcanic eruptions are attributed to these struggles in certain areas. But I knew that Mace would understand the awesome pressure Parmeus bore, for hero worship can be no less weighty, no less burdensome.

True, there were rewards. Mace had enjoyed several parades. But notwithstanding these distractions, he still had a legend to live up to, whereas in truth he was merely a common soldier and a skilled swordsman. How could he, despite the expectation of the people, hope to defeat the battle king?

We made good time, for the rains held off and the ground was firm, and within two days we had reached an area of level ground high in the mountains, a verdant plateau with several villages and an ancient castle built upon an island at the center of a long loch. It was a pretty spot, untouched by war. Fat cattle grazed on the new grass, and sheep and goats could be seen on the hillsides.

We were tired of walking and made our way down to the lakeside. An elderly man approached us; he was carrying a loaf of bread, which he broke into three pieces for us, an ancient Highland custom of welcome. We bowed our thanks, and I described Mace, asking him if such a man had passed by.

"You mean the Morningstar?" he asked.

"Yes," I answered, surprised. "We are friends of his."

He nodded sagely. "Well, if you're his friends, I don't doubt he'll find you," said the old man knowingly.

"He would if he was told that Owen Odell, Wulf, and Piercollo had traveled far to see him."

"And you'd be Odell the wizard?"

It would have taken too long to correct him, so I merely nodded. He said nothing more and walked away to his hut. The three of us sat down and finished the bread, which was a little stale but still tasty.

"He's here," said Wulf, "and I'll wager he won't see us."

As the day wore on and the sun fell lower, it seemed that Wulf would be proved right. Just after dusk the old man came out of his hut, bringing with him a pot of stewed beef and several clay bowls. I thanked him and questioned him about the settlement—how long it had been there and so on. He sat with us for a while, talking of the Highlands and his life. He had been a soldier for twenty years and had fought in three Oversea Wars. But he had come home a decade before and was now a fisherman and content. I asked him about the castle at the center of the lake.

"Been there since before my great-grandfather's time," he said. "No one recalls now when it was built, but it was after them Vampyre wars the stories tell of, I reckon. Never been used for war, though. Armies don't come here. Nothing for them: no plunder, no gain. Been a monastery now for more than a hundred years. Lowis monks. Fine spirit they produce there, made from grain. Take your head off, it will! Not that they allow much of it to leave the monastery. Maybe a barrel at midwinter. By God, there's some celebration around that time."

The name struck a chord with me, and I remembered the conversation with Brackban. Mace had spoken with the Bishop of Lowis.

"Can you row me across the lake?" I asked the old man.

"I could, I reckon," he said, "if I had a mind to."

"I am not a killer, sir. I have no evil intent toward the Morningstar. But it is vital that I see him."

"I know you're no murderer, boy. Been around enough of them in my life. Him, now," he said, gesturing a gnarled finger at Wulf, "he's a rough 'un. Wouldn't want him against me on a dark night."

Wulf gave a lopsided grin. "You're safe, old man."

"Aye, I am. But if I hadn't liked the look of you, I'd have poisoned that stew."

"The way it tasted, I thought you had," replied Wulf.

The old man gave a dry chuckle. "All right, I'll take you across, Owen Odell. But only you, mind!"

I followed him along the shoreline to where an ancient coracle was pulled up on the bank; it was made of dry rushes and resembled my old bathtub back home. "She leaks somewhat, but she'll get us there," he promised, and together we pulled the old craft out onto the dark water. I clambered in, and he followed me, settling down on his knees and picking up a wide-bladed oar, which he used expertly as the coracle moved out onto the lake.

Water seeped in, drenching my leggings, and I began to wonder if this was a good night to learn to swim. The old man glanced back over his shoulder and chuckled. "Seems like I didn't use enough pitch," he said, "but don't you worry, she won't sink."

The island of the castle loomed before us, dark and unwelcoming. The coracle scraped on shingle, and the old man leapt nimbly out, dragging the craft toward the land. I stood and splashed into the shallow water, wading ashore; a cold breeze blew, and I shivered.

"You'll be grateful for the wet," said the boatman. "The monks'll take pity on you and offer you some of their water of life."

I thanked him and set off up a narrow path that led to the main gates of the castle. There were no sentries on the walls and no sound from within. I bunched my hand into a fist and pounded on the gate. At first nothing happened, but after several attempts and a growing soreness in my hand I heard the bar being lifted. The gate swung open, and a small man with a shaved head came into sight; he was wearing a long gray habit bound with a rope of silken thread.

"What do you want?" he demanded gruffly.

"A little courtesy," I responded, "and shelter for the night."

"There's shelter to be had in the village," he told me.

"I thought this was a house of God," I said, my temper rising.

"That does not make it a haven for vagrant ruffians," he replied.

"I am not a violent man—" I began.

"Good," he said. "Then do not allow yourself to fall into bad habits. Good night to you."

Before I could reply, he had stepped back and begun to close the gate. I threw my weight against it—rather too sharply, for the gate crashed into him, hurling him to the ground. I stepped inside. "My apologies," I told him, reaching out a hand to help him up. He rolled to his knees, ignoring my offer of aid, then heaved himself upright.

"Your nonviolent behavior is not impressive," he said.

"Neither is your grasp of God's hospitality," I responded.

"Owen!" came a familiar voice, and I turned and looked up. Standing by an open doorway, framed in lantern light, stood Jarek Mace.

"Yes, it is me," I said. "Wulf and Piercollo are waiting for you at the village."

"You are just the man I wanted to see," he said. "Come up. There's something I want to show you."

The greeting had been cheerful and deeply irritating. Not. "How did you find me, Owen? By God, you must be a skilled magicker." No guilt over his shameful treatment of me during the winter. No apology for the slap or the slights.

I mounted the stairs, fighting to suppress a growing anger. The room he was in was a mess, littered with scrolls and manuscripts carelessly pulled from their protective leather sheaths. "I think I've found it," he said. "I am not a good reader, but I can make out the name Rabain."

"What on earth are you looking for?"

"The Bishop of Lowis told me that I was part of a prophecy. Can you imagine that? Someone, thousands of years ago, named me. *Me!* The whole story. So he said. Well, if that is true, we'll be able to see the ending."

"This is ridiculous."

"You don't believe in prophecies?"

I shook my head. "How can any of us know the future? It hasn't happened yet. And every man has a hundred choices to make every day. It was for this that you scared the wits out of Brackban?"

"What's Brackban got to do with it?"

"You disappeared, Jarek. And without you there is no rebellion."

"Well, if we find the right ending, I'll come back with you," he said, picking up an old scroll and passing it to me. "Read it!"

Sitting down with my back to the lantern, I held up the scroll and unrolled it. The first line explained that it was the eighth copy and gave the name of the monk and the year the copy was made. I passed this on to Jarek, who was singularly unimpressed.

"I don't care who copied the damn thing! Just read the story."

I scanned the opening lines. "It is not about Rabain; he is just mentioned in it. The story is of a knight called Ashrael."

Clearly exasperated, Mace took a deep breath. "Read it aloud!" he hissed.

"These are the exploits, faithfully recorded, of the knight known as Ashrael . . ." I stopped and glanced up. "If they were faithfully recorded, Jarek, then they have already happened. This is not a prophecy."

"Then there must be another scroll!" he stormed.

But I was reading on, idly skimming the fine, flowing script. "Wait!" I said. "This is curious." I began to pick out phrases from the story, reading them aloud. "The lady of the dream told this tale and bade me mark it for future times. The days of the Vampyre kings will come again, and the knight Ashrael will find the sword that was lost . . . Great shall be the grief within the city . . . from the depths of the earth Ashrael will rise . . . mighty will be the king who strides the land . . . Ashrael will light the torch that guides the ancient hero home . . . Rabain shall appear at the last battle, his armor gold, his stallion white, his cloak a cloud, his sword lightning."

"It hasn't got my name on it," snapped Mace.

"But is has. Ashrael, the last star to fade as the sun rises. The Morning Star!" I read on. "It is all here, Jarek: the invasion, the coming of the hero known as the Morningstar. Even the burning of the witch and the rescue . . . and the Vampyre kings reborn, Ashrael coming up from the bowels of the earth. We entered through the sewers. Dear God, it's uncanny."

"But how does it end?" he asked.

"Mighty will be the king who strides the land, his hand a

hammer, his dreams of blood . . . Edmund, the hammer of the Highlands. Ravens will gather above the meadow, and from the past Rabain shall appear at the last battle, his armor gold, his—"

"Yes, yes," stormed Mace. "But what about me?"

"It doesn't say. It just concludes that Rabain will appear and join the attack and that Ashrael's name will live on for as long as men revere heroes."

"Well, that's no damn good!" He slumped down in a chair and leaned forward, his elbows on his knees. "You were right. There's no prophecy!"

"No, I was wrong, I never had a chance to talk of Megan's last words and who she was. Now listen to me." And I told him most of what Megan had said, word for word. His interest quickened when I came to describe her parting from Rabain and his golden armor and white cloak. "That's the answer she was waiting for, Jarek. She wanted to see Rabain one more time. She wanted to know why he had to ride to some battle in the future that should have meant nothing to him. He is coming! Just as the legends always promised. When the need is great, Rabain will live again! Think of it! The Morningstar and Rabain on the same battlefield. How can we lose?"

"Hold on, bard! Megan . . . Horga . . . said he came back. That doesn't mean we are going to win, does it? I'm not going to face up to Edmund just in the hope of seeing a hero from the past and maybe watch him get cut to pieces."

"What will you do, then?"

"I don't know, but I'll tell you this: I wish I had never met you. I would have been far happier, I know that."

"Knowing what you know, would you really change anything?" I asked him. "If you could go back to that day in the forest, would you walk past my fire?"

He sighed, then grinned. "Maybe not. I had my parades, Owen. In Kapulis and Porthside they threw flowers before me. And women? I could have had them form a line. But there's a price to be paid for those few months of pleasure, and it's not a price I can afford . . . even with the prospect of meeting Rabain. Can three thousand men defeat ten thousand in an open battle? Against the finest warlord I have ever seen?"

"There's only one way to find out, my friend. And no one

lives forever. Face it, Jarek, would you want to grow old and toothless, with women looking on you with disdain?''

"I am twenty-four years old. That's a little early to consider losing my teeth! And I expect to mature like fine wine."

I smiled dutifully and then let the silence grow. "I don't want to go back, Owen," he said at last. "It has the wrong . . . feel. I cannot see us winning the battle. And I couldn't watch as men who believed in me were cut down, their dreams destroyed. I couldn't!''

"No one will force you to, Jarek. No one. Tomorrow I will go back to Wulf and Piercollo. I will not tell them I have seen you. We will wait until noon and then make our way back to Ziraccu.''

"Do you think me a coward?" he asked.

"After all that you have done? How could I? Whatever else, you stood your ground and fought the Vampyre kings. You gave the people hope. And because of you they found their courage again, and their pride. I shall tell Brackban that you were murdered by agents of the king. That way the legend will live on. But you must leave this land and never return.''

"I understand that. Thank you, Owen. Will you make up a song about me?''

"If I survive the battle, I shall. And about Wulf and Piercollo. And Ilka, Corlan, and Megan. I think it will be a good song.''

He stood then and extended his hand.

I took it . . . and left the monastery castle.

At the lakeside I found the old man still waiting.

"Did you see your friend?" he asked.

"No," I told him. "The Morningstar was not there.''

"What are we waiting for?" demanded Wulf as I sat quietly in the sunshine, my eyes drawn to the castle on the island. It was more than an hour past noon, and I stood.

"Nothing at all," I asked. "Let's be on our way.''

"Where to?" he asked. "Still northwest?''

"No. Let's go back to Ziraccu.''

"I thought we were looking for Mace," he said. "What in the devil's name is going on, Owen?''

"It was a fool's errand, and I am tired of it," I lied. Wulf swore, and Piercollo stared at me, his one dark eye watching my face. But he said nothing until we were well on our way and Wulf was scouting ahead.

"He was there, friend Owen. Why did you lie?"

"I gave him the chance to join us, and he did not take it. There was no more to be said. Let the world think he died; it is better that way."

"It is hard to be adored by so many."

"You speak as if you have knowledge of it."

"I do. In my country the voice is considered the greatest of musical instruments. We are singers. Every year there is a competition, a great gathering of voices. I won that competition six times. People would travel hundreds of leagues to hear me perform. It began to bear me down. Every day I would practice until the joy was gone. That is why I took the offer to come to the land of the Ikenas. I ran away, Owen. Fame did not agree with me. Perhaps it is the same for Mace."

"I think he is just afraid of dying," I said.

He shook his head. "I do not think you are right. I think he was more afraid of winning."

I stopped and turned to him. "Winning? But then he would achieve all his dreams: riches, power, women."

"No, my friend. That would be the end of his dreams. What is there after a war but rebuilding, reorganizing? Endless days of petitions and laws and all the petty day-to-day running of a state. It is no different from having a shop or a store. Bills to pay, stock to order, workers to instruct. It would be dull, Owen. What need would the people have for a Morningstar?"

His words shook me, for I could feel the ring of truth in them. Mace was in an impossible situation. Defeat would mean death, and victory an end to a life he enjoyed.

"I think," said Piercollo softly, "that it is easier to build a legend than to be one."

"Why do you stay?" I asked him. "This is not your land or your war. And the man who blinded you is dead. There is no need for you to stand at the last battle."

"Evil has no nationality," he answered. "And Piercollo will stand beside his friends. It is all he knows."

We walked on. Wulf killed a pheasant, and we shared the meat by a dusk fire. The hunchback was in a surly mood, argumentative and short-tempered, and well before midnight he had wrapped himself in his blanket and was asleep.

Piercollo was in no mood to talk, and he, too, dozed with his back to a broad tree. My mind was too full for sleep, and I sat by the fire, lost in thought.

Around midnight I thought I heard faint music and strained to locate the source of the sound, but it danced at the edge of hearing, softer than the whisper of a breeze through leaves. Adding twigs to the fire, I leaned back against a boulder and wished I had brought my harp with me. I had a need for music, for the release it brings.

Piercollo stirred and stretched. He saw me sitting there and smiled. "You need to sleep, my friend."

"Not yet." Idly he drew his dagger and began to whittle at a length of wood, cutting shavings for a future fire. Suddenly his knife snapped at the hilt.

"It was poor iron," he said, hurling the broken weapon aside.

"You should have taken one of the enchanted blades," I told him, drawing my own black dagger and tossing it to him. He continued to whittle in silence. "Will you go back to Tuscania?" I asked him.

"I hope so, Owen."

"And will you try your luck at the competition again?"

He shook his head. "I think not. The music is gone from me; they burned it out with my eye."

"That must not prove to be true, for then evil will have conquered you. A small victory, perhaps, but one that should not be accepted lightly. As long as the rest of us are deprived of your voice, then Lykos will have won. But when you sing again, you will know joy, as will all who hear you. And then Lykos will be but a bad memory."

"Maybe one day," he said, "but not yet."

I did not press him.

The fire was dying down, and a strange silence settled on the campsite. I glanced up. No breeze stirred the leaves, no movement. All was utterly still.

"What is happening?" whispered Piercollo. I focused my eyes on the clouds in the moonlit sky. They, too, had stopped, frozen, like a great painting.

A soft light shone between us, growing and swelling, becoming a doorway of gold. And through it stepped Megan, young and dazzling in her beauty, a gown of golden thread shimmering about her slender frame . . .

She saw me and swung her head. "Where is he?" she asked.

"Who, lady?"

"The wielder of the black sword," she answered.

My shock at seeing her was immeasurable. I had watched this woman die from the poison inflicted by an assassin's blade. Yet here she was, in the prime of youth, with no illusion, no magick spell to enhance her beauty.

"Do you know me, lady?" I asked softly.

"No, sir. And my need to find the wielder is pressing. Where is he?"

I rose and bowed. "You seek the Morningstar, but he is not here. We are his friends. How can we help you?"

"You cannot help me," she said dismissively, her gaze raking the trees around us. "You have no idea how far I have traveled or how great the drain on my energy."

"I think I have have, Horga. You have traveled across the centuries, and the spell was mighty."

"How is it that you know my name?" she asked.

"I am also a . . . magicker. And we have already met—in my past and your future. Let us leave it at that. Why do you seek the wielder?"

Piercollo was sitting frozen with shock, while Wulf had awoken but had not moved, his dark eyes drinking in the sight of the legendary sorceress. Horga stepped around the fire and approached me, reaching out her hand to touch my head. My fingers closed firmly around her wrist. "Trust me, lady, and do not read my mind."

She withdrew her hand, and her face became pensive. "I do trust you. I would know if you were false." She sighed and sat. Wulf rose and brought her a water sack, pouring a drink for her; she sipped the liquid from his copper cup and smiled her thanks.

"Tell me about Golgoleth," I said. Her face darkened, her eyes gleaming.

"He thinks he has won, but I will not have it so. He stole the weapons crafted to destroy him and hid them with spells even I could not pierce. Until now!"

"You sent a search spell into the future," I said, amazed. "By God's holy grace, that is power indeed!"

"And I found them. Even his spells cannot linger indefinitely. The weapons were hidden, as I suspected, in the depths of his own castle. The big man fell through the floor—I saw it—and I

saw the wielder leap down and claim his blade. And then I knew
what must be done. But it has taken me time . . . precious time
. . . to cast the magick and travel the roads of future days.'' Her
gaze turned to me, the power of her eyes upon me. ''But you
have not told me how you know me.''

''I *knew* you, lady. In my life we had already met before
today. We were friends. In yours we have yet to become friends.
My name is Owen Odell.''

She nodded. ''I shall remember it. But tell me, Owen Odell.
You must know whether I won or lost.''

''I know. You must not.''

She laughed then, a light rippling sound full of gaiety. ''The
complexity of time. I shall play the game, Owen. But where is
the wielder?''

''He is coming. It is his destiny. I know that now.''

''What is his name?''

''He is known as Ashrael, the Morningstar.''

Her gaze flickered beyond me, and I turned to see Mace
standing at the edge of the trees, longbow in hand, the black
sword belted at his waist.

''By God, Owen,'' he said, ''that is your best illusion yet!''

''It is no illusion,'' I told him, rising. He stepped forward,
disbelieving, and reached out to stab a finger at the golden-robed
woman. Her hand slapped his aside, and Mace leapt back in
shock.

''But . . . it is Horga! You created the image!''

''No, I did not. And this, as you rightly say, is the lady of
legend.''

Mace bowed. ''What can I say, madam? I thought Owen's
images were beautiful enough, but in the flesh you are a vision
of loveliness.''

''I thank you, sir. But now—if I may—I would ask a favor of
you. You have no need to grant it, but . . .''

''Say the word and I will empty the sea with a cup for you.
I'll take a mountain apart stone by stone.''

''I want you to come with me, back into the past. There is a
great evil there that has almost conquered my world. Only a few
heroes remain, ready to stand against the onslaught of the dark.
We need your sword and the skill you have shown in using it.
Will you come?''

Mace turned to me. ''Is this some jest, Owen?''

I shook my head. "This is Horga. And the enemy they are facing is Golgoleth. She has walked the mists to find you. Can you understand what that means?"

"It means that I have to go up against the bastard a second time. Oh, yes, I know what it means."

"I don't think you do. You are being summoned into the past. You are the wielder of the black sword. Think, man!"

"And what do I get for this . . . favor?" he asked Horga suddenly.

"What would you want?"

"I see what I want, lady," he said, his gaze flowing over her body. "But is it part of the price you will pay?"

She did not blush but smiled broadly. "Is that all? Then I agree."

"Wait!" I said, seizing Mace by the arm and pulling him back away from the group, out of earshot of the sorceress. "You have not understood a single word of this, have you?" I whispered. "Do you know who you are?"

"Of course I know who I am. What sort of a question is that? I am Jarek Mace—and the most beautiful woman God ever created has offered herself to me. Now, we both know that back in the past Rabain destroyed the Vampyre kings. All I need to do is travel back with her, give him my sword, and earn my reward. And I don't need to fight a lost battle here. By God, Owen, I cannot believe my luck!"

He tried to move away from me, but I kept a firm hold of his arm. "If you can tear your gaze away from her for a moment, let me point something out to you, that is, if you can still think! You are being summoned. That makes you the *Summoned One*. Are you concentrating, Jarek? The Summoned One? Ra-he-borain? Rabain, Jarek. It is you! When you step through whatever gateway she has created, you will be Rabain."

Suddenly he was no longer trying to pull away. The full force of the argument struck him, and he relaxed in my grip. "I am Rabain?" he whispered.

"You will be if you travel with her."

He laughed then. "How can I lose, Owen? Rabain didn't, did he? He got to be king."

"Yes, he got to be king," I said, holding the sadness from my voice.

He turned away from me and approached Horga, taking her hand and kissing it. "How soon do we . . . leave?" he asked.

"Now," she replied, lifting her arm.

Golden light blazed through the clearing . . .

And I was alone. Piercollo and Wulf had vanished with Mace, drawn with him because they carried the weapons of enchantment.

I built up the fire and waited, my thoughts somber.

After a short while, even before the new wood had burned through, there was a second bright flaring of light and Piercollo and Wulf were back.

Both were dressed differently, and Wulf's beard was better trimmed, his hair cut short. He was wearing a tunic and boots of the finest leather, and a golden dagger was belted at his side. Piercollo looked much the same, save that he now wore an eye patch of silver that needed no thong to hold it in place. He moved to me, hauling me to my feet and taking me into a bear hug that almost broke my back.

"He is the king, then?" I asked as Piercollo released me.

"Aye," said Wulf. "And not making a bad job of it. But he's staying behind, Owen. He wouldn't come back with us. He's living with the sorceress now, like husband and wife. But we asked her to send us back. How long have we been gone?"

"Merely a few minutes."

"Sweet heaven!" he said, shaking his head. "We were there for almost a year. You should have seen it, Owen. Mace was the hero! We stormed the Vampyre keep. I killed one of the kings with—"

"With a silver arrow, I know. And Piercollo slew the second, hurling him from the high walls, where his neck was broken, his head severed upon a sharp rock."

"You saw it?"

"No, my friends, I didn't need to see it; it is a part of history. You were Jerain the bowman, Piercollo was Boras the Cyclops—the one-eyed. It is a wondrous circle. All this time men have been saying that Mace is Rabain reborn. And they were right, after a fashion. All the legends said that Rabain would come again. And in a way he did. And he will."

"Mace ain't coming back," said Wulf. "Trust me on that."

"No, Wulf, you trust me. The Morningstar will appear at the

last battle. There is an old man in the past, a poet, and he will convince Mace that he should return.''

There is a wide, long meadow in a valley eight miles south of Ziraccu. It is flanked by trees and a narrow ribbon stream to the west, with a line of hills to the east. Being old, they are not high hills, mere humps in the land rising no more than two hundred feet. The meadow itself now has a church upon it. They call it the Morningstar Abbey. Pilgrims journey to it, for there is a tomb there—an empty tomb—but legend tells us there is a cloth within the sarcophagus that was stained with the blood of the Morningstar.

For fifty years there have been claims of miraculous healings, and it has become a shrine, guarded now by an order of monks, saying prayers thrice daily by the statue of Jarek Mace. How he would have chuckled to see their set, serious faces.

But I am drifting ahead of the tale.

On the last day of spring, on a cloudy morning—the grass white with dew and mist like the ghosts of yesterday swirling upon the meadow—our army waited. There was no church then, only a long flat area of killing ground.

There were 3,700 foot soldiers at the center, Brackban standing in the fourth rank of seven with a standard-bearer beside him. The standard had been made by Astiana; it was a simple piece, black linen upon which she had embroidered a star of silver thread. Brackban was garbed for war in the black enchanted armor, a raven-winged helm upon his blond head. Almost one thousand of our front-line troops wore breastplates and carried round iron-rimmed wooden shields. Most of them and around half the others also sported helms of baked leather, some reinforced by bronze. But there were still many men who had no armor.

But Brackban was a popular man, and the troops gathered around him, ready to fight and die for their homeland.

He had listened in silence as I told him of Mace's quest, of his journey into the past. He did not, I think, believe me. And even if he did, it meant little to him. For all he took from the tale was that Mace had gone.

"What now, Owen?" he had asked me.

"Prepare for battle. The Morningstar will return."

"You seem confident."

"I am."

"Wulf does not agree with you."

"He does not know all that I know. Have faith, Brackban. Tell the men that the Morningstar will be with them on the day of battle. Tell them he will come in glory, his armor gold and riding upon a huge white stallion. Tell them that."

"I do not want to lie to them."

"It is no lie."

To the left of the battlefield was Raul Raubert with three hundred Angostin knights. These were men who had survived the first invasion, some by hiding, others by running. I was not inspired by them, but Raul was leading them, and his courage was without question. His role was to deflect the enemy cavalry, hold them back if he could.

But all the reports suggested that Edmund's force had more than four thousand heavily armored knights. Three hundred would not hold them for long.

Wulf had stationed himself on the right with the men of the Morningstar, the archers and woodsmen. Eight hundred of them stood ready, their arrows thrust in the earth beside them, an indication for all that they were not prepared to run. Here were their weapons. Here they would stand.

It was noon before Edmund appeared, his column of knights riding along the crest of the hills in a glittering display of martial power. Behind them came the foot soldiers, marching in ranks, disciplined and calm, every man clad in breastplate and greaves, carrying a square iron shield emblazoned with dragons, leopards, or griffins. The king himself could be clearly seen: his armor was polished like silver, and he rode a tall horse, black as jet, its head and chest armored with chain mail and plate.

Slowly the infantry filed out to stand in ranks opposite us, about a quarter of a mile distant.

My fears began then in earnest, and I felt the weight of the unaccustomed sword that was belted to my side and the chain mail shirt I wore. Beside me Piercollo waited grimly, a long-handled ax in his hands.

"There are rather a lot of them," I observed, trying to keep my voice calm.

"Many," he agreed.

The infantry alone outnumbered us by at least three—possibly four—to one. Eight to ten thousand men, battle-hardened and accustomed to victory.

I wondered how the battle would start. For here we were, all of us in a summer meadow, standing silently staring at one another. It seemed so unlikely that we were all about to be embroiled in a bloody fight to the death.

A herald rode from the Angostin camp, galloping his horse to within twenty paces of our center. There was no breeze to speak of, and the herald's words carried to every man in the front ranks.

"The lord of the land demands that you lay down your weapons. He further insists that the rebel leaders Jarek Mace, Brackban, and Owen Odell are to be detained and delivered to him. Failure to comply with these orders will result in the extermination of every man who holds arms against the king. You have one hour to make your decisions. If the men named are brought before the Lord Edmund within that time, no action will be taken against you."

Tugging on the reins, the rider galloped back to the Angostin lines, leaving a silent army behind him.

You could feel the tension in every man. Ahead of us was a mighty foe—unbeaten, seemingly invincible. Fear swept through our ranks like a mist—cold, strength-sapping.

But as the fear swelled, a single voice broke out in song. It was Piercollo, and he was singing an old and famous Highland battle hymn, a deep, rolling ballad, slow and martial. It was called "The Shield Bearer," and it told of a boy going to war for the first time.

Around me I saw warriors looking at the giant Tuscanian, then several voices joined in, thin and piping against his deep tenor. And the sound swelled, the power and pride of the lyrics expelling all fear, until the entire army of the Highlands was singing the battle song. I looked to Brackban, and he grinned, the tension and weariness falling from him. Then he, too, began to sing, and the sound filled the meadow, sweeping out to envelop the enemy army.

At the final verse Piercollo raised his ax above his head, the sunlight gleaming from the huge curved blades. Swords flashed up into the sunlight, and the song was replaced by a deafening roar of defiance.

Edmund did not bother to wait for the hour to pass. A trumpet note blared out, and the cavalry thundered down from the hills.

Raul Raubert led his men to meet them, and Wulf and the archers drew back on their bowstrings, sending a black cloud of shafts into the enemy horsemen. The knights fell in their hundreds.

A roll of drums sounded, and the enemy infantry, lances leveled, began to walk toward us. The drums increased in tempo, the walk becoming a run, becoming a charge.

And the day of blood began, the screams of the dying, the clash of swords and spears, the neighing of horses, the pounding of hooves upon the grass. Chaos and terror, fury and death flowed around me as I stood in the fifth rank. In front of me Piercollo fought like the giant he was, his great ax rising and falling to smash men from their feet. The lines bent and gave, and I found myself drawn into the madness of the battle, where I stabbed and thrusted, parried and countered, desperately fighting to stay alive within the swirl of war.

I don't know how long the initial fighting went on, but it seemed to be hours. Finally the Angostins pulled back, reforming their lines for a second charge. We had lost more than half our men, and many of the others now carried wounds. It took no military mind to realize that one more charge could finish us. Yet no one ran or cried out for mercy. We stood our ground as men.

"Now would be a good time for magic," said Wulf, easing himself alongside us, his arrows gone. He drew his two short swords and sniffed loudly.

"I do not think my illusions would hold them for long," I told him.

"You should have studied better," was Wulf's caustic reply.

I saw the enemy king mount his black stallion and ride out to join his cavalry. They gathered around him, listening to his exhortations.

Glancing to my left, I saw Raul Raubert, his armor drenched in blood, calling his own knights to him. There were scarcely sixty left, but they gathered around him. I felt shame then for doubting them.

The enemy cavalry formed a line and swept down toward our flank. There were no arrows left now, and Brackban tried to set up a shield wall to oppose them. Raul spurred his horse forward, his men around him in a tight wedge. Instantly I guessed his plan: he was trying to force his way through to Edmund.

The Angostins were ready for such a move, and several hundred knights galloped ahead of the king, blocking Raul's path.

The infantry swept forward.

The battle was almost over . . .

A rolling boom of thunder broke above our heads, a jagged spear of lightning flashing up from the hilltop to the east. But instead of disappearing, the lightning held, frozen, white-gold from earth to sky. The charging Angostins faltered, men turning to watch the light.

It widened, becoming a gateway arched by a glorious rainbow. And through the gateway rode a single knight on a huge white horse.

"The Morningstar!" I yelled, breaking the silence.

His armor was gold, and he wore no helm upon his head. In his right hand he carried his black longsword, in his left a spiked ball of iron on a length of chain. I smiled, remembering his first description of the weapon. Jarek Mace had arrived for the battle carrying a morningstar.

Touching spurs to the stallion, he charged at the enemy cavalry.

"Morningstar! Morningstar!" went up the roar from the Highlanders, and they surged forward at the bemused infantry before them. Stunned by this sudden attack, the Angostins fell back in disorder.

I did not join the rush of fighting men. I stood with Piercollo beside me and watched the last ride of Jarek Mace.

His horse reached the bottom of the hill, and several knights rode against him. His sword lanced out, spilling the first from the saddle; the second fell, the spiked ball crushing his skull. The third thrust a lance into Mace's side, but a disemboweling cut from the black sword cleaved the knight's belly.

On rode the Morningstar, cutting and killing, blood streaming from cuts on his face and arms.

Edmund drew his sword and spurred his mount to the attack. There were blades all around the Morningstar now, hacking and slashing, but somehow he stayed in the saddle and the giant white stallion bore him on.

Edmund galloped his black horse alongside Mace and plunged his sword into the Morningstar's belly. I saw Mace's face twist in pain, and then the spiked ball swung through the air, crashing into Edmund's helm. The king swayed in the saddle, losing his grip on the sword that still jutted from Mace's body. Now it was the Morningstar who lifted his sword one last time, slamming the blade forward into Edmund's neck. Blood gushed, and the king fell.

With the Angostin infantry streaming from the field, the knights were in danger of being surrounded. Several of them tried to recover the king's body, but they were cut down by Raul Raubert and his men, who had forced their way through to the Morningstar.

The white stallion, its chest pierced by many blades, suddenly fell, pitching Mace to the ground. I dropped my sword and ran toward him, dodging and swerving among the knights and their maddened mounts.

One knight with lance leveled rode at me, but a second inadvertently got in his way, the two horses colliding shoulder to shoulder. Then I was past them and running toward where Mace lay.

He was still alive when I reached him. Raul was kneeling beside him, holding his hand.

"Get me . . . to the . . . forest," whispered Mace.

Piercollo gently lifted him, and we walked toward the north. Wulf joined us, then other men gathered around.

We halted in the shade of a huge oak, where Piercollo laid the Morningstar carefully down, removing his white cloak and making of it a pillow.

The other men fell back, creating a circle around the dying warrior.

As the sun began to fade, Brackban arrived, his officers with him. I had sat with Mace for an hour by then, and he had said nothing. His eyes were closed, his breathing ragged.

With the gathering dark, men lit torches and held them high, bathing the scene in flickering light. I knelt to Mace's left. Behind me stood Piercollo and Wulf; to the left was Raul Raubert, and beside him was Brackban.

Mace opened his eyes and looked at me. "Surprised . . . you . . . eh?"

"No, my friend. It was no surprise. I was waiting for you."

"Had . . . to come back, Owen."

"Why?" I asked him, leaning in close, for his voice was fading.

"I . . . wanted . . . another parade!" He smiled weakly. "I . . . wonder if they . . . have . . . them . . . in hell."

"You'll never find out," I promised him. "Never!"

"Make it . . . a good . . . song, Owen."

He made me leave him then and spoke quietly to Wulf and then Raul Raubert and lastly Brackban.

I stood back from them in the torchlight and saw that the torchbearers were weeping, and I, too, felt the weight of it as I watched the tableau in the circle of light: the blood-covered warrior in his ruined armor of gold, the hunchback beside him, and the giant standing close by.

I felt humbled by the scene as Mace's blood flowed to the land that had created him. Through him an entire nation had enjoyed a rebirth of courage, a renewal of hope. But then, that is what heroes do, it is not? They make us all a great gift, our lives made larger and more noble by their existence. It matters not a whit that Mace himself was less than legends make him.

For what he gave to the future was far greater than what he took from the past. As long as there is evil in the world, there will be men—aye, and women—who will say. "Stand up and fight it. Be strong like the Morningstar."

And I knew then, as Mace lay dying, that the song would soon be all there was.

He died just before the dawn, and one by one the torchbearers snuffed out their lights, allowing the last of the night to close in over the tableau. We sat with his body until sunrise, and then Wulf, following his instructions, took the body deep into the forest, burying it in an unmarked grave where no man would stumble upon it.

The hunchback would not even tell me where Mace lay save to say that each morning the sun would shine upon him and each night the stars would glitter above him like a crown.

Raul Raubert was acclaimed as the new king, Brackban becoming his chamberlain.

And so what Mace had told me so cynically came to pass. Nothing ever changes . . . The Angostins ruled in the Highlands once more, and order was established in the northern world.

Raul Raubert was a good king, and there were many fine changes to the law. His standard remained the silver star embroidered by Astiana, and from then until this day the kings of the Highlands are called sons of the Morningstar.

And what of the others? Astiana went on to become an abbess, a saintly old woman who cared for the sick. She became the princess of legend, Mace's great love, a warrior woman who helped him defeat the Vampyres. I tried to keep Ilka's memory alive among the people, but no one wants to hear songs about mute whores, no matter how brave. No, Astiana filled their hearts.

Piercollo traveled back to his beloved Tuscania. He wrote me once to say he had entered the contest and won it once more. He dedicated his victory to the memory of Lykos, the man who had blinded him. I was pleased at that, for evil thrives only when it breeds, and Piercollo had neutered its power.

And Wulf? I used to see him in the old days. I would journey into the forest and stay at his cabin for a while; we would hunt together and talk of old times and shared memories. But as the years passed, his memory blurred and he began to remember a different story. He recalled a golden-haired man with a heart of unblemished purity and the courage of ten lions. At first I gently mocked him, but he grew angry and accused me of "slighting the greatest man who ever lived." Mace's dark side, his callousness and cruelty, his womanizing and his greed, all became signs of a reckless youth and a sense of humor.

Such is the way with heroes. Their greatness grows with the passing of time, their weaknesses shrinking. Perhaps that is as it should be.

Wulf died ten years ago. The king—Raul's eldest grandson, Maric—had his body moved to the royal tomb at Ziraccu. A statue was raised to him—a bronze statue. The likeness is almost chilling. Crafted twice life-size, the statue stands facing the south with a longbow in hand, keen bronze eyes staring toward the borders watching for the enemy. Wulf would have liked it.

Perhaps a statue will be raised for me one day soon.

As for Owen Odell, well, for several years I journeyed, staying far from the curious eyes of men who knew me only as a legend. I took passage on a ship that sailed the length of the island and stepped ashore on the south coast, making my way to my father's castle. I found him sitting in the long room behind the stables. He was cleaning and oiling leather bridles and stirrups, and he looked up as his son entered.

"You should have known better than to drop your sword on a battlefield," said Aubertain. "And as for running among mounted knights . . . damn stupid! Lucky no one removed your head from your shoulders."

"You were there?"

"Where else would I be when my king goes to war?"

"You were the knight who saved me," I said, remembering the collision that had stopped the lance piercing my chest. "You charged your horse into the lancer."

He shrugged. "I'm a stubborn man, Owen, but I'll not see my sons killed even if they are fighting on the wrong side. Welcome home, Son. Have you seen your mother yet?"

I don't think I was truly complete until that moment. Megan told me once that there was a man I must meet who would make me whole, and she was right. And now I had found him again. He stood and opened his arms, and I embraced him, the last of my bitterness vanishing.

My brother Braife had been one of the knights slain by Mace in that last charge, but my father bore the Morningstar no ill will.

"He was a man, by God," he said as we sat by the hearth fire on a cold winter's evening. "I'll never forget that ride. And I'm grateful to him for what he did for you. I think he made a man of you, Owen."

"Aye, Father. I think he did."

I stayed in the south until my father died. It happened seven years after I came home and only weeks after the death of my mother from the yellow fever. I moved back to the Highlands then and built my house close to the oak beneath which is buried the skull of Golgoleth.

I have lived long, ghost, and I have seen much, but even I am beginning to believe in the song. Every spring, when the celebrations begin, I think of Mace, his easy smile and his casual charm.

And I listen to fathers telling their sons that one day, when the realm is threatened, the Morningstar will come again.

Oh, ghost, how I wish I could be there when he does!

Epilogue

AGRAINE AWOKE AN hour before dawn, yawned, and stretched. The window was open, the air cold and fresh, stars gleaming in the winter sky. He was cold yet excited by the prospect of a morning meeting with the legendary Owen Odell. Swiftly he dressed, pulling on his warm woolen tunic and trews, his socks of softest wool and his boots of shining leather. He needed a shave and wondered whether the strange old man would allow him the use of one of the servants. Probably not, he decided. These Highlanders were a curious breed.

Hungry, the young nobleman made his way downstairs to the larder, helping himself to a sweet honey cake and washing it down with soured apple juice.

What a loathsome place, he decided as he opened the shuttered window and gazed out over the night-dark mountains. No theaters, no palaces of lascivious amusements, no dances, no readings of the latest works of literature. What clods these people must be, in their primitive dwellings, with their dull little lives.

But the journey would be worth it for the book. He would neither tour taverns nor tell saga stories around flickering camp fires. Oh, no. His father would pay a hundred monks to copy the tale and bind it in leather for sale and private readings among the nobility.

First, however, there was the old man. Agraine smiled. It would be easy to charm the ancient poet—soft words, a honeyed tongue. The story would spill out soon enough. God knows, the elderly loved to prattle!

Taking a second cake, the young man mounted the stairs,

approaching the room where first he had spoken with Owen Odell. The door was ajar, and he heard voices.

Moving silently forward, he leaned in close to the crack by the door hinge, closing his right eye and straining to see into the room. But a floorboard creaked, and the voices within fell silent.

"Come in, Agraine," called the old poet.

Sheepishly the young man opened the door.

"I did not mean to . . ." His voice trailed away, for standing in the center of the room was a golden-haired woman of lustrous beauty, clothed only in a shimmering gown of green silk. Agraine's mouth fell open, and clumsily he executed a bow. "I am sorry, Lord Odell. I had no idea you had other guests."

"It was a surprise to me, my boy," the old man told him. "This is an old friend of mine . . . Megan."

Agraine was sharp enough to spot the lie, but he kept his thoughts to himself and smiled at the woman. "It is a great pleasure, my lady. Do you live close?"

She laughed, the sound like sweet music. "Very close. And I have come to invite . . . Lord Odell . . . to visit my home. I was just explaining it to him when we heard you arrive."

The old man chuckled as if at some private jest. "You will, I hope, excuse me, young man. For I must leave you to break your fast alone."

"It is freezing outside, and there is deep snow in the valley," stuttered Agraine, unwilling to allow the vision to depart from his company.

"You are quite wrong," said the golden-haired woman. "It is springtime, and the flowers are in bloom."

They were both smiling now, and Agraine felt the red flush of embarrassment burning his cheeks. With great effort Owen Odell rose from his chair, his bony hand descending on the young man's shoulder. "I am sorry, my boy; we do not mean to mock. But Megan is right. Where we travel it will be springtime. And there is a young man—little older than yourself—who is waiting to speak with an old poet. It is a circle, you see. Forgive me."

The golden-haired woman was standing beside the open door, and the wind was sending flurries of snow against her bare feet. Taking Odell's arm, she led the old man out into the winter night.

Agraine stood for a moment, unable to gather his thoughts. Then he ran to the door.

The two of them were only a few paces out into the snow-covered clearing, Megan supporting the poet, who moved with slow shuffling steps. They stopped, and the woman raised her hand. Light rose from her fingers in a fountain of sparkling gold, raining down over both figures. Around and around, like shimmering stars, the golden flakes whirled about the poet and his lady. Agraine blinked against the light and the sudden darkness that followed it.

He blinked again. The clearing was deserted.

Owen Odell was gone.

Coming soon to a bookstore near you . . .

WAYLANDER

by David Gemmell.

**The beginning of the Drenai Saga!
Published by Del Rey Books.
Here is the opening chapter of
WAYLANDER . . .**

◊ 1 ◊

THEY HAD BEGUN to torture the priest when the stranger
stepped from the shadows of the trees.

"You stole my horse," he said quietly. The five men spun
around. Beyond them the young priest sagged against the ropes
that held him, raising his head to squint through swollen eyes at
the newcomer. The man was tall and broad-shouldered, and a
black leather cloak was drawn about him.

"Where is my horse?" he asked.

"Who is to say? A horse is a horse, and the owner is the man
who rides him," answered Dectas. When the stranger first
spoke, Dectas had felt the thrill of fear course through him,
expecting to find several men armed and ready. But now, as he
scanned the trees in the gathering dusk, he knew the man was
alone. Alone and mad. The priest had proved but sorry sport,
gritting his teeth against the pain and offering neither curse nor
plea. But this one would sing his song of pain long into the night.

"Fetch the horse," said the man, a note of boredom in his
deep voice.

"Take him!" ordered Dectas and swords sang into the air as
the five men attacked. Swiftly the newcomer swept his cloak
over one shoulder and lifted his right arm. A black bolt tore into
the chest of the nearest man, a second entered the belly of a
burly warrior with upraised sword. The stranger dropped the
small double crossbow and lightly leapt back. One of his attackers was dead, and a second knelt clutching the bolt in his
belly.

The newcomer loosened the thong that held his cloak, allowing it to fall to the ground behind him. From twin sheaths he produced two black-bladed knives.

"Fetch the horse!" he ordered.

The remaining two hesitated, glancing to Dectas for guidance. Black blades hissed through the air, and both men dropped without a sound.

Dectas was alone.

"You can have the horse," he said, biting his lip and backing toward the trees. The man shook his head.

"Too late," he answered softly.

Dectas turned and sprinted for the trees, but a sharp blow in the back caused him to lose balance, and his face ploughed the soft earth. Pushing his hands beneath him, he struggled to rise. Had the newcomer thrown a rock, he wondered? Weakness flowed through him, and he slumped to the ground . . . The earth was soft as a featherbed and sweet smelling like lavender. His leg twitched.

The newcomer recovered his cloak and brushed the dirt from its folds before fastening the thongs at the shoulder. Then he recovered his three knives, wiping them clean on the clothes of the dead. Lastly he collected his bolts, despatching the wounded man with a swift knife cut across the throat. He picked up his crossbow and checked the mechanism for dirt before clipping it to his broad black belt. Without a backward glance he strode to the horses.

"Wait!" called the priest. "Release me. *Please!*"

The man turned. "Why?" he asked.

The question was so casually put that the priest found himself momentarily unable to phrase an answer.

"I will die if you leave me here," he said at last.

"Not good enough," said the man, shrugging. He walked to the horses, finding that his own mount and saddlebags were as he had left them. Satisfied, he untied his horse and walked back to the clearing.

For several moments he stared at the priest; then he cursed softly and cut him free. The man sagged forward into his arms. He had been badly beaten, and his chest had been repeatedly cut; the flesh hung in narrow strips, and his blue robes were stained with blood. The warrior rolled the priest to his back, ripping open the robes, then walked to his horse and returned with a leather canteen. Twisting the cap he poured water on the wounds. The priest writhed but made no sound. Expertly the warrior smoothed the strips of skin back into place.

"Lie still for a moment," he ordered. Taking needle and thread from a small saddlebag, he neatly stitched the flaps. "I need a fire," he said. "I can't see a damned thing!"

The fire once lit, the priest watched as the warrior went about his work. The man's eyes were narrowed in concentration, but the priest noted that they were extraordinarily dark, deep sable brown with flashing gold flecks. The warrior was unshaven, and the beard around his chin was speckled with gray.

Then the priest slept . . .

When he awoke, he groaned as the pain from his beating roared back at him like a snarling dog. He sat up, wincing as the stitches in his chest pulled tight. His robes were gone, and beside him lay clothes obviously taken from the dead men, for brown blood stained the jerkin that lay beside them.

The warrior was packing his saddlebags and tying his blanket to his saddle.

"Where are my robes?" demanded the priest.

"I burned them."

"How dare you! Those were sacred garments."

"They were merely blue cotton. And you can get more in any town or village." The warrior returned to the priest and squatted beside him. "I spent two hours patching your soft body, priest. It would please me if you allowed it to live for a few days before hurling yourself on the fires of martyrdom. All across the country your brethren are burning, or hanged, or dismembered. And all because they don't have the courage to remove those damned robes."

"We will not hide," said the priest defiantly.

"Then you will die."

"Is that so terrible?"

"I don't know, priest, you tell me. You were close to it last evening."

"But you came."

"Looking for my horse. Don't read too much into it."

"And a horse is worth more than a man in today's market?"

"It always was, priest."

"Not to me."

"So if I had been tied to the tree, you would have rescued me?"

"I would have tried."

"And we would both have been dead. As it is, you are alive and, more importantly, I have my horse."

"I will find more robes."

"I don't doubt that you will. And now I must go. If you wish to ride with me, you are welcome."

"I don't think that I do."

The man shrugged and rose. "In that case, farewell."

"Wait!" said the priest, forcing himself to his feet. "I did not wish to sound ungrateful, and I thank you most sincerely for your help. It is just that were I to be with you, it would put you in danger."

"That's very thoughtful of you," answered the man. "As you wish, then."

He walked to his horse, tightened the saddle cinch, and climbed into the saddle, sweeping out his cloak behind him.

"I am Dardalion," called the priest.

The warrior leaned forward on the pommel of his saddle.

"And I am Waylander," he said. The priest jerked as if struck. "I see you have heard of me."

"I have heard nothing that is good," replied Dardalion.

"Then you have heard only what is true. Farewell."

"Wait! I will travel with you."

Waylander drew back on the reins. "What about the danger?" he asked.

"Only the Vagrian conquerors want me dead, but at least I have some friends—which is more than can be said for Waylander the Slayer. Half the world would pay to spit on your grave."

"It is always comforting to be appreciated," said Waylander. "Now, Dardalion—if you are coming, put on those clothes and then we must be away."

Dardalion knelt by the clothes and reached for a woolen shirt, but as his fingers touched it he recoiled and the color drained from his face.

Waylander slid from his saddle and approached the priest. "Do your wounds trouble you?" he asked.

Dardalion shook his head, and when he looked up Waylander was surprised to see tears in his eyes. It shocked the warrior, for he had watched this man suffer torture without showing pain. Now he wept like a child, yet there was nothing to torment him.

Dardalion took a shuddering breath. "I cannot wear these clothes."

"There are no lice, and I have scraped away most of the blood."

"They carry memories, Waylander . . . horrible memories . . . rape, murder, foulness indescribable. I am sullied even by touching them, and I cannot wear them."

"You are a mystic, then?"

"Yes. A mystic." Dardalion sat back upon the blanket shivering in the morning sunshine. Waylander scratched his chin and returned to his horse, where he removed a spare shirt, leggings and a pair of moccasins from his saddlebag.

"These are clean, priest. But the memories they carry may be no less painful for you," he said, tossing the clothes before Dardalion. Hesitantly the young priest reached for the woolen shirt. As he touched the garment he felt no evil, only a wave of emotional pain that transcended anguish. He closed his eyes and calmed his mind, then he looked up and smiled.

"Thank you, Waylander. These I can wear."

Their eyes met, and the warrior smiled wryly. "Now you know all my secrets, I suppose?"

"No. Only your pain."

"Pain is relative," said Waylander.

Throughout the morning they rode through hills and valleys torn by the horns of war. To the east pillars of smoke spiraled to join the clouds. Cities were burning, souls departing to the Void. Around them in the woods and fields were scattered corpses, many now stripped of their armor and weapons, while overhead crows banked in black-winged hordes, their greedy eyes scanning the now fertile earth below. The harvest of death was ripening.

Burned out villages met the riders' eyes in every vale, and Dardalion's face took on a haunted look. Waylander ignored the evidence of war, but he rode warily, constantly stopping to study the back trails and scanning the distant hills to the south.

"Are you being followed?" asked Dardalion.

"Always," answered the warrior grimly.

Dardalion had last ridden a horse five years before when he left his father's cliff-top villa for the five-mile ride to the temple at Sardia. Now, with the pain of his wounds increasing and his

legs chafing against the mare's flanks, he fought against the
rising agony. Forcing his mind to concentrate, Dardalion focused his gaze on the warrior riding ahead, noting the easy way
he sat his saddle and the fact that he held the reins with his left
hand, his right never straying far from the broad black belt hung
with weapons of death. For a while, as the road widened, they
rode side by side, and the priest studied the warrior's face. It
was strong-boned and even handsome after a fashion, but the
mouth was a grim line and the eyes hard and piercing. Beneath
his cloak the warrior wore a chain-mail shoulder guard over a
leather vest that bore many gashes and dents and carefully re-
paired tears.

"You have lived long in the ways of war?" asked Dardalion.

"Too long," answered Waylander, stopping once more to
study the trail.

"You mentioned the deaths of the priests and you said they
died because they lacked the courage to remove their robes.
What did you mean?"

"Was it not obvious?"

"It would seem to be the highest courage to die for one's
beliefs," said Dardalion.

Waylander laughed. "Courage? It takes no courage to die.
But living takes nerve."

"You are a strange man. Do you not fear death?"

"I fear everything, priest—everything that walks, crawls, or
flies. But save your talk for the camp fire. I need to think."
Touching his booted heels to his horse's flanks, he moved ahead
into a small wood where, finding a clearing in a secluded hollow
by a gently flowing stream, he dismounted and loosened the
saddle cinch. The horse was anxious to drink, but Waylander
walked him round slowly, allowing him to cool after the loping
ride before taking him to the stream. Then he removed the saddle and fed the beast with oats and grain from a sack tied to the
pommel. With the horses tethered Waylander set a small fire by
a ring of boulders and spread his blanket beside it. Following a
meal of cold meat—which Dardalion refused—and some dried
apples, Waylander looked to his weapons. Three knives hung
from his belt, and these he sharpened with a small whetstone.
The half-sized double crossbow he dismantled and cleaned.

"An interesting weapon," observed Dardalion.

"Yes, made for me in Ventria. It can be very useful; it looses two bolts and is deadly up to twenty feet."

"Then you need to be close to your victim."

Waylander's somber eyes locked on to Dardalion's gaze. "Do not seek to judge me, priest."

"It was merely an observation. How did you come to lose your horse?"

"I was with a woman."

"I see."

Waylander grinned. "Gods, it always looks ridiculous when a young man assumes a pompous expression! Have you never had a woman?"

"No. Nor have I eaten meat these last five years. Nor tasted spirits."

"A dull life but a happy one," observed the warrior.

"Neither has my life been dull. There is more to living than sating bodily appetites."

"Of that I am sure. Still, it does no harm to sate them now and again."

Dardalion said nothing. What purpose would it serve to explain to a warrior the harmony of a life spent building the strength of the spirit? The joys of soaring high upon the solar breezes weightless and free, journeying to distant suns and seeing the birth of new stars? Or the effortless leaps through the misty corridors of time?

"What are you thinking?" asked Waylander.

"I was wondering why you burned my robes," said Dardalion, suddenly aware that the question had been nagging at him throughout the long day.

"I did it on a whim, there is nothing more to it. I have been long without company, and I yearned for it."

Dardalion nodded and added two sticks to the fire.

"Is that all?" asked the warrior. "No more questions?"

"Are you disappointed?"

"I suppose that I am," admitted Waylander. "I wonder why?"

"Shall I tell you?"

"No, I like mysteries. What will you do now?"

"I shall find others of my order and return to my duties."

"In other words you will die."

"Perhaps."

"It makes no sense to me," said Waylander, "but then life itself makes no sense. So it becomes reasonable."

"Did life ever make sense to you, Waylander?"

"Yes. A long time ago before I learned about eagles."

"I do not understand you."

"That pleases me," said the warrior, pillowing his head on his saddle and closing his eyes.

"Please explain," urged Dardalion. Waylander rolled to his back and opened his eyes, staring out beyond the stars.

"Once I loved life, and the sun was a golden joy. But joy is sometimes short-lived, priest. And when it dies a man will seek himself and ask: Why? Why is hate so much stronger than love? Why do the wicked reap such rich rewards? Why does strength and speed count for more than morality and kindness? And then the man realizes . . . there are no answers. None. And for the sake of his sanity the man must change perceptions. Once I was a lamb, playing in a green field. Then the wolves came. Now I am an eagle and I fly in a different universe."

"And now you kill the lambs," whispered Dardalion.

Waylander chuckled and turned over.

"No, priest. No one pays for lambs."

THE WORLD OF DAVID GEMMELL

Join us in welcoming the bestselling author, David Gemmell, hailed as Britain's king of heroic fantasy, to Del Rey Books. Del Rey will be publishing twelve battle-charged fantasies by this renowned writer.

Look for Gemmell's epic fantasies of ancient Greece, richly peopled with legends and heroes.

LION OF MACEDON

In every possible future, a dark god was poised to reenter Greece. Only the half-Spartan Parmenion had any hope of defeating its evil. And an aged seeress made it her life's mission that Parmenion would become the deadliest warrior in the world—no matter what the cost.

And as the seeress had foreseen, Parmenion's destiny was indeed tied to the dark god, and to Philip of Macedon, and to the yet-unborn Alexander. And all too soon the future was upon them . . .

DARK PRINCE

The Chaos Spirit had been born into Alexander, but the intervention of Parmenion had prevented it from taking over the boy's soul completely.

Now a demon king, in another Greece, where the creatures of legend still flourished, sought the power of the Chaos Spirit that lived within Alexander. And he called the boy into his world . . .

Only Parmenion could hope to rescue Alexander from the demon king— but could anyone save the boy from himself?

Praise for LION OF MACEDON and DARK PRINCE

"Nobody writes better fantasy than David Gemmell . . . A totally engrossing novel . . . It's an enduring and compulsive epic." —*Starburst*

"Gemmell works the reader's emotions adroitly . . . The novel has the potential to be quite popular as a dramatic historical, with fantasy elements . . . It's a satisfying, often exciting fantasy that will thrill many readers . . ." —*Locus*

"This enjoyable historical fantasy set in ancient Greece spans three decades in the career of Parmenion, a Spartan of mixed ancestry whose life is being shaped and monitored by an aging seeress . . . Particularly enchanting . . . is the appearance of Aristotle as a wizard and guide through the underworld . . ." —*Publishers Weekly*

And watch for Gemmell's independent fantasies: KNIGHTS OF DARK RENOWN, a dark Celtic story of lost heroes, and MORNINGSTAR, a medieval fantasy loosely based on the Robin Hood legend—coming in June and October 1993 from Del Rey.

KNIGHTS OF DARK RENOWN

The legendary knights of the Gabala had been greater than princes, more than men. But they were gone, disappeared through a demon-haunted gateway between worlds.

But one tormented knight had held back—Manannan, whose every instinct told him to stay. But as murder and black magic beset the land, Manannan realized he would have to face his darkest fears: He had no choice but to ride through that dreaded gate and seek out his vanished companions.

Praise for KNIGHTS OF DARK RENOWN

"A sharp distinctive medieval fantasy. Dramatic, colorful, taut." —*Locus*

MORNINGSTAR

Jarek Mace was an outlaw, a bandit, a heartless thief. He needed nothing and no one.

But now Angostin hoardes raged over the borders. Evil sorcery ruled, and the Vampyre kings lived once more. The Highland people were in great need of a hero. And when Mace's harassment of the Angostins inadvertently aided the common people, he found himself hailed as that hero, a legend, the great Morningstar returned.

But Mace was an outlaw—not a savior of the people. Or was he?

Praise for MORNINGSTAR

"It is with some reason that he [David Gemmell] is called Britain's king of heroic fantasy. Here [MORNINGSTAR] . . . he looks at the nature of legend—how a man who is basically self-centered and unfeeling becomes the inspiration for a nation in the grip of evil . . . The setting is half-familiar: a place much like the Scottish Highlands at a time like the Middle Ages . . . It is a fine piece of writing. —TIM LENTON, *Eastern Daily Press*, England

"It seems that every time I read a new David Gemmell novel it is better than the last—and MORNINGSTAR is no exception . . . The main difference between the book and the myths it draws upon is that Gemmell includes some of the less savory characters who we suspect may have been at the basis of both Robin and Arthur." —*Starburst*

And look for two of Gemmell's famous heroic fantasy series', coming soon from Del Rey.

Meet the heroes of the Drenai people . . .

WAYLANDER: He was charged with protecting the innocents and journeying into the shadow-haunted lands of the Nadir, to find the legendary Armor of Bronze. But Waylander was an assassin, a slayer, the killer of the king.

LEGEND: Druss was a legend even in old age. And he would be called to fight once more, to defend the mighty fortress Dros Delnoch—the last possible stronghold against the Nadir hordes . . .

THE KING BEYOND THE GATE: Tenaka Khan was an outsider, a half-breed, despised by both the Drenai and the Nadir. But he would be one man against the armies of Chaos . . .

QUEST FOR LOST HEROES: Among the companions, the boy Kiall, the legendary heroes Chareos the Blademaster, Beltzer the Axeman, and the bowmen Finn and Maggrig was a secret that could free the world of Nadir. One was the Nadir Bane, the Earl of Bronze . . .

The Drenai Saga
WAYLANDER
LEGEND
THE KING BEYOND THE GATE
QUEST FOR LOST HEROES

"There isn't a British writer in this area [fantasy] who can hold a candle to his knack for plot-weaving, narrative impetus, and the ability to meld wizardry and high adventure so seemlessly."
          —Fantasy Bookshelf

And more adventures await . . .

Tales of dark magic, sorcery, and conquest in the books of the Sipstrassi Stones of Power . . . A new dark age, a witch queen, a hellborn army, and a man seeking a child born of demon. Bold heroes . . . The brigand slayer, Jon Shannow, known as the Jerusalem man . . . Uther Pendragon . . . Culain . . .

The Sipstrassi Tales
WOLF IN SHADOW
GHOST KING
LAST SWORD OF POWER

And a new Jon Shannow Adventure—going beyond the gates of time itself . . .

THE LAST GUARDIAN

Join Del Rey for the action-filled stories of heroes and battles, of demons and evil armies, for the fantasy novels of David Gemmell . . .